Praise for Richard S. Wheeler

"A master of character and plot."   *—Publishers Weekly*

"A master storyteller whose many tales of the Westward Movement . . . weave fact, fiction, and folklore into pure entertainment."   *—Library Journal*

"No one does it better than Wheeler . . . an extraordinary writer."   *—The Round-Up Quarterly*

By Richard S. Wheeler
from Tom Doherty Associates

The Canyon of Bones

North Star

Richard S. Wheeler

A Tom Doherty Associates Book / New York

This is a work of fiction. All of the characters, organizations, and events portrayed in these novels are either products of the author's imagination or are used fictitiously.

THE CANYON OF BONES AND NORTH STAR

The Canyon of Bones copyright © 2007 by Richard S. Wheeler

North Star copyright © 2009 by Richard S. Wheeler

A Forge Book
Published by Tom Doherty Associates
175 Fifth Avenue
New York, NY 10010

www.tor-forge.com

Forge® is a registered trademark of Macmillan Publishing Group, LLC.

ISBN 978-1-250-16586-2

Our books may be purchased in bulk for promotional, educational, or business use. Please contact your local bookseller or the Macmillan Corporate and Premium Sales Department at 1-800-221-7945, extension 5442, or by e-mail at MacmillanSpecialMarkets@macmillan.com.

First Edition: January 2019

Printed in the United States of America

0 9 8 7 6 5 4 3 2 1

Contents

The Canyon of Bones

For Win and Meredith Blevins

Chapter 1

It was time to take another wife. Barnaby Skye had been thinking about it for a long time, and knew he could not put it off. White streaked his hair and the trimmed beard he wore these days. His youth was gone.

He wanted a child, a boy if God would give him one. All these years he had hoped. But Victoria was barren or maybe he was, who could say? He had no child and thus was the poorest of men.

A man without a child does not see far into the future or care about it; he can live only in the past or present, as Skye was doing more and more. It was as if life had become sunsets rather than sunrises, memories rather than dreams.

He loved to awaken early, even before first light, and slip outside his lodge into the sweet morning air. Then he would stretch, enjoy his own well-rested body, and walk to a nearby hill to greet the day and to pray in his own way.

Now he stood on a ridge, the Absaroka village still slumbering in half-light below him, while he absorbed the blue dawn and the quickening light that began to give color to a gray world. On clear days, such as this one, dawns started out blue, a thin line of blue across the eastern horizon, promising the return of the sun and the stirring of life.

Those were the best moments. Victoria would still be asleep, warm under the thick buffalo robes in winter or a light two-point Hudson's Bay blanket in softer seasons. All the years of their marriage she had been his companion, adventuring where he did, sharing his joys and perils. He loved her.

And now he was aware of the passage of time. The life he had chosen had taken its toll on his body. One could not live as the nomadic Absarokas did without experiencing bitter cold and torpid heat, starvation, poor diet, thirst, and always the danger of war or pestilence. Ancient injuries, some of them going back to the days of his youth when he was a British seaman, would lurk in his body, awaiting the chance to hurt again. And his long thick nose, battered and broken by brawls, was as sensitive to hurt as baby's flesh.

The Crows, as they were called by white trappers, were blessed with a land that usually offered abundant food and hides from the thick herds of buffalo roaming the prairies; that offered strong wiry ponies descended from Spanish Barb stock released by the conquistadors. There were cool mountain valleys to comfort them in summers, sun-warmed river flats to pull the sting out of winter, alpine meadows rioting with spring wildflowers, tumbling mountain waterfalls, and bald eagles riding updrafts, to make a poet of each Crow.

It was a good land if the Crow people could keep it. When Skye thought of the changes that were disrupting the world just over the horizons, he wondered what the future would bring for these cheerful people. Off to the south a vast migration of Yanks heading for the Oregon country and California had decimated grass and wildlife and woodlands for miles to either side of the trail. Riverboats plied their way up the treacherous Missouri, discharging adventurers as well as goods deep in this land where the tribes had been sovereign for as long as their memory knew.

But so far, the life of the Absarokas hadn't changed much. It followed the stately passage of the seasons, and Victoria's people were just as they always were. Her band, the Kicked-in-the-Bellies, drifted from cool mountain valleys in summer to hunting on the plains in the fall to protected river flats in the winter. Its hunters had little trouble making meat; its gatherers had little trouble harvesting buffalo berries, chokecherries, wild onions, various roots and vegetables.

This late summer day, the Crow people would begin their trek southward for their annual encampment with the Shoshones to trade and gossip, and to cement the alliance that helped both peoples to resist the dangerous Sioux and Blackfeet and their allies, the Cheyenne and Gros Ventres or Atsina, and sometimes the Arapaho.

These were festive days. The band would load its possessions on travois, and then meander south past the Pryor Mountains, south past the Big Horn Mountains, then through an arid land along the great river called the Big Horn, to rendezvous with the Shoshones. There they would make sweet the days of late summer, enjoy the cool eves, flirt, smoke the red-stone pipes, and dream. This year the place would be on the extreme west edge of the Big Horn Valley, where pine forests guarded the land of geysers far above. It was a good place.

It would take Victoria only a little while to load the two travois. He and Victoria had a small buffalo-hide lodge and few possessions. He might be a headman, a war leader for her people, but he was not rich the way most Crow chiefs and chieftains were. They had many wives to make them wealthy. A good hunter could keep a dozen women busy cooking meat, making pemmican for winter, and scraping and tanning hides that could be traded at the various posts for all sorts of treasures, such as guns and powder and lead, beads, knives, awls, calico, and great kettles. Some headmen had hundreds of horses that could be traded for valuable things. Skye had only a few horses. Jawbone, his strange, ugly blue roan medicine horse, was chief among them. There were a few more, two riding horses and two travois horses, and a few half-broken mustang colts for the future.

His family was too small. Victoria was forced to do everything, and had no one to share the heavy load of daily toil. Neither did she have any children or sisters or grandmothers in her household to share the day with, to gossip with, to talk about herbs and medicines with, to discuss ailments with, to sew with, to make moccasins with, to dig roots with, to pound berries into fat and shredded meat with. It grieved her, having no other wife to share the toil of this household. It wore her down. Other senior wives among her people were luckier. There were younger wives to share the work. They were like servants, responding to the bid and call of the older or first wife, the sits-beside-him wife. It was a matter of status. It was the right of the first wife to have the company and service of young wives.

Which is why Victoria, as much as she loved Skye, was often moody and even angry, and spent much of her time away from his small and sterile lodge, preferring the society of other women.

But there was something else. No self-respecting headman among the Absaroka people would think of having just one wife. A man's authority was measured by his wives. His wealth was measured in wives. His status as an important man among the people was metered by wives. Even a young and modest youth who had counted coup once or twice, and dreamed of being a great leader of his people, managed a couple of wives. And a chief often had six or eight, and sometimes even more, and had fat lodges, with extra poles to hold up all that buffalo hide, to house his menagerie. And those fat lodges teemed with children too. A chief might have half a dozen, plus two or three pregnant wives to increase his family.

It had taken Skye a long time to realize that Victoria was ashamed of him, for he had but one wife, a small lodge, no children, and few horses. Yes, he was esteemed as a hunter and his Hawken had contributed much meat to the band as well as defending it against horse thieves, Blackfeet raiders, and the ominous and ever-present Sioux.

How often Victoria had hinted, and finally begged for a larger lodge. Far from dreading the presence of another wife or considering one a potential rival, she had pleaded for one or two or a dozen. And there it had stopped. Something in Barnaby Skye had faithfully adhered to the European way of looking at marriage: one man and one woman, bound sacredly together always. He had her and he loved her; why seek anyone else?

He had always been hesitant. How could he split love in two? How could he bring another woman into his lodge and love and nurture her as he had tried to love and nurture Victoria? How could he divide himself in such fashion? How could he spend his nights in the arms of one and not the other? How could he even embrace one while the other lay inert in her robes, well aware of those intimacies that would fill the lodge with soft noises? How did the Absaroka people manage such things, except by indifference, and a sense of wedlock that had more to do with convenience and child-bearing than love? In this tribe the women formed their own nation and society; the men formed another, and little did the separate nations care about one another. Find a gathering, a party, a smoke, a feast, and it would usually be all women or all men.

He had not sought anyone else. At least until now. This dawn he was afflicted with two desolating thoughts. One was that he had wounded Victoria, not heeding her wishes and hopes and dreams. And yet she had faithfully abided in his lodge all these years, even as his own hair was graying and his life was beginning to enter its last chapters. The other, felt just as keenly, was a sense of loss. He would leave no child behind him. He would be a dead end. With him, the race of Skyes would stop. He was a sole son and if he brought no child into the world, the sun would set.

It was an odd and sad moment. Had he grown up in London, secure in its ways, he would have an English wife and family now. But his life had taken a hard and in some ways cruel turn long ago, and here he was, swiftly becoming too old to rear a child, teach a boy how to read and think and reason, how to shoot and live in nature, how to respect women and elders and all helpless things. How to give a boy a name, or a girl a name, and make that name a part of his past and a part of the child's inheritance.

Now he stood on the brow of the hill watching the skyline turn gold, watching the earth turn into the sun, watching the smoke of cook fires rise from the fifty lodges below him. He scarcely knew who or what he prayed to; the old Anglican God he had always known, or some other great spirit, maybe the same great spirit, but one he saw simply as a Father of all things. He lifted his arms to the bright heaven.

A wife, a child, a gift not just to himself but to Victoria. If it was not too late.

Chapter 2

A good day! Many Quill Woman loved to travel. Now she busied herself preparing to move out. Skye had brought in the horses from the herd and they stood quietly near the lodge.

She unpinned the lodge cover, which was held tight by willow sticks threaded through eyelets, and watched the lodge slowly slide to the ground until only the seven poles remained standing. This was a small lodge, truly a hunting lodge, and it grieved her to be so poor.

Her friends always took pity on her because Skye had no other wives and she was alone. It took more than one woman to erect or lower a lodge. Yellow Paint and Scolding Bird appeared at once, and helped her drag the heavy eight-hide lodge cover free, fold it, and stow it on a travois anchored to the packsaddle of one of the ponies.

"It's very sad," said Yellow Paint.

"Maybe someday he will bless you," Scolding Bird added.

"Sonofabitch," said Many Quill Woman, her favorite English expression she had learned long ago from the days when Skye was with the trappers. The other women had heard this phrase many times, always expressed tartly when she was feeling testy, and laughed. They drifted back to their own lodges, for there was much work to do and the Absaroka women did almost all of it. Men hunted and made war and played games and made love and smoked and listened to elders and sought spirit helpers. Women worked.

Many Quill Woman, whom Skye called Victoria after the great woman chief of his English people, lifted three lodge-poles from the skeleton, set them on the earth, and then toppled the four-pole pyramid that formed the core structure of the lodge. It was her lodge, not Skye's. Women owned the lodges. She unwound the thong that bound the four poles, stored it in a parfleche, and then anchored the long, slim lodgepoles to the packsaddle of another pony, a yawning mare that wasn't good for much else.

Skye wasn't very ambitious, she thought. She heaped their remaining robes and blankets and other possessions on the second travois. Some great men of the people re-quired eight or ten travois and many wives to move. It was odd: the people respected Skye as a hunter and warrior, whose Hawken kept enemies at bay and brought meat to them all. But how could any Absaroka respect a man who had only one overworked wife? And hardly any horses? Something was wrong with him. She still loved him, and would always be beside him, but something was plainly wrong with Skye. And not just Skye. All white men.

They all had just one wife except those ones who were heading for the big salty lake. One woman. It made no sense. How could they get along with only one woman? Many Quill Woman pitied those poor white women, living all alone, doing all the work. That was a great mystery. For years after she and Skye had become mates, she never saw a white woman. Where did the trappers hide them? Back East, they said, but why? Why were white women hidden back there?

Then finally she saw one or two who had come west with the missionaries, and knew immediately that white women were so frail and pale that they couldn't stand living away from special shelters the white men called houses. That was it. They were all so weak and sick that they couldn't function.

It certainly made no sense, but white people made no sense at all and she had given up trying to understand them. For years, he had tried to help her with her chores but she had always shooed him away. Nothing could be more shameful than having a man who did women's work. He kept trying to pack things in the parfleches, help lower the lodge cover, pack everything on travois, clean up after meals, while the whole band watched and shook their heads and women came privately to Many Quill Woman and expressed their pity, and hoped she could overcome the shame of it. A man who did that wasn't a man.

So she had angrily chased Skye away and snapped at him whenever he tried to do woman things, such as gathering firewood.

"All I want to do is help you. Make your life easier," he explained.

"Dammit all to hell, Skye, get out."

So he did, greatly puzzled by it. She knew he was trying to be kind to her, loving to her, but he had no idea what a scandal it was among her people. It took a long time, many winters, before she cured him of such bad habits.

She saw him grooming Jawbone and admired him anyway even if she didn't understand him. He was combing the great blue roan medicine horse, while Jawbone snapped his teeth and switched his tail in warning. Never was an uglier horse born; never was a more noble and fierce horse set upon the breast of the earth. Jawbone had narrow-set eyes, flopping ears, an overshot jaw that gave the beast his name, and a nose as formidable as Skye's own awesome beak, which rose from his skull like the prow of a ship, dominating his entire face. There was something strange and fearsome about it all; as if from the beginning of the world, Jawbone and Skye had been destined to come together.

The Kicked-in-the-Bellies were soon ready. Children perched in baskets on travois along with the very old. A great mass of horses had been gathered and young herders were ready to drive them. Women had at last loaded their heavy lodges on groaning travois. Many were festively dressed in fine quilled doeskins, but a few had gotten themselves up in bright calicos from the trading posts. Even the young warriors had taken the time to put on their finery.

The great exodus began without a visible signal from anyone. It simply began its course along the north bank of the Yellowstone, called the Elk River by these bronzed people. Soon it was stretched out a vast distance, but carefully guarded by outriders flanking it on both sides. Many Quill Woman's heart lifted at the sight of the imposing column; the People of the Black Bird were a great people, strong enough to keep the more numerous Lakota and Siksika away.

Skye was among those who guarded this great procession. His favorite place was far forward, where he hunted for surprises and ambushes. That was a dangerous place but he preferred it, and the war chiefs of the Absaroka preferred to see him there. Victoria sometimes saw his shining black beaver hat far ahead. He was like the antennae of an insect, sweeping and feeling the country for danger.

Sometimes he left game in plain sight, a deer or elk he had killed. These were immediately given to the poorest and weakest among the Absarokas. When that happened Many Quill Woman was very proud of her man. His presence was blessing the People.

At night they slept out; in these warm days of late summer, there was no need to erect a lodge unless bad weather threatened, which it never did. At that time Skye would settle beside her in the robes, never forgetting to catch her hand and hold it or to draw her tight for a little while, his love unspoken but profound. Jawbone stood over them like some demented sentinel, letting no one close, not even the People.

They crossed the mighty Yellowstone at a place where the water ripped over gravel, and even the channel was hardly more than ankle deep this time of year. The travois poles dug trenches in the river bottom, but the stream never reached up to the heavy loads securely tied to the poles with thong or braided elkhide ropes.

Skye rarely spoke to her in these times, when his duty was to protect the People day and night. Oddly, she missed his company even though she was surrounded by chattering friends, young mothers with children to look after, boys playing tricks or showing off writhing garter snakes. Secretly, she wished she could ride beside Skye in the vanguard far ahead, before the great caravan had sent every bird winging away, and every rabbit and fox diving for cover.

For three days they passed through starkly arid land, a small desert caught in the rain-shadow of the mighty Beartooth Range to the west, a part of the great Absaroka Mountains named after her own people, but then the majestic mountains seemed to pull back, and they descended into grasslands, and finally into the valley of the Shoshone River. This was still an arid country, but not far upstream the river tumbled out of the noble mountains, and there, in a lush green valley surrounded by timbered slopes, the Absarokas and Shoshones would have their annual rendezvous.

It was easy to see from the marks of exodus that Chief Washakie's Shoshones had arrived ahead of the Absarokas. That only made the trip more exciting. It had been a safe and blessed journey; no child had drowned, no horse had fallen or broken a leg; no thieves had filtered through the night to steal the wealth of her people, whose abundant horse herds were legend among a dozen envious neighboring peoples.

Now she saw her spirit helper, the Magpie, dancing from limb to limb in the riverside cottonwoods. Many Quill Woman had long ago dreamed the vision dream and found this big, raucous, bold bird, white and iridescent black, her helper and guide. She always knew when she saw her friend the Magpie that times would be good or that help was present if times were not good. But now times were good, and here was a whole flock of her birds making loud protest against this invasion. The magpies were like her people, bold and noisy and sometimes reckless, just for the fun of living close to danger.

They paused close to the campground, taking time to don their headdresses, gaud themselves and their ponies with paint, and prepare for a grand entry, in which the Shoshones would howl their delight and cheer the People as they paraded home.

Only Skye did not get into finery. He always wore whatever finery he possessed, which was simply his black top hat and a handsome bear-claw necklace over his chest. And yet, for reasons Many Quill Woman could not fathom, whenever the Absarokas were all dressed in their best it was Skye, on his spirit horse, who always drew the most attention, and those who admired him the most were the ladies. She sighed. Skye was unaware of what great waves and ripples he caused among the women of the northern plains. He only had eyes for her.

Chapter 3

With a whoop the Crows paraded onto the meadow, joyously greeted by the Shoshones. Skye enjoyed the parade. A great column of Victoria's people, all dressed in their finery, wended past the Shoshones. The women flaunted their beaded and quilled doeskin dresses and had gaudy ribbons tied in their braids. The warriors paraded their war honors, their rifles and bows, their colorful lances with a feather for each coup. The chiefs and headmen wore their bonnets, which glowed in the afternoon sun.

Children raced on foot beside the column, the boys in breechclouts, if anything, and the girls in little skirts. The Shoshone hosts were just as brightly gauded for a celebration, all smiles as the allied peoples greeted one another. This would be a festive time, a time of horse races, contests of strength and skill at arms, the exchange of mighty gifts, and also a time when the headmen from both tribes would gather together, smoke, summon the spirits, and cement the old alliance.

Skye spotted the young and noted chief of the eastern Shoshones, Washakie, standing before his great lodge awaiting the arrivals. His gaze was less festive; it was one that assessed the military strength of these allies, the coup sticks, the lances, the number of rifles or muskets, the number of youths who were ready to fight.

Skye had not met Washakie and was eager to do so. The man had grievances against the horde of Yanks flowing along the Oregon Road to the south, but so far had contained his restless people and had chosen diplomacy instead. But the whites neither heeded Washakie nor were his people compensated for the loss of game, grass, and firewood. Even less were they compensated for insults, wounds, shots fired at the Shoshones, and the fouling of watering holes. Skye thought he might add disease to that long, hard list; the Yanks brought all manner of plagues westward upon vulnerable native peoples.

The Shoshones had raised their lodges along the western edge of the verdant meadow here, close to firewood and out of the wind; they had left the center open, knowing the Absarokas would camp on the eastern side, also close to dense forest with an abundance of deadwood in it for fires. The open meadows in the middle would soon harbor dances and drumming, bonfires and feasts, games of skill, races, and a great marketplace where the women, in particular, traded with one another.

There were few Shoshone speakers among Victoria's people, and few Absaroka speakers among Washakie's, yet the peoples got along with a sort of lingua franca, some sign language, and some good guesswork.

Then Skye spotted something else: a white man's wall tent, a wagon, some draft horses, and several white men. Were they traders? Skye, instantly curious, could find no evidence of it; no array of gaudy goods laid out, no shining axes and rifles, no virgin blankets or stacks of pots or cotton sacks filled with beans or coffee or sugar.

He would know soon enough. For now, there were formalities. The Absaroka headmen paused before Washakie, whose own headmen had clustered around them, and there were greetings. The Big Robber, chief of all the Kicked-in-the-Bellies, descended from his pony, embraced Washakie, and then greeted each of the Shoshone leaders. Skye dismounted and did the same, knowing they were as curious about him as he was about them.

For the time being the white men stood discreetly aside, aware that they needed to heed the protocols of this moment. Two appeared to be bearded teamsters or servants; the third, dressed in polished brown boots, a white shirt with a gaudy red silk scarf at the neck, a gray tweed jacket with leather arm patches, and a black, wide-brimmed felt hat, watched cheerfully.

The wagon intrigued Skye. It was well made, sturdy, and light. It was drawn, apparently, by the two homely Belgians, Skye thought, grazing quietly close to the wall tent.

Red Turkey Wattle always selected the exact campsite because his visions offered protection against disease and disaster. Now the old shaman led the parade to a sheltered strand, slightly higher than the rest of the meadow, where the soil was sandy and a rain would vanish into the porous ground. Here he paused, nodded to the four winds, lifted his arms, and then the Crows swiftly erected their camp.

Skye let Victoria select the spot for his lodge. Whenever he interfered, she glared at him, as she was doing now. She would brook no meddling from a white man when it came to something so sacred as a campsite. He knew better than to help her, and indeed her fierce glances were intended to ward him off. Sometimes when they were off alone, she welcomed his help; they would share the toil of making camp, cooking, keeping warm. But when they were among her people, everything was different.

He slid off Jawbone, feeling the ache in his legs as he landed on the meadow. He wasn't so young now that he could leap on and off horses without pain. Jawbone would graze here; the village herders were afraid of him because he'd whirl and kick at them if they approached, so the ugly horse was given leave to wander the village, poke his snout into lodges, and generally offend as many ancients as he could. Sometimes an old warrior, wizened and angry, would threaten to slash Jawbone's throat, but the whole band knew the horse had great medicine, and the old shaman, Red Turkey Wattle, had said that this was the greatest of all horses and must be honored. And no one ever disputed the wisdom of the grand old man.

Skye unsaddled Jawbone and curried him with a bristle brush, while Jawbone shivered and snapped his big yellow teeth and threatened murder.

"Cut it out," Skye muttered.

Jawbone responded by plowing his snout into Skye's belly, a moment of bonding, and then trotted off, snatching at green grass whenever his hunger overcame his curiosity. The blue roan never drifted more than a hundred yards or so from Skye.

Even as Skye busied himself, Victoria wrapped four lodge-poles with thong and erected a pyramid with great skill. Then she laid the remaining poles into the niches, and spread robes over the floor of the lodge. Later, she and the neighboring ladies would help each other to draw the lodge covers upward and pin them in place with green willow sticks poked through eyelets, like buttons.

Skye stretched. This was a glorious late-summer afternoon, not too hot, and the nights promised to be deliciously cool. He lifted the old top hat to let the zephyrs flow through his graying hair, and then began a cheerful tour of the camp. It wasn't that he was looking for another wife, exactly, but somehow his prospects were bleak. Not Missus Crow Dog, no, married and fat and happy. No, not Missus Black Bear, skinny and nervous and unhappy and hard on her little boys. No, not lithe Beaver Nose, youngest child of old

Walks to the Sun; too young, too giggly, too . . . Skye suddenly felt he was not decorous, and recovered his dignity and paced on.

This marriage proposition was not easy. You didn't just up and marry the first nubile lady you saw. At least not if you were a born and bred Londoner. You needed to be a little choosy.

He meandered past Missus Sheep Horns, who was pulling up the lodge cover, along with her friend Missus Black Wolf. Skye knew all about Missus Sheep Horns, who was not satisfied with her husband and was a great flirt. Once, during a war season when the village needed constant protection from the Sioux, Skye was doing picket duty, mostly by watching the countryside from a sun-warmed ridge, when she appeared, smiled, sat down beside him, and made her intentions clear at once. He demurred, having only eyes for Victoria, but not without a struggle. She was a most attractive lady. "Missus Sheep Horns," he had said. "I must keep an eye out for the Sioux."

She had taken offense, got her revenge by telling every woman in sight that Skye wasn't much of a man. That got back to Victoria, who reported it to Skye, who tried to ignore it but couldn't, and never quite lived it down.

That was Crow sport. Trysts were as common as eating a supper. Divorces were the daily entertainment. Which, come to think of it, was reason enough not to marry a Crow woman. He laughed at himself: all he needed to do was join the fun and quit worrying, and everything would be quite fine, and he might have twenty wives, severally and serially, before he departed from this world. Why was he so reluctant?

Romantic, that's what he was. Damned romantic.

Still, the notion that he might find a Shoshone woman swelled up in his head, though he hadn't considered it because he couldn't talk their tongue. But love has its own language and maybe they didn't need to talk. A few smiles would do.

Yonder, across the meadow, there might be a hundred eligible ladies of the Shoshone persuasion. And what better time to go courting than during this great summer festival, this moment of amity between tribes, this period of fun and races and contests?

He saw The Big Robber's women erecting the chief's lodge, but the chief was already padding across the meadow to pay his respects to Washakie. Fires were blooming, pine smoke drifted on the breeze. Tonight there would be the first of many feasts, and maybe some dancing and drumming too. Who knows? These things happened almost unplanned, in some mysterious fashion that Skye never understood.

Then he found himself drifting toward the wagon and the white men. Curiosity drove him; that, more than wife-hunting, was much on his mind. These gents were a long way from anywhere; far from the road to Oregon; far from the river road along the Missouri. Far from any known wagon trail.

He headed that way, at once discovering that they kept an orderly camp. The light wagon was obviously in good repair even though they had crossed rivers and gulches with it, roped it down steep slopes, cleared trails for it through brush and trees. For no ordinary wagon could get here; Skye could scarcely imagine how they managed it, or to what purpose.

The gents were lounging in canvas camp chairs. One stood when Skye arrived, the obvious owner of this outfit, nattily dressed, his face chiseled, his blue eyes bright, his smile genuine.

"Ah, you're Mister Skye," the man said.

It no longer surprised Skye that his name was known even in remote corners. The man continued. "It's a pleasure, sir. I'm Graves Duplessis Mercer, at your service."

A three-piece name. A rich man. But why?

Chapter 4

And some familiar tones in the man's voice.

"Are you British?" Skye asked.

"My father was a captain in the Royal Marines; my mother a Frenchwoman. I grew up in Paris and know France better than my home country. I live in London. And you, Mister Skye, are a Londoner, I've heard."

"Long ago," Skye said. He wondered for a moment whether to reveal more to this son of a naval officer. And decided to put it all before them: "I was a pressed seaman and jumped ship at Fort Vancouver in 1826."

Mercer laughed heartily. "I would have too. Having volunteered for His Majesty's service by press gang, you decided to volunteer your resignation!"

Skye smiled. Maybe the bloke wasn't going to be a pain in the butt after all.

"I've heard a little about you; in fact, Mister Skye, I've been making inquiries. Now, take that Mister that prefixes your name. The story I have is that you require it. Is that the case?"

"It is, sir."

"And why is that?"

"In England, a man without a Mister before his name is a man beneath notice. I ask to be addressed as Mister here in North America, where a man can advance on his merits."

"A capital answer, Mister Skye. I should introduce you

to my assistants, Mister Corporal, and Mister Winding. Floyd Corporal and Silas Winding. They're teamsters and hunters from Missouri and both have guided wagon trains out to Oregon, and know the ropes."

Skye shook hands with both. Winding, in particular, interested him. Beneath that gray slouch hat was a pair of wary hazel eyes set in a face weathered to the color of a roasted chestnut. The man looked entirely capable of dealing with wilderness, and indeed, this pair had somehow gotten a wagon and its gold-colored horses through streams, across gulches, over boulders, up precipices, around brush and cactus and forest, to this remote Eden.

"Never been called a Mister before," Winding said.

"Well, Mister Skye here has set a good precedent," Mercer replied. "I'll follow suit! From now on, you're Mister Winding, if you can stand it."

Winding spat, pulled some tobacco from his pocket, and placed a pinch under his tongue. Then he smiled. "It don't rightly fit but I'll weather it," he said.

Around them, the Crows and Shoshones were swiftly erecting their encampment while children gathered into flocks and raced like starlings hither and yon. The Big Robber and Washakie had settled on some thick robes to enjoy a diplomatic smoke, each of them flanked by headmen and shamans.

Skye itched to learn the nature of Mercer's business but constrained his impulses. If the Briton wanted to talk of it, he would.

But Mercer had a disconcerting way of plunging into the middle of things. "You're wondering why I'm here, Mister Skye. Now, I'm quite happy to tell you. I'm an adventurer. I make my living at it. All of Europe starves for knowledge of the far corners of this great world. A man who can feed them stories about Madagascar or Timbuktu or Pitcairn

Island or Antarctica is able to make a pretty penny, nay a pretty pound, by scribbling away."

"You're a writer, then?"

"Oh, you might call me that. I fancy myself a good and exact chronicler, recording the world with a steady scientific eye. But I'm really a rambler. I go where no one else has gone and write about it. I examine strange people, exotic tribes, bizarre practices, and write of them. I keep a detailed journal, a daily log, in duplicate and in weatherproof containers, in which I record everything. I explore not just the terrain, describing what has never been witnessed by white men, but also the natives. That's why I'm here. These two tribes are unknown in Europe, and here I am to tell the readers of the *London Times* or the *Guardian* what I witness. And the darker and more fantastic, the better. But I also organize my journals into book form. What I see is not for all eyes, of course, and these volumes have an eager readership; people can't get enough of them. I do have a bit of trouble with censors but that only increases the sales. If I didn't have a spot of trouble, the books would hardly fly out of the stalls the way they do."

"A journalist, then," Skye said.

"Ah, you might say it. But it's the least of my vocations."

"What are your larger ones?"

"Explorer, cartographer, ethnologist, geographer, biologist, zoologist, artist, linguist—I have several European tongues, French, Flemish, Dutch, German, Spanish, Portuguese, and a reading knowledge of several others, and by the time I'm done here, I'll have a few thousand words of Shoshone and Absaroka in my notes, and I'll be able to speak to any of these people. Now what I don't have, Mister Skye, is their finger language, sign-talk, and I shall be approaching you for lessons, and especially the nuances."

Skye found himself studying this wunderkind, curious

about the rest: Did he live alone? Alienated from his roots? What of his family? Was he a perpetual boy, living each day for its excitement? Was there a woman anywhere in this life or did he live entirely in this male world he created? How were these exotic articles and books received on the continent? But Skye chose not to be nosy and simply welcomed this remarkable man.

"Actually, Mister Skye, I've been hearing of you for weeks. We came out the Oregon Road, of course, but turned off and headed north, roughly paralleling the Big Horn Mountains. A grand continent, sir. A vast, mysterious land, utterly beyond the grasp of Europeans, who live in little pockets across the Atlantic."

Skye was aware of the sheer energy radiating from this man; it was as if Mercer were a live volcano, brimming with unfathomable powers and exuding energies that would shape not only his own destiny, but those of everyone he touched. It almost made Skye weary just to be in the presence of such force.

The meadow was now lined with colorful lodges, buffalo-hide cones with smoke-blackened tops. Some of their owners had rolled up the lower skirts, letting the playful zephyrs flow freely through their homes, rather like a housewife opening a casement window to air a room.

"See how they make a village out of a meadow, Mister Skye. And in the space of an hour too."

"I've always marveled at it, sir."

"That's why I'm here! I will catch every detail! And after this, we'll head for the geysers bubbling up on that plateau in the mountains I've been hearing about. The headwaters of the Missouri, I believe."

"Not exactly, sir. The Indians call it the roof of the world. Some of its waters flow to the Pacific; some of the waters drain into the Yellowstone River and then the Missouri.

Some of the waters drain into the Madison River, which forms one of the three branches that form the Missouri. But the true headwaters, the farthest reaches of that river, are up the Jefferson, far to the west."

"Ah! You have set me straight. We shall go there. Maybe after we explore the Crows and Shoshones and the geysers, we'll tilt west to the Jefferson, named by the Yankees Lewis and Clark, I remember. Yes, go right on up to the last valley, the final creek, that dumps its waters into the tributaries that carry it to the Missouri, the Mississippi, and at last to New Orleans."

"You have a good grasp of the continent, Mister Mercer."

"How could I write if I didn't, eh? Well, I'll put it on my list."

"List?"

"Things to do. I've a list. It must run to fifty items now. And I'm pleased to have made your acquaintance, Mister Skye. I was hoping to meet you. I need your assistance on a variety of matters, and thought we might work out some sort of accommodation."

Skye was never averse to earning a little cash, so he nodded.

"Ethnography is what absorbs me just now. The Absaro-kas, the Shoshones, most interesting tribes. Religion and all that. I am thinking that you might enlighten me about the Absaroka. I believe you're married into the tribe and know its ways?"

"I am."

"Well, I want to blot it all up, see it, experience it. The shamans, they interest me. I would like to sit in, if I might."

"It isn't something to sit in on, Mister Mercer. The seers have opened themselves to their spirit guides and listen in their own way, and offer thanksgivings. They may or may not share these insights with anyone else. Sometimes a gift is required."

"Yes, yes, of course. But surely there are things about these people to explore. Things you might be willing to share; anecdotes, things you've seen, all that."

Skye sensed that Mercer was driving toward some goal but so far, it wasn't very plain. "I imagine you'll find plenty of material, sir, just by observation."

Mercer leaned forward. "What especially interests me, Mister Skye, is the secret rituals, the nighttime cults, the things that would affront European sensibilities. It's time for Europe to see how the rest of the world lives and thinks. Why, some of the things I witnessed on previous trips to Africa I was forced to describe in Latin in order to pass muster with the royal censors. You get the idea, eh?"

Skye nodded, wondering about the man.

"Actually, I would like to invite you over for some gin and bitters when the sun is over the yardarm. I always carry plenty on my expeditions to ward off the malaria. I've a few canvas camp chairs, and then, over a tonic or two, we can see how this rustic world works.

"I do my research, Mister Skye. In St. Louis I talked to several men of the mountains, inquiring what to look for. To a man, they told me that the Crows are the most lascivious of all the tribes. So I came here! Where better to get a great story?"

Skye listened, startled.

"Why, fidelity is unheard of," Mercer continued. "And a maiden can scarcely get firewood in the forest without being waylaid by half a dozen swains. And even grandmothers tell stories that would make a sailor blush. It's true, isn't it? I want to see it firsthand, record it, lock it in my journal for future use. That's what I'm after. And that's where you come in. You know these people. You can introduce me. You can take me to their rituals, help me befriend them. Tell me where these bacchanals take place. That's where you can earn a pretty penny, eh?"

All the ship's bells were clanging in Skye's head.

Chapter 5

Almost before Skye could respond to Mercer's probing, the man was off in a new direction.

"Mister Skye, they told me that the Yellowstone tumbles over two great waterfalls up there; magnificent falls, scarcely seen by white men. Show me a falls like that, let me measure it and sketch it and I'll have a story. Take me where white men have not been. Take me into that forbidding land of shadows and forests and monster bears where no European has ever set foot, and I'll turn it into something. I'm told there's a geyser up there that blows a hundred feet into the air, and goes off once an hour, and a man could set a clock by it. That and the falls and grizzlies ten feet tall and hot springs where a man can take the best bath he's ever had."

"That can all be done on horseback. It's not wagon country."

"Of course not! I'm sure I could scarcely get a pack mule in there. This wagon, sir, is simply a home base, a portable station where we might resupply. It's been keenly outfitted. I took counsel from a dozen men in St. Louis, friends of yours such as Davey Mitchell, Broken-Hand Fitzpatrick, the Chouteau family, eh? Preparation, that's the key to everything. They all advised me."

"You were in good hands, then."

"Ah, Mister Skye. My list! You should see my list. There's a medicine wheel in the mountains north of here. Very mysterious. I must see it. I hear it's the work of ancient ones and has something to do with astronomy. Maybe like Stonehenge, fitted out to reveal the equinoxes or the solstices. The newspapers love items like that. I can sell it to the *Times* for a pretty penny. And I'm told there's a shy tribe called Sheepeaters up there, now you see them, now you don't. Like the African pygmies or bushmen. They're watching you even if you're not watching them. There's a few stories I'm after. Interview a Sheepeater and I'll sell to half the papers in Europe."

"I've never met one and I'm not sure they exist, Mister Mercer."

"Ah, hoodoo! Vanishing tribes! That's all the better. Well, we'll just look into it. Especially the hoodoo. Find me a tribe with some hoodoo, and I can make a book out of it. Did you know there's some tribes off to the south that make a religion out of the visions they get from eating a certain bean called peyote? Takes a bean-eater right into a different world. The very thought of it would give bishops and archbishops dyspepsia. Yes, sir, I've researched it. Too far south for this trip, but on my list. I should like to sample this bean and see for myself whether I see God, or a reasonable facsimile."

Skye nodded. He was growing dizzy from this man's waltz of mind. He glanced around him, seeing only the peaceful progress the Shoshones and Crows were making toward a festive summer encampment on a cool meadow.

"Yes, Navajos," Skye said. "Some others too."

"Mister Skye, I could sell a dozen stories about polygamy. It's rife here on this continent. The Mormons are on my list. We might just slip down there when the season is colder, and I'll record my impressions, talk to the wives. I'm told that each wife has a separate house, so the husband has separate families. That's how they do it. But in your tribe and other tribes, the chiefs and headmen have several wives and they all live in one lodge. Now that's a cozy affair I want to explore. Suppose one night the chief chooses one wife for his nuptial pleasures. What then? Does he send the others out in the cold, and summon them when he's done? I'm going to find the answer to it. It might ruffle a few peacock feathers along the Thames, but I'll weather it. Answers, sir. I'll get answers to everything. Maybe someday I'll do a paper for the Royal Society."

"Yes, well, you have a world to explore," Skye said, hoping to escape. The idea of escorting this man was growing less and less attractive.

"And that reminds me, Mister Skye, that exploring is at the heart of it. It's all science. All fact. All recording what I find and publishing it for the benefit of the civilized world. You know, Mister Skye, that I am going to be nominated for fellowship in the Royal Society? The greatest honor of all, its fellows selected so carefully that each of them is at the forefront of the frontiers of knowledge. They are the princes of science."

"An honor when it comes, sir."

"Ah, I'll elucidate for you. The Royal Society of London for the Promotion of Natural Knowledge is the most prestigious of its kind on earth. Think of it, Mister Skye. Francis Bacon! Christopher Wren! Edmond Halley! Isaac Newton! Being published in the *Proceedings,* or better still, *Philosophical Transactions.* The papers I write pay the freight, but the goal in this bosom, sir, is to put the whole world, as observed by me, between the covers of those journals."

The odd thing was, Skye thought this bundle of energy would probably do just that if he survived. A man like that could walk into trouble faster than any ordinary mortal and scarcely know he was getting into danger.

"Now, Mister Skye, I do have one small favor to ask.

Chief Washakie brought me, but I have yet to meet the headmen among the Crows, and I would take it kindly if you would introduce me."

"I can do that, sir. And how shall I introduce you?"

"What do you mean?"

"How would you like to be known to them? They don't grasp the idea of explorers. This whole world is perfectly familiar to them and so are the customs of their own people and all the others with which they have contact. They can even tell you a great deal about the religions of their neighbors."

"Well, that's a good question, Mister Skye. What would you advise?"

"I would suggest to them that you are a storyteller, sir. That you want to see everything so that you can tell true stories to your own people. That you keep a journal, just as they keep their histories painted onto a sacred buffalo robe. They call it the winter count, and each year is named and remembered. One year, when there was a great meteor shower that awed us all, they remember as the winter of the falling stars. That's what I propose."

Mercer smiled, revealing even white teeth in the chiseled, lively face. "Good, sir. Maybe they'll put down this year as the winter of the storyteller."

Skye smiled. The man was not without a certain conceit.

"Very well, then." He eyed the teamsters. "By all means, join us," he said.

Skye hiked across the meadow, feeling the thick grass tug at his steps. Or was it just a sudden weariness or reluctance? He wasn't sure he wanted to introduce this amazing man to anyone.

But the headmen saw Skye coming and waited in their circle to welcome him and the other Europeans. Skye paused. It was necessary that he be summoned or invited before he proceeded. The Big Robber examined Skye's entourage, and addressed Skye: "You have brought strangers to us?"

"I wish to make them known to you so that the People will know who is among us."

"That is good. Bring them forth."

Skye brought them to the edge of the circle of the elders and chiefs, and in the Absaroka tongue introduced each man.

"Mister Mercer comes from across the big water, where I come from, and is a storyteller. He makes it his business to see this world, which he has not seen, and meet your people, learn their ways, and then tell these stories to his people. He records what he learns. He is eager to learn of your people."

"And we will be eager to hear his stories. Welcome them. Let them live among us. Tell them to come and tell us stories this night. We will listen. You will translate."

Skye turned to Mercer and his teamsters. "They welcome you. They give you the freedom of the village. They ask that you come this evening and tell them stories."

"I will do that. I will tell them about Africans, or Asians, or crossing the waters in a sailing ship, or a dozen other things. I take it you'll translate?"

"I will."

"We're in your hands, Mister Skye."

With the introductions concluded, Skye returned to Mercer's camp and then excused himself. The truth of it was that in the space of an hour, Mercer had worn him out. Skye could think only of a nap, a rest, an escape from that crackling energy that had engulfed him from the moment he approached the explorer.

He wandered across the meadow intent on rest. Jawbone spotted him, cantered up, and started to butt Skye.

"Avast!"

Jawbone snorted. Someday this free-ranging horse would get himself into serious trouble with these people, Skye thought. But the animal simply would not stay in the herd.

Skye plodded to Victoria's lodge and stumbled inside. Jawbone poked his nose in, checked to see what was what, and retreated. Skye tumbled into the robes, utterly drained and not knowing why. It was not yet evening. Nothing had happened other than an encounter with a man who radiated energy, yet seemed to draw energy out of Skye. What was it about Graves Mercer? Skye couldn't say. Mercer was one of those men who walked along the knife edge of life and yet was rarely in trouble. But there was always a first time, and maybe Mercer's plunge into this world would be a first time.

Skye felt almost drugged, and lay gratefully on the robes until Victoria slipped in, squinted at him, knelt beside him, and pressed a hand to his forehead.

"Dammit, are you sick?"

"No, just worn-out."

"That ain't like you."

"I just am, that's all."

"I saw you with those strangers."

"An Englishman named Graves Mercer. He has two Missouri teamsters for his wagon."

"And big horses. There's fifty Shoshone looking at them."

"Draft horses. For hauling and plowing."

She eyed Skye. "You better tell me what's wrong with you. What's wrong with them. It's them, isn't it. Something wore you out. Who are these men?"

"He's an explorer. He thinks no one's seen this world."

"Typical white man," she retorted. "You rest. I'll go tell him a few lies."

Skye thought that maybe by God she would.

Chapter 6

Victoria was worried. In all the time she had known Skye, she had never seen him take to his robes after meeting someone. He wasn't sick. At least he said he wasn't. She had been beside him when he was fevered, injured, or exhausted. And when he was desolated or angry or starved or thirsty. But he had never been like this, lying in his robes and staring at the sky through the smoke hole.

The visitors had returned to their wagon after meeting the chiefs, so she headed there. Some sort of ritual was under way: one of them was bringing a bucket of icy river water while the big boss was setting out glass tumblers. It surprised her. One didn't see much glass. Half the people in this camp had never seen it. The big boss was lean, tanned, in a clean shirt, clean britches, and clean boots. He wore a wide-brimmed gray felt hat.

She thought some English would do: "Whatcha got there, eh?"

The big boss turned, surprised. "You speak our tongue?"

"Sure, pretty goddamn good too."

"Ah! You're Missus Skye. Your reputation precedes you."

"What the hell does that mean?"

"It means that the men we talked to about this trip in St. Louis made mention of you. You're salty, they told me."

"All I did was hang around trappers a few years. What's wrong with that, eh?"

"I'm sure that would do it. Come join us, Missus Skye.

I'm Graves Duplessis Mercer. These gents are my helpers, Mister Winding and Mister Corporal, from Missouri in the States. They take care of my horses and the wagon. Come join us for an evening libation and by all means summon Mister Skye."

"He ain't feeling so good."

"I'm sorry to hear it. He promised to drop in for gin and bitters."

"What's that, eh?"

"Spirits and a decoction of cinchona, guaranteed to ward off malaria."

She didn't know what the hell that was all about but she liked the spirits part of it. "Serve her up, eh?"

Mercer waved her toward a camp chair and she settled in it.

Mister Corporal swiftly poured some spirits from a cask into a glass tumbler and added some of what they called bitters, whatever the hell that was. He handed it to her, she sipped, and sipped again, aghast at the flavor. It was plainly the most vile flavor she had ever experienced. She sipped again and the bitterness swilled down her throat.

"That's one hell of a drink," she said. "It must give you great powers. The worse the taste, the bigger the powers. Does it make you fly? Do you see visions?"

Mercer grinned, baring even white teeth so perfect it made her ache. No one on earth had teeth like that except for this man. She had heard that all the English had rotten teeth but here was one with teeth that came from heaven.

"It's gin, the favorite spirits of Englishmen," he said.

"I'm going to get drunk," she said. "I'm going to drink this stuff until I roll on the grass. This heals the sick. This makes the lame walk. This cures fevers. It wakes up the dead."

"Ah, Missus Skye, you are true to form. Now I want you

to tell us about your people. I try to learn everything there is to know about a place and the people in it."

"What do you want to know?"

Mercer thought and sipped and thought. "Are there any other tribes here, people hidden away somewhere? People the world doesn't know about?"

"Hell yes, there's the Little People."

"You don't say! Who are they?"

"Only the Absaroka see them. Sometimes they help us, sometimes they play tricks on us like the coyotes."

"Ah, yes, but where are they?"

"Everywhere," she said grandly with a sweep of the arm. She sipped more of that awful stuff, coughed, and smiled. "They could be right here and you'd never see them."

"What do they look like, Missus Skye?"

"About so tall," she said, pointing to her knee.

"Truly they must be taller than that."

"Hell no. They're always hiding."

"This is a joke, isn't it?"

"Ask any Absaroka! Ask The Big Robber, he's the chief. Ask Red Turkey Wattle, he's the man who sees the Other People."

"A good story, Missus Skye. I'll make note of it. What do the Little People do to help you?"

"Hell, anything. Chase bears away, bring water, warn us about trouble, lead us to berries."

"Do they look like Indians?"

"They look like people from under the earth."

"Devils?"

"How should I know. I never saw one."

"Maybe I'll meet someone who's seen one. Now, are there any other strange things here?"

"Damn right. The One With Big Feet Who Walks in Snow."

Mercer stared. "More, please. This is valuable."

"Ain't nobody seen him. But he's a big person, with bare feet twice the size of any of us. Big long steps, up on the snow, any winter."

"Big Foot! Now we're getting somewhere. He is well known and I've been looking for Big Foot for years. He's been seen in Russia, Canada, Siberia, and now here."

"What the hell is Russia?"

"A great northern nation across the waters. This Big Foot has a name. Yeti. Do you suppose there's a tribe of Big Foot?"

"Damn right. Thousands, all over the mountains."

"What does the Big Foot look like?"

"Lots of hair, twice the size of us, big feet, carries a club. Very dangerous, very shy."

"Could you lead me to his footprints?"

"Naw, you just find them when you're not looking."

"Where?"

She sipped. "This stuff, it ain't gonna kill me, will it?"

"It's good. We drink it to ward off the intermittent fever."

"Who knows where? When you're not looking, that's when you'll see the footprints. It'll lift the hair on the back of your neck. You see this footprint, and it's a person, and you peer around, and look into the pines and there's no one there, and something passes through you and you know you shouldn't see this."

"Could you draw the footprints for me with my pencil?"

"I can hardly put quills down straight. Skye's shirts, they look like I got ten thumbs. How about more of this stuff, eh?"

She polished off the dregs and handed the glass to Mister Corporal. This was fun. She would get some booze out of it.

"Are there caves here?"

"That's where the Little People live."

"Big people who make tracks in the snow, and little people in caves. Very interesting. These are Crow, ah, Absaroka stories?"

Victoria was feeling a little resentful. He had to be told everything three times.

"Lots of caves. That's where the Old Ones lived. They made pictures on the walls. These were First People. We don't go in there. Don't disturb the spirits. That is their place, not ours."

"I'd like to see them. Are there any around here?"

"Naw, not here. Long ways away. But there's something not far from here you'd like to see. Big bones in the rocks. Big animals got turned into stone. Some bones south of here, some more up on the big river. The one you call the Missouri. Biggest sonsofbitches you ever saw."

"Fossils. Yes, indeed. In England we have many. Seashells, things like that. Little creatures caught in stone from long ago. No, I don't need to see anything like that."

She shrugged. "You don't want to see a big bone, eh?"

He smiled. "Actually, no. Or let me put it this way: it's low on my list of things to look at. Now, tell me about what the Absaroka do at night. Are there secret meetings out in the woods? What do you do on the night of the full moon?"

"You sure are keeping your eyes shut, ain't ya. This here bone, it's sticking out of rock. It's bigger around than I am and taller than I am. Lots of others around there too."

"I'm sure there's no bones like that. Not even an elephant has bones like that. It's just the way the rock weathered."

"Well, dammit, that's that. I tell you about something around here and you say it ain't so."

He smiled, revealing all those even white teeth. "Forgive me. Tell me about the big bone."

"There's a mess of other bones. This is from a giant bird. Everyone says it's the bones of the big bird."

"How big?"

She stared, finally pointed at a tall pine. "Big as that."

His eyes twinkled. "You love to tell stories, I can tell."

She stood up angrily and dashed the drink in the ground. "I don't want your gin. I don't want nothing to do with you."

He absorbed that. "My most earnest apologies, Missus Skye. Maybe there are such bones. Maybe you'd show them to me."

"Maybe I will, maybe I won't. I don't want you messing with them anyway. Big spirits in there."

"Let me refresh your drink, Missus Skye. In truth, I greatly desire your company because you can translate for me."

"Fill her up, damn good spirits," she said, and sat down again.

Chapter 7

Good stuff. The more Victoria sipped the gin and bitters, the better she liked it. Clean, tart taste, cool drink, just right. These British knew how to live. Wooee!

She sipped and eyed her host. This was good, sitting in a canvas chair with this Englishman. A drink for a story or two. The more stories, the more drinks. Hey hey, things couldn't be better.

Where the hell was Skye? He was hiding. She had never seen him hide before. Not in all the winters they had been together had she seen him hide from anyone. But now he was in the lodge with the robes pulled over his head hiding from this man. That was strange. She would tease him tonight. Make him ashamed of himself.

It worried her. He never missed out on a drink. Something was wrong.

Mercer was enjoying himself too. Sometimes his gaze drifted to the encampment. He seemed not to want to miss a thing. If some boys knotted into a gang somewhere, his gaze followed them. He sipped, totally relaxed, plainly happy to be there.

"Missus Skye," he said. "I consider this a most fortunate meeting. I want to learn all about your people. This is fortunate for me because you speak English. So I hope you won't mind if I ply you with all sorts of questions."

"Then you write it all down?"

"I do. I write it down and publish it."

"I've seen books," she said. "Damn, I wish I could get the meaning out of them."

"Well, I want to record everything about your people."

"Such as?"

"Your rituals, your religion, your demons. When someone dies where does his spirit go? Up to the stars? Down into the ground? Up to the sun?"

"They start their spirit journey by greeting the elders, and then they head east until they get to St. Louis, and then they turn into mosquitoes and bite white men."

He laughed. "Very good, Missus Skye. Now we're getting somewhere. Are there secret meetings in the night? All boys, all girls? All women? All warriors? All virgins? Do you sacrifice prisoners to the gods? Do you sacrifice animals? Do you drive a stake through the heart? Do you drive demons out of your village? Do you bury the old and the sick alive? What do you do with the sick? Do you have herbs and potions? Does a medicine man drive out the evil? What do you do with crazy people? How do you torture enemies?"

"Sonofabitch, you sure ask questions!" She eyed him. "Best damn questions anyone ever asked."

"Is one animal favored over another? Do you eat the flesh of other people? You know, to give you power over them? What do you do with criminals? Banish them? Kill them? Do you have fertility rites? Do men trade wives?"

Victoria sipped her drink. He noticed and smiled. "Have another," he said.

She thrust her half-emptied glass at Winding, who promptly refilled it and handed it to her. That gin was good stuff, oh ho ho! It was making her feel better and better. Damn, how could she answer all those questions?

Then she knew. She sipped, smiled, and sipped again.

"At the beginning of time there was a big raven. Its wings filled the whole sky. It had been born on a mountaintop and pretty soon it was bigger than the mountain. Then it flew here, casting a shadow so big that the world was dark under it, and it decided this was the place for the raven people to be. It settled on another mountaintop and opened its beak and began spilling out raven people . . ."

Now Mercer was scribbling busily, catching everything she said. Good. This should be worth a few more drinks.

"Out they came, many raven people, and they named themselves the People of the Raven, or Absaroka."

"Good," he said.

"They all had black hair, but then one had white hair, and the people knew they had to kill the white-haired one so they cast him into the sun."

"Good, good, Missus Skye. The origins myth."

"What the hell is that?"

"The creation story. All groups have one."

"Well, all right. But the white one didn't die. It became the moon, so at night we see the white one, and know it was cast out of our midst."

"Is the moon evil? Do you gather at night to look at it?"

"Oh, you bet. That's when we do the forbidden things. The nights of the big moon."

He perked right up at that, staring at her with a devouring look. Good. This was fun.

He waited, pencil poised, but she simply sipped. Let him wait. Besides, she didn't know where to go next.

"That's when we sacrifice a baby," she said. "Each full moon, the people give a baby to the pale god, deep in the night when the moon is big and fat."

"Sacrifice! You don't say! How is the victim selected?"

"Not a victim, dammit, an honor. The holiest, most sacred honor. The shamans select the one, and make a bundle and place the bundle before that lodge."

"And then the parents know their baby will be honored?"

"Hell yes."

She had him running now. She finished her drink and edged the empty glass forward. Promptly, Winding filled it with more gin and bitters.

"This is done by the Wolf Society," she said. "That's a secret society of young warriors. It's their task. If a young man really wants honors he will go steal a Siksika baby."

"Siksika?"

"Blackfoot. The Piegans, the Kainah, the Bloods. They are the enemies of our people. A Wolf warrior must go all alone to the land of the Siksika, carry his wolf skin with him so he can wear it, and then wait to capture a baby. He lurks close to the Siksika camp, singing his song to the Wolf so he might succeed, and then when a mother is not looking, he creeps out, snatches the baby, and runs away with it into the forest. This is very difficult. Many of the Wolf Society die; the Blackfeet catch him and take their baby back and kill the Absaroka boy."

"This is remarkable. How often does this happen?" Mercer asked.

"Not often. An Absaroka boy must have a vision, then pledge that he will take a Blackfoot baby, and then do it. After that, there's a ceremony on a big moon night. All the men in the society count coups. Then the baby is left for the wolves to eat. But if a coyote eats it, that's bad luck. Watch out for coyotes. They're bad luck."

Mercer stared, slightly at a loss, and then wrote. The sun had set. A sweet cool evening breeze, scented with pine, drifted down from the slopes.

She was in fine fettle, and hurried on. The next one might be worth two or three drinks. "Now I'll answer another question. The Absaroka have the Wife-Trading Night."

"You do? Then it's true. I heard about this in St. Louis."

"It's true. It's the longest day of the year, when Sun doesn't go to bed but lingers on, and rises early. That's the night when everyone is happy. Wives are honored. It is the Night of the Wives. That's another Absaroka name for it."

"Tell me, what happens?"

"Oh, I shouldn't talk about it. It is sacred, very sacred."

"Please tell me. I'll not mention it or say where I heard it."

"You sure? We don't talk much. It's great honor. Every wife, she wants to try it."

He scribbled furiously, and then the lead snapped. He dug in his pockets, extracted a tiny folding knife, and whittled a new point on his pencil.

"Now I'm ready, Missus Skye. You were saying?"

"Ah, yes, the longest day, the light lingers, and husbands make big deals with friends, and give them their wives for the night, and because it's light everyone knows, everyone knows who goes to which lodge, eh? Sometimes when a wife is plain, the husband, he gives his friend a gift too? An elk skin, maybe. Then the plain wife gets to enjoy the honors too."

"Ah . . . I see."

Mercer looked like he was about to choke.

"You all right?" she asked.

"Fine, fine. Tell me more. Does this happen just once each year, on what we call Midsummer's Eve?"

"Hell no," she said. "It happens all the time."

Mercer was turning an odd red color. "Remarkable. I shall want every detail."

But then the drumming began. She glanced at the meadow, and sure enough, a crowd was collecting at a bonfire, even as old men gathered into a drumming circle and began their plaintive songs to the demanding beat of the drums.

"I must go look," he said. "We'll continue this little talk tomorrow, Missus Skye."

She smiled. She was in a smiling mood. If there was anything the People loved, it was a good joke.

She drifted to her lodge, ready to confess what she had done and celebrate with him, but Skye was gone.

Chapter 8

Skye drifted from the lodge after darkness cloaked the valley. The drummers had begun, their heartbeat drumming throbbed through the camp. A crowd had collected around them to listen to songs of triumph, great events, war, and power.

He was in no mood for that and wished the tribes had some other and quieter way to spend a summer's eve. He had no relish for the company of the explorer, Mercer, either. In fact, he was using the darkness to dodge the man. He had nothing against the energetic Briton who had welcomed him cordially, and yet he did not want further commerce with the man. Somehow, Mercer was an intruder, and few of the Absaroka or Shoshone people grasped that he was noting everything there was to know about them.

It was one of those moments he often experienced, when he felt caught between the European world of his youth and the world of his adopted nation, the Crows; a moment when he was not really comfortable in either.

He did not dislike Mercer, yet he found himself avoiding the explorer and knew he would continue to do so, no matter that they shared a tongue and a world across the sea and the prospect of a few gin and bitters was enticing. He used the thickening dark to drift from camp, reaching darkness and quietness after he reached the Shoshone River. He treasured the quietness of the woods. A three-quarter moon, fat and yellow, was rising in the east and paving the path with glistening light. That was good. It bid fair to be a sweet summer's eve.

Soon the drumming was only a distant throb and then the sound vanished altogether and he was alone. He found a game trail leading upward through forested foothills, and took it, letting the white moonlight filtering through the pines be his lamp. Juniper-laden air eddied down the hill, perfuming the world. The pungence of the juniper, or cedar, evoked the biblical in him and made this place the Holy Land. The malaise he felt in camp left him and he was at peace. He climbed a sharp rise and found an open ridge, its rocky spine lit by moonlight, a place of peace.

And there was a woman. Yes, no mistake, a jet-haired woman sitting on the rock, her back pressed into a shoulder of rock, her gaze rapt. She saw him at once, a swift startled gesture, and he paused. He did not want to frighten her.

"I am Mister Skye. I will go. This is your place," he said in Absaroka, but she did not respond.

He thought she might be Shoshone, but who could say? He made the friend sign, palm forward, the peace sign. She did not move. He felt himself to be the intruder, and turned to leave.

She said something he could not translate but her voice was soft and warm, and she patted the rocky table next to her. He accepted the invitation and discovered a young woman, slim and beautiful, perhaps half his age. She had the strong cheekbones of her people, and almond eyes, and even in the white and glistening moonlight he caught her interest in him. Her survey was as complete as his own and lingered at his gray beard and the beaver top hat. She smiled and spoke again and he could grasp nothing except her meaning: come sit with me and enjoy this sacred place, lit by Mother Moon.

He did, easing himself to the sun-warmed rock beside

her. They sat well above the valley of the summer camp, but could not see it here in this quiet basin, and were alone.

"I'm Mister Skye," he said in English, "and I live with the Absaroka people."

"I know," she said, "and your name is familiar to me. We all know it."

He wondered how he understood her. She said it in Shoshone. Maybe he knew more of it than he had realized. He liked her voice, resonant of woodwinds and wind chimes.

"I am called Blue Dawn," she said. "I am twenty winters, and have turned aside many suitors because I wanted to."

He thought about that a moment, her words meaningful to him, as if a wizard were translating somewhere in his soul.

He nodded. Neither she nor he spoke. It was as if they had already tested the limits by which two people of different tongues could understand each other. She had not used the finger language though she no doubt understood it.

Some night bird glided nearby, hunting the rocky ridge for a meal. A small cloud hid the moon, so he could barely see her for a while.

He thought of things to say to her and then spoke: "I wonder who you are. I wonder why you are here, apart from your people. I wonder how you chanced to hike up this side trail to this ridge."

She smiled, almost as if she understood him. It was almost eerie. But of course she didn't.

"I wonder what your dreams are: each of us has dreams, but yours have taken you away from the drumming, and your people, to this place. It is a quiet place but not a lonely one. It is a place to dream, or seek help from the spirits, or try to find a way through troubles."

She was watching him, so intent that he imagined she was understanding his every word.

"But I think you are not troubled," he continued, imagining she understood. "I think you are seeking something, maybe something the moon can give. I am too. I am wondering what to do. It's my wife . . ."

She smiled. Could it possibly be? Yes, she was smiling.

"I know," she said. He was startled. Had he really heard it? Of course not.

This was getting altogether too odd for his taste. He emptied his mind of everything and settled beside her, letting the sacred scent of junipers drift past him. But now he was imagining what she was saying, maybe because he knew a little Shoshone: it was as if she was talking and by some magic he was receiving every word.

"My spirit helper is the Unknown God," she was saying. "He was made known to me by a white man, a priest of his people, named Father De Smet. Ever since then I have sought this Unknown God who abides beyond the beyond."

Skye couldn't believe he was thinking such things. Once he got back to the camp he would inquire about her. What was her name? Had the great Jesuit, Father De Smet, ever visited her people? Surely this was nothing but fevered imagination at work.

Still, she smiled at him and reached across the rock to touch his hand with hers.

"You want a wife," she said in her tongue. But he caught the meaning.

"No, not I, I'm married, I . . ."

He stared helplessly at her, his mind refusing to accept this mysterious talking, translating without a translator.

"It is known among us. Many Quill Woman has told all the People that you are looking for a young wife."

She sat there quietly, her gaze dreamy, the moonlight flooding her face and revealing friendship in it. She really hadn't said anything intelligible. He must be imagining all of this. There had been only the deep silence of the wilds, the occasional whir of a night flyer, the fat moon slowly crawling upward into a smaller whiter ball, and peace. Not just peace, but a sweet and savory peace.

Now he spoke aloud: "I came here to dodge the white man, the Englishman with the wagons and two helpers. He's a good enough chap. I have nothing against him. But I am not at ease around him."

She listened, her eyes uncomprehending.

"I don't really know what the matter is. We just don't mix. He's a storyteller, I guess that's as clear as I can make it. He's adventuring to the distant corners of the world, looking for strange things. Strange to him, anyway, but not strange to you or me. And he writes all these things down each evening, and then he goes back to England, the country of my birth, and tells them what he has seen. It might be volcanoes or geysers one story; it might be your people or my wife's people too. It might be strange animals, rare birds, who knows? But he tells the stories, and many people know the stories."

She stared. Good. For a while there he swore he was out of his senses, thinking she and he were mysteriously conversing.

They watched swift silver-rimmed clouds play tag with the moon. Sometimes he discovered her gazing at him and sometimes their gazes locked. She didn't smile or seem flustered by it. She was accepting and enjoying this silent encounter. He felt drawn to her, as if she was offering him a circle of sweetness if he would step inside of its circumference.

Who was she? And why did this encounter play out here?

She said something he could not understand, and rose. She was going to leave.

"Would you like my company?" he asked in English.

She nodded, responding to words she didn't know. She smiled, touched his arm, and they started down to the summer camp. She walked ahead of him, lithe and sure of foot, until they reached the river and then they followed it to the moonlit meadows. The camp had fallen into slumber.

She paused at a place where her path would fork from his, looked up at him and smiled. He placed his hands upon her shoulders and drew her close, yet not touching. It was a gesture as ancient and universal as man and woman. She said something, placed his bearded cheeks between her hands, and pressed them gently. That was all.

She left him, walking toward the Shoshone lodges. A dog found her, raced up, recognized her, and trotted along beside her as she fell farther and farther from Skye's sight, until at last she vanished into silver moonlight.

A strange, sweet eve, he thought. He made his way to his lodge, found his way into its blackness, and tugged at his moccasins.

"Dammit, Skye, tell me about her," Victoria said.

An awkward feeling engulfed him, but it passed.

"I don't know her name but she'd make a good wife," he said. "If you want me to."

"Shoshone," she said. "No Absaroka wants a white man with smelly feet."

She laughed, found him, and opened her arms to him as he settled beside her.

Chapter 9

With the first hint of dawn, Skye slipped out of the lodge and into the chill. He always loved this hushed moment in the day, just before the world stirred. In that he was unlike his wife's people, who would sleep to noon if it suited them. For the Absarokas this was still the middle of the night.

Skye surveyed the camp. No cook fires burned either among the Crow lodges or the Shoshones. There was probably no one awake except the horse herders, whose task was to be alert for trouble at all times. It was an honor for a boy to be chosen as a herder. Great was the responsibility, and great was the trust, and it meant that manhood was not far off.

The sun was cutting a ribbon of blue on the eastern horizon, and soon the gray and night-shadowed world would take color into itself. Skye headed for the river, to perform his ablutions, and then he thought he would climb a slope and watch the sun come up.

But at the Shoshone River he found he was not alone: a woman stood silently, watching him. When he drew closer, he was amazed. It was the young Shoshone he had spent time with at twilight. How could it be?

"Good day, Mister Skye," she said. In clear English. "I wait for you."

English? How could that be?

"Wait for me?" he replied, utterly flummoxed.

She nodded. "I know all that you do. You leave the robes before anyone else. You like to see the day begin. I do too."

He could scarcely fathom it. "But last night you didn't speak English."

"Last night I chose to listen. If you want to know some-one, say nothing, and listen and watch."

"How do you know English?"

"My father is called Pompey. My grandmother is named Bird Woman, Sacajawea in my tongue. I learned your tongue from my father and grandmother. They were very careful to teach me many words, saying it would be good for me to know this tongue. Your people are making the world that will come."

"And you?"

"Blue Dawn. Like this." She waved toward the sunrise.

"Then you understood all my babbling."

She nodded.

"And you know me but I don't know you."

She smiled. The widening light in the east lit her face. "I know you. Come. I will make a meal for us."

He had the odd sensation of being drawn into something ordained or planned that he was the last person to know about. She smiled. He thought she was the most striking woman he had ever seen, straight and lithe and proud, with a long-limbed body that arched like a drawn bow.

"We will eat up on the meadow," she said, leading him in the direction of their rendezvous last evening. "I have made everything ready."

He drew his top hat from his head, more and more un-certain about all this. Too strange. Back out. "That's a most thoughtful invitation, but I can't accept. I ought not to be accepting invitations from a lady I scarcely know."

She smiled, her black eyes flashing in the quickening light.

"Come," she said.

He surrendered and followed her as she trotted ahead of him, her doeskin skirts dancing about her calves as she climbed the steep side trail toward the plateau. She moved so fast that it winded him to follow, but when they did reach the high meadow he was glad he came. The whole eastern sky, with a handful of pancake clouds, had turned rosy, and the alpine meadow was gilded in silvery light. It was their private Eden, a place of beginnings.

But he could not fathom what inspired all this. Why she had arisen before light, prepared this place, and waited for him to appear.

She reached the very ledge of gray granite where they had sat only hours before, sitting in what he supposed was a babble of languages. But now she had a fire already burning. She added some deadwood and placed a small black iron kettle over her fire.

"This is all just fine but I'm a little confused," he said.

"Oh, there is no reason to be. Time to be the wife. I decided to marry you."

"Marry me? You decided . . ." This was progressing all too fast.

She smiled, this time shyly. "It is so. It is the word of Many Quill Woman that comes to us. Her man seeks another wife. I think that I am this one. I have always known it. Long ago, when I was little, I saw you."

Skye stared mutely. He could not think of a thing to say. Not one word. She stirred the contents of her small black kettle. Orange flame licked its bottom and a thin gray veil of wood smoke lifted up and drifted across this alpine park.

Now her demeanor was not so certain. "I will be a good wife for Mister Skye," she said in a small voice.

This was taking more getting used to than Skye was

prepared for. He saw doubt in her face, the beginnings of self-rebuke, and swiftly caught her hand.

"Blue Dawn . . ." He wanted to accept, but that seemed odd. He wanted to propose, but it was too late.

She smiled, clamped her fingers over his.

"I've never been proposed to," he said.

"I waited for you," she said. "I knew you would come."

"Everything is upside down."

She frowned. "What is upside down?"

He laughed. "It's when the sky is under our feet."

She stared, a slow smile building at the corners of those young lips.

"I will get used to you," she said. "I will try to be a good woman. A very good woman for you. I will work hard. I will be to you whatever you like me to be. Your beard will tickle my face."

"Where I come from, men propose to women. And they get to know each other first."

She smiled. "I pity the women where you come from."

"It's sacred, you know. It's for a lifetime. You don't rush into it."

"A lifetime! I wouldn't want to live with your people."

"Your father must have told you about all that."

"I didn't believe it. How could people be so savage?"

"But it's civilized."

"Savage. How can a man and woman stand one another for an entire life?" She waved her horn spoon at him. The contents of the pot were beginning to bubble.

"I am glad my father did not take me with him," she added.

"Where is he?"

"In some place called Europe across the sea. He said it's old and cold and I wouldn't like it. So I am glad I stayed here to marry you."

"I haven't said yes yet. I want to get used to this."

"We can wait until tonight if you want."

"Wait until tonight!"

"If you insist. Or, we don't have to wait at all." She stood straight, smiled at him, and waited. "Are you my man?"

He was feeling half crazy. It wasn't yet six in the morning, and apparently he was betrothed. "I want to get the permission of your parents first," he said, hoping that would delay matters for a few months.

She shrugged. "My father, he is far away. My mother," she paused. "She is not here. She is dead. I am with my brother and my cousins. You call them cousins. I call them kin, little brothers, little sisters. You can ask him."

Skye was feeling out of sorts. There she was, desirable, her lithe young body moving under those doeskin skirts, inviting him, provoking him. How could he be an honorable man? How could he do what's right? How could he be proper?

"Well?" she asked.

He lifted his top hat and settled it. "You have to meet my wife first. She has to approve."

She was grinning fiendishly. Victoria had the same grin. Did all Indian women possess that grin in their arsenal? "I already did," she said.

"You met her? You met Victoria?"

"She sure swears, doesn't she?"

Skye began to shrink down inside of his buckskins. This was getting dangerous. Maybe he could bolt for his lodge, leave her stirring her stew.

She touched his arm. "You have a good woman," she said. "She told me about you. She said I should tell you to marry, because you never would. She said you'd be very strange about it at first but you would like the idea. She said I should be called Mary. I think that is a pretty name. You need to name me with one of the names your people give to women. So she said I would be Mary."

"She did, did she?" Skye squirreled his top hat around in his hands. He squinted at her. "She told you that? She set this up?"

"What does set up mean?"

"I don't know what it means," he replied, feeling huffy.

She smiled. "Victoria said you'd be angry, and very strange, and then you would be very happy."

"She said that too?"

Mary nodded.

"Am I Mary now?"

"How should I know? All I do is get moved around like a chess pawn."

"What is that?"

He sighed. She was smiling sweetly. "Let's eat some of that good stew," he said.

Chapter 10

Blue Dawn ladled some of the broth into a wooden bowl and handed it to Skye.

He sampled it. The meat was odd. Maybe dog. But he bravely spooned it into himself and smiled back at her.

"A fine breakfast, yes. Very good," he said. "You'll make someone a fine wife when that person comes along."

"Badger," she said.

"It's badger?"

"My people believe that badger meat makes lust in a man. Give a man some badger if you want to make a baby. They are hard to catch. They have mighty arms to claw a badger hole. I paid two boys to catch one for me."

Skye, always ruddy, suddenly suspected he was ruddier than usual. He chose silence as the best of all responses, and slurped up more of the badger stew.

"Good! Eat it up! We will have a big time."

He thought that maybe eating the badger stew so heartily was a mistake.

"My people don't think there's anything special about badger meat," he said, squinting at her. "It's just meat. Nothing to it."

She smiled wickedly. She and Victoria had the same lustful smile. He thought it would shock all the prissy girls in pinafores in England. But this wasn't England.

"You should finish it," she said. "Then I'll be happy."

"Ah, I think I've had enough badger."

He was feeling more and more snared, and the more he fought the web of cord being wound around him, the tighter it got. She took his half-empty bowl, swiftly ate the contents, and then packed it.

"It works for women too. I asked our prophet, whose name in your tongue is Glow Bug, and he said the meat of the badger is a great, ah, what's your word? Benefactor. A great benefactor. It makes a man and a woman . . ." She laughed winsomely.

Skye thought, it is not yet seven in the morning and already the rest of this day is laid out for me. And I knew nothing of it.

"Don't worry, Mister Skye. When you are old and your belly is cold, I will catch badgers and feed them to you day after day, moon after moon, yes?"

"When I am old I will want to sit in a chair and smoke my pipe and look back on good things."

"Yes! I will do just the same. But we need to find good things to look back upon."

Her bright eyes brimmed with merriment. He sneaked a look at her. He didn't want her to know he was getting interested so he devoured her with small glances from the corner of his eyes, while he pretended to watch a circling crow. She was serenely putting her breakfast gear into the little sack, humming a sweet tune as she worked.

Then she was done.

"Do you want me yet?" she asked.

"I think I should meet your parents first. When Jean Baptiste returns from Europe."

"The badger meat isn't working yet. But it will. Badger never quits. I can feel Badger in me. Pretty soon Badger will take hold of you and shake you."

She was giggling.

Skye ached for some tea. Or even some of the Yank coffee, though he really wanted tea. Some good Oolong would quiet him, let him think. Maybe some tobacco would do it. He wanted a pipe and a smoke. Yes, let the leaf quiet him.

"I will walk with you back to the village," he said, mustering his tattered dignity.

She nodded enthusiastically. "Tonight, then. That will give us a whole day to think about it."

"Ah, no, I'm going to go hunting."

She thought that was pretty amusing. "Badger says no, we're going to get married."

She was so fetching he didn't really mind the idea. Maybe it would work out. Obviously, he had been trapped. Victoria had done it. She had woven this snare and cast it over him as if he were a raccoon. It amazed him, being the object of a great conspiracy between the Crows and Snakes, the intent of which was to overwhelm all his European civility, his pride in being a sensitive and gentle man, his pleasure in being addressed as Mister.

The sun was well up now, casting cheerful golden light across this silent plateau hidden from the camp below. She had collected her things, put out the little fire, and now stood hesitantly, uncertain at last about all this.

The look in her face touched him. It was solemn, almost fearful, as if everything had failed and she would regret this hour for the rest of her days.

He took her hand, peered into those eyes that brimmed with unbidden tears, drew her close, felt her lithe body pressed tight to his own, and then he kissed her. She received his kiss quietly, and slid her arms about his neck, and kissed back, fierce and honeyed.

It sealed everything. If this was the future, then he would welcome the future. This would be good. If this indeed was what Victoria had created by design, then he would welcome it with a full heart. Love? Who could say? Love was something that came out of the south winds, and it would come whenever it blew into his heart. She was beautiful, and felt good in his arms, and held him eagerly as he held her.

"Yes," he said.

"Choose the path and I will walk with you," she said.

"I would like to do this according to the custom of your people," he said.

"I hoped you would."

"What is the first step? How do I make my intentions known?"

"I am in the lodge of my brother. You would bring him a gift."

"A pony? I have several."

She nodded, pleasure suffusing her face.

"Your brother and you are the children of Jean Baptiste Charbonneau. That is good. Two bloods in you will make the life we share easier. You will know my ways better, and I will understand your ways better."

She touched his beard. "It scratches," she said. "Who of the Shoshones has a hairy face?"

"The better to tickle you," he said.

She laughed and clasped his hand as they started toward the village.

"I will bring a horse to your brother. What is his name?"

"In your tongue, The Runner."

"The Runner will take my horse and then what?"

"My people will bring you gifts. The men will smoke with you. The women will spend this day dressing me in beautiful things. White doeskin, fringed skirts, quills, beads, and maybe ribbons in my hair."

"Then?"

"Then, when I am dressed, maybe late in the day when Sun is ready to hide, they will bring me to your lodge. And you will see me."

She gazed anxiously at him.

"See you?"

"You could turn your back and I would be led away."

"Why would I do that?"

"It would mean that I do not please you."

"You already please me . . . Blue Dawn."

"It is Mary. Your older wife is very wise. She says I must be Mary."

"Mary of the Shoshones. Why?"

"It is her wisdom. I will not ask why. I am very pleased with this new name. I like the name. It is a holy name among the white men, is it not?"

"It is."

"Then I am honored. Maybe your first wife knows this and thinks this sacred name is good for me to have."

"Then, when you are brought to me, what next?"

She smiled sweetly. "Then we go into your lodge!"

"And then what?"

"And then your senior wife, sits-beside-him wife, she blesses us."

"How does she do that?"

"Who knows? We'll find out, yes?"

Skye walked with her down the steep trail through scrub trees and grassy parks until they reached the river. He felt oddly unsure of foot, as if the ground might cave in or he might step through thin ice, or a hidden branch of a tree might lash him when he least expected it.

Two wives. This day he would take a second wife. It all seemed so strange, so fraught with peril, he could scarcely imagine it. But it was unfolding now at its own speed, in its own way, almost as if he were a spectator, and this were the work of others. But he knew it wasn't so. He might have been hesitant, might have worried about many things, but he was a willing participant now. He hadn't merely acquiesced;

he had embraced this, and her, and the new world into which he was plunging this sweet summer's day.

He and Mary walked quietly into the bustling village, where children caromed here and there, and youths congregated, and the women, ever-busy, were turning the work of the day into gossip and entertainment, and the sunlight lay golden.

His six horses stood at his lodge, groomed and haltered, their tails switching at flies.

Suddenly he laughed.

"Victoria was very certain how this would end," he said.

Mary laughed too.

"Which horse should I give to The Runner?" he asked.

"The best one," she said.

Chapter 11

She stood there, smiling. He realized suddenly just how beautiful she was. She was glowing. Her glossy jet hair was parted at the center, and hung in braids over her breast. Her flesh, a golden amalgam of two races, glowed in the sunlight. Her figure was slim and ripe. But it was the humor in her eyes that bewitched him. She truly liked him; it was written all over her face.

Around them, the people of the combined villages were enjoying the festive day. Children congregated in odd little knots; young men were already at their archery contests. The maidens were collecting into little groups to share their secrets.

Jawbone eyed Skye suspiciously.

"No, I'm keeping you," Skye said. "Lucky you."

The horse snorted, lowered his head, and threatened anyone to come close.

Skye eyed his best buffalo runner, a line-back dun that had fire in its belly and loved the chase. He would give that to The Runner.

Victoria suddenly emerged from the lodge, eyed Skye and Mary, hands on hips, and began cackling. It was the famous granny cackle of the Crows, lecherous and insinuating.

"Hah, badger meat did it!" she said, and wheezed.

Skye stopped untying the line-back dun. Was this a conspiracy? Had all this been plotted by this powerful woman?

"I told her nothing else would work," Victoria said. "I told her Skye is a desperate case. It would take Big Medicine to make Skye look at another woman. I told her don't go to the damn shamans; their medicine ain't good with white men. She's gotta pull a badger out of his hole and feed you some meat, and if that don't do it, the whole thing's hopeless."

"Hopeless is it? What do you mean, hopeless?" Skye shouted. He didn't know what else to say. He couldn't think of a damned thing to say. "You think I can't, ah, court a woman on my own? That I need some help? That I'm, ah, not a man?"

Victoria was looking pretty smirky and so was Mary. His bride-to-be was smiling blandly, saying nothing, and looking sweeter than ever.

Skye lifted his top hat and smashed it down upon his locks. "Maybe I'll just quit this camp and go off by myself," he yelled.

But his fingers betrayed him. He had loosened the picket line of the dun, and was holding the freed lead rope in his hand.

"Wait," said Victoria. She ducked into their lodge and emerged with the very thing Skye prized most, his bear-claw necklace. "Take that to The Runner too," she said.

"I won't!"

He fingered the necklace. It had been made of grizzly claws, and invested Skye with great powers, the very powers of the most fearsome of all animals. Each claw was six or seven inches long, and had been strung on a thong, through holes in their roots, with trader's beads in between. Defiantly he slid the bear-claw necklace over his neck and tied it in place.

"Dammit, Skye, she's worth it," Victoria said.

Skye was stricken. He looked at Mary, who stared solemnly at him, at the handsome necklace adorning his chest. Yes, she was worth anything he possessed.

"Let's go," Skye snapped. "Show me what lodge."

Quietly, Mary led him across the grassy meadow that separated the two villages, past staring people, all of whom seemed to know what this ritual was about. They entered the Shoshone camp. The lodges rose in a crescent, their lodge doors all facing east as was the custom. A crowd collected and followed, at a respectful distance, with small nods and small smiles directed toward the young woman they knew as Blue Dawn.

Skye soon found himself before a large lodge, artfully decorated with black and brown drawings of successful hunts. Then, suddenly, Mary paused, looked up at him, her face brimming with tenderness. No one emerged from the lodge, but Skye had expected that. The time of meetings and introductions would come. He tied his line-back dun to a stake nearby. Then, while she watched, he undid his treasured bear-claw necklace, fingering those giant polished claws, each one looking like ebony, and then retied the necklace around the neck of the dun. He noticed Jawbone surveying all this from a distance. A silent crowd of Shoshones had gathered. Courting was not done in private, it seemed. There it was; his best running horse, his most treasured medicine item. He turned to her. The look in her face was so loving, so proud, that he would gladly have given everything he possessed at that moment.

"It is time for you to leave me," she said.

He nodded. He didn't want to leave. He was in the middle of something, and he didn't want to wait. But he left. He would know in a glance whether his gifts had been accepted. If they were, his dun would be led away to the herd; if not, it would be returned to him.

She stood before him, while the Shoshones watched their every gesture. Then she nodded, smiled, and slipped into the lodge. He watched as she vanished through the oval door, watched as the door flap fell closed, and then he was there on a grassy field in the middle of morning with twenty or thirty of Mary's people standing politely close by. He nodded, lifted his hat, and hiked back.

Jawbone, in an indignant mood, butted him.

"Avast!" Skye rumbled.

It was odd. He had been nothing but a puppet in this drama. No, that wasn't quite right. Victoria had simply led him through the customs of the two people. The decisions were still all his.

Jawbone veered close and rubbed shoulders with Skye. He reached over the ugly horse's mane and held on.

"We're adding to the family," Skye said. "You'll be a gentleman. You're going to watch over her and protect her. You're going to keep her safe. I will be paying lots of attention to her, and you'll accept that. She's going to be my wife. My wife, understand?"

Jawbone turned his head, eyed Skye, and then walked with his head close to the ground, in abject surrender. Skye didn't like it.

When he reached the Crow camp, he found himself trapped. There, hovering about his lodge, was the one person he would rather not see: Graves Duplessis Mercer, who was practically hopping about.

"Ah! Found you!" he said. "Is it true? You're taking another wife?"

"It might be true; I'm waiting to know."

"Waiting! What's there to wait for?"

"Whether I am acceptable to her family."

"Acceptable! Why wouldn't you be acceptable? You're an Englishman, aren't you?"

"That may be the problem," Skye said.

"I don't understand it. Most of the maidens of the whole world pine for an Englishman."

Skye laughed. The explorer hadn't seen as much of the world as he supposed.

"You old dog! Two wives!"

Skye didn't like the direction of that, so he nodded curtly and kept on toward his lodge.

"Two wives, Skye. But any Englishman can handle six. I suppose you'll keep adding to the menagerie, eh?"

Skye didn't want to confess that this was actually Victoria's idea; that he had been deeply content with one wife; that this was virtually an arranged marriage, worked out in mysterious ways among friendly peoples.

"Now how does this work, Skye. Separate lodges?"

Skye stopped. "It's Mister Skye, sir, and that topic is closed."

"But it's all for science, Mister Skye. I shall write a piece about this. It'll singe fingers at the *London Times*. Two wives! One so gorgeous I had to rub my eyes! You old rascal. Leave it to the English! Now if a Yank tried that, he'd be rebuffed. It's in our blood, you know."

Skye stared stonily.

Mercer subsided. "Mister Skye, I've given offense. I'm truly sorry. It's all a bit exotic to me, and my mind tends to run with the things I see, so far from home. I want to wish you a most blessed nuptial day, and I hope your household is blessed with happiness."

Skye accepted the apology. That was the thing about Mercer. New things, exotic things, were all the same to him. Absaroka marriage custom excited no more curiosity than geysers or giant bones in the earth. The odd thing was, Skye rather liked the man, and enjoyed all his boyish enthusiasms.

"Thank you. My household will be improved. I hope you will be on hand when the moment arrives."

"Capital, capital! I'll have a fine journal entry today. Now what happens tomorrow? How long does this little summer festival go on?"

"Oh, who knows, sir. Until there's no more grass for the ponies. Until the trading and marrying and cementing of alliances are done."

"But a day? A week? The year's well advanced and I have a whole world to conquer, and I rather have plans that involve you, if you're interested."

"I'm not."

"Well, think about it. I would like a guide. I'll pay you handsomely. I earn plenty from my journals and books, and will reward the right man. I'd like someone to take us up to the geysers. And take us to the giant bones. And take us to any other peculiar places. Or show us lost tribes, pygmies, things like that, that might be hidden back in the wilderness somewhere. Is there not a strange rock formation called a medicine wheel, that invokes the sun or solstice? I'm here to record it all, sir. And do it before the snow flies. Maybe end up at Fort Benton, eh?"

"I don't think I'm the man, Mister Mercer."

"A hundred pounds. That'd fetch a man a few things, wouldn't it? Credit any way you want it."

A hundred pounds was a lot of money. Five hundred Yank dollars, more or less.

"That's not for me to decide today, sir," Skye said, suspecting that it was already decided.

Chapter 12

Skye was as nervous as a groom about to walk the aisle of Westminster Cathedral. He twitched and paced. He sighed. He threatened to bolt and never be seen in these parts again.

Victoria sat him down and pulled out a tiny German steel scissor.

"I'm going to trim your beard," she said, and gently began shaping it into a disciplined round form. He submitted peacefully, enjoying the attention.

"White men have too damned much hair," she grumbled. "We see the first white men, we didn't call them white men, we called them hairy men. The hairy men are coming!"

"Are you sure you want me . . ."

"Don't wiggle your head or you'll be cut. Maybe you should be cut. Maybe that's what I'll do."

Skye submitted at once. "Where will you be? What are you doing tonight?" he asked.

"You'll see."

"I need an answer."

"I will be in our lodge."

Skye sank into himself. This was going to be a very difficult night. He didn't know how or when he would ever see another dawn. What would happen in a lodge with his older wife and his new one?

She finished the trim, turned his head this way and that, and proclaimed herself satisfied.

"Now what?" he asked.

"Wash. Your feet smell like a swamp, as usual."

"You don't have to insult me."

"I love swamps."

"Victoria . . . I . . ."

"You don't have to say anything."

He didn't feel particularly guilty. Victoria was the spider who had spun this web; she'd been after him for years to find another wife. But . . . yes, he did feel guilty. Blue Dawn, who would become Mary soon, evoked lust in him. He ached to make love to her. And that was too much for him to cope with.

"I just want you to know I'll always love you," he said.

Victoria broke into that granny smirk so famous among Crow women. It was a lewd, winking smirk. He had seen it thousands of times. Crow grannies could make a soldier blush.

"If you give one thought to me tonight, I'll be mad at you," she said.

At this point he wasn't capable of giving one thought to anything; not her, not Mary, not himself.

He headed for the river, pulled off his moccasins, laved his feet carefully, and the rest of himself as best he could. When he returned, she had laid out his best skins, golden fringed buckskin shirt, with geometric red and black Crow quillwork. And a new pair of moccasins he hadn't known about. The quillwork on them matched his shirt.

She brushed his beaver top hat, cleaned away some mud, popped out some dents, and restored it to him.

"What do they wear where you come from?" she asked.

"A black swallowtail suit. Or gray. Or nothing fancy if a man is humble."

"England is a scandal," she said. "Utterly savage."

Handsomely adorned, he stepped into the late-afternoon sun. An odd hush had settled over the meadow, an air of anticipation. Jawbone squealed and boomed down upon him.

"Whoa," Skye said.

The horse sniffed, bared its yellow teeth, and screeched.

"You get to be Best Man," Skye said. "You going to have a ring ready for me?"

Jawbone reared, pawed the air, settled to earth, and grunted.

It was odd thinking of marriage in white men's terms, brides, grooms, rings, attendants, churches. This was all so different it seemed not to be a union of a man and a woman.

"Ah, there you are, Mister Skye, looking capital, capital," said Mercer.

The man had gotten himself up in his best, which wasn't half bad considering how far he was from a clothier or laundress. He had brushed his trousers, cleaned his boots, trimmed his hair, washed his face, clipped his own beard.

"Thank you. I'll never get used to this," Skye said.

"You old dog. I haven't decided whether to send it to the Manchester paper or the London. Manchester, I imagine. London's too cosmopolitan. A little spice works better out in the provinces, you know."

"Spice, Mister Mercer?"

"Spice, Mister Skye. It's a good thing you are marrying the most beautiful girl in this entire camp. I plan to make note of it."

Skye laughed. One could not escape Mercer.

Victoria herself emerged from the lodge, pulling away the flap from the oval door. He saw at once that she had adorned herself. Her hair was parted and shone bright in the sun. She wore her loveliest gingham, blue with a white pattern running through it, and she had blue-quilled moccasins to match. What would her role be? She wasn't exactly the mother of the bride.

She smiled at Skye, took his hand and squeezed, and then smiled at Mercer, who bowed gallantly.

By some mysterious clockwork known only to Indians, a party gathered over on the Shoshone side of the meadow, a dozen people perhaps, and Skye could see even across that verdant flat that they were festively dressed, and lots of bold reds, sky blues, and creamy buckskin colors filtered to his vision.

There were several women, fewer men. Back a way, much of the Shoshone village followed. So the cathedral would be filled; every pew!

Skye simply stood, not knowing whether to meet this on-coming party halfway. But Victoria simply smiled and waited. Leading the party were two slim people, a young man and a young woman, and Skye knew at once these were The Runner, and his sister, Blue Dawn, soon to become the second Missus Skye.

How handsome they were, their faces bronzed by a be-nevolent sun, their dress breathtaking. He wore fringed elk skins without a single bit of decor, but over his neck hung that bear-claw necklace, its long, lethal black claws curv-ing down in an arc over his breast. Her dress was quite the opposite, for she had been festively attired in every way. Her jet hair was parted at the center and hung in shiny braids laced with scarlet ribbons, and with a white ribbon at the tip of each braid. A streak of vermilion was painted on her amber forehead. She wore a whitened doeskin dress, as soft as flour, and lining each sleeve were jingle-bells that sang merrily in the hush of the afternoon. High moccasins trimmed with red encased her feet. A blue girdle, or sash, caught her waist. It truly was a bridal costume, and her eyes danced with anticipation as she caught sight of Skye.

Behind were other handsomely dressed women, each bearing burdens Skye could not fathom.

They approached.

Jawbone screeched and whinnied. They paused a moment, but Skye smiled, assuring them.

He only had eyes for her. She only had eyes for him.

The Runner stopped before Skye. "Prithee, be thou Mister Skye?"

"Yes, and are you The Runner?"

"Verily, thou knowest my name. My Shoshone name. I am also, in thy blessed tongue, St. John. Thus did my pater christen he who standeth before thee."

"Ah, I see."

"I rejoice to speak in thy blessed tongue. My good father taught me words, and gave me the secret of reading, and left three books upon which I might whet my powers. Thy holy book, and one of a teller of tales, one Shakespeare, and other whose blessed name I don't fathom because his name was torn from the front. From these I have mastered thy tongue."

"You do very well, sir."

"It has taken much practice. But sirrah, thou hast spoken for my sister, and thus cometh I to present her to thee. Is she comely?"

"Ravishing."

The Runner frowned. "You would call her that?"

"Beautiful."

"Ah, that is a comfort. We bring thee emoluments and honors. See? Thou shalt have a quilled shirt, and thou shalt have a holy bundle to wear about thy neck, upon thy bosom, in which shall be the sacred things of the One-God blackrobes, along with our holy things, a turtle stone and an eagle claw."

Skye accepted the small leather bundle, and lowered the necklace over his chest.

"Sonofabitch," said Victoria. "Big stuff!"

"And now, prithee, Mister Skye, dost thee wish to take hold of my sister and carry her away to thy abode?"

"Yes, sir."

"Then we rejoice and sing Hosannas. Take her. She is thine. Be thou blessed. Maketh her fruitful; fill the world with thy children. Seal with her the peace betwixt the Absaroka and the Shoshone, and thy own pale ones from across the seas."

He nodded to his sister, who walked forward to Skye, stood before him expectantly. Skye scarcely knew what was required, so he caught her hands in his, answered her smile with his own.

"To you I am wed; to you I pledge my love and life," he said.

That seemed to fulfill these people. A sudden relaxation swept through this large crowd.

"Well done, old sport," called Mercer. "She's a handful."

Skye found himself so joyous that nothing the explorer might say could possibly mar the moment.

The Runner stepped close, clasped Skye, and smiled. "It is blessed," he said.

And so the moment dissolved, until there was only Victoria, Mary, Jawbone, and himself.

"I guess we'd better go home," he said, uncertainly.

"No, I will go to our lodge. I will carry these things given to you," Victoria said. "You and Mary, you go that way, dammit." She pointed toward a distant lodge, one Skye hadn't noticed, far apart from the Crow village.

"It is a place the People have prepared for you and the Shoshone woman," she said. "It will be a good place."

Chapter 13

The lonely lodge stood perhaps a thousand yards distant, and Skye hurried toward it in the thickening dusk. Mary was as eager as he, and matched his stride with her own. A fine, hot, wild passion was building in Skye, and he knew she was enjoying the moment as much as he.

It was a soft night. The lodge had been pitched beside some larches in a moist hollow, somewhat below the surrounding meadow. A jovial moon was climbing the rim of the world and tossing yellow light upon this Eden. The air felt balmy, somehow more moist than elsewhere in the camp.

He clasped her hand.

Jawbone meandered along behind, not quite abreast but not inclined to abandon his owner, either. The horse was envious. It amused Skye. Where else on earth was such a beast?

They reached the lodge, a small cone nestled in moist grass and screened by the trees, so that the village was invisible.

He handed her through the oval door and into the hushed dark, where only a little twilight filtering through the smoke hole lit their way. The floor was plush with robes.

He couldn't wait, and swept her into his arms, and she hugged him fiercely. But the whine at his ears troubled him. He slapped away a mosquito, and more, and again. The faint humming swelled to a night whine now, and he and she began swatting fiercely, surrounded by scores, and then maybe hundreds. They lit on his neck and hands. He swatted. He felt the sting of several.

She slapped at her neck and her calves.

He yanked the door flap aside and pulled her out, but the mosquitoes found them outside as well as in.

"Mary, head for that high ground. I'll get some robes and follow," he said.

"This is a bad place," she said.

He laughed. "It's a Crow joke. They love nothing better than a joke like this."

"Joke! This is a joke?" She slapped at two mosquitoes that had landed on her wrist.

"Go!" he said.

He dove into the lodge, plucked up two heavy robes, and plunged out, cussing at the cloud of whining bloodsuckers that were tormenting them.

He caught up with her as they raced up a long grade into air that was somehow dryer and scented with juniper from the slopes above. Eventually they were free of the swarming mosquitoes.

"This is a joke?"

"Yes, and probably Victoria's little surprise."

Mary was quiet, and then turned to him. "She is your sits-beside-him woman. Will she be kind to me?"

"You have to understand Absaroka humor," he said. "It is not meant to harm, but to frustrate. There's nothing a grandmother loves so much as a story about lovers frustrated by mosquitoes. Or anything else. It could be a snake or a skunk or a horse. It could be old Coyote. When Coyote frustrates lovers, that's the biggest joke of all."

"Can we play a joke on her?"

Skye laughed. He liked that. "We'll think on it."

"We will make a joke!" she said, delighted at the prospect.

They climbed an arid hillside through thickening juniper brush, the resinous scent sweet to his nostrils. There was something clean and bracing in the scent.

"It is good, here," she said. "Find a place, Skye."

The request was so winsome, so tender, so eager that Skye felt half mad. Ahead, pale in moonlight, was a bluff. He headed that way. Behind, he heard Jawbone crashing through the dense juniper. The bluff proved to be a rocky outcrop, so he followed its base until they happened upon a bower, half cupped by overhanging rock, and surrounded on its lower side by a wall of juniper as high as a man's chest. There were no mosquitoes there, and no harsh wind and nothing but nature's own invitation to lovers. Swiftly he scraped away the debris of gravel and juniper sticks under the overhang until the clay was clean and the ground was sweet.

She stood quietly.

"This is good, Mister Skye," she said.

It was good.

"You are my man," she said.

"And you are my woman, Mary."

It was almost dawn before they tumbled into sleep. Then he dreamed sad dreams: everything a mistake. Victoria, hurt. Victoria, silent. He dreamed of pulling into himself, talking to no one. Going away, never coming back. Cold. He awakened in bright daylight. She was staring at him, sitting bare on her robes, her eyes soft.

"You did not sleep well," she said. "I think you maybe too tired, yes?" Her eyes were merry.

He nodded. She was beautiful, her golden flesh aglow in the morning sun. Yet he felt a sadness he could not define.

It was not rational. He had spent the sweetest night of his life.

But the serenity of the morning swiftly stole through him, that and her sweetness as she settled beside him and pressed her lips to his. The kiss was honey at first, and then paprika, and then as fiery as chili peppers. He thought only of her, and she was thinking only of him. There was nothing else; no warm sun, no sweet morning, no resinous junipers guarding their bower. They captured each other and fell back onto the soft mat of the buffalo robes, and let the world return to their consciousness. A bee hummed past, hunting for blooms hidden under the juniper canopy.

Only hunger could have driven them from that place, and in time Skye was ravenous for a haunch of buffalo. He helped Mary collect the robes, and they wound their way down the foothills to the encampment and their peoples. The Shoshones smiled at them shyly; the Absarokas smiled slyly. Skye sensed he was facing yet another of those small hurdles that a multiple marriage might bring. How would Victoria be this bright morning? How would he feel toward her? Maybe it was all the nonsense of his European ways; maybe not. Maybe there were many men who would wonder whether they could divide their love among two or three wives.

And what else? How would Victoria treat Mary? How would the wives get along? What if one wife tried to ally Skye against the other wife? He suddenly realized he was borrowing trouble, thinking this way. He laughed, and plunged through the Crow camp toward his own lodge. Actually, it was Victoria's lodge. A Crow man rarely owned his lodge.

Victoria was kneeling beside an elk hide she was scraping; women's work never ended, even on festive occasions.

"Well, dammit, now I got someone to help me," she said.

"I started this before the sun rose, while you were busy."
She laughed suddenly, a small cheerful chuckle.

"I will work, grandmother," said Mary, hastily kneeling
beside Victoria, and grabbing a bone scraper.

"The hell you will," Victoria said. She rose, fed kindling
into the embers of a morning fire, and was soon rewarded
with flames licking the black cook pot.

Mary rushed to help, but Victoria shooed her off.

Victoria stood, eyed the fire, and smiled at Skye. It was
a loving smile. He hastened to her, drew her tight, and was
rewarded with a hug. She welcomed his arms and he welcomed hers, and that was all that needed to be said or done.
But Skye wondered how he would ever sort it all out. Mary
was discreetly staring off toward her Shoshone camp.

Victoria plucked up Skye's arm and examined it minutely.

"I don't see any," she said.

"Any what?"

"Mosquito bites. I don't see none on her, either. I guess
you were too busy to get bit." She cackled.

"Is the lodge still there?" he asked.

"Hell no," Victoria replied. She turned to stirring the
stew, and let it go at that.

The wedding night sure had been public.

Suddenly it was fine. They would feast. He was ready to
eat half a buffalo. Mary looked ready to eat the other half.
This afternoon they would leisurely visit friends and family. There would be a good visit with The Runner. It amazed
him: here were Shoshone siblings who could speak English
after a fashion, a legacy of a father living in Europe.

Victoria poured the steaming stew into wooden bowls
and bade them eat. This was a feast. Many a morning Skye
had sawed off some cold venison or buffalo haunch or elk
meat from a cooked roast, and eaten it. But the warmed
meal was Victoria's way of celebrating the new day.

They ate greedily, and then Mary silently collected the bowls, let the camp curs lick them clean, and headed for the river to wash them. Skye watched her go, aware of the lovely body that shifted beneath Mary's skirts.

"You look worn-out, Skye. She wear you out, eh?" Victoria said. "Maybe she's too much for you, eh? Englishmen, they all wear out too fast."

Skye lifted his hat, settled it down on his locks, and roared. "Worn-out! Just try me and see how worn out this Englishman is!"

Victoria made bawdy noises, plainly pleased, and continued with her hide-scraping.

Skye stretched, fed and relaxed and comfortable as the sun pumped some warmth into the morning. Around him the summer's visit was winding down. Skye saw some of the women packing their kitchens into parfleches, while over in the Shoshone camp, the women were hooking travois to horses and loading heaps of robes and bundles onto them. The summer's fun was coming to a close.

That's when Graves Duplessis Mercer threw a shadow across Skye, and stared down at him.

"Well, you lucky dog, I don't suppose you're worth a thing today."

Skye nodded curtly.

"Camp's breaking up. I want to hire you. I need a guide. It's now or never, Skye. There's things to see before the snow falls. You interested? A hundred pounds."

Skye found himself saying yes even before he could weigh the offer.

Chapter 14

Skye waved the man to a log that served as a bench. Mercer always managed to look dashing and now was wearing a broad-brimmed felt hat, a canvas shirt, and short britches that bared hairy white calves.

"Let's talk about it," Skye said. "Where are you heading? What do you want to see?"

"The geysers near here. And the big bones your older wife was telling me about. I also want to meet strange tribes. I want to discover ones that have never seen a white man. There are some, you know. Down in the desert canyons. If you know of tribes that practice cannibalism, that's my meat."

He laughed at his own joke.

"And where are you headed? It's late in the year."

"Why, the Oregon country. After we're done here, I'll hook up with Hudson's Bay, take the first ship out. To the Pacific islands I hope, but I'll take China or Australia or whatever. I have journals to go to London. Need to find a ship sailing somewhere."

"You're too late to get to Oregon, Mister Mercer."

"Too late! How can I be too late?"

"It's August. You need to be on the Columbia a month from now."

"Well, we'll be there."

The man had little grasp of North American geography and even less grasp of its winter climate. He didn't realize how far he had strayed from the Yank road to Oregon, the only practical way over the continental divide, the only way to reach waters flowing west.

"If you were to head this day for the Oregon Road and then head west as fast as you can move with that wagon, you might barely make the Pacific coast before winter shuts you in."

"But, Mister Skye, it's summer. It's hot. I'm dressed in tropical clothing."

Skye was relentless. "You could do some sightseeing in this country, reach Fort Benton on the Missouri River in October, build or buy a flatboat, and reach St. Louis just ahead of bad weather."

"I should turn around? Return to St. Louis?"

"If you want to see the sights here, yes, turn around. If you want to hightail for Oregon, start now, this hour. Don't waste a minute."

Mercer sprang up and paced. He had a boyish quality but Skye sensed the man was harder and more resourceful than his demeanor suggested. Victoria, who had been listening, squinted darkly at Skye. He knew she didn't approve. But a hundred pounds would outfit Skye for years. It was worth the risk posed by this adventurer.

"Oh, pshaw, Mister Skye, I think I'll just do what I planned; see the geysers, see the bones. The weather will hold. You're looking at the luckiest Englishman on the planet. If I'd quit in the middle of half my projects, I'd be moldering as a printer's devil in London. Look at me! I've walked through jungles where bushmen waited with poisoned darts. I've watched Asian cultists lower a little girl into a pit of cobras. I've watched Pacific islanders give a goat to a phallic god. I've seen midnight fertility dances that I can't even write about. I've watched prisoners staked out upon a mound of meat-eating ants. I've watched Afri-

can mutilation ceremonies that I would have to describe in
Latin. I've walked into the bowels of an active volcano. I've
weathered a Sahara sandstorm. I've watched cannibals eat
their guests. I've swum rivers filled with man-eating fish. I
have swum with sharks. I have sailed an outrigger canoe
across the Indian Ocean. I have watched a blind man snare
and eat giant frogs, and catch poisonous eels bare-handed.
I have ridden the backs of whales. Was I afraid? Never."

That did it. "Mister Mercer, I won't guide men who are
never afraid," Skye said.

Mercer didn't even pause. "Why, I was just exaggerat-
ing, old boy. Showing off, you know." He smiled, revealing that row of dazzling white teeth so perfect Skye
thought that maybe they'd been carved from ivory.

"I think you would find none of those things here, Mister Mercer. You're on the wrong continent."

"I'd give my eyeteeth for just a peek at a lost tribe, one
that survives in some canyon somewhere. Or some ruins
like those in Peru. Whole cities rotting away down there.
They're common enough in Mexico. Do you suppose you
could guide me there?"

"I would be as lost there as you, sir."

"Blast. I have to make a living. What is there to say about
this dull place? Someday it will be villages and plowed
fields. And the Indians will all wear calico and leather shoes
and get married by Methodist clergy."

"There's North American wildlife, Mister Mercer."

"No match for Africa. How does this compare with ele-
phants and giraffes? Or Australia. Dingos, kangaroos, and
all that. Pitiful. Who wants to read about bears? Mister
Skye, what I want is strange people who live in strange
ways. That's what sells penny dreadfuls in Liverpool."

"I'm fresh out of strange people, sir."

"There are some. Plural marriage. I've been thinking of

wintering with the Mormons down in Deseret. That should be worth some ink, eh? How do they do it? A few stories from Deseret, and every lusty man in London will set sail. Ho, ho! That's the only interesting thing about North America. Every man on the continent has a spare wife or two stashed away."

Skye laughed. He thought it was time to get the horses and pull out. The Crows were loading their travois. "You'll do fine, Mister Mercer," he said, and stood.

"You win, Mister Skye. I surrender. You take us to the geysers, and then show us the big bones, and I'll head for Deseret for the winter. We'll just ride to the high country and take a few hot baths and then turn it over to Old Man Winter."

"There's a hundred miles of forest, canyons, cliffs, rocky creeks, walls of brush to get to the geysers. It would take a while."

"I have been all over the world. Whenever guides tell me I can't do something, I set out to do it."

"That's fine. I'll draw you a map. You can leave the wagon right here."

"That wagon's my supply depot. If I leave it here, I'll lose everything in it. I can't leave it here. It has to come with me. I want my men with me too. They're good men."

"If you want to stay with your wagon you'd better choose some other sights to see, Mister Mercer."

The explorer had an odd trapped look in his eyes. He wasn't used to being thwarted. "Where are the giant bones?"

Skye turned to Victoria.

"All over hell and back," she said.

"Madam, where is hell and back?"

She pointed southeast. "Some that way, on a ridge near the Medicine Bow Mountains. Near Fort Laramie." She pointed north. "Some that way, near Fort Benton." She pointed east. "Some that way in bad country. Lots of Sioux around there."

Mercer paced back and forth, weighing things, his lust for adventure frustrated by the impending winter and the terrain.

"The bones north of here, then. The ones near Fort Benton." Mercer smiled, that high-energy smile that always seemed to settle things in his mind.

"I'll talk to my men. You get ready to go."

Skye wasn't sure. "We need to address some things. A hundred pounds when? What are my duties? For how long? How will I be paid? Where will my services end? What exactly do you expect of me?"

Mercer seemed to be expecting the questions: "You will be paid at the conclusion of satisfactory service. I can give you a letter of credit good at any fur company post or Hudson's Bay. You will guide us and hunt for us, your women will provide meals and amenities, you'll show us natural wonders known to yourself or your women, you'll translate or use sign language; you'll keep us out of danger and warn me if any sort of trouble looms. You will work until winter prohibits further exploration, and then take us to Fort Benton and get us a flatboat."

Skye nodded. "I have some requirements of my own, sir. In times of danger I will expect you to do exactly what I require, and without delay. If we should encounter some Blackfeet, there may be no time at all to debate. Is that suitable to you?"

"Oh, Mister Skye, those occasions are so rare they're hardly worth worrying ourselves."

"I must have that assurance."

"Oh, have it your way, Mister Skye. Let's be off, eh?"

Victoria was listening and frowning. Mary sat quietly on

a robe. Victoria's eyes were filled with messages, which Skye swiftly understood.

"Something else, Mister Mercer. You will see things and places that are sacred to the people who live here. You respect what you see in any church; you will, I trust, respect what you see here. The bones we will take you to are the bones of the gods and must be treated as such."

"I enjoy writing about the local cults, old boy. The better the myths, the more I like them."

What was it about Mercer that worried Skye? No matter. He would deal with it.

"All right. We'll go to the big bones, and then Fort Benton."

Mercer nodded and headed for his wagon and men. Skye watched him as he addressed his teamsters. They sprang to life at once, collecting the draft horses, packing a mound of gear.

Skye turned to his ladies. "We've been engaged by Mister Mercer. It will earn us a lot of money; there will be good things for all of us at the trading posts." He turned to Mary. "We'll be going to see the giant bones in the rocks. If you wish to say good-bye to your brother and your people, now is the time."

"We will leave my people?"

"Yes. We'll go north with Victoria's people. The man is a storyteller, and is gathering stories to tell people where he comes from."

"Will you give me to him?"

There it was. "Why do you ask?"

"It is the way he looks at me."

"If he tries something like that, I will stop it. You are my wife."

She lit up. "Then it will be a trip to remember!"

"If he doesn't get us in trouble," Victoria said.

Chapter 15

The Absarokas reached the glinting Yellowstone four days later. Mercer and his teamsters tagged along without difficulty as they traversed level and semiarid ground with few creeks to ford. Skye rode Jawbone, keeping an eye on Mercer and his teamsters and the wagon as well as Mary and Victoria, who guided the travois-burdened horses. The wives fell smoothly into companionship. Skye was pleased. Victoria was less crabby than she had ever been, finding that her life had improved.

Mary had offered a tender good-bye to The Runner and her people, and had joined Skye's small household with no visible emotion. Somehow, it all was working and Skye's uneasiness had gradually dissolved. He was also more at ease with Mercer, who proved to be a good travel companion, undemanding and competent to deal with life far from anything resembling civilization as he knew it.

They traversed a grove of cottonwoods and reached the Yellowstone River at a place where it ran through a broad meadow, hemmed by distant bluffs. Even as the Absarokas pulled up on the south bank to water and rest their ponies, they were hailed by a lone traveler heading west, a white man in a gray slouch hat, leading two pack mules.

The Absarokas greeted him with curiosity and asked Skye to translate. Graves Mercer and his teamsters headed toward the stranger even as the Crows flocked around him.

The meeting was all smiles and the stranger doffed his slouch hat time and again, his salute to these people.

The man actually was middle-aged with a trimmed gray beard, spectacles, watery blue eyes, brown canvas clothing, and laced boots.

"This is a surprise," he said. "Nutmeg here. Samuel Storrs Nutmeg at your service."

The man halted his pack mules and acknowledged the collecting crowd. The man's way of clipped and precise speaking awakened curiosity in Skye. Was he a Yank?

"I'm Mister Skye," he said. "My wives Mary and Victoria. This is Graves Duplessis Mercer and his assistants, Floyd Corporal and Silas Winding. And I shall introduce you to our headmen directly."

"Mister Skye, are you? I've been advised that you're the man to hire if one needs a guide. I made some inquiries."

"I seem to have acquired a reputation, deserved or not," Skye said. "And you, sir?"

"A Connecticut Yankee. New Haven, actually. I'm a professor," said Nutmeg. He turned to the explorer. "And you, Mister Mercer. I know your work."

"And I know yours, Professor. Yale College is it?"

"Indeed it is. What a stroke! A pair of wanderers out in the American desert."

Skye peered about, looking for evidence of a desert and finding none. The meadow was mostly sun-cured tan grasses waving in the breezes.

"What brings you to this remote place?" Mercer asked the stranger.

"Science," the man replied. "I am doing a bit of exploration. Maybe you've read a paper or two of mine. Mostly academic journals, my own little sallies against orthodoxy. Took two years off, and spending my last dollar too. I'm heading for the geyser country. You know what's up there?

Obsidian. The stuff has been traded all over the continent. There are regular work yards there, where it was flaked into arrowheads and spear points. It seems to be a prized item among the tribes. I've traced it to the Ohio River valley."

"Natural science! Why, that's why I'm here."

"I don't care to pigeonhole myself," Nutmeg said. "I'm the proverbial square peg. A bit of anthropology, a bit of paleontology, a bit of geology, a bit of zoology, and a dose of botany."

"You have no guide?"

Nutmeg smiled. "Maps and a compass. Two good mules. A field glass. Some interviews a few weeks ago with the mountain men in St. Louis. Some notes and sketches of landmarks. I can't afford a guide, Mister Mercer, not on my salary. So I ramble along quite on my own."

"Quite so. A brave man, sir. I congratulate you."

Skye intervened. "I'd like you to meet our headmen, Mister Nutmeg. They're waiting here, wishing to greet you."

"Very good," Nutmeg said.

Skye, translating, introduced the traveler to Chief Robber and the headmen as well as dozens of Absarokas, who welcomed him. Some of them wanted to know what this lone traveler did and Skye responded that he was a collector of plants and animals and stones. Very like the other one, Mercer.

And in turn, he translated for Nutmeg. "The Absarokas are heading east, downriver, into buffalo country. It'll soon be time for the fall hunt and the buffalo usually are thickest east of here. You are welcome to join them."

"Ah, a pity. I was hoping they might join me for a trip to the geysers but we seem to be heading in opposite directions."

"You're going to the headwaters of the Yellowstone?

Where that geyser is that you can set a clock by?" Mercer asked, an edge to his questions.

"Why yes, it's now or never before the snow flies."

"My man here tells me it's not passable. Rushing rivers and all that."

"For a man with pack mules it is. I understand I'll have no problem if I do it on foot."

"My guide wouldn't take me there," Mercer said.

Skye kept silent. Mercer's statement was not complete or true, but Mercer neither finished nor corrected it.

"All I have to do is follow this splendid river right into the bosom of the geysers, and catch fat trout all the way," Nutmeg said. "Simple enough, eh? Easy way in and out. Why, I'm told once I'm up there I'll see steam rising from geysers everywhere I look. Imagine it. Steam hissing and spitting out of a hole in the rocks. The earth belching a column of hot water and thundering like a volcano. I'm going to take some temperatures, and test the waters for minerals. A little sulphur, I suppose. Who knows what else? I've a kit, you know, a regular laboratory. It's time someone did some work on the geysers."

"All alone. Don't you prefer company?"

Nutmeg paused, eyed Mercer, and slowly shook his head. "I'm a bit of a loner, Mister Mercer. I take my time, go where my curiosity leads me."

"Well, those geysers aren't the only things in the whole area worth writing about."

Nutmeg smiled. "I should think there would be wonders everywhere. But who am I to say? This gentleman, Skye here, is the best man to steer you. That's what I learned in St. Louis."

Mercer responded with one of those toothy smiles.

The Absarokas were restless, impatient to move, unable

to understand all of this palaver. After much consultation they headed downriver. Victoria watched her people go, her face a mask. The Indians forded the Yellowstone at a broad gravelly shallows, the horses splashing through hock-deep water, and continued down the north bank until at last they rounded a bend and vanished. Now there was only silence, bright sun, crows and magpies, and a sparkling river.

"Mister Skye, I've changed my mind," said Mercer. "I think I'll just tag along with Professor Nutmeg. He can teach me lots of things. We'll wagon most of the way. Look at this flat. The river's running through a wide valley, no trouble at all to take a wagon upstream."

Skye stared sharply. Professor Nutmeg had offered no such invitation. "I thought you wanted a look at the fossil bones, Mister Mercer."

"Bones? What bones? What are you talking about, man?" Mercer seemed much put out.

"Fossil bones, Mister Skye?" asked Nutmeg.

"My wife's people know of some, north of here in the Missouri breaks and a few other places. Mister Mercer wished to be taken there."

Mercer dismissed it all. "Oh, I expect they'll be just a few trilobites, ammonites, little stuff caught in a limestone bluff."

"Damn big bones," said Victoria. "Giants from the old days. My people are afraid of them. Their spirits live there, don't like no trouble."

"Madam, I don't believe it is possible to find large bones in fossil form. The geologic pressures are too great," Mercer said.

Nutmeg was absorbing all of this with acute interest. "That would be interesting, looking at fossil bones, Mister Skye. I daresay, some recent discoveries have excited the whole world of natural science. Bones of ancient creatures twenty feet high, giant lizards, so they seem. Obviously extinct."

"Nothing around here, Professor. Wrong strata. Too recent," Mercer said. "A look at the fossils is just a side trip. We're really having a hard look at some of the tribes. Customs, dances, all that. That's what I do, you know, write about people they've never heard of in London."

"Yes, and your pieces are widely read, Mister Mercer. They make their way across the Atlantic."

Skye registered all of this with some surprise. Rivalry. But most of all, secrecy. Nutmeg didn't want Mercer tagging along to the geyser country; Mercer didn't want Nutmeg to know about the bone fields Victoria was going to show to him. Mercer was being deceptive, but not Nutmeg. The professor was straightforward. It was Mercer who had scented a rival.

"Mister Mercer, I think you'll be happy to proceed to the fossil bones," Skye said. "I think you will be delighted by your discoveries. That's where you hired us to take you."

For a moment there was thunder in Mercer's face and then the dazzling smile and the pearly teeth.

"Why, Mister Skye, old fellow, we'll continue on our way. I really wouldn't want to risk a wagon up in the headwaters of the Yellowstone. The geysers interest me not in the slightest."

Skye had a whole new perspective on the man who had employed him. First Mercer wanted to tag along with the professor, a sudden change in plans. Then Mercer tried to conceal what he was up to, lying to Nutmeg about the size of the bones. Clearly, there were sides to Mercer that would inspire caution. Skye wondered if he would last for the agreed-on period, or get paid.

Chapter 16

Navigation was in Victoria's hands. She knew where the giant bones were; Skye had seen them once but couldn't recollect just where. All she told him was that they were not far from the confluence of the Musselshell and the Missouri Rivers.

She led them north across high plains laced with giant coulees, sandstone ridges, and gulches filled with cottonwood trees. To the north and west, distant mountain ranges poked through autumnal haze. It was not a welcoming land. It was a place that made a man feel lonely. Sometimes when the wind quit, Skye could hear utterly nothing. The silence ran so deep that it made a man itchy. It was a land to hurry through.

The party proceeded peaceably enough. The two teamsters knew intuitively where to steer the giant draft horses as they worked up and down long grades and across a roadless sea of grass. The horses stayed fat, devouring the rich fodder.

At night, his women rarely raised the lodge, choosing to bed in buffalo robes under a bowl of stars. This always occasioned stares from Mercer and the teamsters, who put up their wall tent each evening. Let them think whatever they wanted to think. Skye didn't care. The nights were as black as nights could be and how he and his wives lived would be veiled from the men.

Skye roamed wide on Jawbone, training the young horse

to close on buffalo from downwind and then race close to give Skye the lethal shot he needed to down the nimble animal. The great herds drifted across the sky-girt lands in small bunches, as feed and water dictated. Meat was never far away for Skye's party. This was, in its way, a food pantry, but Mercer didn't see it that way.

"When will we get to the bones, Skye?" he asked after several days of steady progress.

"Long way, mate. A week, ten days."

"But, Skye, there's nothing here. This is the most boring land I've ever crossed."

"It's a quiet land, I'll grant you that. But look around you. It's big country. Have you ever seen country so large or the sky so high?"

"But where's the story, Skye? I make my living writing stories. I can't see a story anywhere. I'm wasting time."

Skye hardly knew how to respond. "There's a story in every rock, I imagine. You've seen the way the wind sculpts the sandstone. All those little wind caves make dens for catamounts, nests for birds, cubbyholes for coyotes."

Mercer didn't see it and grew more and more testy.

"Skye, if we were crossing the Sahara, there'd be a story every mile. Dunes as high as mountains. The Berbers! Bright blue eyes, Nordic faces. I'd swear they were Vikings except they have big noses, bigger than yours. Bedouins! Camel caravans! Ancient trade routes known only to those camel drivers. They smoke hashish. They eat sheep's eyeballs. They touch not a drop of spirits. They sometimes lose their trading goods to bandits, swift raiders on fine Arab horses that swirl out of the dust and cut them dead with scimitars. The whole Sahara is a thieves' den, Skye. Murders! Assassinations! Those caravans! The traders enter oases as if they were caliphs, and are welcomed by sloe-eyed women with flashing smiles behind their veils. Well, Skye, where's the story here? Am I on the wrong continent? I ought to have ten sensations a day to fill my journals!"

Skye nodded. A man looking for a sensation here might have a harder time of it. Skye couldn't help that.

The farther north they proceeded, the more he watched for Blackfeet. A war party could hide in any gulch and never be seen. So Skye roamed wide, examined the age of spoor, studied the world from ridges, and checked with his client now and then.

Mercer grew grouchy. "How long, Skye! This was a mistake! I should have known better than to come here! Can't you speed things up?"

"The pace is set by your teamsters, sir. It's the wagon that slows us. Mister Corporal and Mister Winding are making sure those draft horses don't fail you."

"I'll tell them to hurry it up. Those horses are fine, fit as a fiddle, fat. I tell you, this is a wasted time; I'll have to write off the whole business."

"You could study the buffalo, sir. Come with me while I hunt. They're a wise and majestic beast. They can't see well but they can smell. Only the fastest horse can outrun them. When they stampede, the whole earth vibrates."

"Who cares about the buffalo? Just big, dumb uglies, that's all. I don't like the sight of blood. Now if we were in Africa, I could write about lions and zebras and giraffes. There are places on this earth that evoke something mystical in the human breast. Africa is such a place. These endless plains are not."

"You might study the coyotes, Mister Mercer. Crafty fellows, mythic to all the tribes, tricksters, clever and devious, curious about everything."

"Nothing but a small wild dog, Skye. Now the Australian dingos are worth writing about. Predators, eat babies, brutal and cunning. The Aborigines have stories."

Skye sighed. He could not help a man determined to be discontent. Mercer yanked his horse away and rode off to be alone, while Skye stayed for the moment with his small party, his women, his horses, his burdened travois.

Victoria edged close. She had been listening. "I don't like that sonofabitch," she said.

"Oh, he's just restless. Some people truly see the land and its animals and people; others pass through a country and never see a thing. He's one of those, I imagine. But rather a pleasant bloke most of the time. We'll show him what we can, get our money, and have a good winter."

Then one day they reached the Musselshell River, a pallid stream dribbling along a shallow trench lined with willows and cottonwoods.

"What a poor excuse for a river, Skye. Where's the story here?"

"It's sometimes considered a boundary between the Absarokas and the Siksika," Skye said.

"Siksika?"

"Blackfeet. The most restless, proud, handsome, ruthless, dangerous, powerful tribe on the northern plains. They despise Yanks, but might be kinder to an Englishman. They'd butcher me because I'm married into the Crows; take my wives captive, kill your Missouri teamsters, and be content to steal everything you possess and let you hike for the nearest Hudson's Bay Company post."

"Which is where?"

"North of the medicine line. Canada."

"That's all the story here?"

"No; we are crossing the larder of a dozen tribes. This is where they come to eat. They fight over it."

"No story there, Skye."

Skye sighed. Victoria had selected a meadow under a sandstone bluff, well back from the water, where a prairie wind wouldn't topple the lodge. The bluff would also conceal the cook fire. It was a good spot, with natural defenses. Skye wondered whether Mercer grasped that the farther north they traveled, the more Skye sought to keep them safe. That was a story for Mercer if he wanted it. The incessant war between Crows and Blackfeet could fill ten journals if Mercer had wanted to learn about it. But the explorer had slid into a funk and Skye had no desire to tell stories to a man who lacked eyes and ears.

But this night was different. Mercer consulted his teamsters, dug into the wagon, and pulled out a small oaken cask.

"This stream mislabeled a river's got ice-cold water even if it's discolored. It'll give us yellow gin and bitters," he said. "But I suppose we might imbibe. Nothing else to do but stew ourselves to the gills. I've got enough to stew us for a month. I can stew us all the way to Fort Benton and then down the river. I'll stew us at breakfast, I'll stew us at dinner, I'll stew us on the prairies, I'll stew us in the mountains, I'll stew every savage that comes visiting, I'll stew every coyote that pokes his nose into camp, I'll stew the mosquitoes. By God, this American West is a bust, an absolute disaster. How am I to get a living?"

"Aiee!" howled Victoria. She was not opposed to this plan so long as she could be included.

It was a temptation. Skye didn't mind a good sousing. But there was something about all this that was menacing. Big drunks in wild lands were trouble.

"No," he said.

"What do you mean, no? This is my outfit and you're my employee."

"No."

"Are you defying me?"

"I always do what's necessary for the safety of people in my charge."

"Relax, Skye, and have a drink. Enjoy my hospitality. Where else can you get a good gin and bitters around a friendly campfire? The trip's a bust; let's celebrate the disaster."

In a way, Mercer's proposition was delightful. The man was making light of a bad trip and would head for other adventures in other corners of this great globe.

Skye had been there before. At the rendezvous of mountain men, when the fun sometimes turned deadly. At saturnalias where Indians, not used to spirits, came apart and went mad. He eyed Victoria, who would no doubt enjoy the rowdy times, and Mary, new to his life and white men, and vulnerable.

"No," he said. "If you and your party get stewed, I am resigning."

Mercer bared that row of pearly teeth once again. The man could melt the heart of a witch with a smile like that. "Not even one little toddy?"

"Not now. Not here. One would lead to another."

"Oh, come join us, just one, Skye."

"It's Mister Skye, sir. And in your present humor, it would not be one. No, Mister Mercer. Pour and we'll pack up, my family and I."

That's when a voice rose out of the twilight. "Hello the camp," someone yelled.

Chapter 17

Intuitively, Skye and Victoria edged toward shadows even as Mercer welcomed whoever it was.

The approaching man towered taller than Skye thought a mortal could reach. Six and a half feet, perhaps. He had a gray slouch hat over jet hair. He was leading a black mule, laden with gear. If the man's height was striking, his face was even more so. He wore a jet beard as straight as spikes and sawed off horizontally at shoulder level, the shape of the beard as sharp and square as planed ebony. Above that was an aquiline nose and a pair of obsidian eyes. On first glance he seemed menacing, but Skye intuited that the man was not that way at all.

"Well, sirs, I see I am among my own. I'm Jacob Reese at your service," the man said in a voice that rattled out of his lungs. An odd voice it was, rising from the man's belly and reaching Skye's ears as something out of a cave.

Mercer took over. "Why, Mister Reese, I'm Graves Duplessis Mercer." Mercer was plainly waiting to be recognized, but the recognition didn't come, which just as plainly disappointed Mercer. "Ah, this is Mister Skye and his ladies, Missus and Missus Skye, and my assistants, Mister Corporal and Mister Winding. Won't you join us? We haven't started a meal, but soon we will."

"English are you. I saw it coming," Reese said, which puzzled Skye.

The man picketed his black mule and unloaded his gear,

while Skye quietly observed. Reese seemed entirely competent in the wilds.

At last the man finished his chores and settled down beside the low flame. "I saw it coming," he said. "You would be here. I knew it this morning when I searched beyond the ready knowing and into the realm from which I draw gifts."

Mercer smiled, his teeth so achingly white in the firelight that they made almost a beacon of light in the darkness. "Well, sir, you can entertain us with visions. We're about to pour a libation. Would you care to imbibe?"

Reese paused, a certain cunning in his face, and nodded. "Yes, gin and bitters. That's what you're serving. I shall sample one, with gratitude."

"How did you know . . ."

"I don't know how I know. I just do. It comes to me. I have the inner eye. It's a gift and a curse. Did you know, sir, that silver has been discovered in Nevada? Yes, tons and mountains of it! But the word has not yet reached the States. I saw it spread upon the back of my mind. Don't ask me how. I saw it, and I shall be proven right!"

Mercer nodded to Floyd Corporal, the man who usually concocted the bitters and then added them to gin. The teamster set to work. Skye watched uneasily.

The stranger settled by the flickering flame in the twilight, and slapped away a mosquito. Skye didn't know what to make of him.

"What brings you here, Mister Reese?" he asked.

"Gold! Silver! Copper! Right in these northern mountains are giant bodies of ore, so rich it makes me dizzy. I saw it all; I know where to go. Gold, in filaments and flakes, in milky quartz, easy to pluck up if you wish. Fortunes to be made. Gold washing down creeks. Gold and silver buried in thick veins under the earth. Silver, crusted into strange shapes, ready to harvest."

"Where might that be?" Mercer asked.

"I will know it when the next vision is given to me."

"Then you don't know."

"Of course I know! I have come this far, first on a riverboat, and then overland, from Zebulon, North Carolina. I know exactly where I am going. Silver, gold, sir, draw me ever forward."

"But there's been very little silver found in North America," Mercer said. "Mexico, mainly."

"And that has changed! Even now, miners are hitting bonanzas."

"How do you know that?"

Reese sighed. "My inner vision, sir. I see I am not believed. And that's good. For it opens the field to me alone. Where I go, you will not follow."

Floyd Corporal began handing out the gin and bitters in sweating tin cups. Skye held his peace.

"Why do you tell us about the gold and silver? Why don't you keep it a secret?" Skye asked.

Reese fixed Skye with those obsidian eyes. "You do not believe."

Skye admitted to himself that he didn't. The man was half mad. In all the years Skye had roamed the northern lands, mountains and plains and deserts, no one had found gold or even a mineral seam. There was little gold here; little gold to the west where the Rockies climbed to the sky.

"Treasure stories. The world doesn't lack them," Mercer said. "On every continent, among every people. I don't put much stock in them. I couldn't even sell them to the *Times*. But I am looking for stories, Mister Reese. I write little things for British papers. Now, when you were coming up-river, did you see anything out of the ordinary?"

"It suits me that you don't believe," Reese said. "You see, I intend to claim it all and then put it to good use." He eyed each of the people sitting around that fire intently. "There's enough gold and silver and base metals within two hundred miles of here to transform the republic. We're a poor people, we Americans. We scratch livings out of the poor soil. We are roadless. We spin our cloth and hoe our gardens and barely get along. I'm going to change that. I will claim all these minerals before the greedy steal them and exploit them all for themselves. Yes, once I own these minerals, sirs, I will use every cent to bless the poor and the hungry. All a widow will need to do is apply. All an orphan needs to do is apply. The same for the sick and blind and wounded. I'll give a competence to those in need, and better than that, I'll set up people in business. A poor orphan might become a shopkeeper. A lame man an artist. You see? For once in human history, the wealth in the earth will be spent entirely on those in need."

Skye marveled. The man might be mad, but never had he heard such a visionary and noble design.

Reese stopped suddenly, waiting for a response, perhaps waiting for objections, but no one objected.

"I am being led by Divine Providence," Reese said. "Just as surely as I have seen the future, I will harvest the wealth and devote it to the needful."

Mercer seemed amused. The teamsters kept silent. Victoria accorded Reese all the respect that her people gave to madmen.

"This is a fine libation," Reese said. "You might suppose that I would not approve; that I teetotal. You would be wrong. I am not a puritan or a fanatic. Anglican, if you wish to know my background."

"Truly noble, Mister Reese," Mercer said. "But I do have a question. How will you claim these fields and mountains of minerals? Has your republic laws that permit it? This is public land, isn't it? Has it been surveyed? Can you file a claim somewhere?"

Reese sat up. Even sitting, he towered over them all. "What I find will be mine. What I claim will be mine. For I will know, while standing upon a bonanza, where it is and what is there. And once I know, that is all that is necessary. I will drive my corner stakes when I am called to drive them. Until then, the secret will reside in my soul."

"But, forgive me, how will you pass the secret on to others? Surely you don't expect to develop all these bodies of ore in one lifetime?"

"My nature is monkish," Reese said. "It is true that the secret abides only in my bosom. If I had heirs, they would fight over the spoils. So if I perish the vision will perish with me. This, too, I have seen, for it has been given to me to see things in the back of my mind."

"How far are we from gold? Right here, how far?" Mercer asked.

Reese closed his eyes, almost as if he were sliding into a trance. "We are sixty-eight miles as the crow flies from gold. But that is not a large deposit," he said.

Skye had the uneasy feeling the man was exactly right.

"How far from this mountain of copper you mention?"

Again Reese seemed to draw into himself. He closed his eyes, and then opened them. "One hundred ninety-four miles to the mountain of copper, again as the crow flies. But the surface of that place has silver. The copper is lower."

"Where is the best gold?" Mercer asked.

"One hundred and seventy-eight miles southwest," Reese said.

"How do you know that?"

Reese looked affronted. "Have I not told you how I know? I could take you there. We could start this moment and I could take you to the exact place, a river so full of nuggets that it will yield millions and millions of dollars."

"Where is the nearest silver, Mister Reese?" Mercer was obviously enjoying this game.

"Not far. There's a rich carbonate ore of silver one hundred and eight miles distant."

"Very good, Mister Reese. I wish you luck," Mercer said.

"It is not luck, sir. If it were luck, I would spend my life meandering. No, I am being taken where I am being taken, and for the good of the Republic." He finished his cup, stood, and addressed them all.

"I thank you for the hospitality. I cherish a good gin and bitters. Now I'll be on my way."

"At night? You'll not stay for a supper? We've some buffalo tongue."

"Night and day make no difference to me, Mister Mercer. It is all one. Sleep and wakefulness make no difference. When I rest, it is for my mule's sake, not mine."

With that, Reese retrieved his black mule, loaded it, and vanished upriver. In utter silence they watched the man go, and then there was only the night.

"I come to North America looking for a good story, looking for something, anything, to promote science and entertain London, and what do I find? A madman," Mercer said. "There's not a good story anywhere. The trip's a bust."

Chapter 18

The night was black velvet but her flesh felt silky and the welcoming clasp of her arms was as tender as lamb's wool. They lay apart from the others. Victoria slept upriver. Mercer, as usual, slumbered in his stained wall tent. The teamsters were bedded under the wagon. This summer's night was serene but broken by the playful love songs of wolves on distant ridges.

He lay on the thick robe, she beside him, staring at the star-girt sky. So far, his new union had been joyous and yet he worried. He could not help it.

He asked her a white man's question. No Shoshone male would even think of asking such a thing.

"Are you happy?" he said.

"I do not know this. Why do you ask?"

"You are my woman. Is it good? Are you at peace?"

"I have all that I ever dreamed of, Mister Skye."

It was too much a white man's question, he thought, but then she slid her hand across his beard, toying with it.

"It is good. I am the woman of Mister Skye. How could it not be good?"

"I am glad. I am very happy too," he said.

"Maybe you will tell me what we will do next," she said.

"We'll take Mercer to the big bones. It makes my head ache to think of the creatures when they were alive. Lizards bigger than the tallest lodge."

"We must be very respectful. Their spirits will linger there. The spirit of an animal so big must be very strong."

"I think Mercer wants to measure them, sketch them, take a good look, and then guess what sort of beast they were."

"Why is this?"

"He likes to find things his people have never heard of, so he can write about them, tell stories about them."

"Our storytellers like to talk about the things we have always known."

Skye stared at the mysterious heavens. "Just now, bold men are looking everywhere for new things and new places, things unheard of, animals unknown, plants strange and exotic. They sail the seas. They go to the south and the north. They go to islands where no one has ever been. They go to a place called Africa and see strange people. And all this is being carefully recorded. Mercer is doing that, and has become a great storyteller there in England, and is making much money from it."

"He is strange himself," she said. "He says this trip is no good and yet his eyes don't see."

Skye liked that. He slid an arm around her and pulled her close until her head nestled in the hollow of his shoulder, her raven hair tumbling over his chest. "It's because he has an idea of what he wants and keeps looking for it. In other places he saw strange animals and strange people, and oddities of nature. In Africa there are horses with black and white stripes called zebras. But here, the animals are familiar, and the people, your people, have been known to English people for two centuries."

"He will be happy when he sees the bones."

"I think so. The geysers would have fascinated him too. Who in his land has ever seen hot water and steam explode from the ground?"

"He makes happy smiles but he is restless," she said. "Mister Skye, in my heart I fear that he will get us into trouble, and I am afraid of him."

Skye thought about that, seeing some realism in it. "We will need to be careful, then," he said. "It will only be for a while. And then he will buy a boat and go down the Big River."

A twig snapped near the stream and Skye instantly grew alert. Something was passing through. He sensed a large animal, and waited to hear more, but there was nothing to hear. He peered into the darkness and saw Jawbone looming over him.

"Go eat," he said.

The horse snorted softly, nudged Skye, and meandered away.

Mary relaxed too. On a summer's night the whole world moved from place to place. Over the years of living outside he had learned to sort out the shifting of animals, and could sometimes even tell which animal, but most often he knew only that some creature was making its way through the darkness. Somehow, human movement was different. Night sounds ceased, as if humans moving through the night were entombed in silence. He did not sense this silence now.

She was sitting up, the pale light reflecting off her bare shoulders, so he pulled her close again, and she responded with delight.

The Musselshell turned north here, and they would follow it clear to the Missouri River, enjoying its flowing water and whatever game might be lurking in its bottoms. It would be a pleasant trip even if Mercer didn't much like the pace.

With the dawn, the explorer was up, shaved, and restless as his teamsters heated water for his tea and began some biscuits in a Dutch oven. Skye washed in the river, studied himself for a moment in the shimmering water, finding himself grayer than he had supposed, and then joined Victoria and Mary at the cook fire.

As Skye somehow expected, Mercer headed his way as soon as it was proper.

"I say, Skye, I'd like to hurry this along. Can we make better time? I'd like to get across this wasteland in a day or two and get on with it. If I have a peek at the bones, I can be in St. Louis in a few weeks and England before Christmas."

"With your wagon, sir, it's four days, maybe five to the Missouri, and a couple more to the bones."

"That long? Gad, Skye, I'm trapped."

"All right. We can go much faster if you abandon the wagon."

"No, unthinkable." He smiled. "It's got a hogshead of gin in it. And a cask of bitters decocted in a mountain stream. You wouldn't want to ditch that now, would you?"

Skye nodded. Mercer would have only himself to blame for the lumbering progress across the anonymous plain.

They toiled down the river and didn't seem to make progress. Ahead a vast land rose to meet the sky. To the east the land vanished in haze. Skye rode Jawbone to any prominence where he could get a good look at the surrounding country. It all seemed too quiet. The midday heat discouraged even the ravens, and drew sweat from dust-caked horses and humans alike.

Skye pulled up beside Mercer, who was stretching his legs and walking beside his horse.

"We might happen on some buffalo. Not just a cluster, but a herd that could run miles wide and more miles long. They drift south and north with the seasons right through here. If you saw a herd like that, Mister Mercer, you'd never forget it. I imagine there are hundreds of thousands in one herd. If they run, or stampede, you'd see something rarely seen by a European. You would have a fine story."

"I'm glad you think so," Mercer retorted.

But they spotted no giant herd. In fact, Skye saw no sign of buffalo, no broad pathway of torn-up short grass, dung, and dust. This day the August heat built up to unbearable force, and Skye called a halt at a copse of willows on the bank of the Musselshell. The teamsters unhooked the big draft horses and let them drink. Big black horseflies were tormenting man and beast, so Skye pushed on, hoping to find a windswept bench where the cloud of flies wouldn't drive them half mad.

The sun didn't relent and no cloud offered mercy. But just ahead, on a grassy flat beside the river, a dozen vultures lifted into the sun-bleached blue and flapped away. Skye halted at once and watched the vultures flap blackly into the heat of afternoon. Victoria halted too, studied the black birds, and slipped off her horse. She trotted swiftly toward a river bluff and scaled it to gain some perspective on what lay ahead.

Behind, the wagon drew to a halt, and Mercer sat his horse impatiently. "Well, what's the slowdown this time?" he asked.

"Vultures."

"Something is dead."

"It would seem that way."

At Victoria's signal, Skye proceeded the remaining half mile to the flat, his rifle at the ready. And there, close to the river, were bodies, four in all. Indians, young men, so newly killed that nothing had damaged their flesh except for the arrows protruding from each of them.

"Mister Mercer, look to your safety. Make sure your men are armed and keeping an eye on the bluffs."

"An attack?"

"The warriors who did this aren't likely to return. They dread the spirits of the dead. But never take anything for granted, especially in war."

Mercer reached for his rifle, a handsome Sharps model that evoked envy in Skye.

Victoria, ever bold, slipped into the carnage and studied the dead.

"Assiniboine," she said, poking a moccasin. Then she tugged gently until an arrow pulled loose from a man's thigh, and she squinted at it. "Atsina! Sneaky thieves!"

"What on earth are Atsina?" Mercer asked.

"Gros Ventres, Big Bellies," Skye said. "Allies of the Blackfeet, famous for begging and thievery."

"Never heard of them," Mercer said. "Not much of an item for my journal, I'm afraid."

"Not the same as a giraffe," said Skye, tartly.

Here was evidence of tragedy, of war and death, yet the explorer dismissed what he saw. Skye dismounted, studied this place for its story, and soon understood what had happened.

Mercer watched impatiently, eager to be on the road again.

Chapter 19

A great sadness tore through Skye. It was all easy to read. Three Assiniboine boys and an older war leader had camped for the night here. They were on a horse-stealing raid, the first test of a young warrior and the classic medallion of maturity among the plains tribes. And here their dreams came to a brutal end.

They had been jumped by Gros Ventres, perhaps also young men looking for war honors, and the Gros Ventres had killed every Assiniboine and made off with the Assiniboine ponies. And it had all happened only a few hours earlier. Rigor mortis had not yet stiffened the bodies. The Gros Ventres could be only a few miles distant. They could even be watching.

There were signs of struggle. The older one, whose gray hair was worn in coarse braids, had four arrows in him, two in the abdomen, one in the chest, and one through the neck. His bow was shattered. He had several ancient war wounds, puckered flesh that spoke of bloody fighting. The ground around him was disturbed. He had not surrendered easily. The neck wound, which must have pierced an artery, had bled and now bright blood, not yet browned by time, covered his flesh.

The others had come to swift ends. One youth's skull had been split by a war axe. Another had died of an arrow through his mouth. Another had a belly wound and had been mutilated in a way that suggested revenge or maybe triumph. Another had been cleaved at the back of the neck, and probably had been trying to run away from his pursuer.

Victoria knew better than he did what people these were and who the attackers had been. Each tribe made moccasins its own way, and signed their arrows their own way. Trying to memorize all that made Skye dizzy but she knew at a glance. The Gros Ventres had few arts; everything from arrows to clothing was coarse. The Assiniboine were gifted workers of leather and bead and all the bone and flesh and hair of the buffalo. These boys wore handsome moccasins.

Mercer stood at the edge of the bloody field, not wanting to get too close, his gaze on the hills, vigilant against attack. Maybe this was more story than he or his London readers wanted to read over their breakfast tea.

"Are you sure we're safe here?" he asked.

"I'm not sure of anything."

"They could be lurking over the hill."

"They could, but probably aren't."

"I'll keep watch," Mercer said, his gaze resolutely on the ridges.

Death draws the eye, even if one doesn't want to look. The four bodies seemed to blot out everything else; the bright hot day, the green of the river bottoms, the copses of willows and chokecherry, the flight of birds.

"Well, we'd better be going," Mercer said. "Losing time."

"No," said Skye. "I will bury them."

Victoria looked sharply at him. She didn't want to bury these enemies.

"But they mean nothing to us; I understand these tribes were enemies of your wives."

"The death of anyone is an occasion for grief," Skye said. "Their families would want us to care for these men."

"But shoveling four graves—"

"I will put them on scaffolds; that is how these people bury their own."

"Well, as long as you're in my employ, I'll ask you to push on. We can make another ten miles today."

Skye ignored the man. He probably would do this task all alone. Victoria would be wary of the lingering and angry spirits of the dead. Mary would watch quietly.

He fetched his axe and headed for a great cottonwood tree with overspreading limbs, some of which were horizontal. Nearby were green cottonwood saplings, still straight and true.

Victoria caught up with him, hatchet in hand. "Damn," was all she said.

They hacked and limbed the poles, working steadily while Mercer paced and glared. The adventurer would not discharge Skye; not here, Skye thought. Mary dug into the skimpy possessions of the Skye household and found a ball of thong. When twenty poles had been readied, Skye lifted each one onto the cottonwood limbs and the women anchored the poles to the limbs with thong. It was taking a long time, and Mercer was watching thunderously but saying nothing. He drifted closer now, studying the dead, putting them into his mental notebook if not his journal.

There were ancient blankets lying about; some half ruined by blood. Blankets not even the Atsinas wanted. They would do.

Skye spread one next to the older warrior, the war leader, and then cut away the arrows with his Green River knife. He nodded to Victoria. Together they lifted the warrior onto the center of the ancient red blanket, covered the man's empty face, and tied the bundle tight with thong.

Skye wished someone would help him lift this burden, but the two teamsters were on the nearby bluff, rifles ready, keeping an eye out, and maybe that was best.

It was hot and getting hotter. Hard to breathe. Flies swarmed around the bodies. Slowly, he and Victoria wrapped the Assiniboine boys in their tattered blankets. One had an ancient buffalo robe that would serve as a shroud.

"What is this turtle thing he's got around his neck?" Mercer asked, studying the youngest of the dead youths.

Skye saw that the boy was wearing a turtle totem, a small leather pouch that rested on his bronze chest.

"It's his natal totem," Skye said. "His umbilical cord's probably inside. It's who he is, all compressed into that totem."

"I want it," Mercer said.

"No! It belongs to this boy."

"Do not take it," Victoria added. "The boy's ghost will follow you the rest of your life, and bad things will happen."

Mercer smiled, even white teeth, his chiseled features lighting up.

"All the more reason for me to have it. I love to own the things that have stories in them."

With that, he knelt, slipped the leather turtle totem up and over the youth's head, and put it into his pocket.

Victoria muttered. Mary cast her gaze elsewhere, not wanting to see what she had seen.

Skye paused. "Mister Mercer, out of respect for the dead, you'll wish to place the turtle totem inside the boy's funeral wrapping."

Mercer smiled. "I carry a good-luck coin, a shilling, actually. Here. Put that in. We'll trade luck." He withdrew the coin from his britches and dropped it on the blanket.

Skye stared at the coin. All right, he thought. A fair trade. Maybe.

Victoria stared, uncertain about the swap. Skye wrapped the youth in the old blue blanket and quietly tied the bundle shut.

And then they were ready: Skye slid his arms under the bundle containing the war leader, the enemy of his wife's people, who was far heavier than the boys. He staggered under the weight, and Victoria helped by lifting the warrior's feet. But finally Skye had the body in hand, and he struggled to the benevolent cottonwood, with its deep shade and noble height, and they hoisted the warrior to his grave, just above Skye's own height, and straightened him out. The other three would barely fit.

Mercer paced but did not assist. That was fine. Skye somehow didn't want him here under the funeral tree, thinking of journal entries instead of burying the dead and respecting the lives that were lost this hot and windless day.

One by one, Skye and his women lifted the youths, carried them to their aerial grave, lined them up side by side, until at last all four rested on the scaffold. Skye removed his old top hat.

"Rest in peace," he said.

Their bones wouldn't. The carrion birds would be at them soon, tearing through the tattered blankets.

"That was touching," Mercer said. "A wilderness massacre, a burial, the possibility of another raid always with us."

Skye thought that he was beginning to understand the soul of the man. He was hungry for a story and that hunger trumped everything else including ordinary compassion. Did Mercer have any feeling at all for these dead men? Did he see them as mortal? Did he see them as boys with mothers and fathers and brothers and sisters? Did he see them as youths hungry to be men, out on a raid for the first time, only to lose everything?

"Let's go," he said to Mercer, who smiled brightly with the three-hour delay ended.

Skye rode ahead. If there were hostile Indians about and they were in a fighting mood, he would need to be on guard.

The teamsters got the wagon rolling. Mary and Victoria started their travois-laden horses.

Mercer spurred his sleek horse and pulled up beside Skye, who didn't want the company.

"Mister Skye, I've come to apologize."

That surprised Skye.

"You did the right thing, burying those chaps. That's the golden rule, isn't it? Treat 'em as we'd like to be treated."

"It is."

"I was going to discharge you. Disobeying and all that. I won't. You've taught me a thing or two."

"You've taught me a thing or two, Mister Mercer."

"Do you really think bad luck's going to follow me because I've got the chap's turtle in my pocket?"

"My women think so. They think you'll regret it."

"But I don't believe in that stuff. You could never get me to believe in a ghost even if half of England's got a dozen in every attic. The dead are dead. But that isn't it. I didn't just take the chap's turtle; I traded for it. I gave the chap a shining shilling, a good bit of cash to get him where he's going, wouldn't you say? He's not going to haunt me. The chap's going to be my guardian. If a man needs a friendly ghost, this chap will do just fine, eh? You just watch. From now on, everything that happens will be lucky. Hired me a genuine Indian chap to keep an eye on me."

Skye nodded. Then he smiled. What was it about Mercer? You couldn't dislike the fellow for more than two minutes even if there were a dozen bad patches in every day.

Chapter 20

The day turned hot. Not much air was moving. The sun pummeled them. Black horseflies circled like dreadnoughts waiting to bite. The blue was bleached out of the sky. The mountains to the west slid into white haze.

It was the time of year Skye liked least of all. The land was parched. The spring monsoons had ended in June, and now the grasses had been toasted to a tan color, and the stalks of dried-out weeds skipped over the ground with every gust of furnace air. The heat sapped the horses and slowed the caravan as it struggled north. The Musselshell River water wasn't cold enough to refresh man or beast, but it helped to pour it over one's head. Skye soaked his hair in it and clamped his black top hat over the soggy hair and got some relief out of it.

The teamsters took the wagon along the higher ground west of the river, where there were fewer impediments such as fallen logs to stay their progress. Away from the stream the way was easier. Skye roamed ahead, wary of trouble, while his women trailed their ponies along their own route, different from the wagon's. Mercer had fallen into deep silence, wearing his frustration like a hair shirt. This would not be a good trip, and his plain objective was to get it over with as soon as he could manage it.

Burying the bodies had turned the day sour, but the unbearable heat worsened the mood of them all. Skye yearned for some mountain valleys with icy creeks tumbling through them. But as far as he could see there was only haze and white skies and air so hot it sapped his will.

It also made him edgy. He couldn't say what it was, but the whole world seemed poised at the edge of disaster.

Mercer rode up to Skye.

"It's bloody awful. It drains me. How long do these hot spells last?"

Skye shrugged. "Long time, sometimes."

"You mean we're stuck with it."

"I don't know of any way to escape it unless you want to head due west into those mountains and find a cool valley. But that's fifty miles at the least."

Mercer shook his head. "Take me to the Missouri. At this point I don't care about seeing some bones. I don't care about anything except floating my way out of here."

"As you wish, Mister Mercer."

The adventurer turned his sweat-stained horse away and retreated to his wagon and the patient teamsters.

Skye spotted an antelope racing north, and then a pack of them, maybe a dozen. Something had stirred them up. Some crows flapped due north.

There was something on the breeze that troubled Skye, some portent of trouble he could not pin down. As always, when his instincts were jabbing him, he paused to consider what danger there might be. He sucked the hot air into his lungs and then got it: fire. Smoke. The first tendrils of smoke hastened along by a quickening south wind.

Now he saw mule deer racing north, and some coyotes loping steadily north, and a nervous bull elk on a crown of a hill. At a high point he turned in his saddle to take a sharp look at his back trail, and saw what he dreaded most. Maybe ten or fifteen miles to the south, a gray wall of billowing smoke crossed the whole horizon, and he could see no break or end to it east or west. It was a prairie fire, a grandfather of all prairie fires, loping along.

Just about then Victoria and Mary figured it out, and Victoria spurred her pony to reach Skye. She pointed. Skye nodded. He needed to find a safe harbor. He needed a wide river or a massive cliff. He needed some place to shelter the livestock and protect the wagon. And he saw none at all. Whatever decision he made now would determine their fate. If he chose wisely, they might have a chance. If not, they would die the most miserable of deaths, not necessarily of flame and furnace heat, but of asphyxiation. A prairie fire sucked oxygen out of the air; there would be nothing left to breathe.

Now Mercer spotted the ominous dark wall behind them and so did the teamsters. The sinister wall, sometimes yellow-gray, sometimes almost purple, was rolling along and would overtake them soon. Who could say when?

"Where, Skye?" Mercer yelled.

"I don't know."

"Tell me, man. Are we dead?"

Skye shook his head. His gaze raked the rolling plain, the river bottoms, the horizons. Jawbone shifted under him, his terror evident in his every twitch. It was all Skye could do to rein him tight.

"Head for the river. Don't head for an island. An island in a narrow river's worthless. Head for a pool deep enough for your horses. Deep enough for your wagon. Make it a pool in a grassy area. Not a pool where the river runs through woods or brush. Then unhitch your draft horses. Go!"

Mercer didn't argue. The teamsters had already made their own decisions, and were veering downslope toward the river, toward a broad island in the braided stream.

Skye heard Mercer yelling at them.

Jawbone trembled.

"River's all we've got," he said to Victoria. She would do the best she could with whatever she had.

But the next mile of stream bottom was packed with dense cottonwoods and willows and chokecherry brush, all of which would turn into a furnace that would snuff life out of anyone or anything trying to shelter in the river itself. A ten-yard-wide shallow stream would hardly shelter a mouse. If they could get to the river downstream, where the bankside forest thinned and gave way to brush, that would help. If they managed another mile, where the river flowed through a grassy flat, that would be best, especially if they hit a hole where they could stay submerged.

He pointed, the best he could manage, and the whole caravan careened toward the north. Now small animals raced by them; frenzied hares, raccoons, otter, skunks, all of them oblivious of the men and livestock. Rattlesnakes coiled and slithered, thousands of them, racing north.

Victoria's ponies began running, their travois careening and bobbing and threatening to pitch out everything in Skye's household. Victoria and Mary fought the animals, barely keeping them from bolting. But one of the travois snapped loose, dumping parfleches of pemmican and kitchen supplies.

Behind, the gray smoke to the south had climbed the sky, rising into a giant wall that would soon obscure the sun. The teamsters had the worst of it, working their way down the bluffs to the floor of the valley, doing their utmost to keep Mercer's heavy wagon from toppling over. Behind them, the smoke advanced like the shadow of night, streamers of gray extending far in front, and reaching directly overhead.

Skye felt parched. Jawbone's sweated flanks had dried, leaving a white rime on them. The horse wanted to run. But prairie fires often moved so fast they overtook everything in their paths. And this one, riding the hot wind out of the southwest, was wasting no time. Gusts of hot smoky air coiled through the river bottoms. A breeze rattled the parched cottonwood leaves. Skye steered toward the teamsters, who had gotten the wagon down from the high plains and were heading toward water.

"Get beyond the woods," he yelled. "Look for a hole. Cut the horses free if you have to."

"Can't. Got to save the wagon at all costs. Orders. Mercer's journals," Winding yelled.

Mercer's journals. They could kill the teamsters, kill the horses, and perish anyway when the wagon burned. But there was no time to argue.

Still, these were savvy, trail-hardened men and Skye liked what he saw. They were keeping the draft horses at a steady trot, steering them away from boulders, fallen trees, ditches and ridges, somehow in control of twelve-hundred-pound draft horses.

Now live sparks began dropping, each an angry hornet capable of starting fires in advance of the main blaze. Skye watched Victoria and Mary race the ponies forward. Another travois had fallen apart, this one carrying the lodgepoles. And the lodge cover was working loose from the third travois.

A dry cottonwood tree to the right suddenly exploded into flame, as if lightning had struck it. Skye felt heat at his back, sucked smoky air, and heard for the first time a rolling thunder behind him, the roar of a conflagration that was rolling down on them, eating everything in its path. Above, blue sky had vanished and a gray smoke cast deep shadow over the land. The sun died suddenly, and a great darkness slid over them. Still, the fire was far enough back that Skye saw no flames.

A deer burst from a thicket startling Jawbone, who reared

and danced and then bolted ahead, while Skye hung on. Ahead, the woods surrendered to brush, walls of choke-cherry lining the stream, as dangerous as the wooded bottoms they were leaving.

Mercer's wagon fell behind. Skye feared the teamsters would stick with it, killing themselves and their horses. But they were far from succor, far from a hole in the river, far from meadows. He heard shouts, turned, and saw Winding and Mercer yelling at each other, while Floyd Corporal was unhitching the big draft horses. Mercer was screaming. Then the draft horses were loose, and they lumbered for-ward at speeds Skye had never dreamed possible in such beasts. They raced past, with the teamsters and Mercer just behind. The wagon stood forlorn, cocked to one side, its wagon sheet smoking on the bows, doomed.

Skye took one last glance, lamenting not the journals but the cask of gin, and then spurred Jawbone ahead. A half mile up was open land where the river narrowed and ran quiet, a sign of some depth. A place of salvation. A slim chance, but the only chance. Behind and gaining every sec-ond was a streak of orange flame higher than the tallest bankside trees, boiling into the heavens, ascending higher and higher until Skye thought the flame touched the sun.

Flight. Now it was a race to that pool. Heat behind them, heat beside them, a moving furnace gaining on them. Jawbone needed no encouragement, but plunged pell-mell toward the quiet waters ahead. Victoria rode a pony that trailed a broken travois behind it; Mary's pony bucked and leaped, but she held on.

Mercer, on a lean roman-nosed beast, sailed past, and amazingly the big Belgians thundered by, even as heat blistered hair. The teamsters were riding too, but one's hat was smoking and embers were driving their horses mad. A flash and boom behind them told Skye that the powder keg in Mercer's burning wagon had detonated. Some smaller booms from his own travois debris told him that fire had consumed his own powder, save for what was in the horn on his chest.

They reached the pool all at once. The draft horses plunged in, splashing deep into cool water. Jawbone hit the water with a giant splash, and Skye was shocked to discover him plunging straight toward a black bear sow, with two cubs, up to their noses. Two deer and an elk stood nervously at the far side of the pond, their heads barely visible. With a great roiling of water, the rest plunged in. Skye dismounted, filled his top hat with water and poured it over himself. Then he poured more water over the horses' backs. Victoria dropped straight underwater and emerged draining water from her braids. Mercer and the teamsters struggled to dismount in all that turmoil and dipped themselves in water. The horses splashed furiously as fiery missiles dropped from the black sky frying any flesh they touched.

Skye coughed. It was hard to breathe. The air was so bad one wanted not to suck it into lungs. He filled his top hat over and over, splashing water on Victoria, on Mary, on Jawbone. The heat was so brutal it evaporated water as fast as he threw it on the horses; it pushed itself straight through their hair, his clothing, his beard.

The bears slid lower and lower in the frothing water, until their snouts barely showed. The deer and elk writhed in pain as a storm of embers blistered their backs. He saw rattlers swimming in every direction.

Now they were surrounded by orange walls, no succor, no air, no relief. But here the river ran through meadow, not woods, and Skye had been counting on that. The grasses flared briefly and moments later there was only charred earth as the wall of flame rolled past them, driven by sharp dry wind out of the south. But heat and smoke followed, the streamside trees and brush still burnt furiously, casting blankets of choking smoke straight over Skye and his party.

It was each to his own safety. Skye dipped under the water, which was clogged now with black debris, burst upward, tried to breathe air that would not support life, felt his lungs ache, threw water over the suffering horses, and plunged under again.

Jawbone shrieked as a burning missile landed on his rump, and he bucked furiously in the water, which actually sprayed lifesaving water everywhere.

Skye felt himself weakening. No air. He was gasping and drawing only brutal, acrid smoke into his lungs. A quick glance told him that the others were done for too. They hung on to horses' manes, worn-out, not far from doom. Skye saw the future clearly. They had escaped the worse burning but were going to die of asphyxiation. And there wasn't anything anyone could do.

He slid backward into the roiling water, and discovered blue sky above him. The black wall of smoke had vanished. The hot south wind had driven most of the smoke to the north. But it didn't matter. He couldn't breathe. None of them could. He clung to Jawbone's mane. He saw Victoria faint, and somehow reached her before she slid into the water and drowned. He tugged her close and kept her head up and tried to keep her from sucking water into her lungs.

The river itself had turned hot, as if it would soon begin to boil, and there was no more coolness to comfort a body. So this was how it would end. Rattlers swam by. His mind was so fogged that he no longer cared. He could not think. Thinking required air and without air his mind simply drifted toward oblivion.

And so life was suspended. He didn't know how the others fared. Black river debris slid past him, bumped into his arms. He was holding Victoria above the surface with his last strength; that is all he knew.

Then oddly a tendril of clean air reached him. He knew it was good air. He sucked it into his chest, exhaled it, sucked again, exhaled again, and did not cough as much. The merciless south wind that had driven this galloping fire was also driving clean air past this place of death.

Yet no one moved. Not an animal stirred. The bears remained submerged, only their snouts showing. The horses, half out of water in that shallow pond, stood stock-still. They had terrible burns on their backs where the fire had scorched away their hair and fried their flesh.

"Help me," said Mercer. He could no longer keep his head out of water, and slid under the surface. Skye bestirred himself, as if coming from some distant shore, and waded toward the explorer, catching him as he drifted downstream.

Skye yanked Mercer's head up, clapped him on the back until Mercer coughed and began to breathe again. Skye held him up. He counted heads. Mary, Victoria, Mercer, Whiting, Corporal. Alive. Draft horses alive and suffering cruel flesh wounds. The ponies all suffering.

There was little he could do. Little anyone could do. He hadn't the strength to help himself, much less help the others. In every direction there was nothing but char, blackness, black earth, black rock, black forest debris. A blackened earth cleaved by the shallow river, under a harsh sky.

Some unfathomed amount of time passed. The river water cooled and cleared somewhat, but it still carried a full charge of charred limbs, logs, and debris, along with dead animals, rabbits, a skunk, a porcupine, an antelope, belly-up snakes, slowly floating and whirling as the waters carried them toward their final destiny. An acrid smell hung over the whole area, the smell of charred wood and grass, smoke-saturated clothing, ash that clogged one's nostrils and ears and collected around the eyes.

The bears were the first to leave. The sow herded her cubs out of the pool and lumbered downstream without a glance backward toward those who had shared the refuge with her. The deer stood frozen, not ready to move anywhere. There was no place to go. Not a blade of grass or a leaf to succor the creature. Skye felt the need to return to hard ground, and pulled his way out, feeling dirty water run off his soggy buckskins. He fell to the charred ground and lay there. The act of getting out of the water had exhausted him.

The women seemed more resilient, pulled themselves out, wrung their skirts, and began walking upstream to see what might be salvaged. But one of the teamsters, Floyd Corporal, was in a bad way. He pulled himself out of the water and fell down on the black ground and wept softly. Mercer and Winding were better off. But no one was ready to look after the animals, and they spent another hour beside the Musselshell just recovering what they could of their strength and wits.

At last Skye led Jawbone out of the pool. The horse had a blister on his rump that looked ugly. There was little Skye could do about it. The saddle was charred but intact. Skye's old Hawken still rested in its sheath. It was soaked and Skye would have to pull the wet charge. He hoped he still had dry powder in his horn. The others were now unarmed unless some of their weapons had survived the conflagration that consumed their wagon.

Skye discovered that most of the hair on his head had been singed, and now it fell off whenever he touched it. Still, the hair had protected his neck and head. He could grow more. Much of Victoria's jet hair was gone. Mary's hair had survived. Somehow, Mary had done best of all, and except for some ruined buckskins and moccasins, seemed much the same. Mercer and Winding began to look after their horses. The big Belgians had several blisters, and their other horses were little better off. No one would be riding them for a long time.

No one talked. Skye didn't want to. He nursed his thoughts deep down inside of himself, as if talking would shatter a healing process that had to occur in silence. He stood wearily, pulled the rifle from its sheath, and began to pull the wet charge. It involved a complex process in which a spiral worm on a hardwood stick was screwed into the lead ball until it could be pulled free.

He sat quietly, working the wet charge loose, and finally succeeded. Then he ran a patch down the barrel to wipe it clean, poured powder, which had stayed dry in the horn, patched a ball, and drove it home. The fulminate cap was still good, so he let it stay on the nipple. He was armed, but there were no animals to shoot and no defenses needed.

Skye had no intention of shooting the deer that had shared the pool with them. The deer had survived; let it live.

Off to the north the wall of smoke continued to roll away, burning everything before it. They could no longer follow the river. There was not a blade of grass for the horses, not a deer or antelope or buffalo to eat. Nothing for man or beast. Blackness ahead, blackness behind. They would need to cut sideways, either east or west, and Skye already knew the answer. They would head west where the mountains still were dark green, unburnt. There, life could continue if they could find a way to start over.

Mercer broke the silence. "We don't have a thing. Everything in the wagon's gone. The blankets, stores, my journals, some tools. The rifles are twisted and worthless. We have only the clothing on our backs and some horses we can't use or ride. We're going to be hungry and haven't even a pound of flour. It seems to me we survived that fire, only to perish in a few days from every imaginable want."

Skye lifted his soggy top hat. "It's bad," he said.

"Worse than bad. We have nothing. How will we live? You don't have anything either."

"We might not live," Skye said. "Then again, we might."

Mercer stared, annoyed at such enigmatic conversation, and wheeled away.

Skye didn't feel like talking. He studied the mountains lying to the west perhaps thirty miles, a hard day's walk in the best of conditions, but two or three days in the shape they were in. Two or three days without food or water or grass for the animals, under a brutal sun.

Chapter 22

A sorrier collection of people and animals Skye had never seen. The backs of the horses were peppered with blisters. Both of the teamsters had lost most of the hair on their heads. Skye had lost much of his. Victoria had lost most of hers. Somehow most of Mary's hair had survived. Corporal had a blistered neck and hands. Mercer himself had blisters across his neck. Their lungs hurt. They wanted nothing more than to curl up in shade and rest.

Mercer, hollow-eyed, patrolled the banks, looking for anything that wasn't ruined. Victoria worked back along the bank to the place where the travois had fallen apart and discovered an axe head minus its burnt handle, and a hatchet with a half-burned handle. Actually, they were treasures. But the lodge was a smoking ruin, the lodgepoles gone, the parfleches of clothing and food lost.

She returned, showed the metal to Skye, who took note of it. Those two items could save their lives.

They were all caked with soot, their clothing a black ruin, their moccasins soggy. The waters of the Musselshell were undrinkable and filled with floating corpses.

Mercer, his face haggard, approached Skye. "We're dead men. That's plain. Dead men."

"How so?"

"Nothing but charred ground. Horses can't be ridden, blistered backs. No feed for them. Smoke's ruined our lungs. I can't walk a hundred yards. Same for my men. Not a thing left of our wagon. Even the iron wheels are twisted. No food. No drinkable water. Clothing falling off. The blisters will mortify. Nights are cold now. We've not a blanket among us. It's all plain enough."

It did look that way, and Skye knew that there was little he could say to hearten the explorer. "We'll try for grass. It's a hard day's walk. Day and a night, maybe."

Mercer stared at Skye as if Skye were daft.

"I'm taking my women and horses to grass. You want to come along?"

"I'd like to stay here. At least there's water."

"There'll be water where I'm going. Place I once trapped long ago, called Flatwillow Creek."

"It'll be burnt."

Skye pointed. "Those are the Little Snowies. Big Snowies beyond that. They didn't burn."

Mercer squinted. "How can you tell?"

"Are they smoking? Forest fires burn for hours, days, weeks."

Mercer whirled away and settled beside the river. "Go ahead," he said. "I'm staying."

"You're quitting."

Mercer turned his back on Skye.

Skye and his women collected what little they had, herded the horses into a group, and started west, cutting across scorched earth that was sometimes hot under their moccasins. He didn't know whether they would make it. He knew it was the only choice. The brutal sun swiftly pummeled the wet out of their clothing, and then it really got hot.

He heard a shout and discovered Mercer and his teamsters a hundred yards back. He let them catch up. They had collected their few things and were pushing the horses ahead of them. The draft horses, in particular, were badly blistered; their backs were the highest out of the water. Not a horse in the whole party could be ridden.

Skye nodded. For some reason he liked Mercer though he often wondered why.

They hiked west through a dehydrating south wind, pausing every little while to breathe. Not a blade of grass nurtured the horses. Not a chokecherry bush, not a willow thicket. The fire had scraped the earth naked, and there was only yellow clay and ash and a brassy sky.

For a long while they struggled west, even as the sun marched west, as if to impede them. Skye rested frequently. His feet were bloody. Corporal had stepped into the remains of some prickly pear and was nursing a painful left foot. But no one complained, least of all Mercer, who had that British grit to him.

Then, as the sun began to slide, they struck a broad coulee issuing out of the mountains, and suddenly there was grass on its south slope, while the north slope was charred. The wind-driven flames had leaped over half the coulee.

They paused in grass. It seemed a miracle, tawny brown grass as high as their calves, something at last that wasn't ash. The horses spread out and devoured it. But soon it was time to push on. Skye led them straight up the coulee, which was going where he wanted to go more or less, and the horses nipped grass along the way. At one point they scattered a herd of antelope that had found refuge in the unburnt strip of land.

"I say, Mister Skye, it's a rule of exploring to find a trustworthy guide and follow his counsel," Mercer said.

Suddenly there was Mercer's mile-wide grin.

Skye nodded, smiled, and something was healed.

But now thirst loomed. He felt parched. He saw Victoria slip a pebble into her mouth and suck on it to activate the saliva. The murderous sun could kill them if nothing else did. And Corporal was slowing down, not able to keep up.

Skye found a shaded place and halted them. "We'll wait for twilight," he said. "Water ahead five miles; creek I know of."

Five miles seemed a continent away but that was the only choice they had. Corporal pulled off his boot, wrapped his injured foot in some shirttail, and tugged the boot on again.

"All right, we're going to cut northwest over burnt land again," Skye said. "I think we'll strike a creek in about two hours."

"Are you sure, are you absolutely sure?" Mercer asked.

"No, sir. I'm never sure. A man roams this land and makes a map in his head. In the beaver days we came through here a few times. But maps fade, and so does our memory. No, I am not at all sure."

Mercer's two teamsters stared, waiting for a decision from their boss. But then he nodded.

"We'll have a time of it pulling these horses off the grass," Skye said.

They did have a time of it. Two of Skye's ponies curled around to the grass; both of Mercer's draft horses refused to budge.

But then Jawbone set to work, snapping and snarling and sinking teeth into blistered butts, while Skye marveled. There were times when he swore Jawbone knew his mind. They set off at a good clip, covering three miles in an hour, always over burnt land as desolate as the Sahara. But a half hour later Jawbone, and then the ponies, and lastly Mercer's horses, began trotting, and then loping, and finally the whole lot of them raced ahead, down a grade, into a burnt-out valley where leafless trees stood in wintry death, and poked their heads into a clean, swift creek.

Skye and his hobbling bunch found the horses sated and

THE CANYON OF BONES 137

comfortable, standing beside the creek in the twilight. The men drank. Skye's women retreated around a bend and washed themselves. In purple twilight they all started up the creek, plodding toward the looming mountains, and then suddenly they hit grass. It was if a knife had severed the land; burnt black to east, placid golden grasslands with thickets of cottonwoods dotting the creek bottoms to the west.

Mercer stood at the knife edge of the fire and marveled. "Mister Skye," he said, "we're not out of it, but you brought us here."

Indeed, before them was succor and water, deadwood for a fire to drive the frost away at night and cook meat. The horses tore into the long grasses, eating as they all ambled westward into the twilight.

Skye was thinking about food. So were they all. He checked his Hawken. He had a fresh charge in the barrel and a patched ball pressed hard against the load.

"I'll go ahead, mates," he said. "Stay back."

They saw he was ready to hunt, and knew as well as Skye did that this grass-lined creek would be a haven and refuge for plenty of animals driven there by the fire.

But it was growing dark. Skye could only hope that if he found game it would be at once, and not when he couldn't see to shoot. He walked only a few minutes when he made out great dark beasts ahead, so many that it startled him. His heart lifted. He was downwind and had a good chance. Up there were meat and robes, tools and clothing, moccasins and steaks.

He drifted close, knowing the shaggies did not have good hearing and only mediocre sight, but did have a keen sense of smell; that one whiff of him would send them running. But he had hunted them many times before, and slipped his way toward the shifting herd, maybe twenty or thirty; plenty of meat, plenty of everything they might need. He slipped toward the creek and settled behind a downed cottonwood, using the log for a bench rest. There were three cows he wanted, each grazing quietly. He set his horn beside him, uncapped it, readied some patches and balls, pulled out his ramrod, and then leveled his rifle, sighted on the heart-lung spot of one farther back.

The first shot dropped the cow in her tracks. She caved slowly while he dumped powder down the barrel, rammed a patched ball home, slid a cap over the nipple, and aimed at the next cow. The herd had shifted restlessly but had not run. The cow turned toward him, ruining his aim. He lined up a shot at a young bull, and squeezed. Again the boom shattered the peace. The bull trotted a few dozen steps and collapsed. Skye swiftly reloaded, and dropped a second cow, just as the herd decided, in some collective and mysterious judgment, it was time to run. The big animals raced upslope, out of the intimate Flatwillow Valley, and vanished into the night. One of the cows was thrashing on the ground, and then he saw Victoria cut its throat. That was a dangerous thing to do, but she did it.

By the time the others arrived, all three buffalo lay dead.

"Three, Mister Skye? Why so much waste?"

Skye reloaded, pondering an answer. "No waste at all, sir. There are six robes, two to a hide, to keep us warm. Meat for a few days. Tools to make from bone. Moccasins for your feet, a shirt or vest for your body, a hat to keep the summer sun from blistering your head, saddles and girth straps to replace the horse tack and harness you lost, and if you want to make a pillow out of the beard of the bull, it's there too."

"I'll settle for some hump meat," said Winding. "I'll eat one shaggy and you can share the rest."

Chapter 23

People seemed to know what to do without being asked. All set to work except Floyd Corporal, who was too sick to do anything at all. Winding looked to the horses. Mercer gathered deadwood from the patches of cottonwoods and pine near the creek. The women began sawing out the buffalo tongues, the easiest meat to get at fast, and one of the most delicious parts.

Skye studied this haven, bathed in lavender twilight, and decided to have one last look. Too many trappers he knew had come to a bad end by unwittingly camping close to trouble. He clasped his Hawken, slowly and painfully climbed the north slope of the Flatwillow Creek valley until he reached a ridge above it where he could see the bright blue sky in the west where the sun had vanished. To the east, the burnt-over land spread blackly to the horizon. A sharp line separated the burned from the lush valley grasses they had made their haven this night. He studied the lonesome land, so big and empty it sometimes made his heart ache. He saw no trouble. No smoke from other camps. No new flame on the horizon. No burning mountain. No storm clouds. Just a vast, quiet, and achingly sweet land that flooded him with gratitude.

Below, a bright fire flared. The women had collected tinder from beneath rotted cottonwood bark and had ignited the wood that Mercer had collected. They were jabbing green willow wands through two buffalo tongues to suspend them at the fire, and in a while everyone in this ragged band would be fed.

Skye was reluctant to come down from the ridge. As cruel as this land could be, it was his own land, now bathed in soft and gentle light that made the whole world serene and quiet. But there was much to be done. He tore himself away from the views that entranced him, made his way down to the camp, and found the tongues sizzling beside a lively fire. The horses grazed peacefully on good grass. Their backs were a mass of suppurating blisters, and some might never be good saddlers again. But they could pull travois.

Even as the fire licked the tongues, the women had tackled the first cow with their skinning knives. Pulling a hide free was hard, messy labor. But ere long they had cut the belly, spilled entrails, set aside the intestines that would make a great feast, severed the head, cut the legs loose, and had started the tugging and cutting that would gradually pull the vermin-infested hide free of the great bulk of the cow. Three hides. Six robes, and plenty of hide left over for moccasins, which would be the most urgent of their needs. It would be a long time before anyone rode those horses.

The tongues sizzled; Mary occasionally rose to turn the meat, or see to it that the tongues didn't burn. Mercer and Winding stared hungrily. They all had food on their mind. Skye thought to go after a liver, always a choice piece eaten raw by Indians and mountain men. Indeed, Corporal had revived enough so that he began poking into the stomach cavity of the eviscerated cow, and did finally produce the purplish slab of meat. But instead of eating it raw, he skewered it and began to cook it alongside of the two tongues.

That suited Skye. Buffalo liver was legendary for its powers of rejuvenation. Let Floyd Corporal devour the whole of it. The man wheezed and coughed, and Skye wondered if the teamster would make it.

Oddly, no one spoke. And yet there was a silent language that flowed between them all. An occasional smile. A bright nod toward the cooking meat. A sigh as they glanced at this demi-paradise, the quiet groves of trees, jack pine, lodge-poles, willows, chokecherry, rushes, and a narrow creek of clean, cold water rippling boldly through the narrow valley. Only a mile or so away was a far grimmer world.

When the tongues were more or less cooked, Victoria pulled one from the fierce fire and carried it with her skinning knife to a slab of rock, and there she began sawing, one juicy slice after another, hot, steaming meat that fell to the rock.

Winding came first, but she shooed him away.

"Burn your fingers," she said.

He grinned, pulled out his Barlow knife, and stabbed a fat slice. He began whirling it around and around, letting the air cool the tongue, and finally sank his incisors into it, making obscene noises as he chewed.

That was the start. They all stabbed their pieces of meat, cooled them, and began gnawing. They ate both tongues, and Corporal ate the liver too, sharing small pieces with Winding, their fingers dripping.

"A respite, anyway," Mercer said, licking his fingers. "What's the old saying? Eat, drink, and be merry, for tomorrow we die."

Skye finished his tongue and wiped his hands on the tan grass. He felt so weary he could barely stay awake.

"Tomorrow the hard work starts," he said. "If we all work hard, we'll pull through."

Mercer smiled, but there was something fatalistic in the smile, as if he believed that Skye was simply trying to boost their spirits. Mercer was about to get a lesson in living Indian style.

"These downed buffalo will draw predators," Skye said.

"I want each of you to collect a pile of rocks, something to throw at the varmints. Coyotes are no problem. Wolves could be. A catamount might be trouble. But I'm worried about bears. We haven't the means to hoist any of the meat into a tree; there's not a rope among us. The one other prospect is to bury each of the carcasses under pine limbs. Do you want to do it?"

"I don't have the strength left," Mercer said.

Skye didn't think he did, either. "All right, it's rocks, then." He turned to Floyd Corporal. "Tomorrow, I would like you to whittle a new haft for the axe head we salvaged. Not from pine. Try willow or aspen. That's mostly quiet work, something you can do while your lungs heal."

"It'll be done," Corporal said, and then coughed violently.

"Good. Tomorrow we'll pull hides, start fleshing them with the hatchet blade, braid some rawhide rope, try to raise some meat up high to keep it safe, start making some rawhide harness and packsaddles, and a few other things I have in mind."

Mercer laughed. "Factory workers."

Skye decided not to let it pass. "That's what tribes do, Mister Mercer. They are factory workers, turning what they hunt and gather into everything they need."

The flames dimmed to orange coals. There would be little comfort this night with no robes or blankets to warm their bodies against a night breeze that would drop close to freezing. There would be no spare clothing, no sheeted wagon overhead to stop the wind.

"Let's keep this fire going," Mercer said.

"That's good. It'll throw heat and maybe keep animals at bay. Did you bring in enough wood?" Skye asked.

Mercer hadn't. "Maybe when the moon comes up I can find some."

"Maybe you can," Skye said. "You'll be in charge of keeping us warm."

Mercer laughed again. He was, it seemed, a pretty good sport.

The night passed quietly. Perhaps there was too much of the acrid odor of fire in the air. Perhaps predators were having a banquet upon all the fire-wounded creatures elsewhere. Mercer managed to keep a flame going all night, and asked no relief from anyone. Skye slept soundly; he was far too exhausted not to sleep, even if his backside was freezing while his front side roasted. He was awake at first light, as always. He studied the ridges for danger, as always. Around him lay the rest, each in a place hollowed in the turf. The great carcasses of the buffalo lay untouched, at least by large predators, thirty or forty yards distant. He arose stiffly, wishing he had some tea. But there wasn't even a kettle, much less a tin cup. He saw that Mercer had finally fallen into sleep, the explorer's face somehow soft and innocent.

Victoria was staring at Skye. She arose softly, padded to him, and he drew her tight. It was something they always did. They greeted each other with a fierce hug as each day began. She vanished into the bush while he washed his face in the flowing creek, which offered up the music of soft laughter. Then he washed his Green River knife and settled beside the buffalo cow. This fine morning they would all enjoy the most succulent and tender part of a buffalo, the hump meat. The women had pulled as much hide free as they could, but now the cow needed to be turned over so they could tear the rest of the hide free. It was a task beyond his strength, but when Mercer suddenly appeared, they tugged on the legs and finally flipped the cow over, so Victoria and Mary could continue.

Slowly and carefully, Skye sliced a rib roast out of the cow while Mercer gathered sticks and built up the fire from its coals. Skye hurt; yesterday's ordeal had left his body aching in every muscle. His lungs ached. The smoke had done something terrible to them. But he was used to it. No man lived close to the wilds without pain.

He cut two roasts out of the hump and set them to cooking while suspended on green willow sticks. As the meat sizzled, he continued butchering, gradually building a great heap of meat that would nourish them all this day. The women would find time to start jerking some of it for future emergencies. A lazy smoke lifted off the wavering fire while the meat sizzled. The scent woke up the teamsters, and then Mary. A feast at dawn. An odd breakfast, but just fine this big, hot day in paradise.

Skye watched them all. People were different at dawn, shaking sleep out of their bodies, and sometimes shaking the pain away too. But one by one they settled near the fire while the flame blackened the outside of the roasts and the fat dripped steadily from the meat.

They had a boss rib breakfast, and it was as fine a meal as any Skye had ever enjoyed, though he might have savored a pinch of salt on the tender meat.

Mercer ate heartily and seemed as ready as the rest for a day of toil. And strangely, he no longer talked about the certitude of perishing in the wilds of North America.

Factory indeed. The want of everything was so urgent that Skye scarcely knew what required the most attention. But these things sorted themselves out their own way. The women swiftly pulled hides off the remaining buffalo and staked them to the ground, hair-side down. Then, using the hatchet blade, Victoria began fleshing the hides while Mary brain-tanned them, using a rounded river cobble to grind the fatty brain into the hides.

Graves Mercer turned to joking, but at least he stayed busy butchering meat, which he did so poorly that Skye feared the man would sever a finger. Still, the amount of salvaged meat that could be turned into jerky or pemmican began to grow.

Silas Winding turned to what he knew best, and began slicing strips of rawhide from one of the hides and braiding it into rope. Some of this new rope would soon hang haunches above the reach of bears, while the rest of it would become lead lines, halters, bridles, reins, and other tack. Floyd Corporal, the weakest among them, was still able to whittle a new handle of willow and fit it to the axe head, gather firewood, tend camp, cook meat, and keep an eye out for danger. But he looked bad, haggard, and Skye wondered about him.

Skye patrolled the hillsides periodically, looking for trouble, but then he helped butcher for a while and found along the creek abundant chokecherries and sarvis berries to make pemmican. The horses grazed peacefully in the valley, content to stay near water. It would be many days before they might be healed enough to drag a travois.

After Corporal had fashioned a workable axe, with wedges pinning the head on the haft, Skye felled young lodgepole pines and turned them into usable travois and lodgepoles. It felt good to draw upon the world around them and make shelter and transportation from whatever nature provided.

When the women finished fleshing and brain-tanning one hide, they headed for a nearby tree and whipsawed the stiff hide back and forth around the trunk, softening the leather. There would not be time to turn it into velvety soft leather, but this hide, severed in two, would provide warm robes for two of the party.

Because one of the hides would be devoted to horse tack and parfleches and clothing, they were still short of leather. Skye hoped to remedy that the next evening, when he would slip out at twilight, heading up the creek in search of an elk or at least a mule deer. He wouldn't mind finding a moose or a black bear, either.

Floyd Corporal took over the cooking, and kept meat broiling all day. So hard was the labor, and so ravenous were the toiling people, that they simply stopped now and then for another slab of buffalo roast that rested on a flat rock, ready for all comers.

By the end of that first day there were crudely tanned robes for two, plus the remaining hides to shelter the rest of them against the sharp cold of late-summer nights.

"Let's rest and have a bite, mates," Skye said.

They collected around a table rock where Corporal had piled the cooked meat, and helped themselves. It was a messy business, gnawing at large slabs of dripping hot meat held in bare hands. But a satisfying repast.

"Well, Mister Skye, we've survived another day," Mercer said. "I'll be the first to say you've opened my eyes."

"The Indians opened the eyes of many a trapper who came here," Skye said. "Here was everything they needed and they knew what to do with it."

"But the work! All I've done is slave all day," Winding said.

"And we'll slave for another week," Skye said. "Then maybe one or two of the horses can pull a travois."

"We'll head straight for Fort Benton," Mercer said.

"Why?" Skye asked.

"Because we lost everything. This is all make-do. We need to outfit."

Skye shrugged. "If that's what you want, I'll take you there. But there's no need. You came to see what you could see, and there's still two months of good weather."

"But, Skye. There's only one rifle among us. A few belt knives. Makeshift tools. No paper for a journal. I lack even a pencil."

"Then I guess we'll just have to live like Indians," Skye said.

"I shall want a dozen wives," said the explorer, and then laughed at his witticism. Skye did too. There was that quality about the man that made him good company.

"Ain't no damned Absaroka that would marry him," Victoria said.

"No Shoshone," Mary said.

"No Nez Perce. No Hidatsa. No Lakota," said Victoria.

"No Piegan. No Assiniboine. No Gros Ventre," said Mary.

"Maybe a damn ugly Arapaho with warts," Victoria said. "Someone with her nose cut off."

The women laughed merrily. A cut-off nose was the punishment some tribesmen imposed on adulterous wives.

"I don't know what's so funny," Mercer said.

"They're having a very good time with your ambitions," Skye replied. "In some tribes, a woman with a severed nose is a woman punished for unfaithfulness."

"Ah! Then I shall look for half a dozen of the bobbed nose beauties!"

Floyd Corporal thought that was capital, and wheezed cheerfully.

Skye found his ancient Hawken, checked the load, and slipped into the twilight. Behind him, the party sat around the fire, enjoying the evening even as chill air slid down from the mountains. He felt the soft rush of air as something silent flapped by and realized it was a large owl. He would not tell Victoria. An owl was an omen of big trouble.

He padded softly up the creek valley, looking for those shapes of large animals that would offer him more meat and hide. Elk hide made especially fine moccasins as well as good waistcoats or pantalones. A man could live just fine in a cotton shirt, elk-hide vest, elk leggins, and moccasins.

He was a fine hunter who glided softly through the cottony dark, pausing to listen, instinctively understanding where animals might water or graze or simply stand quietly. Jawbone had not followed, so Skye slipped along as silently as that owl.

Then he froze. Ahead was a cow elk and a late-born baby, scarcely two months old. The little one butted her bag and suckled. He lowered his Hawken intuitively, but stopped. It was not in him to kill her and orphan that baby. He might if he were desperately hungry but that was not the case. He watched quietly as the calf suckled and then meandered away from his mother. She sensed his presence. Her head jerked upward, she stared at him, sniffed the air, and then hightailed away, dancing ahead like a proud trotter. The calf froze, ancient instinct telling it not to move. Then a soft whistle, or was it just an odd breath, and the calf tripped away into the gloom.

"Hope you grow into a big fellow," Skye muttered.

He worked his way into deep night, following the melodic creek, and then turned back toward camp, empty-handed. Jawbone whickered softly, trotted up and bumped his massive head into Skye's chest.

"Avast," he said softly. He scarcely dared touch the animal. The horse's mane had burnt away in places, and there were painful blisters on Jawbone's rump. Big black horseflies were tormenting all the horses now, crawling over the blisters, and Skye wondered what to do about it. Maybe river mud plastered over the blisters would help. He would try in the morning and hope he didn't get kicked to death.

He found the camp still busy. Mercer and Winding had hung two haunches of buffalo from a stout willow tree. The women toiled on the next hide, now staked down where the previous hide had been worked. Corporal, whose wheeze had worsened, was fitting together a little rack next to the fire where he intended to smoke-cure some buffalo meat. With indefatigable people like this, Skye thought, they would soon be outfitted and on their way.

That night Skye and Victoria shared one hide, spread out under them. The hair warmed them and offered protection from the hard earth. And they warmed each other. Floyd Corporal gladly took a robe. His wheeze had shifted to a rattling cough and Skye worried about the man. Too much searing hot air, too much smoke, too much chill and hard living and walking through corrosive ash, had taken their toll. Skye didn't like the black flesh around the man's eyes, the rasping of his breath, the desperate look in the man's face.

Mary gratefully took the other new robe, while Graves Mercer and Silas Winding settled on the remaining uncured hide, finding some comfort in it. This night was even colder than the previous one. It was that time of year when days remained hot but the nights turned icy. Several times, Skye awakened and added wood to the flickering fire, but its faint heat did little to drive away the chill, and Skye got more comfort out of stirring about than he got from the miserable flame.

He eyed the night heavens anxiously. The worst thing that could happen now, when they were so ill prepared, would be a cold rain or worse, an early winter storm. But for the moment, their luck held.

No predators showed up that night, either. The fire probably kept them at bay. But when Skye pried open his eyes at dawn, he swore he was staring at a wolf not far distant. Whatever the case, by the time he was fully awake, the wraith had vanished.

The camp was slow to awaken. A cold blue dawn slowly expanded into daylight. Victoria sat up suddenly, alarm in her features.

"He is dead," she said.

"He was all right a while ago. I checked."

"Dead."

She arose, padded softly across dewy ground, and knelt beside the still form of Floyd Corporal. Slowly she lowered her head to listen. Then she slipped the robe open and touched the man's face. Then she shook him.

There was no response.

Skye knew that they hadn't escaped the prairie fire after all.

Chapter 25

Death in their midst. They gathered around Floyd Corporal, absorbing the great silence of him. It had happened suddenly and mysteriously. Yesterday, he had been well enough to whittle an axe handle and gather firewood. Late in the day he was wheezing. This morning he was gone. Of just what cause no one could say, but surely that fire and its lethal smoke had much to do with it.

He looked smaller in death than in life. Alive, he had been a quiet, able teamster who was well versed in wilderness ways, kept his livestock in good shape, knew what could be gotten from a horse or mule or ox, and said very little. There he was now, dark-haired, hollow-faced. His eyes were closed.

"This is bloody awful," Mercer said.

"Floyd Corporal was a good man," Skye responded. "He got you here."

"What'll we do? We haven't a shovel."

"We're living by Indian ways," Skye said. "We will give him to the sun rather than the earth."

"A tree burial! But that's for Indians, not white men. I wish I had a journal to record it."

Skye was put off by the remark. "We will bury him with respect," he said.

Corporal was some mother's son, perhaps someone's brother, maybe someone's father. He would be missed by someone, somewhere.

"Do you know his family?" Skye asked Winding.

"I can't say as I do. Missouri folks."

"I would like you to make it your mission to get word to them, whoever they may be."

Winding nodded. "I have that in my mind."

"Let's be about it," Skye said. He took the axe and headed for a grove of saplings, where he began to harvest poles. Mary slashed branches from the poles with the hatchet. Victoria cut rawhide strips. Mercer and Winding, not knowing what else to do, watched.

When Skye had cut eight poles, he and his women built a scaffold in a willow tree whose limbs overarched the meadow. The rawhide strips anchored the scaffold to two horizontal limbs, and in a while a bed of poles rested aboveground, under a leafy canopy. It would be a good place for a mortal to meet eternity.

Without hesitation, Mary and Victoria wrapped Corporal in the brand-new buffalo robe, the very robe that had cost them a day of hard labor, and tied the robe tight with the thong, making a snug leather coffin for Corporal.

Mercer looked like he was about to protest; to say that the robe was needed and valuable. Skye could almost read the man's mind. But Mercer held his peace. The dead deserved whatever honor could be accorded them, including the precious robe.

Skye nodded, and he and Winding and Mercer lifted the body and carried it slowly to the willow tree, and then hoisted it as high as they could reach, until they settled it evenly on the poles.

Skye pulled his battered top hat from his graying locks and addressed Mercer. "Do you wish to say anything?"

Mercer looked about, at Victoria and Mary and Winding and Skye, all of them suffering from fire blisters, scorched-away hair, soot-blackened clothing.

"Floyd Corporal was a fine man. May he rest in peace," Mercer said. "I know little enough of the man. He kept to himself. But a man reveals himself in his work and his conduct. He left no task undone, angered no man, wounded no man, and gave his best at all times. I should be proud to call him a noble Yankee."

Skye liked that. He found himself gazing into the eyes of that other teamster, Winding, and found tears there in that sun-blasted chestnut flesh under his eyes.

"The Lord is my shepherd, I shall not want," Mercer said, and recited the psalm.

Then it was finished. And still a mystery. Corporal's life had played out almost before anyone grasped how close he was to death.

The sun had not yet transcended the surrounding ridges.

"We have a few more days of work here," Skye said.

The next days were devoted to hard toil. The women fleshed the remaining hides, brain-tanned them, softened them, and sliced them into robes. Mercer gathered buffalo berries and sarvis berries, shredded the cooked meat, collected bone marrow grease, pounded the berries with river cobbles, and made pemmican. Winding looked after the horses and made horse tack from the remaining rawhide. Skye hunted, at last bagging a mighty elk. It took a combined effort to drag it into camp, with Jawbone providing most of the motive power.

"Moccasins!" Victoria exclaimed.

And more. Before the women were done, there were moccasins for two men, a parfleche to store the pemmican, and enough left over to make a vest.

Mercer was growing restless, but Skye and the women were far from done. Mary harvested pieces of buffalo small intestine, washed it, turned it inside out, and stuffed it with shredded meat, which she then roasted. Victoria sliced the lean meat into strips and set them to drying in the hot sun on racks of her devising.

Bits of rawhide became belts or hobbles. A piece of green rawhide wrapped over the head and haft of the axe, soaked and left to dry, anchored the axe head to Corporal's improvised haft.

Skye cut the buffalo horns free, hollowed them out for ladles and spoons, while Winding swiftly learned to weave the shaggy hair of the bull into braids that would end up as halters for his horses. The women carefully freed the sinew from the backbones of the great beasts. The sinew would have various uses as a form of thread, and could be turned into bowstrings.

But at last the day came to move along. The carcasses were reeking. The surrounding meadows had been grazed down to bare earth, and the horses were wandering farther afield to feed themselves. One of the draft horses seemed well healed, and the simple belly-band harness for a travois would do the beast no harm. Skye and the women had fashioned a long travois, poles and crossbars, and now hooked it to the draft horse. They piled the new robes and the parfleche and tools onto the crossbars, and carefully anchored everything down. During the fire everything had been lost; now the robes and tools and emergency foods needed to survive rested on those poles.

Mercer had slipped into a respectful silence. From the aftermath of the fire unto this day, his perception of events had changed. He thought himself doomed after the fire, when every one of his European tools, save for a belt knife, had been consumed. But now much had been restored. To be sure, an axe head and hatchet had contributed. And Skye's salvaged rifle and powder had helped. Robes and clothing and tools and food had been extracted from nature. The lesson of living Indian style had sunk deep into Mercer's mind.

They looked at one another, and at the brook and meadow that had nurtured them.

"Fort Benton?" Mercer asked.

"Why there? I thought you came here for stories."

"My notes are ash. I haven't a scrap of paper."

"Then record your stories Indian style. On the back of your robe."

Mercer thought about it. "I've seen these," he said. "Pictographs, each evoking an episode. Each triggering a communal memory." He walked to the creek and stared into the babbling water. And then returned. "Would your ladies teach me?"

Mary nodded shyly. She was a good artist.

Mercer brightened. "Then we're off to see the big bones."

Silas Winding spent one last moment, head bowed, his slouch hat in hand, at the scaffold and then began driving the horses before him. The blisters had scabbed over, but the horses were far from being useful.

Skye took the caravan straight north, out of the intimate valley, over ridges dotted with pines and into brush-choked coulees. There were unnamed mountains to the west, clad darkly in pine, but he steered through open country as much as he could. They were on the move but defenseless against a host of troubles, most notably a cold downpour, and unless they could make peace with passing bands of Indians, they could find themselves in big trouble.

Skye rode Jawbone, who seemed none the worse for wear, and stayed well ahead of the rest, scouting for trouble and hunting game. He shot an antelope and left it on the trail for the rest. The meat would be fine; the hide would make a new parfleche or a vest for someone else. The summer was waning, and leather clothing would be welcome.

For days they toiled north through open country. Graves Mercer was growing restless again. He was an adventurer, and when no great adventure greeted him, he fell into distemper. This took the form of small complaints about food, or lack of shelter, or the slow progress.

"Find me a tribe, Mister Skye. I wish to meet them."

"You won't wish it if we run into Piegans, Mister Mercer."

"Piegans?"

"The southernmost of the Blackfeet. And deadly enemies of Yanks in particular. But they buy their weapons from Hudson's Bay, and suffer the British."

"What would make a good story about them? You know, for London readers? Do the chiefs have a dozen wives? Are they lecherous?"

"I think, Mister Mercer, that no tribe has social arrangements that Europeans think are proper."

"That's what I'm after! Find me some."

Skye laughed.

The next day, while riding up a ridge well ahead of his party, he stopped suddenly. On the ridge were two mounted warriors, waiting for him to reach them.

He did what he usually did in those circumstances, spurred his horse straight toward them, his hand high, palm forward, the peace and friendship posture of the plains.

When he reached the ridge he found two young men, both with bows and nocked arrows, but these were pointed away from Skye.

Gros Ventres, Big Bellies, or Atsina, allies of the Blackfeet, famous moochers, famous thieves, famous tricksters, famous for their endless visits. And maybe the killers of those Assiniboine youths back on the trail.

Chapter 26

The young warriors were wreathed in smiles. They eyed Skye, studied Jawbone, who stood with his ears laid back, and then examined Skye's party, visible a mile back from that ridge.

"Come. Visit. Smoke. People that way," one of the warriors signed. He pointed northwest.

Skye would rather not, but saw little choice in it. All he could do was warn his people to keep an eye on their horses. There wasn't much else that they could call property or that the Gros Ventres would prize.

Skye nodded. His hands worked swiftly. He would return to his people and guide them to the village.

The sign-talker's hands responded. "We go with you."

Skye acknowledged it and turned Jawbone back to his party, trailing along behind.

When he rode in, flanked by the Gros Ventres, his women watched warily, ready for trouble. But Skye possessed the only weapon among them, something the Gros Ventres swiftly realized.

"Mister Mercer, these gents are Gros Ventres, a tribe allied with the Blackfeet. They want us to visit them," Skye said.

"Well, we'll do it."

Skye studied the two warriors, who sat impassively on good ponies. They didn't grasp English.

"We'll go. Not much choice. These people can be very friendly or not, as the mood strikes them. Watch your possessions. Especially the horses."

"Thieves are they?"

Skye shrugged. He wouldn't single out the Gros Ventres as being any more light-fingered than many others.

But Winding knew these people. "They've a reputation as moochers."

"That's a Yank word I'm not familiar with."

"They are known to overstay their welcome," Skye said.

Mercer chuckled. "Very like us all. Let's go."

Escorted by the young Gros Ventres, the party topped the ridge, descended into a grassy bowl, and discovered the village camped along Box Elder Creek. They had obviously had a successful hunt. Buffalo hides were staked to the grass, jerky was drying on racks, and the women were busy fleshing hides, making pemmican, and cooking.

The party was soon being scrutinized by the whole band, who crowded around, examining the blistered horses, the sole travois, the lack of weapons, and Mister Skye, the one person they knew.

"Sonofabitch!" said Victoria, walking beside Skye. She didn't like any people allied with the Blackfeet, and Skye guessed she despised these most of all for their sticky-fingered ways.

"I feel like a rabbit in an eagle's talons," Winding said.

Nonetheless, the throng seemed perfectly cheerful, and Skye spotted plenty of smiles along with rank curiosity as they all studied Skye's harmless and near-desperate group.

There would be the ritual visit to the chief or headman. He hardly needed to explain what had happened. The singed hair on horse and man, the soot-smeared clothing, the blistered backs of the horses, the makeshift tack, all told a story to anyone with eyes to see.

"Is there anything I should know about these people?" Mercer asked. "Do they worship a dragon goddess? Eat sheep's eyes? Sacrifice virgins to the sun god?"

"They're cannibals, mate. You'll end up in their stewpot."

"Ho, ho. You make dangerous jokes, Mister Skye."

"Anything for a good story, Mister Mercer."

This was an ill-kempt camp. The lodges were scattered in random clumps. Latrine odors sifted through it. Middens of offal and bones lay everywhere. Mangy mutts circled the newcomers, some of them yapping or howling. The lodges sagged in the sun, many of them fashioned of ancient buffalo skins that had seen their day. This was a place of castaways. Still, this was not a permanent camp; it was a hunting camp, intended to serve its purpose for a few days. But Skye found himself aware of poverty here. These people had no wealth, unlike the proud Blackfeet to whom they were allied. He wondered if they were simply shiftless, or whether misfortune had afflicted them.

But they seemed cheerful enough. The crowd throbbed along beside them, scampering children, the boys naked; bronze women in summer calico. Chestnut-tinted old men wrapped in grimy white and red and black trade blankets. Toothless grandmothers, built like barrels, smiling through wrinkles in their corduroy faces, their faded dresses hanging loose.

The chief's lodge proved to be no larger than the rest. The headman waited, dressed only in a loincloth and moccasins, some scars of battle puckering across his ribs and arms.

Several elders flanked him. Clearly, they had received word and had arrayed themselves for guests.

The chief held up a hand in welcome, his face crinkled in pleasure. These people plainly were enjoying the prospect of guests. Then he signaled a word, bear, and pointed at himself.

There was no one who could translate, so Skye found himself using the time-honored sign language of the plains. Swiftly, he introduced his party. The Englishman, the Missouri man, the Snake woman and Absaroka woman who were his wives. He recounted the fire that had destroyed nearly everything. And told the chief he was glad to be welcomed among the Atsina. He used the name they gave themselves, not the French name trappers had bestowed on them.

The chief rambled, barely accompanying his long talk with signs, so that Skye caught little of what was being said. Still, there were scraps of information. The great prairie fires had pushed the buffalo this way, and hunting was good here. The People had no enemies, only friends. The visitors would be welcome to share the meat. Everything the village possessed now belonged to the visitors for their use, and everything the visitors possessed now belonged to the Atsina for the People's use.

That gave Skye pause. Was it rhetoric? Was it something larger, a justification for copping some horses? Uneasily Skye worked his way through the welcoming ritual, and then the chief summoned a pipe-bearer to bring him the peace pipe. There would be a smoke, a sacred affirmation that no harm would be received or given, and then his party would be free to make camp.

"And what have our visitors brought us?" the chief asked, his fingers filling in for words.

Skye knew at once that a gift was required. A gift he and Mercer didn't have.

"Nothing. We are poor. The great fire took everything."

"That is a good horse." The chief waved at Jawbone.

"You would find him dangerous, Chief Bear."

"Then he would make good meat."

Victoria watched, horror in her face.

"What's he saying, Mister Skye?" Mercer asked.

"He is expecting a gift and has his eye on Jawbone."

"Tell him I will give him the giant horse. Not the one bearing our travois, but the other."

Skye felt a flood of gratitude toward the explorer. "Chief Bear, grandfather," he signaled. "It is our wish to give you the largest horse of all, that giant standing there. You will have the biggest horse you have ever seen. He is recovering from some wounds caused by fire, but in a short while, you will have a giant. He can pull twice as much as other horses."

"Ah! So it will be! Welcome. The Atsina welcome our friend Skye. Welcome. Be our guests!"

"What's he saying?"

"He's welcoming us. He accepts the draft horse. He wants us to be at home among the Atsina."

Skye felt momentary relief, but worries crowded his mind and he wanted nothing more than to escape gracefully, without arousing trouble that seemed to lurk in every corner. He wondered how many more horses this visit would cost.

Mercer led the great animal to the chief, who waved a hand and one of the younger of his family took the line. They peered at it, stood beside it, marveled at its height, carefully scrutinized the crusted-over wounds, talked much among themselves, and seemed pleased. Now everything was smiles again.

Some tension dissolved and Skye's party was led to a place just outside the village where there was some grass remaining for their stock. Mercer and Winding picketed their remaining draft horse and saddle horses while Skye turned Jawbone loose. If an Atsina tried to catch him, he'd have his hands full. And they had all been warned. Jawbone was no horse to trifle with.

Mercer seemed content to wander the village, study men, women, and children, his sharp eye missing nothing. Skye was plenty hungry, and so were they all, but so far they had not been invited to any feast.

But at twilight all that changed. Chief Bear summoned them all to a feast of buffalo hump, the finest meat available on the plains, and soon Skye and his wives were gorging on well-done, succulent meat that was roasted in such plenitude that they all ate more than their fill.

"Skye, this is the best boss rib I've ever sampled," Mercer said.

And so it was. It came without adornment, no prairie turnips, no greens, no berries, but it sufficed this pleasant evening, as the sun swept toward its bed behind the western hills, and a lavender darkness crept over the cheerful camp.

He began to relax. Tomorrow, early, they would slip away, probably before any of these people stirred. They were not known for industry, or getting up at dawn to spend daylight at toil.

"I say, Mister Skye, this is capital. But I haven't a story. Can you think of something worth writing about?" Mercer asked, gnawing on a stem of grass.

"You could write about the white men wandering these plains. You've met two unusual sorts," Skye said.

But Mercer dismissed the thought with a grunt.

Then an emissary arrived from Chief Bear, summoning Skye once again to the headman's lodge, where he sat upon a reed backrest, enjoying the company of half a dozen comely women.

"Mister Skye," the chief signaled. "Night comes, the owl flies. And at night we think of other things. I will give you a gift. Take one of my wives this night. Send your men here and take them all. Enjoy them. They are very beautiful."

Skye was afraid of that.

"And, Mister Skye, send your wives to me. The younger one catches my eye."

Chapter 27

Over many years, Skye had learned to cope with practices and beliefs of the native people of North America. Often they didn't accord with his own. And now he was caught in a dilemma that instantly tortured him. Chief Bear was being hospitable. Lending an honored guest a wife or two was a mark of esteem. Offering the chief a wife or two was a mark of the visitor's respect. All this was simply the commerce of the plains, ordinary except to a European like Skye whose instincts were utterly different.

"Sonofabitch," said Victoria.

"What did he say, man?" Graves Mercer asked.

Skye could hardly bring the words to his lips. "He's offered us the pleasure of his wives and wants me to reciprocate."

"No! Really?"

"Hell yes," said Victoria.

"Ah! At last! Something to write about! I've wandered over half of North America looking for a sensation, and finally I've found one!"

"Mister Skye," said Mary, "I am honored. I will be the one-night wife of this fine Atsina chief. I will bring smiles to him, and feel rewarded by his happiness."

"Dammit, Skye, tell him I am old and full of bad diseases," Victoria said.

Skye lifted his top hat and settled it on graying locks, for once not only wordless but with no plan rising to mind.

Beside Chief Bear, a dozen women smiled broadly. They could read the chief's sign language as well as Victoria and Mary could. Skye spotted the sits-beside-him wife, older, stern, gray, with great authority in her demeanor. She showed no pleasure in the honor of sleeping with guests but the younger ladies trilled and cooed and smiled broadly.

Skye surveyed them all and admitted to himself that Chief Bear had an eye for comely young women. In fact, most of these Atsina ladies were gorgeous, with flashing brown eyes, glossy jet hair in braids or hanging loose, golden flesh, and trim ankles. One in particular stared at him quietly, her young, golden face warm with anticipation, even as she stood higher and prouder that he might notice her. One glance at her, slim and sweet and eager, stirred him.

Skye puckered his lips. He wished to speak, but all he could manage was some fierce puckering of lip.

"By the Lord Harry, I hope you'll spare me a pair of them," Mercer said. "What a dainty dish to set before the king."

"Serially or at the same time?" Skye asked.

"Ho, ho, ho," Mercer retorted.

Matters were getting out of hand.

"You must realize, Mister Mercer, that some of these lovelies might be infected. The venereal is common among them, and white men are more vulnerable to it than they are."

"Trying to scare me off, are you, Skye?"

"What you do is up to you, Mister Mercer."

"Will they expect anything from me, Mister Skye?"

"A baby."

"Baby? Surely you don't mean it."

"The Atsina would be enchanted if you were, ah, to father a child among them."

Mercer began to shuffle, one foot and another, contemplating that. "Do I have my choice of lovelies?"

"You might offer another horse, seeing as how you don't have a wife to bargain away."

"And Winding?"

"I imagine a horse would do it."

"Absolutely delightful. How do I proceed? I can't even signal them, unless I just point at the lady . . . maybe that one there, standing behind the rest. A slim beauty, solemn, not a bit of eagerness in her face."

"I'm afraid, Mister Mercer, that the object of your desire is the chief's daughter. If you ask for her, you might get her for life."

"Oh. Blast. Bad luck." But then he brightened. "But good story. Shock London, you know. Old boys'll turn beet-red over their tea. Oh, what it'll do the prime minister. Ah, what it'll do in every rectory! Oh, what a stir at the Royal Society! Half the old dogs will run snuff up their nostrils, the other half will be envious of me."

"Confession is good for the soul," said Skye.

"How'm I going to write all this down? Have they paper and pencil?"

"Not likely. You can record it on your robe, using the greasepaint Victoria gave you, and a reed."

"I'd have to smuggle the bloody robe into England."

"Mister Skye, just choose a few," Victoria said.

He knew she wouldn't mind it a bit if he wandered into the night with three ladies on his arm, even if she herself didn't want to become Chief Bear's paramour. But the Crow were like that.

"Please, Mister Skye, give me the honor," said Mary, aglow.

Around them eager Atsina had collected. This was a good

show, and word had spread through the whole camp. They would enjoy seeing who Skye selected, and would enjoy Skye's presentation of his ladies to Chief Bear, and maybe Bear's sons and sons-in-law.

All in all, it seemed a cheerful prospect.

But something was raking Skye's soul.

He stepped forward, and immediately the merriment and gossip stopped. What he would say with his fingers would be there for all to see, all to interpret. It would not be easy. The finger-talk lacked nuance and was unclear, sometimes dangerously unclear.

"My medicine," he signaled, "is to live only with my wives. It is not in me to share them with you. It is not in me to take any of yours. It is the way I am. It is in me to believe this comes from the Great Spirit. You are good to offer these things to me. This is good according to your medicine. I wish you happiness and peace."

"What's all that about?" Mercer asked.

"I was turning down Chief Bear. I said it isn't my medicine."

"But, Skye, what about my story?"

"I impose my own rules of life on no man but myself," Skye said.

"But you're employed by me. You didn't ask me."

"Yes, sir, I am. No, I did not ask you. My domestic arrangements are my own."

The chief thought about Skye's response for a while, frowned, and nodded. But there was grudge in his nod. Plainly he had been affronted. And plainly Skye's party was on perilous ground. But it was an ironclad rule of the plains tribes that hosts treated their guests with respect. Nothing would happen within this village. Probably nothing would happen at all. And yet Skye found himself ill at ease.

Mercer seethed all the way back to their campsite. As soon as he was out of earshot of the Atsina, he lashed out.

"I've walked across this continent looking for a sensation. I've suffered indignities, lost my outfit, lost a man, and lost my journals. Nothing happens over here. It's not like Africa or the Near East. All I've found is a big blank. What will I send to the seven newspapers that employ me? What sort of papers will I present to the Royal Society? Answer me that, eh?"

Skye stood stock-still.

"Now at last something happens. A chief with the morals of a rutting dog wants to trade women. A sensation. I can sell the story ten times over. At long last, after squandering months and a small fortune, we have something worth writing about. And what happens? You scotch the whole thing. I never thought I'd be hiring some missionary. I never imagined you'd wreck this entire trip. What's left, eh? Bones. I don't want fossil bones. I want sensation. You've taken a year out of my life. That's what this is about. A year out of my life. Lost. Gone. Dead."

Skye had hoped for good pay, but now he knew he would get nothing at all.

"If you're discharging me I think we will head for Victoria's people, Mister Mercer."

"What? And leave me here? Without a guide? Without a translator? Without anyone who knows the hand-talk? Without a weapon? You signed on for the whole trip. You'll take me through."

"Very well. My advice is that we pack up and leave immediately. There's trouble here."

"Don't be absurd, Skye. They're fixing to do some drumming, have a party, throw a fandango in our honor, and you want to sneak out."

"Do you reckon one of those blistered saddlers which

ain't ever gonna be good for much would fetch me a lady?" Winding asked. "I'm plumb lonesome."

Winding's yearnings seemed to settle it for Mercer. "Are those nags good for anything?" he asked.

"Not for saddling, anyway," Winding said. "Maybe you and me, we'd be getting the real bargain, eh?"

Victoria laughed; it was her rowdy, raucous laugh, the sort of laugh that evoked midsummer saturnalias among the Absaroka people.

"I don't know as how I'd want the chief's sits-beside-him woman anyhow," Winding said.

Skye nodded. His women were already drifting into the village, full of merriment, full of devil-may-care, ready for a howl. And Mercer and Winding were headed for the horses, which were picketed on grass alongside some trees two or three hundred yards away.

Skye found himself alone. The whole world, in all its diverse tribes, enjoyed a happy time. Fiestas, potlatches, parties, balls, dances. He wondered why he felt so ill at ease about all that. Maybe it was because he had ended up a man without a country. His only land was not a place, but lay in the heart.

Chapter 28

Skye wasn't going to have a night by himself after all. Victoria came for him and told him he was needed.

Reluctantly, for he was not comfortable with these people, he followed her into the village, where a great congregation had collected before the lodge of Chief Bear. The wrath of the earlier hour had melted away and he eyed Skye affably.

"Ah, Mister Skye. Help me, please," Mercer said. "They've inquired what I do, who I am, and I thought to tell them I am a storyteller. That's as close as I can come to a journalist. Victoria did the sign-talk. And now, nothing will do but stories. They're gathered here, the whole bloody village, to hear me tell stories!"

"We will have stories!" Victoria said. "They have a young man who knows English."

"Then why me?"

"Just a little English. He worked at Fort Benton a few moons."

"Two sign-talkers and a translator?"

Victoria grinned.

Spread on robes in every direction was a great crowd, some wrapped in blankets against the chill, most of them eager for this delightful event to begin. A small fire cast up gray smoke and shot wavering light into the multitude.

"What'll you talk about, Mister Mercer?"

"I don't know a thing about stories but I can tell them where I've been, what I've seen. Monkeys. Zebras. Giraffes. Lions. Crocodiles. Anteaters."

Chief Bear, seeing Skye at hand, rose and lifted an arm, gaining attention swiftly. He was going to orate first, and Skye hoped the young translator could convey the gist of it.

Bear began in a monotone that somehow projected outward to the farthest reaches of the crowd.

"He says, storytellers are the greatest of all people. He says storytellers bring us the rest of the world. They give us mighty lessons, and show us good and bad. They fill our minds with wonders. And here is a man who is said to be the greatest storyteller on earth, this man Mercer. So listen well my children, for there is no one else like him."

The young man was converting the Gros Ventre tongue into English well enough, which relieved Skye. He had no idea how he would convey the idea of a giraffe or a hippopotamus to these Atsina people.

"Ready, Mister Skye?"

"No, but go ahead."

Graves Duplessis Mercer stood gracefully among the Indians that cool night, lit only by the flames of a fire before him. He spoke in a loud sonorous voice, thanking them for inviting him, and expressing his wish that they would all profit from his talk.

Skye knew at once that Mercer possessed some sort of magic. It would not matter what he said, but that he was there among the Gros Ventres, making a memorable night out of a fall evening.

"I have sailed across the great waters. I have been to lands we call Asia and Africa and South America. I have been to a vast land called Australia where there are strange animals. I have been far north to an island covered with ice called Greenland. I have been to small islands in the south seas, where the waves crash on white beaches, and everyone is beautiful."

Skye intuitively followed the dialogue with his hands, even as the youth who knew a little English intoned his translation. No one consulted Mercer about the accuracy of any of it; it didn't matter. A good story did not need to be true.

"I have seen snakes called anacondas and boa constrictors so big that they are as thick as a tree trunk and five or seven paces long. I have seen animals called anteaters that have a long snout and dig up ants."

"Ah!" said someone. People laughed politely. This man's stories were becoming more and more strange, and that made them all the better.

"There is a tribe in Africa that pierces the flesh below the lower lip of young women and puts a wooden plug in the hole. And then every little while they put a larger plug in, until the lower lip protrudes outward like a small platter. They think this is beautiful."

Women clacked and giggled at that.

"I have been among people who tattoo their whole bodies. Do you know what a tattoo is? It is body art, pricked under the skin, and some people have covered all of themselves with body art. It cannot be washed off. It is their medicine forever," Mercer said. Clearly, he was reaching for anything exotic, and was getting exactly the result he hoped for.

"Zebras! Horses with black and white stripes! Can you imagine it?"

No one could.

"And pygmies! Little people, only this high." He gestured in the direction of his waist. "Little people, great warriors.

"Some people in Africa have blowguns. I suppose I'll have to tell you what a blowgun is. It's a big reed. The little people put a poison dart into it and blow it toward their enemies and kill them with poison."

Ah! That evoked a stir. Skye's fingers were incapable of telling these stories but he kept up manfully. The Gros Ventres were getting most of it from their translator. Whenever the fire flickered low, a young woman fed its flames, so all could see Skye's sign language and watch Mercer talk.

The man had a genius for it. He paused dramatically to let his interpreters translate. He gestured. He didn't try to tell stories, the kind with beginnings and endings, but simply described the wonders he had seen, and that was more than enough.

People edged closer, so they could study the sign language and hear the translator, who stumbled along, as taxed as Skye was. But somehow they got it, or something close to what Mercer was saying.

The explorer catalogued all the wonders of the world. Giant lizards, parrots as bright as sunsets, scorpions, camels with great humps on them that could walk across deserts and go for a while without water. He talked of fierce tribes of marauders in North Africa, blond people in Scandinavia, striped tigers that prowled the jungles. He talked of naval battles between big wooden ships with cannon on them. His talk roamed everywhere, the seas, the deserts, the woods, the mountaintops, the jungles, the rivers a mile wide.

Then, finally, as the chill turned to sharp cold, he stopped. By now, the whole village had edged close, jammed together for warmth.

The hour was late but one could not know that from watching Mercer, who had an odd glow about him. He was a storyteller, and he had recounted many of the wonders of the world.

Chief Bear stood. He seemed oddly animated, as if Mercer's great catalogue of wonders had triggered some excitement in the seamed old man. He spoke quietly in the Gros Ventre tongue to some youths who slipped away, and there was an air of expectation.

After a while, the boys returned leading two horses. These were handsome ponies, each equipped with a saddle and hackamore.

Chief Bear made the sign for a gift.

"These are gifts to you," Skye said.

"A gift? I thought they were moochers. Isn't that what you told me?"

"A gift," Skye said. "Accept them."

Mercer stepped forward, accepted the reins, and nodded to the chief.

But more followed. Now others in the village brought three horses to Mercer and Skye and his women, two of them saddled. Others brought lodgepoles. Then a group of Gros Ventre women dragged a whole smoke-darkened lodge into the circle of light, and presented it to Skye's party. Others brought parfleches filled with pemmican or jerky. Young men brought bows and quivers and left them at Mercer's feet.

Mercer accepted them all gratefully, making his delight known to these people. Skye signaled his own great pleasure and offered the friendship sign to them all.

"What's the protocol, Mister Skye? How do I thank them? My Lord, what have I done?"

"All the world loves a storyteller, mate. They're honoring you. This night they heard of wonders they'd never imagined. Creatures beyond anything they'd heard of. People different from any they'd seen. Customs they never knew. Foods they never tasted. Weapons that sent shivers through them. But yes, you can return a gift or two. Good idea. It's called a potlatch, and it's very big among some of the tribes. Maybe the nags blistered by the fire. These people could use them after they're healed."

"Done!" Mercer said.

Winding needed no instruction, but plunged off toward Skye's camp to collect the animals. They now had six new ones, all sound and saddled, and could surrender the blistered ones. And now they had a lodge and lodgepoles. They had gone in one evening from fire-chastened poor to rich.

Soon Winding returned with the nags, and Mercer gave them to Chief Bear, who was pleased to have them.

The evening was over. Skye's party lugged all their new-found wealth toward their own camp. Mary and Victoria swiftly spread the lodgepole pyramid, and laid lodgepoles into it, and then raised the soft, worn buffalo-hide cover. They would have shelter that chill night. It wasn't large, but it would house the five of them.

"What have I done? I still don't quite grasp all this," Mercer said.

"You gave them wonders. You do just the same in England. Why do all those papers and journals pay you well? You give them, in your words, sensations. You even hunt for sensations to write about. This is no different. The person who can tell stories is the most valued of all among many peoples."

"Well, that's a bit of a twist, eh? I thought I was a tale-bearer to the English, but now I'm a tale-teller to the Indians. The only trouble is, there's hardly a blessed thing to write about in North America."

Skye kept his thoughts about that to himself.

"I say, Skye, will we be intruding? There in the lodge

with two women?" Mercer asked. "A little bit too close for comfort, eh?"

"You are gentlemen," Skye responded.

"Not exactly, Mister Skye. When I'm pressed, or desperate, I can be a gentleman. But don't push your luck."

Chapter 29

Suddenly they were affluent. Each had a saddle horse. The remaining draft horse pulled one travois bearing the buffalo-hide lodge; another horse pulled the lodgepoles. Spare horses carted the rest of the gear, the robes, the parfleches, on packsaddles.

They pulled out at dawn while the Gros Ventre camp slept. Those people were late risers and their village would not come to life until nearly noon. A few horse herders silently watched them leave. In the quiet chill, Skye led his party north through broken country, largely open range land, a paradise of deer, antelope, and elk.

"How far is it to Fort Benton, Mister Skye?" asked Mercer.

"I thought we were heading for the bones," Skye said.

"But I am unequipped to write about them. I lack even a blank page and a pencil for my journal. Those pictographs won't do, you know."

"The bones are not far now."

"Oh, well, I'll have a glance."

"I've seen them only once but I won't ever forget them. You can't imagine how big. Victoria tells me they're the bones of giant birds, three times taller than a man."

Mercer laughed. "Never let the truth get in the way of a good story. I believe that's your motto?"

"We'll see," said Skye. He didn't blame Mercer for doubting.

They were crossing an empty land where a man could

watch cloud shadows scrape across the breeze-bent grasses, cured tan now by a hot summer's heat. The clouds sometimes took the form of animals, bizarre heads, horned creatures floating through the blue. There were shapes to heat the imagination, clouds to trigger campfire stories.

Victoria's people swore that some clouds reflected the world they were passing over, and one could see buffalo or a migration of some other tribe mirrored in the bottoms of the clouds. But Skye had never seen any such thing.

They nooned at a willow grove beside a slow spring that fed water into an algae-topped pool. The horses nuzzled the water but drank little.

Victoria approached Mercer with a request: "You let me shoot that bow a little?"

"You know how to shoot it?"

"Hell yes."

"You're a warrior woman?"

"You want to bet? Make a match?"

"I should warn you. I'm very good with a bow and arrow," Mercer said.

"Whoever wins gets the bow and quiver, eh?"

Skye watched all this with joy. Victoria coveted that bow and quiver that the Gros Ventres had given Mercer. It was a handsome reflex bow of yew wood, strung with buffalo sinew. The quilled quiver contained a dozen arrows wrought from reed and tipped with Hudson's Bay sheet-iron points. That bow and its arrows could down an elk or deer; maybe a buffalo if the shooter was close enough to the heart-lung spot.

"And what'll you give me if you lose?"

"My robe."

"Oh ho, this will be a contest."

Victoria smiled. "You pick a target."

Mercer studied her, noting the thin arms, the wiry frame,

the feminine hand. "I think I will go for some distance," he said. He selected a willow tree perhaps thirty yards distant and gashed an X in its bark. Ninety or a hundred feet, Skye judged. For a plains Indian bow, an ample distance.

"Three arrows apiece? Closest one wins?" Victoria asked.

"Do we practice first?"

She smiled. "Practice one arrow if you want."

Winding finished watering and picketing the horses and watched quietly. Mary was digging into parfleches, extracting some jerky for their meal.

Mercer easily flexed the bow with his knee and slid the bowstring into its slot. He pulled back the string, getting some sense of the bow's power.

"It pulls easily, but I'll wager it'll put an arrow some distance," he said. "Mister Skye, will you join the competition?"

"I couldn't hit an elephant," Skye said. He hoped Victoria would win. She was a fine hunter and many a time made meat, especially when rain had ruined his powder.

Mercer slid an arrow from the quiver, eyed it, and frowned. "This shaft isn't exactly true," he said.

Victoria smiled.

"I suppose you mastered a bow and arrow as a young woman," Mercer said. "I shall have to redouble my effort. I learned, actually, in the Near East. No one thinks of that as a place of bowmen, but it is."

He nocked his arrow, took a long time aiming, and let it fly. It buried itself in the old willow trunk only a foot above the center of the cross scraped in the bark. He smiled and handed her the bow.

"I will shoot four," she said. "The first for practice. The rest will count."

She took no time at all. Some ingrained instinct made her draw the string and loose the arrow all in one swift movement. The practice arrow was about as far from center as his; the next three grouped closer, within seven or eight inches. She had hardly squandered thirty seconds at it.

"Oh, my," said Graves Mercer. "The lady can aim."

"Let's mark her arrows," Skye said. "Pull the practice arrow and tie a bit of something to these."

They did that. Victoria tied a little doeskin thong cut from her skirt to each of her arrows.

"Ah, here goes your robe, madam," Mercer said. "It'll keep me warm."

He drew and aimed slowly, taking his time, settling his body into steadiness. He loosed the first arrow, and Skye saw at once that it was true. It plunked home only an inch farther out than the best of Victoria's.

"Two more," he said. There he was, those even white teeth bared in a cheerful smile.

He aimed the next one carefully, taking all the time in the world, only to see it miss the target willow altogether.

"That means it all rides on this one," he said. "I'll keep that in mind."

He nocked that arrow after studying it, and took his time once again, lifting and lowering the bow, flexing it, studying that distant crude X clawed out of the gray bark of the tree. Then, when the wind had died and the sun was burning down on them all, he loosed the arrow. It slapped squarely into the center of the X, easily the best shot.

"Oh, ho! You owe me a robe!" he said, unstringing the bow. They all walked to the willow tree where his final arrow had sunk true into the very place where the bars of the X joined. They patiently retrieved the valuable arrows, working the metal points loose, and restored them to the quilled quiver. Then Victoria headed for the packhorses, found her robe, folded it, and carried it to Mercer, who accepted it.

"Time for a little potlatch of my own," he said. "These both belong to you." He handed her robe back, and then added the quiver and the yew-wood bow.

"Sonofabitch!" she said, accepting the gifts.

"Well put, madam. You get right to the heart of it with your pithy remarks. The truth of it is that I'm no hunter. By the time I line up a shot the deer would be over the hill."

That was true, Skye thought. It felt just fine to have Victoria armed and able to help defend them if need be.

They rested through some midday heat and then headed north once again, toiling through an empty, lonely land that seemed never to change. Some landscapes were boring. But Skye knew that the best hunting was often in the dullest country. The coulees ran north now, the dry washes steering their occasional charge of water toward the mighty river that had cut its way deep below the level of the tumbling plains to either side of it.

They camped that night at a seep that supported a few cottonwoods. Winding cleared out some debris from a hollow and let the water form a tiny pool scarcely two feet in diameter. It would do. With a little patience, they could water all the stock and themselves. The savvy teamster set to work, deepening the pool even as he brought the horses one by one to the cool water.

Skye could have used some real meat that night, but they made do with pemmican and some prairie turnips they roasted beside a fire. Not much of a meal, but a thousand times over the years Skye had fared worse. And it only made the promise of some buffalo boss rib all the more delicious.

Jawbone drank heartily in the twilight and began gnawing the short grass, making a meal of almost anything that grew. Then suddenly his head bobbed upward and he snorted softly. That was all Skye needed to grab his rifle and begin a slow, steady search of distant hills, soft in the twilight. He saw nothing. Victoria and Mary saw nothing either. Winding noticed that all the horses were pointed in one direction, their ears forward, and finally it was he who spotted whatever there was to see.

It was a mustang, plainly a wild stallion, standing erect, silhouetted by the fading blue of the day far to the northwest. And flowing below him as grazing dictated was a band of mares and foals and yearlings. The stallion lifted his head and sniffed the wind, a noble animal with an arched neck, a long broom tail, a proud demeanor. Now the mustang mares were alerted. The old lead mare stared squarely at the camp, her ears pricked forward, ready to run. That was how the mustangs lived. The king stallion would fight; the mares, under the old boss lady, would retreat.

Nothing happened for what seemed an eternity. No animal moved. The stallion stood there, the setting sun dropping below the horizon behind him. The mares and young stuff stood stock-still, assessing trouble.

Then everything happened at once. Jawbone squealed and broke straight toward the mustang stallion. The mares saw him coming, and bolted to the south, driving their young with them. But the stallion didn't move.

"No!" yelled Skye, but it was like bawling at the wind.

Jawbone loped straight at the old mustang, and Skye knew that blood would flow.

Chapter 30

Winding raced for the horses, which were tugging on the picket pins. Skye followed the teamster, grabbing a lead line just as a young stallion yanked free. Victoria and Mary each caught a mare before it bolted, and Mercer, last to act because he scarcely grasped what was happening, caught two yearlings. All the horses tugged and fought their lines in wild-eyed excitement.

"Hang on," Winding yelled. The livestock man had taken charge. That mighty mustang stallion out there was fixing to pirate the whole herd and had sent shocks of terror through the horses in camp. There was something eerie about it; his screech on that distant ridge had galvanized the horses, as if lightning had struck nearby.

The mustang stallion danced on the ridge, its neck arched, its nostrils flared, looking to make all the trouble it could. With each of its bellows, the domestic horses reared and danced and snorted. It was all Victoria and Mary could do to hold on, and Skye feared that those braided lead lines would snap.

The world of wild horses was a cruel one. Stallions fought for mares; a powerful stallion acquired a harem. He killed rivals, kicking and biting them to death. He drove away yearlings and old horses. The lead mare, and every such mustang band had one, was his partner, leading the mares and younger animals to safety, disciplining the other horses with kicks and bites. But it was also nature's way of preserving the bands. Horses relied on flight, and everything in the behavior of the band was geared to flight.

Now Jawbone danced outward, his very soul reverted to the primitive instincts of a young stallion about to square off with an older one. This was not the Jawbone Skye knew, but some brute of a horse, murder in his eye, ready for deadly combat with the intruder. Skye could no more stop him than he could stop the sun in its tracks.

Skye's and Mercer's horses quieted suddenly. The boss mare of the wild band stopped, and nipped the rumps of the mares that didn't stop. They knew somehow to await the outcome. This was going to be war, horse against horse, to the death. The stallion, lit red by the setting sun, stood stock-still, a statue on a ridge, while Jawbone slowed to a mincing walk like a boxer circling around his opponent. The old stallion bore the scars of battle. Half an ear was missing. Its flesh was puckered. Its broom tail reached the grass. Its burr-choked mane rested in lumps on its neck. There was nothing beautiful about this wild animal, but rather something sinister and proud. Its tail switched back and forth as it waited patiently to slaughter yet another rival.

Jawbone slowed, and then walked up the ridge until the setting sun limned his gray body. The wild stallion watched almost quietly, except for the arch of its neck and an occasional shuffle of its feet. He was magnificent, far more handsome in his raw fashion than Jawbone. The low sun glinted off the dun coat of the wild one, setting it afire or so it seemed to Skye's eye.

The two horses stood a few feet apart on the ridge, just out of kicking range, studying each other. Time stopped. Jawbone lifted his neck, bared his teeth, and sawed the air, his head bobbing up and down in some act of challenge known only to horses. The wild stallion did much the same, its lips forming a rictus, its head sawing the air, issuing his own challenge. And then things quieted. The two stallions stared at each other. Skye wondered if there would be a fight at all; whether Jawbone might turn tail and walk back to camp.

The wild mares and young ones stood two hundred yards distant, ready to bolt. High in the evening sky a large hawk of some sort rode the breeze. Skye found it easy now to hold on to the lead lines of the three horses under his control. They stood as quietly as the two rivals on the ridge.

Then the wild stallion slowly turned around until its rump was to Jawbone, and seemed to gaze into the deepening twilight, ignoring his rival. But Skye knew better.

Jawbone sawed the air again and stepped closer. The wild dun whirled, squealed, and planted rear hooves squarely into Jawbone's chest, with such shock that Jawbone staggered, seemed paralyzed a moment, and then righted himself just as the wild one's lethal teeth bit into Jawbone's neck. Now the mares stirred.

But Jawbone did not flee. That was the thing about Jawbone. He ran straight toward trouble. Instead of stumbling away, chastened and defeated, he sprang straight for the wild one, slamming the wild one with his chest, staggering the wild one. Now it was Jawbone's turn, in close, too tight to receive a lethal kick, slowly crowding the stallion off the ridge, pushing forward steadily, impervious to the wild one's bites. Once the wild one reared upward, intending to crush Jawbone under falling forehooves, but instead, Jawbone plowed into the belly of the rearing wild horse and unbalanced him so he tumbled to earth, rolled, sprang to his feet even as Jawbone's own hooves crashed down on the wild one's rump.

The wild stallion staggered up and retreated. Jawbone followed relentlessly, crowding inside those brutal hooves, always chest to rump, chest to belly, chest to neck. And then the stallion fled. Jawbone followed, crowding the wild one with every bound, not letting him escape. The wild one would not walk away from this fight. Jawbone ran him hard, over the ridge and out of sight, and suddenly Skye and his party hadn't the faintest idea what was occurring out there in the twilight.

They stared at each other, still mesmerized by the drama they had witnessed. The sun vanished, leaving rosy light in its wake, and a cloud the color of blood. Silence crept over the land. Jawbone had disappeared. Minutes passed and they seemed longer to Skye; as if each were an hour. The mystery deepened. Wherever the stallions were, far to the south, their combat was veiled to Skye's party.

Then, as the day turned dusky, Jawbone reappeared alone, nipping at the wild mares, disciplining the boss mare with teeth planted in her neck, driving the wild one's entire harem straight toward Skye's party. They clearly didn't want to approach the human beings there but Jawbone was making them, doing it brutally, knowing he was king of the herd and intending to let every animal know it. The lead mare veered away from Skye's party, but Jawbone cut her off, his teeth snapping, until her fear of him was larger than her fear of the people watching this amazing spectacle.

Then, as swiftly as it had started, the run ceased. The wild ones milled before the group, terrified of both the human beings and of Jawbone. The domesticated horses jerked on their tethers, excited by all of this.

Jawbone quietly circled them, a living corral that prevented escape. Proudly, calmly, he proclaimed his lordship over them, even while his sides still heaved from a long run.

"Mister Skye, I do believe that you are suddenly a rich man, if wealth is measured in horses," Mercer said.

"It appears that way, if Mister Winding can gentle them."

"I think I can," said Winding. "Most, anyway."

"You will be rewarded for it," Skye said.

"Wasn't that something! Damn, Mister Skye, you should have ten wives, like Jawbone," Victoria said.

"It appears that Jawbone is going to leave his progeny all over the northern plains, Mister Skye," said Mercer.

Jawbone knew they were talking about him. He abandoned his guardianship of the harem for a moment, walked straight toward Skye, and gently butted Skye in the chest. It was his way of giving Skye the gift of mares and foals and yearlings.

"Avast!"

"Ah, Mister Skye, he has more ladies than you do," Mary said.

Mary was teasing him! He was used to it from Victoria, but now Mary was doing it too.

"I prefer quality to quantity," he retorted.

"What do them damn words mean?" Victoria asked.

"They were compliments." Skye was feeling testy.

All that evening the mares looked ready to bolt but Jawbone disciplined them. The slightest infraction won a nip or a kick. By deep dark, the wild bunch was grazing quietly. Everything depended on Jawbone. It would be a long time before any human could touch that bunch or turn them into saddle horses. Skye's and Mercer's own horses were allowed to drift among the wild ones. The sooner they became acquainted, the better. As long as Jawbone remained the king of this herd, there would be little trouble.

They built an evening fire and roasted some antelope. The meat tasted just fine.

Every now and then the wild horses stirred in the darkness, and sometimes Jawbone's policing squeal drifted through the darkness.

"Jawbone has his work cut out for him," Mercer said. "But I think he's equal to it."

"He's a lucky stallion," Winding said.

"Luckier than you, Mister Skye." That was Mary, of all people, but Skye ignored the insult. The women were giggling. He lifted his top hat and settled it, contemplating whether to rebuke them. But their laughter dissolved his displeasure.

They put up the lodge by firelight and moved the robes and parfleches inside.

"I say, old boy, it's a fine night for sleeping out. I think Winding and I'll just catch our robes and hightail away for the evening," Mercer said.

There it was, right out in public, but Skye didn't mind. "Get yourselves a good rest, mates," he said.

The Briton and his teamster drifted into the night, laden with warm robes.

From out of the darkness, Jawbone squealed. Skye knew that squeal. So did his women.

Mary and Victoria were grinning at him and he thought that was just fine.

Chapter 31

No one slept well that night, least of all Skye. The quiet was punctuated with squeals, the clatter of hooves, snorts, nickering, and the sounds of passage.

Jawbone spent the whole night patrolling his new harem, disciplining rebel mares, sinking teeth into rumps and necks, kicking the unruly, and above all circling the whole herd to keep it from bolting. The wild mares and yearlings and foals weren't used to the presence of human beings. Neither were they used to the domestic horses in their midst and spent the night taxing Jawbone's energies.

Skye and his two wives spent the night side by side in their buffalo robes, Victoria on his left, Mary on his right, his own arms catching them both. But the night did not turn out in the way of Mercer's imaginings. Skye and his women rested peacefully, protected from weather and cold by the Gros Ventre lodge, happy to share a quiet moment. It was, in that respect, a sweet night, except for the hubbub outside of the lodge as Jawbone established his command over his new family.

As always, Skye awakened at dawn when the first light shone in the smoke vent at the top of the lodge, silhouetting the poles where they collected together. His women breathed quietly. Skye slipped out of his robe and into the chill predawn, sucked cold air into his lungs, and studied the country. Off a few dozen yards, Mercer and Winding lay in their robes beside the ashes of a small fire they had built. Dew lay on the grass. Patches of fog blanketed the hollows. The air was cold indeed to have condensed moisture out of the air.

Jawbone stood guard over his herd but he was plainly exhausted. His head hung low. His alert and fierce gaze had vanished under the obligations he now faced. The wild mares shifted nervously as Skye drifted toward them, and Jawbone's head popped up. The mares didn't run but edged away from this alien thing in their lives, and Jawbone minced along beside them, each step taken as if on springs, his way of telling the mares that he would catch and punish any runaways.

All but one. A yearling stood awkwardly, and staggered when it tried to follow the drifting mares. Even in that soft gray light, Skye knew at once that its foreleg was broken. As he edged closer he could see that the shinbone had splintered and pierced flesh.

Skye knew what he had to do. It was never easy, but he never asked anyone else to do these things for him. It was a part of being a citizen of the wilds. He feared the day might come when he would have to do this very thing to Jawbone. It was why he tried not to love an animal, but he did anyway. He remembered horses he treasured, a dog he once owned, and his deep respect for Jawbone, whose mysterious medicine made him an animal he would honor all of his days.

The yearling tried to limp away as Skye approached, but finally stopped, quivering and in obvious pain. The night's uproars had destroyed him. A night spent racing around on treacherous ground, a night bumping into fleeing mares, tumbling under Jawbone's onslaught, had finally snapped this fellow's leg. And there was nothing anyone could do except end its suffering.

Skye slipped his Green River knife from its sheath at his waist.

"Whoa, boy," he said.

The yearling was too far gone to resist, but it trembled as Skye approached.

The wounded leg was terrible to look at. Splintered bone stabbed through flesh. Black blood soaked the pastern and hoof.

That didn't make it any easier.

Skye lifted a hand to the colt's mane. It trembled. Then swiftly, hoping to give swift peace and not lingering agony, he jammed his knife under the ear, sliced downward under the cheek and across the throat, feeling his keen blade sever life from death. The horse shook a moment, and then tumbled down.

"Well done, Mister Skye," said Winding, who was standing ten yards away.

Death is never well done, Skye thought. But he nodded, acknowledging the teamster's expert opinion. The swift sharp knife had lessened the torment of the wounded animal, offering a merciful death, and that was what the teamster meant.

Skye wiped his blade on grass and restored it to its sheath. It was a rotten way to start a new day.

He would not ride Jawbone. The young stallion would be busy this day and many more herding his harem, and the task would draw on the horse's last reserves of strength. It would be good to put one of those fine Gros Ventre ponies under saddle and see what sort of gift those people had given Mercer for the magical night he gave them.

Jawbone was young. He had whipped a proud old mustang and driven him away. Skye wondered how that old horse must feel this dawn. Yesterday, he was king of his little herd. Yesterday he was a lord of all horses, breeding mares, stamping foals with his own nature, disdainfully chasing away all the young stallions who meant to steal his band from him. Today he was a broken old stallion, an out-cast who had surrendered to the law of life: the young re-place the old; the young conquer from the old.

Was he quietly grazing somewhere, nursing the wounds Jawbone had inflicted on him? Did horses have feelings? Was he bereft? Or was he merely a bundle of instincts, with-out understanding of his new and humbler condition? Skye didn't know, but he wished he might find the old stallion and wish peace and comfortable old age upon him. Maybe now, free of responsibility, the old fellow would graze peace-fully, enjoy the warm sun, look upon his world as a good place, and think upon his own glory. It was a fanciful thought, so Skye set it aside. There was much to do this morning.

The light was quickening now. Mercer swung out of his robe and stretched. Skye's women emerged from the lodge and headed toward the seep. Skye remembered there was little water here; not enough for a herd of horses. They would need to move on.

"Didn't sleep. Not a bloody wink all night," Mercer said. "Jawbone was breeding, I take it."

"No, it was more than that," Skye said. "He was making himself king."

"A monarch! Well, whatever. It spoiled my night," Mer-cer said. "The horse world is no democracy. God save the king."

With that, he smiled, those even white teeth flashing again.

He caught up his robe and brought it to Skye, turning it over so the hair side was down. "Now, what'll I record for yesterday, eh? The day Jawbone captured a harem? And how do I paint that, eh?"

Mercer had indeed kept a pictograph journal of sorts on the fleshed side of his buffalo robe, very like the winter count of many a tribal elder. Mary had shown him how to make paints of grease and colored clay, usually ochre, and how to turn various fibrous reeds or twigs into brushes. She had even sewn a tiny bag for Mercer, so tightly done that he could store his greasepaint within it and tie it shut.

"Not much to record, Mister Skye. Nothing that would cause a sensation in London. Just horse doings. Anyone in England is entirely familiar with horses."

"Wild horses, sir? You could make something of it. I'd be interested in reading it."

"Well, it's not the stuff of a good story. I should have headed for Salt Lake. A piece or two on the Saints would've rocked London on its heels. This North America, sir, it's a bust. There's not a story in the whole continent."

Skye had heard it all too many times.

Nonetheless, Mercer opened his little paint bag, softened the fibers of his stick brush, and began to draw some stick-figure mares and foals, and two stick-figure stallions rearing. It was not bad art. Mercer could be expressive with a few strokes of brown paint. There was, actually, an impressive collection of symbols and figures known only to the adventurer himself. But the saw-toothed fire symbols were plain enough.

"There now. I'll take this moth-eaten thing to London. But I'll write most of the stories on board ship across the Atlantic and pop them onto desks when I get back. Not that my scribbling will ever pay for this trip."

Mercer rolled up his robe and put away his little paint bag.

"I say, Mister Skye, what do the bones look like?"

"They're poking out of rock. There's a skull several feet long, teeth six or eight inches high."

"What do the Indians think of them?"

"Hard to say, sir. Each tribe has its own stories. But Victoria's people think they are the bones of a huge bird, maybe the big black bird of their people, their namesake."

"How big did you say?"

"Bigger than any animal known to modern man, sir. Maybe three times the height of a tall man."

"These birds, did they fly?"

"I can't say. Ask her."

"Well, bones are bones. I hardly think there's a sensation in them."

"The tribes all have legends about them, Mister Mercer. The Crows do. I'll wager you'd get a different story from the Sioux or Blackfeet or Assiniboine. It's also a sacred place, sir. We won't touch those bones. The spirits of those animals are there, ready to destroy anyone who tampers with them. That's the story one gets from the people who live here. It's taboo. It's forbidden."

"Forbidden! I have been to a hundred forbidden places in Asia and Africa. At last I might have a story, Mister Skye."

Chapter 32

Skye's party continued to cross broken prairie in autumnal weather, as if it were all a picnic. Maybe Graves Mercer was simply a lucky man, Skye thought. Everything seemed to go right, just because he wanted it to go right.

The man lost an outfit in the fire and won another one. The gods were smiling. It was as if Mercer, the great explorer, could conjure up whatever he needed. And now he needed a sensation. A bigger sensation than anything that other explorers might uncover. The man had rivals. Who could find the most exotic thing lurking in the unexplored world?

Skye thought about that as they pushed northward toward the great ditch of the Missouri River. What the man really meant by a sensation was something that would shock his English countrymen. Shock was in the air. In modern times the queen's men had radiated outward to the farthest reaches of the unknown world, penetrating into the Amazon jungles, pausing at South Sea islands, probing toward the poles, trekking up the Nile, climbing higher and higher toward the peaks of the Himalayas. But it was the customs of foreign peoples that shocked the English. Wicked things. Erotic things. Cruel things. Sacrifice a virgin to the morning star and the civilized world would be duly horrified.

Mercer was really engaged in shock. Whatever he could unearth that would rattle his countrymen, that's what would ensure his own fame. How different this was from other times, when people sought the comforts of orthodoxy, or the healing of faith, or the blessings of a strong crown.

Even as Skye mused, a good buffalo runner gotten from the Atsina chief was carrying him northward ahead of the rest of the party, the horse lithe and young under him. Skye never stopped scanning the open country, for it was his duty to keep his people safe, to spot trouble, to give those behind him time to regroup or defend. His women were riding now, thanks to the plenitude of horses. They kept the travois ponies and packhorses moving steadily along. Winding and Jawbone brought up the rear, keeping an eye on the wild bunch.

Mercer, also riding now, never seemed content and was forever spurring forward, or pulling off to one side or the other, or dashing somewhere to examine something. But now he urged his pony forward and joined Skye as they crossed an empty land.

"When you say forbidden, Mister Skye, what do you mean?"

"I meant that the Indians revere these bones, respect them, and would not want anything to damage them. In the case of the Absarokas, these are the bones of creation, the bones from which they derive their visions of where they came from, and who they are."

"Ah, mythology! I suppose most people have some of that to explain themselves. The Greeks and Romans did. All those stories were displaced by Christian religion but they linger on, half submerged, and one still sees villagers at the old pagan shrines. I've seen them myself. I suppose when Europeans settle this country, these old stories will linger in the hollows and hills."

"They are more than stories, Mister Mercer. The tribes feel a kinship to these bones. The bones are their ancestors. And I should tell you, there's never been warfare at the place of the bones. Blackfeet, Crows, Sioux, other tribes that fight each other, they gather here, enemies at all other times, but quiet and respectful and at peace. Parties come and go, camp there, sit for hours before these giants, and are perfectly safe. The next day, a mile away, they might kill each other but not there where the bones poke up from rock. That's how powerful this place is."

"Well, I'm ready for it. There's nothing else around here. Of course I discount all the stories about the size of the bones. Those things get exaggerated, you know. The more sacred they are, the bigger they get. It'll be a guffaw or two when I start some measuring and find they're maybe as big as an ostrich. Now that's a big bird, an ostrich. And I'll probably end up writing about this very thing: the natives worship at a pile of fossilized ostrich bones and have turned them into the bones of giants."

The man was saying he didn't believe Victoria or Skye, but there was no point in protesting it. He would see for himself. But Skye supposed that was all part of being a sensationalist writer. If you debunk a local legend that's quite as good as confirming it.

"I say, Skye, these bones. They're caught in sandstone?"

"Fossils, yes."

"How do you suppose that happened?"

"They are very old, Mister Mercer."

"How old?"

Skye had no answer. "Older than anyone imagines; what else can one say?"

"Maybe a trick of God to fool the unfaithful? Wasn't the world created in six days, about six thousand years ago?"

There were things Skye did not feel he could respond to, and that was one. He scarcely grasped theology. But he had a few notions.

"Some things are written as poetry, Mister Mercer,

because they were too much for the prophets to explain. Genesis is poetry, I imagine. I read Genesis once, and saw that it was fanciful."

"Ah, you're a heretic, like me!"

"No, sir, not that. I am a faithful man in my own way. Let me put it this way. Most of the natural world has yet to be revealed to us. Someday maybe God will open our eyes."

"That's a gracious response, Mister Skye. How did you get here, in this corner of the unknown world?"

"I was a pressed seaman, ended up in the Royal Navy, snatched as a boy right off the streets of London. I made my escape when I could."

"Ah, a deserter."

"Think what you will. I consider myself a freedman. My liberty was taken away; I took it back."

"But you cannot return to England."

"Never."

"I've met wanderers like you from one end of the world to the other, Mister Skye. England has its exiles. Convicts sent to Van Diemen's Land, the refuse of the Napoleonic wars, criminals who fled the island, and republicans at war with monarchy, or Irish opposed to English rule. But mostly, Mister Skye, outcasts. Social transgressors. Women who became enamored of another man and paid for it by fleeing from disgrace. Men who professed atheism and found themselves ostracized. Bigamous men. Banished men. Odd quacks who declare themselves nobility. I met a chap in Spain who said he was pretender to the throne and he was collecting a fleet to topple the queen. Of course most Englishmen flee to France, but there are exiled Englishmen in every corner of the world. And you're one."

"By accident, sir. I would probably be an import-export merchant like my father if a press gang of laughing sailors had not pinned my arms behind my back and dragged me

over the cobbles to the wharf. I have no very great quarrel
with England. It's still my land, my people. In fact, after
meeting a few Yanks, I prefer Englishmen. I won't make
myself a Yank. I'm a man without a country."

"That answers my next question, Mister Skye. What a
good day this is. We've been weeks on the trail, and only
now do I sense that I know you."

"I guard my privacy, Mister Mercer."

"Out here, beyond society, beyond law? But why?"

"I'll respond with a question: Are you planning to write
about your guide Skye in the North American wilds, the one
with two Indian wives, one young and very beautiful?"

Mercer grinned. "You have me, Mister Skye."

"And shock London with it?"

"Yes, but what difference does it make?"

"I have not seen my family for decades. I don't know
whether my parents or my sister live. I don't know whether
she married or has children. I haven't heard about my cousins, either. Would you make sport of me?"

"Probably. If it's true, and if it catches the eye, I would
publish it."

"Then say that I love my wives. Both of them. Say that it
is the Indian custom. Say that when native women's burden
is shared they are happier. Tell them that I was and am an
Anglican. And tell them that a man yanked off the streets
and stuffed into a royal sloop deserves his liberty."

"As you wish, Mister Skye." Mercer's tone was earnest.
Somehow, he always managed to redeem himself.

They rode on in silence, though no antagonism remained
between them. The land forms changed. Now great grassy
gulches tumbled northward. Skye consulted with Victoria,
who pointed westerly. Skye turned their caravan down a
long trough where the grass was thicker in the bottom than
on its sides.

The horses seemed eager, and pushed ahead almost without urging, so that sometimes the travois bounced. The walls of the great trench of the Missouri River rose higher and higher as they plunged into a giant ditch that seemed devoid of all life.

They came at last to narrow bottoms and beyond a slender flat the great cold river purled its way to its union with the Mississippi. Skye dismounted and let the buffalo runner poke his ugly nose in the icy, clear water. Skye studied the bluffs, looking for trouble, and found none.

The women dismounted and let their horses drink. And then, one by one, watered the packhorses and the draft horse and the spare mounts, while Winding ran a well-versed teamster's hand over pasterns and fetlocks and shins.

A narrow trail ran west here.

Victoria spotted the broken arrow and summoned Skye.

Directly ahead, on the trail they soon would take, was an arrow plunged point-down in the ground, with its back broken and the feathered part lying beside it.

Mercer hastened to the spot.

"What's that about, Mister Skye?"

"It's a warning. It says, do not go farther."

"For us?"

"Yes."

"But we will, of course. I haven't come across an ocean and a continent just to be put off by this."

"You would be risking your life, Mister Mercer," Victoria said.

"Well, I'll just risk it. Missus Skye," he said. "What tribe's arrow is this?"

She picked up the feathered end, and pulled the shaft out of the moist earth.

"I don't know," she said. "I have never seen an arrow marked like this."

Chapter 33

The arrow was unlike any Skye had ever seen. The entire shaft was enameled bloodred. Large feathers, maybe hawk or falcon, adorned it. It lacked an arrowhead or iron point. A ceremonial arrow, then, and all the more ominous for it.

"This is big medicine, Mister Mercer," he said. "See how it's made. No point. All red. This is a medicine arrow, a message arrow."

"Who made it?"

"Damned if I know," said Victoria. "Makes me unhappy, I don't know. Maybe the spirits made it."

"Spirits?"

"Stuff you and me don't know about."

"Surely you don't . . ." Mercer stopped himself.

Skye smiled. Mercer was dismissing Indian legend but was being polite about it.

Victoria studied the arrow, cussing softly. "Owl feathers. Owl feathers! That's what these are. This is very bad, owl feathers."

"And what does it tell you, eh?"

Victoria squinted at him. "We better damn well stay away. That's what."

Mercer studied the red arrow, turned it over and over. "A taboo. A message. Oh, this is delightful. I love a taboo! I shall record it on the backside of my robe tonight. This makes the whole trip over here much more promising.

Something to scribble about. There's nothing like a good taboo to titillate a Londoner over his morning tea."

Skye was growing restless. "I think maybe we should consider it a threat, Mister Mercer. Someone might have some rather lethal plans for you."

"Oh, pshaw! This is legend, and legend is my meat! We shall carry on."

"I think not. You should not take this lightly, sir."

"Don't be a tiddlywink, Mister Skye. This is grand. I haven't seen the like since a human head the size of my fist was set in my path in the Mato Grosso of Brazil." He turned to Winding. "Have you an opinion on it?"

"It would be more comfortable if we were armed, sir."

"But I am armed in ways unknown to you. I know how to deal with all of this. Why, I've dealt with bushmen, cannibals, Zulus, and Lord Admirals of the Fleet. And never had to draw so much as a pocketknife. Here's the secret. We're big medicine ourselves. I make magic. My magic is bigger than their magic, eh?"

He thumped his head and then his skull as a sort of exclamation point or two. "I am the great Wazoo, Moomumba, Atlatl, Kitchikitchi Bugaboo, Lord of the Universe."

"Wazoo, I ain't going," said Victoria.

Mercer's smile was all teeth again. "Very well, then. The men will carry on."

She glared at Mercer.

The explorer mounted his nag, nodded to Winding, and the pair of them proceeded upriver, past the threshold of warning. Skye knew he could either try to protect his client or turn back. There was no stopping Mercer. Uneasily, he climbed aboard the buffalo runner and followed. The women resolutely started their pack animals upriver too.

The going was peaceful enough. Here there was enough bottomland for a river road. Here and there the Missouri was hemmed by great cliffs, often weathered to odd formations, and at these points the trail climbed to the high plain and then down again to the bottoms.

Skye kept a sharp look for ambush, for a glint of metal along the bluffs, or movement around the crenellated rock, or the startled flight of a bird, or a sudden shadow. But he saw naught but silent bluffs and he was tempted to think the warning wasn't for his party. He knew better. He kept his old Hawken across his lap ready for use. But whatever befell them would be larger than a lone man with a lone rifle could cope with.

The river flowed quietly here, the icy water hurrying on its way to the Gulf of Mexico an impossible distance away. He saw an eagle floating above, an osprey, an otter, and something he couldn't identify. The canyon narrowed but a trail carried them to the plains above. The day was utterly peaceful. Mercer was enjoying himself; the thought of doing something forbidden had transformed the man into a daredevil, but also into a sort of invincible, invulnerable purveyor of magic.

They paused at a place where the trail dived downward into the gloomy valley, where the rock changed from chalky to tan, and then oddly blue. The bones were not far ahead. Victoria squinted at Skye.

"Maybe we will walk the star-path together," she said.

She was saying she loved him and also saying good-bye. This plunge into the forbidden was tormenting her far more than she let on to Mercer or anyone else. Skye saw Mary sitting resolutely on her pony. She had kept her feelings to herself and would go wherever he went, be with him wherever and whenever she could be with him. Hers was utter faith.

He turned to Mercer. "The bones are close now. Maybe a mile ahead."

"Good. And no lightning bolts have struck us yet, Mister Skye."

But square on the trail before them was a blue arrow, this one unbroken, erect in the ground, made by the same arrow-maker as the red one. Skye dismounted and pulled it up. Its shaft was a deep blue, a dye not easily found in nature; maybe trading-post dye. It, too, had been fletched with owl feathers.

Victoria studied the arrow and sagged. "I don't know what the hell it means. It means something bad, but I don't know it."

"Ah! More taboos! More mystery! Skye, old boy, this is getting better and better," Mercer said.

"It's *Mister* Skye."

Mary studied the arrow. "This is an arrow of respect," she said. "We must honor what we see and maybe the spirits will not torment us."

"How do you know that?" Mercer asked.

Mary shrugged and turned silent.

Skye didn't know. He thought he would need to know what blue meant to whoever fashioned the arrow. He liked the color. The Blackfeet used it a great deal on their lodges, in their clothing, beadwork, and quilling. For him, blue was the color of liberty. When he thought of himself as a free-man, it was always somehow associated with blue.

"There you have it," Mercer said. "What does blue mean? Anything. We will be respectful." He nudged his horse forward, and suddenly they were all descending a rough path down into the shadowed bottoms of the Missouri past layers of blue-tinted sandstone, dropping precipitously, so much so that Skye worried that the travois might topple or twist the ponies off the trail. But soon they were at the river and entering a broad flat south of the water, a delta that had been carved from a tributary canyon and deposited there.

This was the place. Skye recollected it now from his sole trip there years earlier. And he had the same eerie feeling now that he had then, a sense that indeed he was trespassing. It was quiet here, perhaps because no wind found its way into this sunken vault far below the high plains. There was blue sandstone layered up the south slopes, topped with tan sandstone streaked with red. He had the sense that this was an ancient place, one where the river itself was a newcomer, slowly sawing its way downward.

They paused. Victoria pulled up her pony, and Mary did too. They were alert for trouble even without having any real reason to be alert. A great and old serenity lay upon the land. Skye felt a sort of sadness in him, and couldn't say why. Maybe it was because he was about to experience the world's darkness, something in these primeval bones that spoke of blood and ferocity and struggle.

Mercer pulled up too, and Winding.

"This is it?" the explorer asked.

Skye nodded. He pointed toward a far blue escarpment.

They rode quietly across the flat, which was sparsely vegetated with a coarse grass, and came at last to the blue sandstone wall.

"I don't see a thing," Mercer said.

"You will."

Skye noted evidence of other visitors. There was a medicine bundle hanging from a stunted cottonwood. On closer examination he found several amulets and totems, each suspended from a limb.

He pointed these out to Mercer. "This is a holy place. This is a place the Indians come to when they are looking for guidance or needing the story of their people."

"Medicine bundles. Why are they here?"

"They are put there in reverence," Skye said. "They are offerings to the spirits that live here."

They dismounted. The horses stood quietly, content to be in this sheltered flat. Skye led them slowly across the flat to the tumble of detritus that had fallen from the blue stone above. The strata were actually layered in stair steps, with the higher strata farther back from the river, and the lower strata closer.

Victoria knew the way better than Skye, and veered left toward a sector where the ancient tributary had cut its own passage through the sandstone.

She began climbing slowly, working past talus that erosion had tumbled from above. She reached a bench that lay at the foot of an overhang that sheltered everything that lay below it, paused, and decided to head right. The rest followed, somehow silent as they approached what amounted to a shrine carved out of a cliff.

Then she stopped, and stretched to the balls of her feet, proudly. The rest caught up and stared at what lay before them. Protruding from the rock was a long skull of unimaginable size, the head of a monster.

Chapter 34

It was oddly quiet. No breeze penetrated here. There was nothing to say. They stood side by side, studying an elongated skull that rose only a little out of the sandstone in which it was embedded, revealing perhaps ten percent of its mass. But it was enough. The ancient jaws held monstrous teeth, each larger than a man's hand, and shaped to pierce. The powerful jaw could catch large prey if indeed the beast was a meat-eater.

A huge eye socket, the hole larger than a human head, peered up at them. Slabs of humped skull bone formed a lengthy nose. The back of the skull stopped abruptly, almost as if broken off. Behind the skull, the spinal bones lay disordered, half buried in the stone. From the vertebrae rose flat-topped dorsal ribs, with smaller curved ribs below. From there, the fossil vanished into the stone, only to reemerge ten feet farther along. There were more vertebrae all in disarray, beyond the imaginings of the most learned doctors of nature. But here were giant ribs, familiar bones now that spoke of the chest cavity. And an array of tiny bones that formed forepaws. These were so small that Skye could not believe they belonged to the same animal. Maybe this was all an ancient boneyard, the grave of all sorts of strange beasts.

There was a pathway that took them farther along, a path worn by countless visitors. A pathway recently used, with faint imprints in the dust. Next was a few square yards of disorder, a great jumble of ribs and vertebrae, and then odd-shaped pelvic bones, broken into several pieces, mostly buried in rock. And then the shocking thing: monstrous leg bones, each taller than a tall man, mostly buried in rock, but the outlines visible. These were impossible bones, larger than wild imagination could fathom. Bones of an animal as tall as a house. And a few yards away, a well-preserved three-toed foot, a bird's foot, delicately formed but still a pedestal that could support this monster. Beyond was a scatter of other bones, smaller and smaller, yard after yard, as if this strange beast had a twenty- or thirty-foot tail.

Skye had been here before, and now had the same response as before. Did this come from God?

Now he watched Mercer; watched the man visibly abandon the notion that this was a carved shrine, some religious artistry worked by an ancient sculptor. This beast had perished beside a river or on a beach and had been gradually covered with sand, and over aeons had become a fossil caught in sandstone until some giant upthrust had pushed this rock high, and erosion had worn through the sandstone and bared these unimaginable things.

Mercer took off his hat. He was not smiling this time.

"How old, do you think?" he asked.

Skye shook his head.

"There's more," Victoria said. She led them silently along the worn path that skirted the sandstone outcrop, until they came to another ledge jammed with bones, these disordered so much a mortal could hardly put them together to mean anything. But there they were, a carpet of bones, mostly broken into small pieces, and yet parts of a beast as formidable as the more complete skeleton they had just visited. But no, this was not the same beast, for when they came to the skull, or the fragment left of it, they found a peculiar horn rising from its snout, a blade where no blade should be, an illogical blade that would serve no fathomable purpose. So here was another monster of the deep, another nightmare to float through a man's soul when sleep beckoned.

"How would you like to run into one of these on your path?" Winding asked.

"Why are they here?" Mercer asked.

Who could say? The sandstone overhang protected them; that was all Skye could make of it.

Mary was careful to touch every bone she could reach. She ran her small brown hand over the rock, her fingers into creases and over bulges, as if the bones were there to give her strength, and the more she touched them the stronger and wiser she would be. Victoria frowned. For her, the bones were sacred relics of her own origins, for she was one of the people of this bird. But Mary saw these bones her own way. Skye smiled at her and she smiled back. Touching the bones was giving medicine to her and she was harvesting the strange powers that lay within them.

"Many more," Victoria said, pointing. Indeed, the trail ran another fifty yards through the mortuary of giants somehow trapped here and hidden from air and sun and wind until recent times.

Slowly Mercer hiked to the end of the bone yard and retraced his steps back to the monster that lay almost intact, the very first they had seen.

"So you suppose the earth, the whole universe, is very old?" he asked. "I mean, hundreds of thousand of years. Maybe a million years. Do you imagine that God is recent; the universe is older than God?"

Skye smiled. "That sort of thing is beyond me." He would not speculate on things that seemed forever beyond understanding.

"Well, I've seen the bones," Mercer said. "Now let's measure them. As it happens, the length of my belt is exactly a yard, and I've marked off feet on the belt. It's my wilderness measure."

He pulled the belt from its loops. There indeed, on its interior side, were foot markers, and half-foot markers, and a set of six inches marked in some sort of ink or dye.

"How am I going to record all this when I lack so much as paper and pencil?" he asked.

It was a good question.

"I will bring your robe. We will put the marks on the robe," Mary said. The Shoshone was dealing with the bones a lot more easily than Victoria, who turned tight and silent and maybe angry.

Skye watched Mary head back to the travois. But Mercer was already heading for that giant skull.

"I say, Skye, I owe you an apology. I didn't imagine these bones could be real. Just a mystery or some madman's art. Not something that taxes my limited grasp of geology. Not something that turns my world, my theology, my universe, inside out. I'm glad you brought me here."

That was the thing about Mercer. He was always redeeming himself. Skye nodded and smiled.

Mercer crawled up on the shelf and began measuring. Victoria looked ready to explode. He ran his belt over the skull and finally pronounced his verdict: "Six feet four inches from the extremities." Then he measured the eye socket. "Over a foot. No make that fifteen inches." And then he measured the largest of the exposed teeth. "Can you imagine it? Eleven inches or so!"

Mary returned with the robe, some reed paintbrushes, and the small sack of ochre greasepaint. These she handed to Victoria. "I do not know how to make the marks," she said.

"Don't give it to me," Victoria snarled. The explosion was so dark and pained that Skye and the men paused.

"We'll be leaving directly, Victoria," Skye said. "We will be very respectful and do no harm."

Victoria sullenly turned her back on him. Skye had never seen her in such a state, and it worried him.

"Oh, not quite that fast, Mister Skye," Mercer said. "I'll want some sketches. Blast it for not having paper. But I'll do what I can on the back of the robe. What else can a man do?"

Mercer laid the robe, hairy side down, directly on the bones and began the slow process of painting line drawings of what he saw. There was little room left on the robe, which now was filled with stick figures and pictographs. Mary cheerfully helped him but Victoria stormed away.

Skye saw the depth of her anguish and headed her direction, catching her at last well out of earshot of the others.

"He will doom us," she said. "He has no respect."

Skye didn't argue.

"That is the Mother of my people. That is the great bird that came out of the heavens and gave birth to my people. That is the bird the ancient ones, the storytellers, speak of. We are the people of the great black bird. And whoever touches those bones will perish."

Skye didn't believe the legend. It was ingrained deeply in her very soul but he could not share it with her.

"You and I have not touched the bones or shown them disrespect," he said.

"But Mary has! And so have the white men."

"What will happen, Victoria? What does the legend of the Absaroka say?"

"We should not even be here. We should not even approach these bones without a purifying. A sweat and the smoke of sweetgrass and gifts to the spirits. You saw the gifts as we came here, bundles given to this spirit. The spirits of these birds are here. They are offended. Now we will perish, all of us, and I am at fault. I brought you here. I am a daughter of the People, a daughter of these ancient ones. They are my fathers and my grandfathers."

Tears filled her eyes.

"I'll fetch Mercer and the rest. We'll leave the grandfathers alone, Victoria."

"It is too late."

Skye left her and went back to the bones, now resting in deep and cool shade under the sandstone ledge. Mercer was busy painting ribs and vertebrae.

"I don't know what half these bones are," he said. "How am I going to persuade anyone I ever saw them? London is a city of skeptics. The Royal Society is a body of squinting old men."

"Time for us to leave, Mister Mercer. This is a holy place."

"Leave! I just got here. I don't have much to dig with, but I'm going to take a tooth. That'll shake a few timbers."

Chapter 35

Mercer began hunting for a tooth he could pry out with his belt knife but Skye tried to stay him.

"Mister Mercer, don't. This is sacred to Victoria's people. And other people who live here."

"Skye, it's nothing but a boneyard. Bones scattered everywhere. I plan to take a few with me. It'll be my contribution to science."

"Mister Mercer, let's think about this. If you took a tooth back to London they'd say exactly what you said before you got here. It's a fraud. Someone carved it. A few fossil bones won't make believers of them."

Mercer grinned. "Have to try, Skye. This is the biggest find of my life. My Lord, this'll make me a Knight of the Garter. Sir Graves Duplessis Mercer, K.G." He laughed. The idea tickled his fancy. The ancient order was the highest civil honor the crown could bestow and entitled the recipient to be called "Sir," and to add the K.G. after his name.

So Mercer was hell-bent to make himself a knight. Skye chose another tack. "Mister Mercer, this is a holy place. If you pry up bones it would be no different from someone sacking Westminster Cathedral for relics."

"Oh, pshaw, old boy. The cathedral's a work of man. This is just an old boneyard that got covered with sand, and eventually the bones fossilized. Now, that's not a bit like someone walking into a cathedral and digging up a dead king or duke or two to steal a molar."

"I'm afraid it's just like that. For people who find their religion in nature, this is their cathedral. Those prayer bundles hanging from the limbs over there are oblations, sacrifices, gifts to the spirits here."

Mercer listened impatiently. "Well, I'll carve a few bones anyway and no one will know the difference. Why aren't you curious? Why aren't you excited? The biggest bloody bones in the universe. We've found a monster! Why aren't you dancing? Itching to share this treasure with the whole world? I am all of those things. What do you think these bones are? What sort of beast? I'm absolutely at a loss. A bird? Three-toed feet, eh? A lizard? How do you make out the little front paws and giant rear limbs? Is this some sort of giant kangaroo? By gad, Skye, these beasts are something unknown. Unimagined. Maybe the bones of a dragon? Who would have thought that Mercer would find a prehistoric dragon, eh? But the reality is, sir, that this monster from the deeps is nothing known to mortals. Not a bird nor a lizard, not a mammal nor a fish. This monster will shock the world, shock every single member of the Royal Society. What shall I do? Pretend that these are nothing, not worth the attention of science, not worth bringing to the attention of civilized people?"

Skye tried again, quietly: "As a favor to me and a favor to Victoria—"

Mercer shook his head. "We'll not impede science. Nothing will come of it. I've seen superstition on every continent I've visited. I've seen strange rituals, sacrifices that civilized people abominate. I've seen strange peoples worship a stone or a toad or cut open a carp to examine its entrails. I've seen a thousand religions and superstitions and this is just one more in the long parade."

"Then do this: Be an observer. Leave them alone. Don't dig them up. Measure them. Record them. Sketch them.

Gather witnesses. I'll verify what you record. I'm sure Mister Winding will. But leave the bones alone. If you leave the bones unharmed, I believe you will leave here unharmed. If you harm these, I cannot say what will happen or which of us might get hurt. Maybe all of us."

But it was over. Mercer was shaking his head all the while that Skye pleaded with him. The adventurer had already made up his mind and no argument could stop him.

"Lend me your hatchet and your axe, Mister Skye."

"No, you're on your own."

"I'll use our knives if that's all that's available to us. It'll take longer, that's all. Some good hot fires over these bones will crack rock and loosen the bones. That and some careful digging. I'll get some bones, whether or not you're here to help."

Mercer smiled, that bright, relentless smile that announced he was going to have his way no matter what. "I refuse to argue. If you feel so strongly about it, we can part company here, Skye. I can make Fort Benton on my own. It's simply upriver. Winding and I'll go there after we're done. I'll send you a letter of credit for services rendered, care of the factor at Fort Laramie, or whatever you choose. What was it? A hundred pounds? Yes, and well spent. I'll thank you for services rendered. You and your lovely wives. Excellent service, Mister Skye. You've been a fine guide and companion, and here we are. This is the finest of all my discoveries on four continents and nothing will put me off."

Skye saw that this was how it would end. He eyed Mercer and Winding, thinking of all they had been through, the fire, the loss of all equipment, the odd quest for sensation, and now the sacrilege. Of course Mercer didn't see it as sacrilege, and for that matter Skye didn't either, but over his long years in the wilds he had come to understand how his wife's beliefs governed her life, her choices, her tastes and feelings and very character, just as his own faith, however residual it might be, governed his own.

"Very well. I'm sorry to part company with the mission incomplete. I had hoped to deliver you safely to Fort Benton and with ample material for you to write about. There's one thing more, sir. I should like a receipt or financial instrument."

"But there's not a sheet of paper here, Mister Skye."

"You may write it on my robe, sir. And sign it."

"Well, that's fine, I'll do it. I'm a man of my word and you'll have your receipt for services performed, even if we're parting a few dozen miles shy of our destination."

Skye nodded. There was always that redeeming quality about Mercer. Mary, who had followed the conversation, was already heading back to the packs to fetch Skye's robe, and now she returned with it and spread it on the sandy pathway before the terrible bones.

Mercer knelt, and with his stick brush and little sack of greasy paint, dated and began his instrument. For services rendered, Mister Barnaby Skye shall be entitled to one hundred pounds, to be collected at an exchange of his choice. Signed this day, Graves Duplessis Mercer.

It took a while. Scratching text with a fibrous end of a stick required time. A midday brightness began to flood the canyon and its flat, even throwing light upon the great field of bones under the sandstone overhang.

"There you are. Present this at a post and they'll aim it toward Barclay's Bank in London via Hudson's Bay or Chouteau and Company."

Mercer lifted the heavy robe and handed it to Skye.

"I will do that." Skye lifted and settled his old top hat, as he always did when at a loss for words. "We've been through a lot together, sir. I wish you a safe passage home."

"Wish me a boatload of bones, Mister Skye!"

Victoria sprang at him, bristling, saying not a word, her glare so fierce that Skye wondered whether she would strike the Briton.

"We will never see you again. No one will ever see you again," she said.

Mercer, used to more politic language, was plainly at a loss for words but he nodded and bowed slightly.

But there were tears in Victoria's eyes. It was not just anger, but some anguish, some deep sadness that was moving her now.

Skye slipped over to her, wrapped an arm over her shoulder, but she violently shook herself free. Just then, white men were her enemies.

He hoped this great sadness would repair swiftly. There was little to do but collect Jawbone and lead his family and horses away from this quiet canyon off the Missouri River, and hope the high plains and wind in the waving grasses would brighten her heart.

An odd cloud drifted overhead, a momentary gray on a dry, brittle autumnal sky. An equally odd roll of distant thunder slipped into the canyon, muffled and low, as if it had come from a great distance, maybe aeons away through time and space. Victoria stood rigidly, hearing things that Skye could not hear, and then she stared long and sorrowfully at Mercer. For her, the gods had spoken.

Skye thought maybe the gods had spoken to himself as well, for the odd cloud was vanishing before his eyes and there was naught but hard blue heaven at last from one rim of the canyon to the other. Maybe, when they reached the high plains, they would discover the odd cloud drifting away.

Things did not feel right. He furtively eyed Mercer, wondering if he would be the last person ever to see the explorer alive. And Winding. He collected Jawbone, whose flesh shivered when Skye touched it. What was the matter with the horse?

He mounted, and felt the horse turn leaden under him, devoid of all energy. Mary seemed cheerful enough, but Victoria looked small and shriveled, temporarily an ancient woman as she collected her horse and made sure the travois were readied.

Then, softly, from some other passage into the river canyon mounted Indians came in a long file, all of them painted in ghastly fashion. There was no escaping them. The newcomers took in Mercer and Winding as well as Skye's party, and continued toward them, never pausing. Some wore black on one side of their head, red on the other. All were hideously painted. And for the life of him, Skye could not make out the tribe.

Chapter 36

Skye glanced at Victoria. She shook her head. She didn't know either. Mary studied the Indians and shook her head also. None of them could identify this band of painted men walking their ponies toward them.

Mercer saw them too, and hastily moved his robe so it did not cover any of the bones he was rendering to pictographs.

"Who?" he asked Skye.

"Don't know."

Mercer began his own preening, straightening hat, adjusting his shirt. Winding stood, watching the painted Indians, a certain resignation in him.

Now the warriors, walking their ponies single file, were close enough so Skye could make out details. The ponies were painted too. The lead horse had a set of pointed teeth across his chest, like an alligator jaw. The hideously painted warrior held a staff burdened with feathers. Not a weapon was visible among any of them. They were all splashed with umber and red, black and tan, with circles and giant eyes painted on their chests, and chevrons on their arms.

"Mercer. Stay quiet. They're not painted for war."

"Got it, old boy."

But Skye wondered whether the explorer did get it. The band now rode toward Mercer and Winding, parading their ponies along the path that bordered the bones, studying Mercer's pictographs painted on his robe.

Skye held up his hand, palm out, the peace sign, and then did the friend sign. The chief of this band did likewise. For the moment, anyway, trouble receded. Skye beheld about fifteen young men of unknown tribe, all silent, all dressed in outlandish ways, but plainly exhibiting the most powerful medicine they could manage from their paint pots.

They reined their ponies to a halt and stared at the white men.

"Who are they, Mister Skye?" Mercer whispered.

"No idea," Skye replied.

"Well find out, blast it."

The explorer who had just discharged his guide suddenly had need of him. Skye allowed himself a moment of amusement.

"I am Skye," he signaled, pointing to the sky and his chest. "Who you?"

"No Name here," the leader signaled back. A man who concealed his name.

"What people?"

The leader gave the sign for Sarsi but Skye didn't recognize it.

"Sarsi!" whispered Victoria.

"Sarsi? They're Sarsi," Skye said to Mercer.

"Never heard of 'em."

"Canadian."

"Ah, the queen's very own!"

"I doubt it," Skye retorted laconically.

He knew little about them. The band had lived on the Saskatchewan plains, been driven west by Cree about the turn of the century, and had found protection and support from their friends the Blackfeet.

"Sonofabitch," muttered Victoria, who was no friend of anyone associated with her mortal enemies.

"Who him?" signaled the one who owned no name, pointing to Mercer.

"He storyteller, makes pictures, from the land of the Great Mother."

Skye's hands flew, his fingers formed and re-formed image after image. Sign language was never easy.

"Why here?" No Name pointed at Mercer.

Skye paused. He had to be very careful.

"To tell story of bones."

No Name dismounted and stooped over the robe to study the pictographs.

"What's he doing, Mister Skye?" Mercer asked.

"He is reading your signs as best he can."

Others dismounted and crowded around the robe, pointing at this or that image. Mercer was plenty nervous and kept smiling, flashing a row of white teeth at one and another of the Sarsi. Then they began arguing in a tongue Skye could not grasp.

"What are they saying?" Mercer asked.

"Who knows?"

"I have to know!"

Skye smiled. "Mister Mercer, at this moment your life depends on the way you behave. Give no offense."

All of our lives, Skye added silently.

"What do you make of it, Victoria?"

"Secret society. Sarsi come here to get big medicine from bones. Maybe bone society. All young sonsofbitches, eh?"

"What are our chances?"

"No one ever got killed here. What you call it, a truce here. Big truce."

"But if they decide Mercer has done evil?"

She shrugged, not wanting to answer that one.

The dispute among the Sarsi seemed to escalate. And it

involved the robe. That was plain from the gesticulating and pointing.

Skye signaled Mercer to be cautious but Mercer mixed right in with the young men, smiling, making friends or so he thought.

Finally, the Sarsi headman approached Skye, hands and fingers moving swiftly once again. "The storyteller. Does he know the story of the big bones?"

"No."

"But he has told the story on his robe."

Skye nodded.

"He will tell the story to us."

"He does not know the story."

"But he has painted it on his robe."

Skye sensed he was trapped. "Mister Mercer, they believe you know the story of the bones because of what you've put on the robe, and now they want to hear it. I'll have to use sign language."

"But, Skye, I'm really not a storyteller."

"I told them you are one."

"What'll I say?"

"Tell them what Victoria's people believe the bones to be."

Victoria glared at Skye and retreated into herself. But Skye sensed she was secretly pleased.

No Name signaled Skye. "We will learn the story of the sacred bones. The Storyteller will tell us. We will dance and pray. We have begged the four winds for the Storyteller and now he is here. This is a great omen. The Mystery of the Bones will be opened to my people. This day will be re-membered for all times."

"What's he saying, Mister Skye?" Mercer asked.

Skye pondered how to put it. "Mister Mercer, they have

waited a long time to learn the mysteries of the big bones. This is a pilgrimage. They come from the north. They have come here to pay their respects to the bones and learn about them. And now they will find out from you. For a long time they have pleaded for you to come here and now you are here. You are the high priest of the big bones. Perhaps one of their shamans prophesied that you would be here. I don't know. This evening they will listen to you, and dance and pray to the big bones."

"High priest?"

"You, yes. Behave accordingly. Consider yourself the archbishop of bones."

"Gad, Skye, I am not a high priest of anything except women." He was grinning again, even white teeth on display.

"Sir, take this seriously. I repeat, your life depends on it. False priests are the first to feel the battle-axe."

"But I am to make up a story? How can I take that seriously?"

"A myth is not made-up. The story of Victoria's people, the people of the great bird, is not simply manufactured. It's an ancient tradition to explain their origins."

Victoria absorbed that solemnly.

Mercer sighed. "Storytelling is my calling, it seems."

It was eerie. The Sarsi clearly believed this encounter was preordained, fated by the gods, and clearly had foreknowledge of Mercer's visit. There were powers of the universe that Skye didn't grasp, this understanding of the hours and days and months ahead.

The secret bones society of the Sarsi made camp on the flat close to the river. They had brought no tents, only a sleeping robe each, and necessaries. Some of the young men had drums; each had his own paints. They carried only a little jerky, just enough to stave off starvation.

That afternoon, they lionized Mercer, bringing gifts to lay at his feet. The high priest of the bones received two robes, a Hudson's Bay axe, a battle hatchet, an awl, a knife, a King James Bible from who knew where, a small medicine bundle carefully strung over his neck, a fringed elk-skin jacket, and a sacred pipe with a red pipestone bowl.

"Gad, Skye, I'm rich! Now I can dig bones!" Mercer said.

A cold fear coursed through Skye. "Leave them alone if you wish to live."

The great ceremony began at sundown, when chill suddenly pervaded the gloomy canyon of the Missouri and a soft lavender light replaced the bold blue of day.

Skye grasped that there would be no food; these Sarsi were fasting, and expected their guests to fast. This was the moment of the big bones and it would be remembered in their tribal history for all time.

At last No Name summoned his men to sit close to a fire, where they could see Skye's gestures and learn the story of the bones. One by one, these young men settled, mostly cross-legged, some of them with their robes cast over their shoulders.

"The floor is yours, Mister Mercer," Skye said.

"Blast it, Skye, I have no story to tell. So I'll tell them some science, at least as far as my addled mind can come up with some science. They want truth. From me, they'll get science, and not wild stories."

Skye waited with dread for the explorer to begin.

Chapter 37

There was this quality about Mercer: he stood there like a Greek god, gathering the light about him, so confident and whole and magical that the expectant gaze of every Sarsi was upon him. What was it that Mercer radiated? Skye could not say. This man was Hermes, god of travelers, luck, roads, music, eloquence, commerce, young men, cheats, and thieves.

Mercer smiled at Skye and his women and then turned calmly toward his hosts, but now his gaze was different, mysterious, as if he were tapping some powers of heaven that eluded lesser men.

"The world is very old. Older than any person can imagine," he began, and Skye had no trouble translating that into hand-signs. The Sarsi followed easily enough.

"The world changes. Long ago there were oceans here. Mountains rise and fall. Rivers cut through rock and carry land into the sea. Ice carves valleys and cuts down mountains. All this happens so slowly that no one can imagine it. But there are fossils of seashells high in mountains. Nothing stays the same."

Skye marveled at this strange tale of a world so plastic that mountains rose out of seas and ice and rain wore them down again. The Sarsi were marveling too.

"The world is so old that people are newcomers. We have been here only a little while," Mercer continued, while Skye turned that into the universal language of the plains. Good.

If Mercer stuck with simple words and ideas, Skye knew he would have no trouble conveying them.

Mercer spoke quietly, yet his voice carried easily to the farthest Sarsi, a boy sitting well behind the others.

"Long before there were people, there were creatures, large and small, creatures of the skies, the oceans, the land. They are all unknown to us. Many disappeared. Some became other things."

Skye suddenly realized that Mercer was flying a long way from the biblical beliefs of the English, the creation story found in Genesis.

"There were giants among them such as the giants whose bones you see here. They are gone forever. They lived before our type came. We do not know what they were or why they went away."

This was certainly not Genesis. This world was not made in six days. Skye meant to inquire about it, when he could catch Mercer afterward.

"These bones we have here, the bones you have come to honor, are the bones of that which has no name. But maybe these bones are the grandfather bones of creatures we know. Maybe these bones are the first bird or the first lizard."

How could that be? How could any species change? What God wrought was what God wrought. Was Mercer some sort of heretic?

Mercer talked of these things another little while, of creatures forming and dying and changing into other creatures, of land rising and falling, of ice and rivers changing everything, of those bones and shells found in rock all over the world, the bones of creatures unknown to anyone.

The Sarsi were rapt. Mercer, whatever his other gifts, had the magic of the storyteller in him, and the stranger the story, the more attention he won from his auditors.

If the Sarsi were rapt, Skye was even more so. For this man was not talking about eternities, a world forever the same from beginning to end, but a world in endless flux, as if God could not make up his mind, and was forever erasing continents and species, and creating new ones. Was the world made of India rubber? Were creatures, including mankind, here today and gone tomorrow? Skye had never heard of such a thing, though his own observations had hinted at them sometimes. Who was Mercer? How could he know these things? Or even theorize about them?

By full dark, Mercer was done.

The Sarsi expressed their thanksgiving at this great revelation, and made camp down beside the river.

Skye was done with the sign language and it had become too dark for the Indians to follow his fingers and gestures anyway. He glanced at his bemused women, who were absorbing Mercer's strange talk of a world in flux, where nothing was permanent, and monsters of old became something else.

"I say, Skye, thank you. I was in a bit of a bind, you know, not being able to talk with those chaps."

"Yes, Mister Mercer, you were in a bind, all right. You are still alive."

"Right you are, old boy. You saved my bacon. That's an expression I got from the Yanks. What do you suppose it means, saved my bacon, eh? The thing I want to talk to you about, sir, is my mistake. I shouldn't have let you go. I need you. That was a scrape, all right. I simply must have someone with me who'll translate."

"I will take you to Fort Benton and you can hire a translator there, sir."

"Ah, you still object to my taking a few specimens."

"Exactly."

"Then we can't resolve it. I am going to take some specimens and thanks to these Sarsi chaps I have some tools to do it."

"Then I cannot be associated with you, Mister Mercer."

The explorer smiled. "I'll go it alone, eh?"

"This place is still a church to these people and I will not desecrate a church. But speaking of that, sir, would you tell me where all this came from? I've heard things this night that I never thought I'd hear from an Englishman or a Christian."

Mercer nodded and settled on the ground near the dying fire. "There's a ferment in England, sir. Seems most everyone looking at the natural world is objecting to the Genesis account of how it came to be. Blasphemy, my friend, and subject to action by the crown, you know, but that has hardly slowed anyone down."

"Tell me of it."

"You've been out here, far away from England, so I don't suppose you've heard of it. There's a fellow named Charles Lyell who's done a bang-up book about geology. I pretty closely followed his ideas when I talked to these Sarsi chaps tonight. He thinks the world is truly ancient, and there have been enormous changes wrought in it by natural forces. Land masses rising and falling, oceans now where they weren't before, and land now where it wasn't before. Mountains coming up out of the bed of the sea and that's why you find fossil seashells on mountaintops. A world of constant geological change, Mister Skye, but over aeons of time."

"How much time?"

Mercer shook his head. "No one can even fathom the time. But there's more. Chap named Darwin, Charles Darwin, one of that bright Wedgwood tribe, been on a long sea journey to South America. He's a keen observer and he's shared a few of his ideas with me, but cautiously. He doesn't want the crown on his neck. He's admitted to the Royal Society, 1839 that was, and also the Athenaeum, 1838 that was. That's a little club for the leading minds in the arts and sciences. And of course the Royal Geological Society. He's a man of parts, sir, and he's working on something that'll rock the world. It was 1842 that he did a little sketch about what he's up to, and he tells me he's about ready to publish his outline of a whole new hypothesis, drawn from observation of all forms of life, about species and where they came from. He thinks that they evolved from other forms of life. Too long to go into here but let me put it the other way. He doesn't think God thought up a bug or an elephant and plopped the creature down on earth full-made and ready for life."

"Heresy, then?"

"Oh, I wouldn't say that. But you might find most of the men in the natural sciences thinking that Genesis is a poetical account of creation, and not a literal one."

"This is what you call science, Mister Mercer?"

"Yes, exactly. Observation, analysis, deduction. Rational examination of a phenomenon."

"And that's what you brought to the Sarsi?"

"You have it just right, Mister Skye. You've called me a storyteller, and that's a good way to letting those fellows know what I do. So what does a storyteller do? In London, I'll tell them about the creation story of your wife's people and their belief that these are the ancestral bones, and let them marvel at the banquet table when I'm done. But here, among the Sarsi chaps, I'll tell them about Lyell and Darwin, and let them marvel. That's what a storyteller does, you know. I bring them new things, meat they never tasted before."

That was an insight into Mercer. Skye, who knew he had no storytelling gifts at all, felt a faint surprise at Mercer's ways of dealing with radically distinct audiences. Tell the creation legends of the plains tribes to Londoners; tell the latest ideas raking scientists to the tribes. Skye laughed. It took all types to make a world.

"Who's this Darwin, sir?"

"He's got a fine brain, if you ask me. He found the fossils of seashells at twelve thousand feet in the Andes and began asking the right questions. He found species on the islands off South America unlike others, and well adapted to their environment, and began asking questions. I tell you, sir, I can barely wait for his outline to come out. Last I know, and I talked to him just before coming to North America, he was ready for the printer. I hope it's out when I return. I tell you, Mister Skye, this man Darwin's going to rattle every cage."

"Rattle the idea of God?"

Mercer smiled. "It might. Some will argue that it might even overthrow God."

"That is not something I want to hear."

"Of course not, Mister Skye. I don't want to hear it. I'm a good Church of England man myself. Everything we are in England, it all flows from our beliefs and our faith. That's why I dread this a little, even while applauding it. There's Darwin and another chap named Wallace who thinks the same way, and many others asking questions. We're on the brink of an earthquake, I'd say."

It was odd, sitting there beside the embers of a campfire in one of the most remote corners on earth, listening to all the latest ferment in London. For a moment or two Skye wished he could be there, in his old home, following all of it. But he saw Victoria and Mary, sitting pensively, blotting all this up, and knew his home was here and always would be here.

"Well, Skye, are you going to help me pry up some bones tomorrow?" Mercer asked.

"No, sir, I won't," Skye said. "And we'll be far away."

Chapter 38

Skye awoke to a sharp pain in his chest. He stared upward, found a Sarsi warrior over him, the man's lance stabbing into Skye's breast. He was one quick thrust from eternity.

He lay very quiet but stared up at the warrior. He could see that the women were similarly impaled. It was light; well past dawn. They had not erected the lodge but had made their beds in a private corner of the flat, well away from Mercer and Winding.

Now he stared in terror at the young man whose lance pinioned him to the earth. The Sarsi was not painted this morning. He and the others had scrubbed away the hideous designs and colors that had marked yesterday's ceremonial visit to the bones. He was simply an alert young man, dressed only in a breechclout, his hair loose around his head and neck, a red headband holding it in place. Suspended about his neck was a small medicine bundle shaped of leather.

All Skye could do was wait and pray. Even to open his mouth, to yell, to explode in anger, could be fatal. The warrior seemed to be waiting for something, and as the seconds ticked by, and Skye wondered whether this was his last day, he began to fathom what this was about.

He was not wrong. In a while more armed Sarsi warriors appeared, pushing Mercer and Winding before them with their lances. Other Sarsi men had arrows nocked into their strung bows, ready for anything.

Mercer was putting a brave face on it, smiling, standing erect, ignoring the half-dozen lance points that were hovering inches from his body; points that could turn him into a pincushion in no time at all. He carried a piece of rock in his hands.

"They don't take kindly to my digging, do they?" he asked.

Skye did not respond but his stare caught Mercer and somehow subdued the explorer.

"I went for a tooth, just one old tooth," Mercer said. "I tried the war hatchet and the axe, but all I did was shatter the blasted tooth. A man needs stone mason's chisels to cut out a bone or two."

"Westminster Abbey," Skye said.

Mercer managed a smile. An acknowledgment.

Skye felt the iron point dig into his chest and swiftly returned to silence. He waited, his pulse climbing, waited for death.

The older Sarsi, the only one with graying hair, appeared before Skye, and nodded to his young warriors. They withdrew the lances. Skye didn't dare sit up but a nod from the warrior told him he should. Slowly, he sat up. Slowly, the women were sitting up. Mary was very still. Victoria glared at Mercer with such heat in her face that Mercer could not escape the scathing rake of her gaze.

The chief began to say something in sign language, and Skye followed carefully. The two men had taken the tooth of the ancient one. They had desecrated a holy place. They had offended the spirits. They had offended the Ancestors. They were worse than an enemy of the Sarsi; they were worse than a witch. They were the Evil Ones. The Sarsi would put them to death. Then they would decide what to do about Skye.

Skye turned to Mercer and Winding. "You've desecrated the ancient one, the holy place. You are more evil than enemies. You are more evil than a witch. You will die. They will decide what to do about the rest of us."

Mercer absorbed that bleakly.

No one spoke. The Sarsi were all watching Mercer, watching to see whether he was a god-man, a prophet of the bones. Mercer wilted as the reality gradually pervaded him.

"Tell them I'll give back the tooth! I don't want it!"

He thrust the tooth fragment toward the headman, No Name, only to see it fall to the clay. The broken fossil lay there, an accusation, the proof of evil. No one picked it up. Skye wondered whether these people were even allowed to touch the sacred bones.

He surveyed the scene. The light was quickening though this deep canyon of the Missouri still lay under shadow. Several lancers guarded the prisoners. Several more bowmen backed them. Two of the Sarsi had caught up the lines of Skye's horses and the one holding Jawbone was likely to get his head kicked in. But Jawbone, whose ears lay flat back, was behaving for the moment.

There was no escape.

Mercer must have been working from the earliest gray light, maybe hoping to chip out a tooth of the monster before anyone noticed. And now he was standing before the Sarsi, a condemned man.

"Tell them I will make it up. Tell them I am a priest of the bones."

Skye shook his head slowly, but the headman caught the gesture and wanted a translation.

"He says he is a priest of the bones and will make everything right," Skye translated, employing gestures.

The one with no name stared bleakly at Mercer.

He barked some sort of command to his group and they withdrew except for half a dozen who were guarding the prisoners. Skye watched them retreat out of earshot, toward the place of the bones, where they all paused to examine the ruptured rock, the damaged skull where the giant tooth had been torn out, taking some of the lower jaw with it judging from the rock still clinging to the tooth.

"What are they going to do, Mister Skye?" Mercer asked. He was now truly alarmed. It had taken him this while to grasp the trouble he was in; to understand that his luck, which had been with him across several continents and in all sorts of strange circumstances, had suddenly run out.

"They are going to decide our fate."

"But I've offered to make it up." It was a plaintive whisper from a man who had never grasped how different peoples are and how sharply they vary, and how goodness to one people is evil to another.

"Sonofabitch," grumbled Victoria. This time the expression was directed toward Mercer.

Skye didn't know what to do or whether he could do anything. Powerful warriors stood ready to slaughter them if they showed any signs of trouble.

Over at the bones below the sandstone overhang the Sarsi sat in a circle and began a discussion, sometimes animated, sometimes so quiet it was hard to know whether anyone was saying anything. But Skye gathered that an intense debate was in progress there, and he guessed the debate had much to do with Mercer's fate. The Sarsi did not want to anger the spirit whose bones lay just a few feet from them.

The sun rose, bathing the tops of the bluffs north of the river with gold. Mercer, weary of standing, slowly sat down. Winding joined him. Skye thought that Mercer's fate would

234 RICHARD S. WHEELER

probably be Winding's fate if both of them had been caught ripping the fossil tooth out of the sacred site.

The guards watched warily. Their lances had flat iron points made by Hudson's Bay Company, points that could pierce flesh as well as slice sideways. One point was caked in black dried blood. The guards were veterans, not a youth among them. They eyed Victoria and Mary, identifying the tribes by what the women wore.

The women would live. Skye was sure of it. He also suspected that they would become prisoners, maybe virtual slaves of the wives of these warriors. They might never see their own people again and might die far north in British possessions.

Skye drove such thoughts from his mind. If he focused on a way out of this, perhaps he could do something. But he didn't have the slightest idea of an escape.

As was often the case among plains Indians, the Sarsi took their time. But eventually the headman, who declined to reveal his name, rose, walked to the prisoners, and addressed Skye, his hands and arms forming quick, sure gestures.

"Not long ago a blackrobe came to us and told us about the religion of the white men," he said.

Skye nodded. That probably was Father De Smet, or one of his assistant priests, who had done so much missionary work among the Blackfeet and other tribes.

"He told us about the god-man, the high priest of the people. Is this man here, who destroyed the bones, the god-man of your people?"

The question startled Skye. Where was this chief's thought running?

"No," Skye signaled. "This man is a storyteller. He goes into strange lands and learns about them and goes back to his people across the big water and he tells his people what he has seen."

"But he called himself a priest of the ancient bones. He is a grandfather, is it not so?"

A grandfather could be a revered elder. Reluctantly, Skye acknowledged that it was so.

"The white men hung their god-man from a cross, is it not so?" the headman asked.

"It is so."

"Then we will do this. He must die. He angered the spirit whose bones these are."

"But it is not the same."

The headman stopped Skye's protest with a savage wave of the hand. "We will put him on a tree like the god-man of the whites."

Skye stared at the headman.

"What's he saying? Tell me!" Mercer said.

"I don't think you want to know," Skye said.

Chapter 39

Mercer whitened. "Am I to die?"

Skye nodded.

"But why?"

"You already know."

"You must stop this! I didn't offend anything."

"I will try." Skye caught the eye of the headman and began the language of the signs. Let this man go. Do not hurt him. The spirit of the bones does not want him.

The headman, the one with the secret name, growled and abruptly slapped Skye's hands and arms with an arrow. The blow stung. It was a command: no protests, no resistance, no signs, no words. Skye felt rage boil through him, found himself staring into three lance points and a nocked arrow, and he subsided.

The morning sun caught the cliffs high above the river bottoms and painted them gold.

"What are they going to do to me, Skye?" Mercer asked.

But Skye simply shook his head.

Several of the Sarsi headed for a willow grove with axes and cut two stout poles, each about six feet long. These they laid on the ground and forced Mercer and Winding to lie across them, so the poles were under their shoulders. Then the Sarsi bound the arms of each man to his pole with sopping wet rawhide. Their arms were anchored at elbow and wrist. Skye knew that the rawhide would dry into a steely binding, and shrink in the process, gradually cutting off circulation at wrist and elbow.

Victoria muttered softly. Mary was horrified.

The Sarsi lifted each man to his feet. Now their arms were outstretched to either side and firmly anchored to the pole across their back. They could not eat or drink or perform any function with their hands. And in time the pain in their shoulders and arms would become excruciating.

Sharp commands from the headman made it clear that the Sarsi were leaving and taking their prisoners with them. A Sarsi youth collected the Skye horses. Jawbone had sense enough not to fight the cord that drew him. With a word, the headman started them all up a winding trail that climbed steeply through juniper to the rimrock high above.

"Where are they taking us, Skye?" Mercer asked.

Skye quickly shook his head. Silence was best just now.

It was hard for Mercer and Winding to climb that trail with their arms outstretched and tied to the pole. They were utterly helpless to balance themselves. Skye and Mary and Victoria followed, watched carefully. All of Skye's possessions followed, on the packhorses.

The Sarsi traveled quietly, padding up the steep grade, sometimes over rock ledges, sometimes up cliffs that were hard for the horses to negotiate.

"My arms are killing me, Skye. Make them cut me loose. Beg them. I'll do anything they ask. I'll be their slave if they want a slave. Just cut my arms loose."

The headman listened, no doubt surmising what Mercer was saying without requiring Skye's translation. But he said nothing. The trail was steep and just staying upright occupied all of them. Then suddenly it topped the bluff and they stepped into harsh sunlight blazing out of the east. It was already heating the sandstone. In a few minutes the whole party collected on the flats at the top of the bluff. Below, the Missouri River ran its silvery way toward the east, still caught in deep shadow. The river flat and the sandstone ledge that protected the bones lay directly below, perhaps three hundred feet. Skye could see the high plains stretching toward the heavens at some hazy horizon an infinity away. Every rise in the land cast its long shadow as the sun struggled upward from its night-bed.

The headman studied the cliff below him. About twenty feet below was a narrow sandstone ledge that capped a stratum of rock. A game trail led down to that ledge. He motioned Mercer and Winding to follow him down there, and motioned Skye and his women to stay put.

Mercer warily slid down the game trail, obviously knowing he was helpless to stop the descent if he should lose his balance. Winding followed. Several Sarsi followed them, carrying more of the well-soaked rawhide thong. On the ledge they bound Mercer's ankles and knees with the rawhide and tied the sopping leather tight. And then they did the same to Winding. Then they swung Mercer's legs around until they dangled over the ledge. And Winding's. Now both of them were poised on the lip of the ledge, their arms tied to the poles across their backs. They could not walk or stand. They could not untie themselves and escape. They could only sit on the brink of eternity..

Skye suddenly knew how this would end. When the deepening pain in their shoulders, or the tightening rawhide cut the circulation in their hands or forearms, or their thirst, or the heat of the midday sun, became more then they could endure, they would do the one thing they could manage: kick themselves over the ledge and fall a hundred feet free and clear and then bounce another hundred or more over scree and talus. They would end up on the sandstone overhang protecting the bones, and add their bones to the bone-

yard. The Sarsi had arranged it so that Mercer and Winding
would, of their own volition, give themselves to the spirit
of the bones.

Mercer saw it all now, and craned his head upward to
Skye.

"Good-bye, then," he said.

"I will do what I can, any way I can."

"You were right, Skye."

"We can go fast or slow," Winding said. "Our choice.
They ain't killing us. We'll be doing the job ourselves."

"Tell the Royal Society. Write them. Don't leave out anything."

"How much time have we got?" Winding said.

Skye shook his head. How thirsty would they get? How
hot? How long could they endure the pain in their shoulders and arms?

"Do not give up hope. I will return if I can, as soon as
I can."

A sharp rap from the headman's arrow, which he employed as a nasty little club or crop, lashed Skye's face.

Then several of the Sarsi brought twists of sweetgrass,
coarse and dry, and laid them between Mercer and Winding.

"What are they doing, Skye?"

"Sweetgrass smoke purifies you, cleans your bodies for
the sacrifice to the spirits."

The headman glared at Skye but did not lash him.

The Sarsi struck flint to steel, showering the dry sweetgrass until it began to smolder. A pungent and pleasant
smoke began to rise from the small pile, curling outward,
drifting over Mercer and Winding. Skye had sometimes
burned sweetgrass himself and bathed in its smoke. It was
a tribal custom that he found comforting and cleansing,
though he could not say why.

The sun rose higher, blinding the two on the ledge, who

could not protect their eyes or turn away from its glare. Skye pitied them and felt sheer helpless anger roll through him. He searched wildly for a way, for a club. He would find a stick and wade in, crack heads, push Sarsi over the cliff, until the lances found him. But what good would that do?

It was all about religion again. Offend another man's religion and hell would break loose. Challenge belief, question faith, desecrate an altar, violate a taboo, laugh at rituals, and you would stir the most volcanic emotions residing in the soul. Mercer had violated a religion. Skye doubted he would ever see the man again, and hoped he would push himself over the edge sooner rather than later; avoid suffering rather than torment himself to the last. By afternoon, at most, if the day was hot, both men would be out of their heads.

The Sarsi sat quietly, watching the sweetgrass smoke wash the sacrificial victims, knowing the smoke would prepare the two men for their rendezvous with the spirit of the big bones. The Sarsi were in no hurry. It was well to sit and watch, and know how perfectly the two suffered from heat and pain and thirst and hopelessness.

The sun climbed until the sandstone around them radiated its heat. And then the headman, he of the secret name, rose, gestured, and the Sarsi bone worshipers collected their own possessions as well as Skye's laden horses, and prodded their other prisoners away from the fatal ledge. That country was impassable, and it was necessary to retreat from the headlands back to the high plains and pick up a trail there. Skye had no idea where he and Victoria and Mary were being taken. They were on the south side of the Missouri; the Sarsi lived far to the north. Fords of the Missouri were few and often dangerous.

He had been so absorbed with the explorer's fatal circumstances that he hadn't given much thought to his own or those of his wives. Now, back from the ledge, the prisoners were given their horses and Skye found himself astride Jawbone, who itched and twitched under him. He had all his possessions except his Hawken and axe, which the Sarsi wisely kept.

Victoria rode silently, her face stony, and Skye knew she thought the punishment was just and proper. Mary was far more anguished, fighting back her grief.

They rode west for miles, and then the headman of the unspoken name halted them at a high plains seep to water their horses and rest in the shade of two or three willows there. This was coulee country, a land of giant gullies each leading down miles of prairie to the Missouri River.

The women retreated to find some privacy down one of those giant grassy gulches, leading their horses with them. The Sarsi didn't much care. Eventually Victoria returned with her horse, but not Mary, and in the milling of packhorses and Jawbone's wild bunch no one noticed as they started west again, except Skye.

Chapter 40

Mary's absence was soon discovered. The man whose name was secret approached Skye.

"Where wife?" he signaled.

"Don't know."

"Gone to bones?"

Skye shrugged.

The headman issued a sharp command. Several Sarsi trotted their ponies back toward the coulee where Mary was last seen. Skye waited quietly. Victoria looked grim. She probably didn't approve of Mary's rescue attempt but it was her code to let anyone do what he or she would, and bear the consequences.

In a few minutes the Sarsi returned and consulted with the headman. They plainly had lost Mary and the rock-hard clay of the area wasn't providing a track. Skye figured that Mary might even have a mile head start by then if she had urged her pony into a lope.

Still, she was four or more hours from the bones. And the sun this late summer day had been relentless. If she did escape, she probably would find Mercer and Winding dead at the foot of the bluff. But she would try, and he marveled at that quality in her. His Mary, so newly his wife, had the same courage and spirit as Victoria.

The Sarsi were engaged in debate, probably whether or not to return to the bones, catch Mary, prevent her from saving those who had been sacrificed. Skye eyed them, eyed his pack animals, eyed his rifle snugged on one of them, wondered how to make use of this, wondered how to escape the four bowmen and lancers who were steadfastly guarding him and Victoria.

He edged Jawbone toward the impromptu conference and signaled: "Permission to speak."

The headman stared, then nodded.

"Let us go. We have done you no harm. We did the bones no harm. Why do you keep us?"

The assembled Sarsi watched his hands work. Fingers were poor substitutes for talk, and he doubted he could do or say much that would persuade them. There were only a few hundred words in the sign language, and they had to do, and often didn't do.

The headman stared at the sun, which was heading west now, well after noon. It was very quiet. Skye could pretty well read his mind. If he released the white man now, could they return to the sacrificed ones in time? Why keep them longer? Keep them? Kill Skye and his wife? Chase Skye's younger woman who had escaped them?

The flinty headman stared proudly at Skye, and Skye wished he could befriend this one. He liked the man who had led a small group of young Sarsi to pay homage to the big bones. Maybe the headman liked Skye. He and his family had been treated with care and respect.

A bee hummed by, surprising them.

The headman with no name spoke abruptly to two of the boys. They trotted their ponies to the herd, cut out Skye's horses but not Mercer's, and brought them to Skye.

Skye lifted his hat. There was no good sign for thank you, so Skye signaled blessings.

The headman nodded. Skye took the reins, gave Victoria the lines of the pack animals, and turned away. For the briefest moment his back itched as if it would receive arrows, but nothing happened. Skye and Victoria walked their horses slowly back along the path they had taken, and in a while the Sarsi turned the opposite way, and receded from view.

"Oh, Skye," whispered Victoria.

He saw the tears.

With the pack animals they could not hurry, but Skye thought they did not need to: Mary was hurrying. She had her moccasin knife. She would do what she could do if she was in time.

They rode steadily through the heat and the waning day. The sun was plunging below the horizon earlier now but Skye thought they would reach the bluff by daylight.

They paused briefly at a seep in a coulee, and Victoria dismounted, stretched, and smiled.

"I am going to put the tooth back in the jaw of the grandfather," she said.

"Where is it?"

"Where it was dropped by the one whose name I will not say."

That would be Mercer, whom she believed was dead now. Once the spirit had fled no plains Indian would name the departed.

"I will help you if you want me to."

"It is for me alone. The bones are my grandmother."

"We will watch for it, Victoria."

Something in her face touched him just then. She loved him as much as he loved her. She loved him through best and worst, through times that challenged everything she clung to, believed in.

They mounted and rode steadily east, along the trail south of the Missouri River basin. The closer they came to the place of the bones, the more they rode deep inside of themselves. Familiar bluffs hove into view and finally the one that overlooked the flat, far below, where the monster lay in layers of sandstone, its bones a shrine to many peoples of the plains.

It was not easy to find the exact cliff; so many places like it crowded the river canyon, but slowly Skye and Victoria examined the likely places, one by one, until they did find the spot, and found fresh hoofprints in the dust. They dismounted. No one was sitting on that ledge below. Heat from the ledge still radiated fiercely, though the sun was now well to the northwest, and adding nothing to the temperature.

Skye walked down to the ledge itself, treading carefully because a misstep could send him sailing to his doom. He saw nothing there. He peered over the lip, and far below detected something crumpled, something he was sure was a body. He studied it, not knowing who, or whether the cloth heap down there was two bodies or one.

"Someone died," Victoria said when he returned to the top.

"Maybe both."

He stood a moment, feeling grief.

They mounted, followed the perilous trail down the cliff, and eventually reached the shadowed flat that lay very still, very lonely, in the late light of the day.

Skye was puzzled. Surely Mary would be here.

Then Victoria pointed. Mary was not near the big bones but some distance away, at the bank of the river, doing something. Her horse stood quietly near her.

Jawbone whinnied and Mary's horse responded. Mary looked up, and then stood gently.

Skye and Victoria rode slowly there, through gloomy shadow.

At Mary's feet was the body of a man, legs dangling in the river. Skye and Victoria hurried close. It was Mercer, and he was alive, his body writhing now and then. They gazed down from their horses at a man whose limbs were monstrously swollen, whose shoulders had puffed up, whose hands were purple, whose face was sun-blistered, whose whole body was sun-poisoned, and whose blue eyes were filled with madness.

Mercer stared up at them from eyes sunk in puffed flesh.

"Ahhhh," he said.

"This man, I find him up there and cut him free. Somehow we get down to the river," Mary said.

She had been cooling him, pouring water over his shirt and trousers, finding a way for him to drink. But he plainly could barely move his tormented arms and hands, which projected out like bloated sausages to either side, in much the way they had been tied all day.

"Ahhhh," Mercer said.

Skye knelt, felt the man's forehead, and found it feverish, as he had expected.

Victoria headed for her packs. She kept herbs in them for many an illness, including some that broke fevers.

"Winding is gone?" Skye asked.

"Ahhh."

"You will survive this. You will be all right."

Mercer groaned.

Skye and Mary pulled Mercer's feet out of the water and laid him flat beside the river. The explorer stared.

Great shadows filled the canyon of the bones. Victoria returned with some bark in hand and began steeping it in a buffalo-horn cup.

Skye stood slowly, his gaze on that brooding cliff. Winding was somewhere partway up it. He felt saddened. He liked the teamster, a man excellent with horses and filled with the sage wisdom of the wild trail.

"I find him there, and he is still talking a little. I cut him free and help him down. Very hard, he cannot walk, so we drag down together. He falls into river, and I pull him out and get water into him. At first he talks a little, enough so I can get his words. The man who died, this man lasted until around the middle of the day. But the rawhide it tightens, making him crazy, and then bees come and sting, and he screams and pushes himself, and he goes down the cliff and his spirit leaves him," she said.

"Bees?"

"Bees sent by the spirit of the bones."

"Is Mercer bitten?"

"No, just the other." She, too, would no longer name Winding out of respect for his spirit.

Mercer gazed wildly upward at them, struggling for air and life, and sanity.

"How long has he been like this?" Skye asked.

"He is mad, his spirit gone to be with the owls," she said.

"The bones did it," Victoria added. "That was what happened."

Chapter 41

Mercer was out of his head. Sometimes he wailed. Sometimes he glared at one or another of them. "You have no right!" he said once. "No story," he muttered. "Knight of the Garter."

Skye wondered if the man even knew where he was or who he was with. Victoria tried to draw Mercer's swollen arms to his sides but he howled with every gentle tug. He simply would not fold his arms to his sides; something about it was too painful.

The women began to make camp. Mary was propping up the lodgepole pyramid and laying the rest poles into it. They were going to get Mercer out of the night air if they could.

Skye saw he was not needed and decided to tend to the next business. He hiked slowly past the bones and then climbed the steep slope laden with scree at the foot of the cliff where Winding had jumped. Enough light remained to hunt for the teamster. Skye hoped to offer the man a respectful burial. He had no spade; it would have to be another scaffold burial but at least it would be that much.

He did not see Winding in the talus, and stumbled about the base of the cliff hunting for the body. But it was not there, nor visible in either direction. He was mystified. Then, looking up, he saw Winding dangling seventy or eighty feet up the cliff, caught by the pole across his arms that had wedged into stone there. He saw only sheer rock, gouged by cracks, and no foothold or handhold.

He could not bury the teamster. The birds would soon reduce that hanging flesh to bones and then indeed the last of him would tumble.

He pulled off his old top hat and stared upward. "Mister Winding, I'll send a letter to your folks in Missouri. I hope they'll get it. I'd do more if I could," he said.

A breeze turned the dangling feet.

A black bird, raven maybe, settled on Winding's arm. Skye found a rock and threw it upward. The bird flapped away.

It didn't seem right, didn't seem finished, but he didn't know what else to do so he retreated carefully down the talus, taking great care not to stumble and twist an ankle. Winding gone. Mercer out of his head. Corporal gone. What was left?

Slowly, in fading light, Skye descended the slope to the place of the monster bones and paused there. He felt the sacredness of the place. Generations of Indians had come to this place of mystery, taking away some intuition of the origins of life, giving something, reverencing the great bones projecting out of rock. Someone had restored the broken tooth. The piece, including the chunk of jaw, had been carefully restored to the monster's skull. Odd. He didn't remember Victoria or Mary coming to the bones to do that since they returned. They had been busy setting up the lodge and caring for Mercer.

Skye stood in the quiet, feeling the sour song of the bones churn in him. How old they were. It occurred to him that this monster might be one of God's mistakes. Maybe God didn't fashion creatures he was satisfied with and kept throwing them out. Maybe this one was evil, cruel and wicked, and God cast it into hell, or into oblivion, which might be the same thing. Maybe heaven was merely the place for what was selected to survive, a place for what proved to be good. These seemed older than a hundred thousand lifetimes. God's early mistake, not a recent one.

His mind drifted back to the idea that these were sinister monsters, much older than God, that when God came along he destroyed the evil ones, including this huge creature with the enormous skull and long tail. Maybe the whole world was hell until God vanquished hell and all its monsters, such as this one.

Skye marveled. The sacred bones had started feverish speculations in him, things he had never thought about. He could not explain it. Why would giant bones make him so itchy, so unhappy with his paltry store of understanding? He had paused at the bones only a minute or two and yet in that time, his mind had catapulted into realms he had never dreamed of before. Suddenly he knew how Victoria's people must have felt when they first saw the bones; how the bones fevered their minds, fired their imaginations, and soon enough the giant bones were sacred to them, and had to do with their own origins. Skye wondered whether other tribes had found their origins in these bones. And what had they seen? A big bird, like the Crows? He left the shadowed crypt and returned through a peaceful twilight to the camp.

"The man who cared for horses?" Victoria asked, carefully.

"Dead. I can't reach him. He's hung high up."

"The spirit put him there," she said.

It was as good an explanation as any. "Did you put the broken tooth back?" he asked.

She stared blankly, then shook her head, and that was answer enough. He found Mary starting a campfire. "Did you put the broken tooth back in the skull? The one Mercer chopped out?"

She stood, and slowly shook her head.

"Someone's been here and did it," he said.

But they saw no evidence of anyone.

"Very strange," he muttered. He thought maybe one of the Sarsi had done it before they all left.

Their task was to move Mercer from the riverbank to the lodge. Skye brought a robe, and he and Victoria slid the man onto it. The explorer groaned and uttered one long wail.

"Is it all right with you if we shelter him?"

Victoria eyed him coldly. "I would not want it any other way. We will take care of him. Those who are mad must receive the greatest respect."

"Filomena, will you ever forgive me?" Mercer said. "I could not help myself."

They waited but the explorer made no more mention of Filomena.

Victoria slipped into twilight, toward a slough filled with chokecherry brush, and there harvested the last of the cherries as well as more of the bark and roots. She mashed the roots and set them to steeping in water that Mary had heated in a leather bag, using hot rocks. This decoction she slowly fed to Mercer, who sipped, gasped, sipped again, and gradually swallowed much of what she was giving to him using a horn spoon.

It was an old Crow remedy to quiet a person and settle an upset stomach. Skye thought it would have to do; there was little else growing there.

"Who are you?" Mercer asked.

"I am Victoria."

"Where am I?"

"You are in the lodge of Mister Skye."

"Who is that?"

Mercer didn't wait for a response but closed his eyes and slipped into quietness. Victoria stood, her work done. Mary covered the explorer with a buffalo robe and they all crawled into their beds. It had been a brutal day.

Skye slept restlessly, something nagging him about camping so close to the great bones. If Mercer was able, they would leave for Fort Benton in the morning.

Some time in the night, Jawbone screeched. Skye awakened, and in one swift move lifted his Hawken and slipped into the night, the quarter moon his lantern. The horse was untouched and standing calmly. None of the other horses had been stolen or hurt. It was not uncommon for a horse to startle in the night but Skye ached to leave this place of the bones.

"Nothing," he whispered to his women.

"The spirit," Victoria said. "Jawbone saw the spirit."

They slept fitfully the rest of the night except for Mercer, who seemed to sleep the sleep of the dead, never stirring. But when dawn's first light began to collect in the smoke hole, Skye discovered Mercer sitting up and staring. His arms were still grossly swollen but dropped to his sides now.

"Where am I?"

"On the Missouri River."

"How did I get here?"

"We brought you here."

"Who are you?"

"I am Mister Skye. These are my wives, Victoria and Mary Skye."

"Why did you bring me here?"

Skye hesitated. "You asked to be brought here, to see some large fossilized bones."

Mercer stared. "Why would I do that?"

It was plain to Skye and his wives that the explorer had no memory of recent events. He wasn't incoherent, just blank.

"We lost Mister Winding, sir," Skye said.

"Who is that?"

"Earlier, we lost Mister Corporal. Floyd Corporal."

"Sorry, the name's not known to me. Should I know it?"

Skye scarcely knew how to reply. "Have we met, sir?"

"Graves Duplessis Mercer at your service, Mister Skye. But I am a little hazy about how I ended up here. Am I a prisoner?"

"No, not that."

Up to a point, Mercer seemed himself, but that was only if he spoke of events long past. It became clear that his ordeal on the cliff had blanked his memory. Engaging Skye and his entourage, the trip, the prairie fire, and the long trek to the bones before returning to England simply eluded Mercer.

"This is an odd place to camp, Mister Skye, down in this gloomy trench."

"We came here because you wanted to see the bones, sir."

"That's very strange. Now tell me, why do my arms torture me? They're swollen. My shoulders are unbearable. My fingers thick as sausages."

Skye hardly knew how to proceed. "The Sarsi Indians here took offense, sir."

"Took offense? But why?"

Skye decided that moment to hold off. "Let's get ready for travel, Mister Mercer, if you're up to it. We'll head for Fort Benton and they can put you on a flatboat going down the river."

"Why would I do that?"

"It was what you had in mind, before . . . this."

Mercer struggled to his feet, and stepped out into the hush of predawn.

"It's all very odd," he said. "I seem to have lost some time somewhere. What is Fort Benton?"

"We'll talk about it on the way, sir," Skye said.

Chapter 42

Skye and his women thought Mercer would be able to travel at least a little while. It would be good to get him out of the gloomy canyon where sunlight didn't arrive until midmorning and departed midafternoon.

It was Victoria who saw what to do next. She began packing Mercer's robe and then realized it contained memories. She found Mercer sitting patiently, awaiting whatever would occur next, and quietly laid out the robe before him. Skye and Mary swiftly caught on, and joined her.

There, before the explorer, was a pictograph chronicle of events since the prairie fire had destroyed his journal, done in his own hand. Most of the marks scraped into the hide with umber greasepaint could be deciphered only by Mercer but some were plain to anyone. His sketches of the skull, his measurements, his drawings of bones. His record of daily passage through the high plains was more obscure, yet plainly intended to trigger memories.

Mercer gazed blandly at the robe, set hair-down before him on the ground.

"What is this, pray tell?"

"It's your journal, sir. After the prairie fire destroyed your journal, you kept a log of events here."

"How quaint. I'm no artist, Skye."

"No, no artist. Neither am I. But each of these little drawings has meaning for you. These mountains here, those are the Snowies, shown from the east. I daresay this is the Musselshell. These figures here are Indians on horseback, wouldn't you say?"

"Why would I do this?"

"You are an explorer and a journalist. I believe you intend to write up your experiences when you return to London."

"Well, that's an entertaining little twist, eh?"

"Look at each of these, and tell us what it means."

Mercer suddenly smiled, that famous toothy grin. "That's a good game, but not today, Skye."

"We'll bring out this robe again, then."

Victoria rolled it carefully. Somehow, the robe would be the key to Mercer's recollections.

"One last question, Mister Mercer. You're in North America looking for material to write about, correct?"

"Quite correct."

"You came out the Oregon Trail and left it accompanied by some Shoshones, correct?"

"Perfectly correct."

"You planned to write about Mormon polygamy, correct?"

"I believe so, but one learns to follow one's instincts."

"You were present at the moment Mary's family gave her to me as my second wife?"

"Was I?"

"You were curious about it."

"Who wouldn't be, sir? There's a fine little yarn to be told in it."

Skye continued to grill the explorer. It was plain that he hadn't lost much; mainly the period from the time his wagon burned to the present. Yet he could not remember either Winding or Corporal.

That was enough for one session. They helped Mercer up; his arms and shoulders hurt so much he gasped, but his legs were all right. Victoria would lead his horse. Mercer could not rein it.

Skye started them up the precipitous trail to the open country south of the river, and felt relief when they escaped that gloomy, mysterious valley of the bones. He preferred the great open vistas where he could see as far as tomorrow, where he could follow a cloud's passage for a hundred miles, where a man was not hemmed by anything.

Mercer began to howl. It sent shivers through Skye. The man bayed like a wolf, the voice eerie and lost. Skye kept his party going, thinking that Mercer's howling would subside, but it didn't.

The explorer was plainly in distress, and Skye began hunting for a campsite. North, the ancient trench of the Missouri sliced through the high plains as if the foundations of the earth had been ripped apart. He descended a giant coulee to a small flat where a spring purled out of a crack in the underlying sandstone and fed thick brush and cottonwoods for half a mile below it before the runoff vanished. It would do.

They lifted Mercer down. The man was fevered, his face ruddy, his breathing coarse. Victoria and Mary silently began making camp though it was only midafternoon. Skye knew he needed to hunt; they were down to pemmican and jerky. There was spoor from antelope and mule deer here, and a calling card from a black bear. He hoped to surprise a deer.

They settled Mercer on his robe. Mary began collecting wood for a fire. Victoria would soon decoct one or another of her herbal remedies and let him sip.

"Skye, why do my arms hurt?"

"Because they were tied to a pole across your back,

straight out, with rawhide that shrank in the sun as it dried. It stopped the blood."

"Did you do that?"

"Some Sarsi Indians did."

"But why, Skye?"

Skye's gaze lifted to the ridges. "You had offended their beliefs, sir."

"How could I do that?"

"The tooth, sir."

"I have all my teeth but one."

Skye laughed. "The monster's tooth, sir."

Mercer exploded. "You'd bloody well not make jokes. I hurt so much I can't even think. My shoulders! If you had my shoulders right now, the pain in them, you'd be lying on this clay weeping. I keep a stiff upper lip, and I don't need jokes."

"As you wish, sir."

"Monster's tooth! You low-bred dog! You off-scouring of London's alleys! You damned deserter! You barbarian, fleeing all that's right and proper! You degenerate! You seditionist! Skye, you should have been shipped to Australia long ago!"

"It's Mister Skye, sir."

"Mister! Mister! You? Mister Skye, is it?" Mercer cackled.

The explorer's manner brooked no further talk, so Skye set about his camp chores. He watered and picketed the horses and inspected their hooves and pasterns. He slid the packs off the pack animals. He dragged the lodgepoles to a level spot where Victoria and Mary would raise the lodge. He unsaddled Jawbone, slapped him on his rump, and Jawbone screeched and bared yellow teeth, and then headed for the spring water and the thick brown grasses nearby, scattering his wild mares just for the joy of it.

"What was that?" Victoria asked.

"He hurts."

"Sonofabitch, so what?"

"His memory is returning. He knows who I am."

Victoria stopped wrestling the lodge cover, slipped close to Skye, and touched his lips. "So do I," she said softly.

Skye plucked up his Hawken, checked his possibles, and walked down the endless coulee. He felt like walking. He would hunt and he wanted to sort things out. But there was nothing to sort out. Whether from pain or fear or something else, Mercer had turned on him and the trip to Fort Benton would not be pleasant. Skye would do his duty, take the man to safety, and endure whatever the man pitched at him or his women. It would soon be over. Skye's responsibility ended at Fort Benton, and then he and his wives could drift south to Victoria's country, his own country now, along the Yellowstone.

It was a quiet afternoon, without a breeze, the sort of breathless weather that comes just ahead of fall. The afternoons were plenty hot, but the long eves and nights made this September time pleasantly cool. He struck a brushy spot not fifty yards from camp and found himself staring at a sleeping grizzly, a brown giant with unkempt hair, sprawled in a bed she had scraped clear under some protective deadfall from cottonwoods. He froze. He studied the trees, looking for one he could climb but there was nothing.

She awakened, sniffed the air, and turned her massive head. He studied the area and found the cub twenty yards off, its head up, watching Skye.

He hurried back to camp. It would not do to camp so close to a grizzly sow.

"What?" asked Victoria.

"Big brown sow down there a bit. Cub with her. Taking a nap. Woke up, sniffed, and didn't like us here."

"You going to kill it?"

"Ten men with ten rifles couldn't kill it, and my gun is the only one in camp. I don't like having horses around here."

Mary was already undoing the lodge cover and letting it slide back down.

"What are you doing, Skye?" Mercer asked.

Skye's temper was a match for Mercer's. "It's Mister Skye, and we're getting away as fast as we can. There's bear."

"Wave your arms and chase him away."

"It's a sow grizzly, not a black. And she's protecting a cub."

"Well, I'm not moving."

Skye ignored that, saddled Jawbone, loaded the packs on the ponies, saddled Victoria's and Mary's horses, and helped the women load.

It came time to load Mercer.

"I'm not going," he said. "I hurt too much."

"Then we'll have to leave you."

"I'm in command here, Skye, and I say we stay. If we leave that bear alone, it'll leave us alone."

"That's probably true. But I'll not take the chance."

The explorer didn't resist when Skye, Victoria, and Mary all helped him up.

"I don't tolerate insubordination, Skye, especially from a degenerate hiding from the civilized world."

"We'll leave you here if you want. You and your robe and your horses."

"I am dependent on you, and loathing every minute of it. Get me to Fort Benton," Mercer said. "Then I can be rid of you and your unwashed wives."

Victoria stared.

Skye led his party up the coulee to the trail. The grasses shimmered in the breeze, and as far as he could see was virgin land. But this little party was no longer harmonious. One man had turned bitter. It was like a great cloud bank obscuring the sun.

Chapter 43

Skye led his party upriver on a well-formed trail over high ground. The world was silent. Barely any breeze sifted through his shirt. He watched distant ravens circle and a hawk soar by, looking for dinner.

Mercer rode sullenly, radiating a heat that kept the rest at a distance. They passed from grassland to hills covered with jack pine, resinous in the midday sun.

He kept a furtive eye on Mercer, whose swollen arms and shoulders were tormenting him with every bounce in the saddle. The man rode alone. The women hung back, and Skye kept well forward. No one wanted to be near the explorer.

Mercer stood it for a while, and then kicked his pony forward.

"How far to Fort Benton?"

"I don't know. Maybe fifty miles. Seventy miles."

"How many days?"

"That depends on you, sir."

"I want a direct answer, Skye."

"How many miles do you plan to go each day?"

"Damn you, Skye, what kind of guide are you? Have you ever been here?"

"Yes."

"Then you should know."

Skye put heels to Jawbone until his horse pulled ahead a

bit. It was better not to respond to a man itching to pick a fight.

"Find a campsite, Skye," Mercer yelled at Skye's back.

Skye nodded. Mercer was fevered and hurting. This was dry country, with desolate shoals of pine collected on slopes and no sign of a spring or river. They would need water for Mercer. Victoria's decoctions were all that made it possible for Mercer to be moved. She had that splendid knowledge of nature's own pharmacopoeia and was making liberal use of it to treat him.

"I want to rest!"

Skye halted. Mercer tumbled off his horse, unable to use his hands or arms dismounting, and headed into some brush.

Skye turned to Victoria. "Any water nearby?"

"River."

When Mercer returned, he glared at the three of them. "Well?"

"We'll follow the next coulee to the river," Skye said.

"Help me up."

Skye and Victoria lifted Mercer. It was not easy. His arms were useless. They handed him the reins, knowing he could barely hold them, and started off once again, Skye leading his company.

A while later they hit a giant canyon running toward the river and Skye turned into it. This was white-rock country, with crenellated bluffs along the skyline.

They reached a flat with a fine cold spring bubbling out of a white cliff, and plenty of brush and trees below it. Skye stopped there. This was as close to paradise as a camper could get and there was the promise of game.

"Go on, go on," Mercer said.

Skye reached up. "Time for you to get some rest. I'll hand you down."

"Go on, go on, damn your cowardly hide."

Whatever Skye did, Mercer contradicted. Find a camp-site. Don't find a campsite. Stop here. Don't stop here. Keep going. Don't keep going. Skye ignored it all.

This was a good place. Skye rode Jawbone around the meadow, finding thick grass for the domestic and wild horses. He checked the brush, finding no bears or other trouble. He returned to the others just in time to hear Mercer berating Mary.

"Keep your greasy hands off me," he snarled.

Mary, who was helping him down, paused.

"Get me off this nag, Skye," Mercer snapped.

Skye stared.

"You do it, Skye. Your women are full of vermin. I don't want them touching me."

Victoria and Mary stopped cold.

"That got your attention, didn't it, Skye?"

Mercer decided he could dismount himself and almost managed. But he lost hold and tumbled into the clay.

"Help me up, Skye."

"I think you can stay right there, sir."

"East London scum. Deserter. Louse-ridden squaws. Degenerate. I thought you were an Englishman. How did I get tied up with this lot?"

Skye resisted the rage welling up in him and nodded to the women. They turned away, collected deadwood, and soon had a fire going.

It was a temptation to leave the man and his horse to fend for himself, but Skye knew he would not. There are obligations and duties and one of them is to get a feverish man to safety, and another is to fulfill a contract. He had promised to deliver this man to Fort Benton and so he would.

They rolled the cursing Mercer onto his robe and dragged him into the shade of a giant willow tree.

Stonily, Victoria began preparing her medicinal tea for

the explorer. She had one bark to calm him and a root to mitigate his pain. Skye wished she had one that would heal his distemper.

Mary heated stones she had collected and placed next to the crackling fire. These would be lowered in a small well-greased leather sack containing Victoria's herbs and water. The stones would bring the water to boil and Victoria would have her tea. They had lost their metal pots in the great fire, and the women were resorting to ancient methods.

It was a splendid day but for the sourness emanating from Mercer. Skye studied the horizons, where puffball clouds rose and marched across the heavens and slid out of sight. The weather would change soon. There were mare's tails high in the sky, a forerunner of change. It would turn cold and cloudy, and maybe rain some. Maybe they would have to put up the lodge if the weather turned. Skye checked the site to make sure it was well above any flash flood watercourse. It was well placed, ten feet above the gully that might carry water in a deluge. He had chosen a good place. That was his business. His skill. His way of life. His communion with the whole natural world had meant survival and safety for all the while he had been in North America.

Mercer's distemper spread like a miasma and Skye and his women steered clear of him, keeping out of shouting range. But in time Victoria had her tea, so she filled a horn with it and carried it to the shade of the willow, where Mercer glared up at her. He sat up, and she held it to his lips because he couldn't use his arms.

"This is an abomination!" Mercer yelled.

Skye heard Victoria responding quietly. She was telling him her tea would comfort him and reduce his pain and swelling.

"Filthy squaw!"

He heard disorder over there and hastened to the willow tree. Mercer's robe was soaked. The horn lay on the earth, empty. Victoria's leather skirt was splattered.

"Get this wahine slut away from me!"

Victoria bolted. Skye stood, staring at the explorer, whose face reflected triumph. The man was enjoying every moment of this.

"Afraid of me, aren't you, Skye. You won't even defend the virtue of your women. I insult them and you don't even respond. I insult you, and you just let it pass. That's because you're a degenerate."

The bright light of day filtered through the willow leaves, giving the shade a dappled, friendly light. But it was not a friendly place.

Skye patiently considered this fevered man's transgressions. "If I respond softly or say nothing, and take whatever guff you dish out, you'll enjoy it. That would mean I'm your servant. If I say anything at all about your conduct, you'll take it as proof that you're a well-born Englishman dealing with an insolent underling. If I don't seem to mind the offenses to my wives, that means I'm a degenerate, as you put it." Then he offered his own mysterious response. "Address me as Mister Skye, sir."

"Mister! Mister! What fun you are, Skye."

"Victoria will try again to give you some tea. It helps. I've sipped it time after time when I needed help. It's an anodyne for pain. It quiets your distemper. You can knock the horn away again or drink up and feel better."

"Don't let that pile of filth in here, Skye."

Skye plucked up his hat and retreated into the clean sun and sweet air. It was as if he had the Black Plague in his own camp, lurking there, impossible, cruel, rude, and full of white men's conceits.

"Don't go over there, Victoria."

She laughed, suddenly and unexpectedly. "White men are such savages," she said.

"I will try to help him," Mary said.

"You'll be abused."

She shrugged.

Mary dipped the hollow horn into the steaming tea and then carried Victoria's potion to the tree sheltering Mercer, and knelt beside him. There was some muffled talk at first.

Skye waited, ready to do whatever was required. It didn't take long. He heard hard male laughter, a surprised feminine response, and she stormed away. The stain of the tea was spreading across her skirts. She was straightening them as she fled.

She stood in the sunlight, tears welling in her eyes, her small fists clenched.

Skye hurried to her and took her in his arms. "You did what you could," he said.

"That ain't it," Victoria said, obviously annoyed at Skye.

"What do you mean?"

"Don't be so blind," Victoria retorted. "He insulted her."

Skye felt Mary collapse into him, cling to him, and felt her tears soak his shirt. Skye held her for a long while but she seemed taut.

Finally, when Mary had calmed, Skye slipped over to Mercer and found him flat on his back on his buffalo robe, his eyes fevered and merry.

"If you touch my women or insult them, I'll kill you," Skye said.

"But why, Skye?" Mercer asked, his eyes bright. "What don't the three of you do each night?"

Chapter 44

As that day waned, so did summer. Skye watched a gray mass rise on the northwestern horizon, and knew the seasons were changing. This land often received an equinox storm and this would be it. Whippets of cold air snaked through the coulee.

The women wordlessly undid the lodgepoles and erected them on the flat, well above the dry watercourse, but they stayed as far from Mercer as they could go. Gusts of air made it hard to raise the lodge cover. Skye wanted to help, but they had always chased him off. They soon tugged the heavy cover upward and pinned it together with willow sticks. Victoria, squinting into the rising wind, began collecting the heaviest rock she could carry and pinned down the lodge. Mary collected armloads of deadwood and stored most of it within the small lodge.

Skye looked to the horses, checked their pickets, released Jawbone to discipline his wild bunch, and headed for Mercer. The explorer had wrapped his robe tightly about him under the willow, and stared malevolently up at Skye.

"Maybe you'll have to drag me into the lodge if it rains, Skye. Then I'd ruin your sport," Mercer said.

Skye wheeled away. He had no intention of sharing his lodge with Mercer if he could help it. But an icy rain would change matters. He would do what he had to do. He would shelter the fevered man even if that man was as loathsome as any Skye had ever met. Not many days past, Skye mused, he had liked the man.

He walked away from the willow to the sound of Mercer's cruel laughter resonating behind him.

There wasn't much to eat. They were down to a little pemmican. Skye knew that the eve of a storm was a very good time to hunt so he pulled his old Hawken from its sheath, checked it, and headed down the coulee hoping to scare up some meat. Jawbone trotted behind, an uninvited guest, but Skye let him come. The horse might be handy to drag a carcass to camp.

The farther he got from Mercer, the better he felt. He worried not so much about Victoria, who was tough, but Mary, who was open and vulnerable to Mercer's cruel taunts. Tonight in the darkness of the lodge he would gather his younger wife to him and simply hold her, and let his embrace tell her all that there was in him to say to her.

He saw the yearling buck frozen across the dry watercourse, its two spikes all the antler it could manage at that age. He lifted his Hawken, aimed at the heart, and squeezed the trigger. The old Hawken barked, its voice lost in the whirling wind, and the young mule deer crumpled where it stood.

"I am sorry," Skye said. "You will give us meat and life."

It was the Indian way to apologize to an animal just killed, and Skye had gotten into the habit of it. It was good, and was a reminder to spare life, take only what was necessary for food.

Jawbone trotted beside Skye across the rocky dry wash and up the grassy slope beyond, where the deer lay. It was dead. Skye's shot had gone two or three inches below where he had sighted, a fault of that particular weapon, but it had killed cleanly.

The young buck was too heavy to lift or drag but Skye was not three hundred yards from camp, so he returned, saddled Jawbone, collected some woven elk-skin rope, and returned to his meat.

It took Jawbone no time to drag the deer, by its hind legs, back to the camp. Skye looked for a place to hang the carcass, wanting any spot other than the willow tree where Mercer lay. He finally settled on a cottonwood near the cold spring. With the help of the women he raised the buck and began work. There was little time before full dark and maybe rain. He gutted the deer, scraped out the cavity, and then butchered a rib roast. It was cold and bloody work and the deepening dark made it dangerous too. But both of the women were with him, peeling away hide, sawing into tender meat, and soon, just before utter blackness overwhelmed them, they collected some venison steaks and ribs, and carried them to the lodge.

Skye raised the carcass several feet higher, and hoped that would discourage uninvited guests. But he doubted that he could lift the carcass out of bear range. It had grown so dark he could scarcely make out the lodge, and he hastened that way, aware that the temperature had dropped in minutes. Just before, it had been a mild summer's eve. Now it was wintry, not much above freezing.

Maybe it would cool off Mercer's fever.

The rising wind made it impossible to start a fire outside the lodge, though that would have been preferable for cooking meat. The sparks from their flint and steel flared and died without igniting any tinder. Victoria, muttering, gave up and headed into the deep dark of the lodge, heaped some tinder under the smoke hole of the shuddering lodge, and nursed the tinder into flame.

The women fed tiny sticks into the fire while Skye

marveled at the bright warmth. One moment the world was dark and alien; now a tentative blaze was blooming in the lodge, casting friendly bouncing light everywhere.

They would need to cook the meat by suspending it over the flame on green sticks. Victoria sliced the bloody meat into thin strips, jabbed sticks into them, and set them beside the small fire. It would take a long time.

Looming out there in the night was the presence of the explorer, the ghost under the willow tree. Skye hoped the rain would hold off. He hoped this night not to suffer Mercer in close quarters. But he knew, somehow, it was a futile hope. There was rain-smell in the breeze and before long the rattle of rain would be heard on the lodge cover. He hoped the old lodge given them by the Atsina would turn the water and had been kept well greased.

It was odd. There in the sweet warm intimacy of their lodge, the world was good. Just outside, not eighty yards distant, lay a man who exuded evil: whose eyes and tongue were evil, whose sweat and spit and urine were evil, whose foul breath was evil. Mercer had not always been that way, but now he was a man unloosed from all restraint.

The rain hit as suddenly as a thunderclap. One moment the wind was eddying; the next, a roar thundered down on the lodge, spitting water through the smoke hole, each drop hissing in the fire.

Skye arose, wrapped a robe around him, and plunged into the night. He could scarcely get his bearings. He headed toward the willow tree, found it, found Mercer sitting against the trunk, wrapped tightly in the robe.

"Come," Skye yelled over the roar.

"Ah, the degenerate Skye is going to let me live!"

Skye whirled at him. "You will keep your silence. If you offend my women, I will put you out. Your fate is yours. Live or die."

Mercer laughed. Even in that darkness, Skye could see those even white teeth all in a row.

Skye helped the man up and then plunged into the driving cold rain. Mercer followed.

"Bloody cold," he yelled.

Skye didn't answer. He was done talking to Mercer. The next words he would say to the man would be, *Get out.* They made the lodge and stumbled into its warmth. The rain was driving at enough of a slant so that little was entering the smoke hole. Victoria had adjusted the wind flaps well, as always.

It had been eighty yards, but Skye's and Mercer's robes were drenched. Mercer stumbled in and Skye pointed to a place at the door, on the right, the place of least honor. This guest in Skye's lodge would not be given the place of honor next to him, at the rear.

"Bloody wet evening," Mercer said. He slid to the ground and cast aside his robe, its pictographs suddenly visible in the wavering light. Then he had the sense to stay quiet.

Victoria fed deadwood into the fire. It flared, and the meat roasting on sticks next to it bled juices. Skye settled back in his damp robe. He was thinking of a fine chill fall, with air crisp and clean, the sun warm on his back, heading toward Victoria's people after depositing this man in Fort Benton. He was thinking of his newfound wealth, a hundred pounds, money to buy a new rifle, some blankets for his women, maybe some spectacles if one of the posts had some ready-mades. His eyesight was changing. It was harder to read and harder to see things at great distances. A hundred pounds would buy him a fine pair of cheaters.

The women busied themselves in deep silence. Neither they nor Skye could escape the presence of that man lying there next to the door of the lodge. Now and then the lodge shuddered under the impact of a gale wind, and always the staccato roar of rain drowned out everything but the thoughts in one's head. The lodge began to drip in a few places, single beads of water slowly collecting, trembling, and then falling to earth. Skye rose, cut some white fat off the meat, let it soften in the heat, and then began rubbing the leaking spots. It did no good. This rain would drive through a pinhole.

The meat finally was brown and hot, and its savory fragrance filled the lodge. Victoria silently pulled a stick free, its slice of meat pendant on it, and handed it to Mercer, who accepted it with clumsy hands. It fell to the ground. He stabbed it and lifted it up.

He cleared his throat. "Mister Skye, Madame Skye, and Madame Skye," he said. "I apologize to you for offensive remarks and equally offensive conduct. Thank you for letting me stay in this lodge."

That was as startling as an earthquake.

"I am very sorry," Mercer concluded.

No one spoke.

Time had frozen.

"Well, eat up," said Skye. "Plenty of meat here, killed a buck, enough meat to fetch us to Fort Benton."

Mercer bowed his head. "We thank thee, Lord, for these thy gifts."

Skye paused. The women stared.

They ate in silence.

Which person residing in that body was Graves Mercer?

Chapter 45

The Missouri River is a tough stream to ford, even at low water. Skye had to get his party across it to reach Fort Benton. He didn't know which ford to use so he followed the trail most heavily worn, and found it winding into an ancient bed of the river and then around a bend to the actual channel where the river sparkled. The adobe fort loomed across the water on a broad flat, its bastions guarding its walls. Lodges were scattered around it.

This trail took Skye and his party upriver a mile and then it dropped straight toward the water's edge close to the smaller opposition post, Fort Campbell. The river ran low now but that was a lot of river between the south bank and the north, and the water wasn't moving slowly, either. It was hurrying here, sucking at anything in its way.

Skye turned to Mercer. "I'm going to have Victoria lead your horse."

Mercer nodded. He had been subdued ever since that night of the storm. His hands were all but useless, and Skye didn't want him trying to rein a horse, especially if the ford involved a drop-off and the horses had to swim a channel. It would be all Mercer could manage just to stay in the saddle.

Victoria took Mercer's reins. Behind them, Mary was herding the packhorses and the wild bunch trailed along at its own pace. They were all on the bank, staring at the icy water, which showed not a ripple that might suggest a ledge or a ford.

"Let me sound it out," Skye said, steering Jawbone toward the cold water. The horse hated cold, laid back his ears until they were flat on his skull, and then minced in, high light steps that splashed water everywhere. The ford descended quickly until water was pushing at Jawbone's belly, and Skye was keeping his feet high and forward. The flow threatened to push Jawbone off balance but the determined young animal bulled ahead and then suddenly the bottom rose. They could traverse the river there without swimming.

Jawbone clambered up the north bank and shook himself so violently he almost tossed Skye to the ground. Skye watched the others plunge in, start a hundred-fifty-yard passage. It went smoothly. Mercer kept his balance even when his horse began sidestepping under the pressure of the flow. Victoria made it, but her moccasins and lower skirts were soaked. Mary had a hard time dragging the packhorses into the river, and in the middle, when the current was wetting their bellies, two of them bolted forward, the packs rocking on their backs, the lodgepoles and lodge careening behind them. The wild bunch simply swam. Then, suddenly, they were on the north side, water rolling off them, thoroughly chilled. The sun had lost its summer's potency and now was a wan and subdued friend.

The American Fur Company post stood downriver, its flag flapping quietly. Skye had worked for the company back in the beaver days. Now its business was buffalo hides and peltries of all sorts.

There it was. Civilization of a sort. It basked in the bright light, snugged under yellow bluffs. It had been erected maybe fifty yards back from the riverbank.

Every hour of every day the clear cold water of the

Missouri, fed by mountains upstream, hurried past on its way to the Gulf of Mexico. For Yanks, it was passage home. For Skye and Mary and Victoria, it was just another big stream.

This was a sleepy afternoon hour. Skye saw no one moving through the scatter of lodges around the post, or anyone entering the massive, and wide open, front gate. He rejoiced. His long hard journey was done. He would soon have Mercer settled there, awaiting transport downriver. Then Skye and his wives would stock up. Five hundred dollars was a lot of money. It would buy rifles and blankets and tools and kettles and horse tack. It would fix his family's fortunes for a year or two.

He had done it: taken the London explorer where he wanted to go, shown him what he wanted to see, saved him from fire and other disasters, nursed his health, shared stories. Skye had faithfully done what he was hired to do and had done it well. Now would be the harvesttime, a farewell to the adventurer. They would outfit and head south. Who knows where? Victoria's people, maybe. Fort Laramie, maybe. There was work to be found at Laramie, on the Oregon Trail. People wanted guides with them.

But all that could wait. He watched Victoria wring out her skirts, Mary smooth the doeskin and let its water drip away. He watched Mercer, who sat quietly, eyeing the fur post a mile distant.

It was time to move. Skye led them along the riverbank, past the opposition post, over level meadow worn by the passage of countless horses. They reached the scatter of sagging buffalo-hide lodges that dotted the plain. Then Victoria urged her pony forward until she was alongside Skye.

"Sarsi!" she said.

He studied the lodges, not certain of it. "You sure?"

"The same ones!"

Skye was suddenly grateful they were in the powerful reach of the post. He slowed until Mercer caught up.

"Victoria says those are Sarsi lodges and likely the same bunch. It makes sense; come south to visit the bones, come here to trade before going back to British possessions."

"You don't say! Will they . . ."

Mercer's sudden fear was palpable.

"Posts are safe ground. They won't touch you."

"But, Skye. Sarsi? Protect me! What if . . ."

"Mister Mercer, sit up. We'll ride in there and you have nothing to worry about."

But as they approached and were recognized, they had plenty to worry about. Sarsi swiftly congregated around them, their gaze on Mercer, following along with every step of the horses, even as Skye's party pierced the great gate and entered the post's yard, a small rectangle girt by high adobe walls, the warehouse, and other rooms.

They were the same band of Sarsi, all right. There was the headman, he who had a secret name, and there were the others. Mercer began chattering and shivering. He seemed half wild. A few of the post's engaged men materialized from various rooms, their dress drab compared to the brightly clad young Sarsi.

Skye looked for trouble and saw none. The Sarsi stood in deep silence, their gaze riveted upon the one back from the dead. Skye spotted a man who might be in charge.

"Can anyone talk the Sarsi tongue?" he asked.

"Yes. And you?"

"Skye, sir. Mister Skye."

"Ah! I should have known. I'm Ezekiel Lamar. Let me fetch the trader."

"Good!"

Skye hoped it might be Alexander Culbertson, who had

governed this post for a generation but had retired to Peoria, Illinois, with his Blackfoot wife Natawista. Culbertson had come upriver frequently since then, sometimes bringing the annuities the Yank government gave to the Blackfeet, sometimes bringing the post its resupply from the American Fur Company. Officially, he was still the post's factor even though he was largely an absentee one and in charge of all the upper Missouri posts for American Fur.

But it was no man Skye knew: a beefy Scot, Andrew Dawson.

Skye dismounted and shook hands.

"What brings these Sarsi in here? Why do they stare at that man? Who's this fellow?" Dawson asked.

Skye made the introductions. "Mister Mercer is the explorer, here from London, collecting stories."

"Fine, fine, but why are these Sarsi staring at him?"

They were indeed staring, their gazes riveted on Mercer, who shrank under them, rubbing his arms, and looking about ready to leap off his horse and flee.

"Long story, Mister Dawson. But would you do the honors?"

The trader nodded.

"Tell their headman, whose medicine is to reveal no name, that Mister Mercer lives. See what the man says."

Dawson conducted a considerable conversation with the headman, using no hand-sign that Skye could follow.

"It seems that his people sacrificed Mercer to the spirit of the big bones but here he is. That can only mean that Mercer has powerful medicine. They have gathered here to see the medicine man, dead and now alive, bearing the bruises of his death. This makes not a bit of sense to me, Skye."

"I would be most grateful if you called me Mister Skye, sir."

"Yes, yes, your reputation precedes you. But here they

are. There's Mercer. And now he's the object of their veneration, it seems."

Mercer began laughing wildly. "Bloody savages, almost murdered me, left me to die, killed my teamster too. And now they think I'm bloody immortal. Hang the whole lot, I say, string every one up, send them all to hell."

Skye started to object but Dawson suddenly loomed large, standing close to Mercer and his horse. "Mister Mercer, they're in awe of you. They have their own beliefs about life and death. They are friends of us all. There will be no more of that talk. They trade here. Friendly people, friends of the Piegans and Bloods. Do not make trouble for yourself."

"Make trouble for myself! My God, man, they made trouble for me! They tied me up and left me to perish! Hang the lot!"

Dawson was not pleased. He turned to the headman and spoke at length and listened at length. Then he turned to Mercer.

"You are absolutely safe among them."

Mercer nodded curtly, dismissing the Sarsi. "When can I get transportation downriver?"

Skye stared. Mercer had turned abrupt and demanding again, his gaze imperious, his manner imperious, his posture lordly. He was addressing underlings and servants and rabble.

"No one is traveling that I know of, sir. Not until spring."

"Then find me a boat! I'll go myself!"

Dawson smiled. "Mister Mercer, dismount, I pray. Come join us for a supper. We've much to discuss."

"I will not abandon this horse until these vermin are driven out of this place."

Dawson saw how it was with Mercer.

"They wish to place gifts at your feet. They wish to be

touched by the man with medicine. They wish to bestow a name, He Who Has Come from the Bones."

Skye helped Victoria and Mary off their ponies and began putting his horses into the pen with the help of Lamar. Out in the yard, Mercer sat his horse, gazed imperiously at the young Sarsi quietly collected around him, and the minutes ticked by without any change at all.

Chapter 46

Sundown resolved the impasse. Always at that hour the gates of Fort Benton were closed, and Lamar or another of the engaged men invited any tribesmen within the post to leave.

"Sundown, sundown," the man bawled, and wordlessly the Sarsi retreated into the quiet flat surrounding the post. Mercer watched imperiously, and when the last Indian walked through the massive gate the explorer stepped down, handed his horse to the nearest employee, and headed toward the chief trader's handsome house, which snuggled against one wall of the fort.

Dawson was sitting on its veranda, smoking his pipe, keeping an eye on events. Skye had settled his wives in a small room reserved for women. He would stay in the company barracks along with the engaged men and now sat beside the chief trader. A peace descended on the post along with a sharp chill.

"I shall want a room, sir," Mercer said.

The tone instantly troubled Skye. The man had slipped back into his imperious ways.

"I will be pleased to accommodate ye, Mister Mercer," Dawson said. "The gentlemen bunk just over there."

"A room, Mister Dawson, a room."

"I wish we had one, Mister Mercer."

"You do. Your dwelling here has several rooms."

"This is a private home, sir. It houses either the factor or the chief trader." Dawson suddenly relented. "Ye may have one, if ye wish."

Mercer smiled, a row of white teeth again. "You are a gentleman, sir, welcoming me in this manner."

Dawson rose from his hand-hewn chair, went inside, and a moment later a handsome young Indian woman materialized.

"Letitia will show ye the way, Mister Mercer," Dawson said.

"Good. Just the ticket. What time is dinner, Dawson?"

Mercer scarcely noticed the woman, who picked up the parfleche containing the small sum of Mercer's possessions. But Skye knew intuitively what Dawson's household arrangement was. She was a tall, striking Blackfoot.

Dawson considered it a moment. "We will put food on the table whenever ye are ready, sir. Shall we say an hour?"

"I shall want some duds, Mister Dawson. I shall write you a draft. Let us proceed to the trading room, eh?"

"Can it wait until morning, sir? The room is closed and the day's accounts are in the ledger."

"Surely you can accommodate a man in need of a few items of clothing. I haven't a shirt to my name."

Dawson stirred unhappily. "Very well," he said.

He knocked the dottle from his pipe, left it at his chair, and headed across the yard to the trading room, which was on the river side of the post next to the great gate. He turned to Skye:

"Long as we're about it, is there anything you need?"

"Yes, sir, if you'll accept Mister Mercer's draft."

Mercer hurried up. "What's all this? A draft?"

Skye nodded. "I'll get it."

Mercer laughed oddly.

Skye headed toward his gear, stored in a heap beside his bunk, found the robe with Mercer's debt instrument painted

on it, and headed for the trading room. Dawson had lit an
oil lamp, which cast yellow light into the far corners. This
was a pungent, pleasant place, with thick blankets stacked
on shelves, bolts of gingham, trays of cutlery and arrow
points, sacks of sugar and flour, barrels of hard candy, a rack
of new and used rifles, strings of bright beads, plugs of
tobacco, and a hundred other items that Indians bought in
exchange for the furs and pelts they heaped on the trading
counter each day.

The explorer had already heaped clothing on the hand-
sawn counter when Skye pushed in, carrying his heavy
buffalo robe.

"A dollar for a ready-made shirt? This is madness! I won't
pay it," Mercer was saying. He had a blue chambray shirt
in hand, waving it so that the sleeves danced.

"They come a long way, Mister Mercer. At great risk. The
company loses ten or fifteen percent of everything in tran-
sit, every year. We've had entire boatloads vanish in the
river."

"Bosh. I've heard that before. What you do is charge the
most you can get away with, and offer the least."

Dawson took it easily. "Yes, and the Opposition upriver
does just the same. And if they charge a bit less than we do,
or pay a bit more for pelts, we feel it here."

Skye waited quietly while Mercer complained about most
of his merchandise. The courteous Dawson nodded and absorbed it. Then the chief trader dipped a steel nib pen into
an inkpot and scratched out a bill of sale. Then he pulled a
pad of preprinted debt instruments.

"It comes to eighty-seven and forty-two cents, Mister
Mercer. I've filled out this instrument. What we need is your
signature and the name of your bank, and your endorsement
of the clause that says there will be collection fees."

"It's Barclay's Bank," Mercer said. "All right." He signed, initialed the proviso.

Dawson, finished with Mercer, turned to Skye. "What may I do for you, my friend?"

Skye hoisted the robe to the counter, fleshed side up, and showed Dawson the carefully worded instrument painted there. A hundred pounds on account, and signed by Mercer.

Dawson studied it. "A rather unusual draft, wouldn't ye say, Mister Skye?"

"There was no paper."

"Come hither, Mister Mercer. Here's a draft for a hundred pounds on the back of this robe, and it carries your signature. I can cut this out of the robe and ship it to St. Louis, and the company can forward it to London for collection. But I should like your guarantee."

"What's this! What on earth is this?" Mercer glanced at the robe, over which he had spent so much time. "A damned forgery, sir."

Skye felt his blood rise. Suddenly he knew, he *knew* what was coming. "You guaranteed it," he said tautly.

"Guaranteed what? What did I get? You almost got me killed. I got nothing out of the whole trip. You were so incompetent you got me into a fire, failed to protect me from savages, and bungled everything so badly you're lucky I even talk to you."

Skye choked back his mounting rage. "Did we agree on a hundred pounds and did I bring you here safely?"

"We agreed on nothing! I had my own men. I didn't need a bloody guide or some lice-ridden sluts. You claptrap bunch of parasites hung on like leeches, wanting handouts, charity. I couldn't find any way to get rid of you."

Skye tried hard to stay calm. "It's owed me, sir. You were taken where you wished to go."

4 RICHARD S. WHEELER

Mercer grinned. "My gawd, a confidence man of the wilds!" He snatched the inkpot and carefully poured a black puddle over his painfully wrought signature on the leather.

Skye sadly watched the ink spread and sink in.

Dawson looked solemn. "The company asks two-bits a sheet for paper, but I'll donate a sheet. Here, Mister Mercer. Draft a payment for Mister Skye."

"This bloody impostor? This bloody degenerate? For what? Tell me, for what?"

Skye thought to count the ways. For saving Mercer's life just a few days earlier. For showing him strange things, introducing him to strange people worth writing about. For keeping a prairie fire at bay. For putting food before him. For showing him how to survive without white men's tools. For sheltering him from weather. For nursing him through grave illness. For translating among the Indians. For his knowledge of the American West.

But the man was leering at him, triumph in his eyes, enjoying every moment of it. Here was the man, his soul naked.

Dawson intervened. "Mercer. I don't think I'll let ye out of here until ye pay the man."

Mercer's smile was dangerous. "Oh, is that how it is, eh? I'm going to enjoy this. Come along, Dawson. Let's have dinner. Just you and I, eh?"

"I have invited Mister Skye and his wives."

"Squaws? That reprobate at my table?"

"My table, Mister Mercer."

Dawson herded them out of the trading room and locked it with a heavy iron key. He spotted one of his men in the yard and beckoned.

"Mister Mercer will sleep in the yard, or wherever he wishes, and I want you to extract his things from my bedroom."

"Yassum," the man said, hurrying to the house.

"Mister Skye, bring your ladies to dinner."

Skye nodded. The chief trader was the absolute master of this small world and Mercer was finding that out. "We are pleased to join you, Mister Dawson."

"What? What?" yelled Mercer.

"Ye have chosen not to enjoy our company, Mister Mercer. Ye may bed where ye choose. The manger, in the horse pen, makes a good bed, I'm told, if ye pitch in some hay first."

"Oh, Mister Dawson, you think you're god out here, lord of your own world. How little you know."

Dawson ignored the threat. Skye nodded, knowing that no dinner with the chief trader could ever assuage the loss he was undergoing, the demolition of dreams, the brutal discarding of ordinary justice.

Dawson clapped Skye on the back. "A little of Scotland's finest will work a little warmth into ye."

Skye was in no mood for a little warmth. But the darkness evaporated as he fetched his wives from their room. They met him at the door, refreshed, beautiful, and glowing in the evening light.

"We'll be dining with the chief trader," Skye said.

"Something's wrong," Victoria said.

"I'll tell you later."

They were swiftly welcomed into Dawson's home. Mary had never seen a furnished home, every shining piece of furniture in it brought upriver. There were oil portraits of Dawson's ancestors on the wall. She marveled. Victoria had seen such things but that didn't allay her curiosity.

"Where's the explorer?" she asked Skye.

Dawson replied. "He chose not to join us. He chose to bed down out in the horse pen, madam. Welcome. Now, madames, and Mister Skye, shall we have a wee drink, just to whet the appetites?"

They had more than a small drink. They had more than they should have and the next day they didn't remember much.

And the next day they heard that Mercer had been forcibly booted out of Fort Benton at dawn.

Chapter 47

Gone. Skye learned about it the next day. Graves Duplessis Mercer had hied himself to the Opposition post, Fort Campbell, discovered that an express was leaving for St. Louis within the hour, traded his nags for passage, and hopped aboard a large voyageur's canoe paddled by an engaged man and floated down the river.

If all went well, Mercer would be in St. Louis within a month and reach London in November. Skye absorbed that numbly. Now there was nothing in his purse and nothing to show for hard and dangerous service to the explorer.

He found his women loading the packhorses.

"He's gone," Skye said.

Victoria nodded stonily. "We should not have taken him to the bones. The spirit has repaid us."

Skye plucked up his robe and headed for the trading room, and waited patiently while Dawson completed a trade with a Blackfoot woman, a robe for some hanks of beads.

"I owe you for putting up the horses," he said. "Would this robe do?"

Dawson shook his craggy head. "It would not do, and put it away, man. The bastard skipped, did he? It is a bad thing. I'll send word down the river and maybe something'll come of it."

"We're going to head south," Skye said.

"Not for a little bit."

Skye waited grimly. The chief trader would ask for some labor to pay for horse feed.

"A man gets stiffed, and it's like an arrow through my own heart," Dawson said. "I can lend you a little bit. Pick what you need."

"How'll I pay you?"

"Some robes at any American Fur post. Or one month as an engaged man. After that it's nothing but a bit of book-keeping."

"I'll do it. Thank you, Mister Dawson."

"Ah, ye'd do the same, would ye not?"

Something unspoken passed between them that made them brothers of the wild.

Skye needed powder and shot, a few tools, an axe han-dle, and then he indulged in four-point blankets for the three of them, and a bit of foofaraw for the ladies, particularly some bright blue beads they cherished.

Dawson smiled. "It comes to nineteen and a quarter, and ye needn't be in a hurry about it."

"I'm always in a hurry to pay debt."

"That bastard," Dawson said. "He'd better not show his face in any post run by American Fur."

The women had his small caravan readied in the yard and even had saddled Jawbone, ignoring the laid-back ears and snarls emanating from the young stallion.

He handed them their four-point blankets and blue beads. Mary ran her hand over the smooth nap of the wool, her eyes shining. Hers was cream with blue bands at the ends; Vic-toria's red with black bands.

"Dammit all to hell, Skye," she said. "Dammit all."

They forded the Missouri and rode into a golden autum-nal day, with the air crisp and sweet. The cottonwood leaves were starting to turn. The sun's light sparked off the river. The land seemed clean without Mercer in it.

Leisurely, they drifted south toward the land of Victoria's people, enjoying the rhythms of the horses under them, the cold nights and bright days. Nature was bountiful. Skye shot a buffalo cow and they spent a few days jerking meat and making pemmican, employing chokecherries growing abundantly everywhere. They feasted on hump rib and tongue, watched Jawbone's wild ones fatten, fleshed and tanned the buffalo hide, repaired the old lodge, but always kept a wary eye out for marauding war parties or hunters.

They found the Kicked-in-the-Bellies band of Victoria's people on the Yellowstone, enjoying a fall hunt when the hair was thick and the animals were fat. They wintered that year north of the Yellowstone beneath the Birdsong Mountains, peaks sacred to the Absarokas, a range that stood apart and north of the main chain of the Rockies. Lewis and Clark had called this place Rivers Across because streams debouched into the Yellowstone from north and south there.

It was a good winter, with many guests filling their lodge. Skye and his wives had no trouble preparing a dozen buffalo robes, which would more than pay his debt to the fur company. The cold sometimes enveloped them, and they were forced to bury themselves under a heap of robes in their lodge. The women braved frostbite to collect deadwood to keep the lodge warm. There was never enough wood to keep the north wind at bay. Between the hard work, the elders told stories and passed along the story of the Absaroka people to the next generation. Sometimes they talked about the mysterious bones. Young men prepared themselves for manhood, learned the arts of war, made their vision quests, so they might receive the spirit helper who would guide their lives henceforth.

Skye worked all winter at subduing the wild horses, and eventually he succeeded. These he gave to Victoria's family; they would return the favor if Skye was ever in need of horseflesh.

When spring was just around the corner and the ground was still frozen so passage was not difficult, Skye packed up his goods and his lodge, and began the long trip south to Fort Laramie on the Oregon Trail. Times were changing and Skye knew it would not be long before this life, lived so amiably by the Crows, would come to an end. Not far away was the time when these people would be placed on reservations. He wanted not only to prepare his women for that but to make a living. The idyll would not last. The time when he could take his rifle out upon the plains and feed and clothe himself with it, and care for his women with it, was drawing to a close.

He knew a certain sutler at Fort Laramie, a Colonel Bullock, who often arranged matters for wayfarers who needed a guide or a responsible party to escort them west. Skye could do that. Many an old trapper was doing it. The Sublettes, Jim Bridger, Broken-Hand Fitzpatrick. It was a living.

So Victoria hugged her family, Mary hugged them too, and they started toward the army post far away on the North Platte River. He knew it well. It had been a fur post for decades before the army bought it and turned it into a supply base and entrepot on the Oregon Trail.

They worked their way around the Big Horn Mountains, up and down giant shoulders of land, ever southward. They were a solitary family on the move across an endless and hollow land. But one day they struck the Platte and turned east along its well-worn trail, the very trail that had carried thousands of Yanks to the Oregon country, a flood of them each summer. But now there was not a soul on that worn trail. In the mornings the trail was ice-bound and hard; by afternoons soft and exhausting.

Then one afternoon they reached rough country and found themselves in the military reservation of Fort Laramie, crammed into a jaw of land between the Platte and the Laramie Rivers. Mary and Victoria saw the soldiers, cavalrymen in blue, details collecting firewood to feed those hungry stoves or working the cavalry mounts in close drill, or constructing outbuildings.

"They're all the same damn blue!" Victoria said. "Can't tell one from another."

"Army likes it that way," Skye replied.

Victoria grunted. How could a warrior fight if he was the same as every other warrior?

Other groups were receiving instructions in firearms and the tactic of volleying from drill sergeants. A great many of the blue-bellies were caring for horses. A farrier corporal was operating a smithy where horses were being shoed for spring campaigns.

They progressed toward the old adobe and log post, entered a yard, and Skye suddenly headed toward a log structure with a great verandah at its front.

He watched Mary and Victoria absorb all of this. They had little experience with the Yank army, and most of it bitter. Both of his wives were suddenly subdued, aware of power, aware of some sort of medicine in the flapping flag and guidons.

A hitch rail had been planted before the post's store, and there Skye dismounted, tied the other horses, but let Jawbone stand. That horse would not submit to tying, but neither would he roam.

The sheer ugliness of the beast drew the gazes of some of the cavalrymen, who flocked close.

"Better not get too close," Skye said.

"Does he kick?" asked one.

"No, he kills."

The trooper laughed uneasily.

A door clapped, and a black-suited, silver-haired gent boiled out on the verandah. "Well, bless my eyes, sah, it's Mister Skye and his ladies!"

It was Colonel Bullock, the Virginia-born sutler, retired from active service but still in the West because he liked it.

He invited the Skyes to his bailiwick, and they walked past burdened shelves and bags of goods that would put any trading post to shame, back to Bullock's cramped office, where he hastened to supply chairs for his guests.

"Well, Mister Skye, sah, you have magnified and amplified my day. It is good to see you! Now, introduce me to your lovelies."

Skye did. "This, sir, is my dear Victoria and here is my beloved Mary. They both speak excellent English and in that I am most fortunate."

"Worthy wives for a worthy gentleman," Bullock said. "Mister Skye, sah, your reputation abounds. You honor us by your presence. There's not an officer here who doesn't know of you. There are stories told of Mister Skye around every campfire, in each barracks, among all the guests and travelers who drift through this post."

Skye nodded, embarrassed. What had he done that was different from what hundreds of others had done?

Mister Bullock slid his monocle into his eye, much to the alarm of Skye's ladies. "In fact, sah, I have a bundle that arrived by army courier just a week ago. Addressed to Mister Skye, Fort Laramie. It's from the American Fur Company agent in London, I believe. Monsieur Borchgrave. The company does a heap of business there, you know, all through Borchgrave. Well, sah, he sent the bundle here, confident that it would wend its way to you before the year was out. Let me get it."

Bullock dug into a pile of materials behind his desk, and

extracted a well-worn package wrapped tightly in butcher paper, its surface begrimed by months of slow passage from England to this far corner of the known world.

Skye reluctantly cut the twine, fearing bad news from his family. But when at last he popped the wrapping off, he discovered a number of newspapers. The *London Times, Manchester Guardian,* and several others. Nothing more. Intuitively, Skye knew what he would find within each one, and he wasn't sure he wanted to read any of them.

Chapter 48

Skye leafed through the yellowed papers. Those around him sat solemnly, awaiting what was to come. These were dated from late November, 1857, to early December. These were about five months old. Mercer had found swift passage to London.

He tried to read but his eyes had changed. He could barely read the print, even at arm's length.

"Do you have some ready-made spectacles, Colonel?"

"A tray of them, Mister Skye."

Colonel Bullock swiftly produced a tray of wire-rimmed eyeglasses, which Skye sampled one by one, and finally settled on one that fit his right eye perfectly and his left eye less sharply. He jabbed the wire around his ears, and found himself able to read. He would buy these as soon as he could.

"This is the *London Times*. It says its correspondent, Graves Duplessis Mercer, is freshly returned from North America, where he spent a season beyond the borders of the Republic, observing strange native cults, odd natural phenomena, and things unknown to the civilized world."

Victoria was frowning. Mary looked rapt, marveling that Mister Skye could examine the marks on this paper and turn them into words and ideas.

"'In late summer, I witnessed an extraordinary event: a renegade Briton, a deserter from the Royal Navy named Skye, lives like a lord of the wilds beyond the borders. He took it upon himself to acquire a second wife, though his first is perfectly serviceable. Of course I use the term wife loosely, this being a purely whimsical transaction involving female slavery.

"'The brief transaction proceeded as follows: Skye, a shaggy, degenerate sort who fashions himself a Beau Brummell of the wilderness, adorned with a battered top hat that he believes grants him status, transacted an arrangement with the girl's father, a Shoshone savage with several such daughters to spare. I wasn't able to ascertain the exact purchase price, but young wives go for a pony or two, or maybe a blanket, or a hank of beads. At any rate, the arrangement complete, our wilderness Brummell, with no evidence of so much as a trim of his tangled gray hair, collected this second wife, and hied his way to his ill-kempt lodge, a conical tent made of skins.

"'Now, here is the mystery: what are the arrangements among wives and this rustic Lothario? The odd cult of the polygamous Mormons, currently settling around the great lake of salty water, is clear enough: each lady has her own household and the master of these domestic nests visits each in turn. But here, hundreds of miles from civilization and law, matters are somewhat different. This master of two wives has but one lodge and was not seen evicting either wife at any hour.

"'Now, among savages it is a matter of prestige for a headman or chief to acquire several of these willing wives. It is quite common to find an important man possessing half a dozen wives, and these fill his lodge along with his numerous offspring. When the lodge is too small, his wives build him a larger one, so that some lodges house a veritable crowd of all ages, including a few parents and grandparents as well as squalling infants.

"'The wives prefer it because it lightens the burdens of

maintaining the lodge. It falls to women in these rude societies to do the heavy labor. They collect firewood, slaughter game brought to them by their hunter-mates, flesh and tan hides, fashion clothing out of them, produce not only the daily meals, but also the preserved food, dried meat known as jerky, or a mixture of berries, shredded meat, and fat called pemmican. What's more, the senior wife in these savage societies gets to sit beside the master of this odd household, and is called the sits-beside-him wife. She is the boss; the junior wives, often her sisters, are at her absolute mercy. So just what advantage this wretched Shoshone woman gained by being sold into this carnal servitude is not easily fathomed. Nonetheless, on this occasion she was all aglow, having been sold by her father for a fancy bride price and handed over to the degenerate who bid for her.

"'Skye himself, though once an Englishman—he claims to be born in London but I could not detect it in his voice—has now given himself over to the wild lands and wild practices to be found out beyond the rim of the known world. . . .'"

"Liar," said Victoria.

"You must tell me what those things mean," Mary said.

Colonel Bullock was caught between two impulses, the first to gaze politely on Skye, and the second to guffaw. Skye saw the colonel subside into cautious politeness.

"Let us not pursue this any further," Bullock said, stiffly.

"Do you make me to be a degenerate, Colonel?" Skye asked.

"Of the very worst sort, Mister Skye."

"And am I a rude Beau Brummell?"

"Unsurpassed, sir."

"I note that Mercer alludes to our private arrangements but dodges the matter."

"Censorship, Mister Skye. He could not very well discourse in a public newspaper on the subject without incurring the wrath of the crown's censors. It might even get him in trouble with the church, or the sedition laws, or the blasphemy rules."

"Yes, you have it, Colonel."

"What the hell is this stuff?" Victoria demanded.

Skye turned to her. "Mercer is aching to tell his readers in London that he thinks I . . . ah . . . take my pleasure of both of you, but he can't quite manage to say it."

Mary sat straight in her chair. "Ah, Skye! I wish you would!"

She began to howl happily. Skye was amazed. He thought such a sentiment might rise from Victoria but in Mary it was an astonishment.

Skye suddenly felt the need to steer the conversation elsewhere. That was all too intimate for Colonel Bullock's ears, no matter that the post sutler was an old friend.

"Ah, I shall see about the rest, here," Skye said, rattling papers to restore decorum. "Let me see. There's a piece or two about the prairie fire. It seems he and his teamsters might have survived it without loss if the renegade Skye had not insisted on staying put rather than outrunning the flames."

Victoria looked grim.

"Find the story of the bones," Mary said.

Skye opened several more, and finally found one that might be about bones.

"A Savage Shrine on the Missouri River" was its heading. Skye delved into it, and soon found absorbing material:

"'When the wretch Skye, who was always angling for a small tip with which to buy whiskey, suggested he could take my party to a place on the Missouri River that was sacred to the savages in the area and a great mystery, I immediately was all ears. This was a place of fossil bones buried in sandstone, and known but to a few tribesmen, it having been hidden for aeons from others. He would probably demand a shilling for it, but I succumbed, always on the search for new discoveries.

"'"What sort of religion?" I asked, fearful that we would be invading someone's Westminster Abbey.

"'"Why, lord love a duck, matey, it's just a heap of bloomin' bones and they have invented mighty stories to explain them," says this rude philosopher of the wilds.

"'With that we proceeded across uncharted country, the oaf getting us lost time after time. I had to straighten him out by employing a compass. But in due course we did strike that mighty trench, after crossing a vast country never before seen by Europeans. Once we hit the river valley, he sobered up enough to know where to go, and in due course we ended in a sinister little flat, shadowed from the world by huge bluffs, and there, under a protective ledge shielding the bones, were the remains of an ancient beast, protruding slightly from the stone.

"'I measured these extraordinary remains, a task which alarmed the older of Skye's squaws, who thought I was somehow violating the spirit whose bones these were. With some sharp questioning, I ascertained that her people believed the bones were those of a monster bird, and out of the beak of this bird her people had come to populate the world. So she considered the bones to be those of her grandfather. Other tribes, it seemed, had similar explanations.

"'Indeed, these bones were unusual. The skull measured more than six feet in length from snout to the back of the tiny cranial sheath. There were monster femurs and tibia, and the remains of a long tail. One three-toed foot was visible. I took detailed measurements, employing a buffalo hide for a ledger because my journals were destroyed by fire. In due course, having studied the bones, I discerned that they were of a lizard nature. Not a new species, but a sport, a singular anomaly of nature, in which a creature becomes something other than what it was intended by God to be. And so this ordinary lizard simply grew to truly gargantuan proportion and it was easy to see how the superstitious savages could turn the bones into the remains of their gods.

"'Now about this time, a party of Sarsi, a small band living in crown possessions to the north, came to visit the bones, and this brought peril to me, as they considered my scientific observations to violate some savage taboo of their own. If that lout of a translator, Skye, had been more accurate I might have been spared the ordeal to come, but in fact he was in his cups and botched the whole business and I soon found myself a captive . . .'"

"I have heard enough," Victoria said.

Skye had his fill too, and folded up the papers. "I'll read these some other day. Perhaps you would keep them for me, Colonel."

"May I read them?"

"Just don't believe them."

"How could I possibly believe them? Were you paid?"

"Not a cent."

"Were you tagging along looking for a handout?"

Skye stood. "They all have their stories, don't they? We invent stories to explain everything. Even the way we cheat others."

"If I find clients for you to guide, the first thing I'll do is make sure you'll be paid."

"That would be helpful."

Skye knew the colonel would devour the British papers and during the next days would brim with questions, and maybe some sly humor too. That was all right. Mercer was writing more about himself and his reputation as a great explorer than about the world he had come to explore, and Bullock would understand that.

Skye wondered whether this bundle of half-truths and untruths would hurt him, and decided they would. Truth sometimes hurts, but all lies eventually hurt someone or something. There were people in England who might still remember him, and what would they think now? Mercer had not only cheated him, but had wounded him. But it was not something to brood upon. Mercer was far away.

"I shall entertain myself with these," Bullock said. "Are these to be kept secret?"

"No. They're published."

Bullock considered a moment. "The temptation is to make a fool of Mercer. All I have to do is show these pieces to a few people. But when I reflect on it, Mister Skye, I think I will say nothing. For your sake, and for the sake of your ladies."

"You are a friend, Colonel."

"I mean to be, sah. You are a man of reputation, and I mean to honor it."

Chapter 49

They erected their lodge in a quiet place up the river a bit from the post, out of sight of the fort and its blue-shirts and its gossip. He was at peace. That night, in the sweet dark, he and his wives lay on their backs looking at the stars parading across the smoke hole.

"Mister Skye," said Mary, "I have something to tell you."

"Yes, Mary?"

"We have made a child."

"Made a child? You'll bear a child?" he asked, full of wonder.

"Our child," she said. "Yours and mine. And Victoria's too."

"You lucky bastard," said Victoria.

Skye thought that was as good a verdict as any.

Author's Note

Graves Duplessis Mercer is based on the real Sir Richard Burton, British explorer, ethnographer, translator, and journalist. In 1860 Burton visited North America, focusing on the polygamous life of the Mormons in Salt Lake City. Burton eventually published forty-three volumes dealing with his explorations, provided thirty volumes of translation, and was fluent in many languages. He was fascinated by the mating practices, rituals, and cults of various tribes and peoples in the Near East, Africa, and Asia, and recorded these in his diaries and journals for many years. He so affronted Victorian sensibilities that he was forced to live the last decades of his life away from England. When he died in 1890, his wife burned the journals.

North Star

A Barnaby Skye Novel

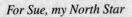

For Sue, my North Star

Prologue

Jawbone was stumbling now and then, but Mister Skye didn't mind. The ugly old horse still had a great heart and was as eager as he always had been. Skye was hunting high in the Birdsong Mountains this November day, and on the trail of two elk whose hoof prints unwound in the rain-dampened earth.

Except for a dusting of snow on the craggy peaks, there was little sign of impending winter. The snow and cold of the uplands had not yet driven the elk and deer down the long shoulders to warmer and safer habitat. A sharp wind cut into Skye's leathers, chilling him, but he had endured harsh winds and rain and snow and cold for half a century, and he could endure this wind too. But it made his bones ache.

Skye led an empty packhorse with a sawbuck saddle on it. If he killed an elk, he could carry most of it back to his wives and his lodge far below by quartering it and loading some of it on both horses. If that happened he would walk. He wouldn't mind that, either, because he would be bringing good meat to Victoria and Mary, his two Indian wives, and there would be some to give to the elders and the widows in the Kicked-in-the-Bellies winter encampment on Sweet Grass Creek.

He rode easily, his old mountain rifle cradled in his arm, ready to use. He knew the two elk were not far ahead, in this sheltered upland valley. Most of the timber was well below.

He didn't see the bear until it was too late. The giant, humpbacked grizzly had been denning, clawing its way into a steep hillside to prepare for its hibernation, but now it backed out of the hole, swung around, eyed Skye and his horses with small pig eyes, and didn't hesitate. It lumbered down, amazingly fast for so big an animal, an odd hiss slipping from its mouth, and Skye suddenly had no time at all. Skye swung the octagon barrel of his rifle around, but the bear rose up on its hind legs, even as Jawbone screeched and sidled away and the packhorse broke free and fled.

The blow knocked Skye clear out of his saddle, and another caught Jawbone and raked red furrows along the old horse's withers. Jawbone reeled sideways, stumbled, and then fell on Skye, who had landed on his shoulder. Skye yanked his rifle around, pointed, and fired. The rifle bucked, slammed into his ruined chest, but it caught the huge brown grizzly in the shoulder, plowing a red furrow into the caramel-colored hair.

The grizzly paused, snapped at the wound on his shoulder, where blood was swiftly rising into the hair, and then whined. It paused and licked its wound, mewling and crying like a child, sobbing and licking. It sat on its hind legs, upright, furiously working at its wound, unable to slow the blood or subdue its pain, its sobbing eerie and sad.

Skye watched from the ground. Jawbone had clambered off of him and stood, head down, shaking with his own pain. Cruel red lines gouged his flesh. Skye's own shoulder ached, and he bled from a few places. He had no wind in him, and his arms didn't work, and he had trouble breathing. He couldn't lift his rifle even if he needed it again. He would need to make his old body work, or he would perish here. He would need to return seven or eight miles to the

Crow camp, and he would need to do it without help, for there was none.

The bear, still whimpering, limped toward its almost completed den and pushed into the hillside. Skye knew it wouldn't come out until spring. Skye lay helplessly on the grade, staring at the blue heavens, which had mare's tails corduroying it now. The weather would change soon, maybe for good. He tried to inventory his body. He had a few scratches but those six-inch, lethal claws had only scraped him. They smarted but weren't bleeding. Wind eddied into the slashes left in his leather hunting coat. His pain made him faint, but he was used to pain. A half a century in the North American wilds had brought him more than his share of pain, but also inured him to it. But he could not lift his arms, or twist his body, or get himself to his feet.

He knew that time would help. He eyed Jawbone, who stood with legs locked, head low, going through his own torment. The blood on Jawbone's withers had stopped flowing and was coagulating in the cold. He couldn't see the packhorse, but it wouldn't be far away. Time, little by little, restored some control of his limbs to him, and he rolled onto his side. It was then that he saw his bearclaw necklace lying in the grass. It had been given to him when he was young, a sacred symbol among his Absaroka People of his bear medicine. His brothers were the grizzly bears, and during the whole half century he had never shot a grizzly, nor had one ever attacked him, until now. Maybe his bear medicine had finally failed. This ornery old grizzly male had come at him, and he had shot it. And now the medicine bond between Skye and the bears had been shattered. Skye gathered the remnants of the necklace. The giant gray claws had been separated by blue trade beads, and the whole ensemble had never failed to win admiration and respect among those who examined it. He picked up the beads and claws that had scattered when the necklace was torn from his chest, and these he tenderly folded into his coat pocket.

That was oddly disturbing to him. It was an ending, a shattering of an ancient bond that had made the grizzly bears his brothers and sisters, his spirit helpers in time of need. He lay quietly another while, but the wind was picking up, and he knew he would either get up now or not ever get up. He found his rifle and used it for a crutch, slowly pulling himself to his feet. He stared around the serene upland valley, its grasses brown now, its aspen bare-limbed, the gray rock and tawny earth naked to the elements. He saw his packhorse grazing downslope, dragging its lead line, undamaged.

Jawbone limped close and gently pressed his muzzle into Skye's chest. They were a pair, and they had survived yet again.

It would be a long walk back to the winter camp, but Skye knew he would make it, would have to make it. There would be no elk roasting over the fire this night.

Chapter 1

One bitter dawn in 1870, Barnaby Skye realized he had not lived in a house for fifty-two years. He was thirteen years old when a press gang snatched him off the cobbled streets of East End, in London, and he found himself a powder monkey in the Royal Navy. For seven cruel years he had lived in the bowels of frigates, and after that, in the wilds of North America. But never again in a place with a kitchen and hearth and bedroom and parlor.

He wrapped his blanket tight about him against the brutal cold, crawled out the door of his buffalo-hide lodge, and slowly made his way over trampled snow to the red willow bushes, where he might find relief. More and more, as he aged, he needed to get up in the night. No matter that he was inured to discomfort after a lifetime spent out-of-doors. It was getting harder and harder to live in this fashion, among his wife Victoria's Kicked-in-the-Bellies clan of the Absaroka People, drifting through the seasons to wherever the buffalo ran or the berries ripened. Twice a night now, sometimes more, he stepped into cold, or heat, or rain, or snow, or wind. He had no choice.

He stumbled once as his moccasin plunged into a soft patch, but finally reached the willow brush away from the lodges, where he waited and waited for the slow stream to begin and comfort to return to his belly. He was sixty-five, and feeling it. The changes in his body had come on cat feet, and he had missed or ignored them, until now. The cold stung his cheeks and bit his ears, no matter that a dense gray beard now covered his weathered face. By the time he was done, he was cold.

A deep silence pervaded the winter camp of the Crows on Sweet Grass Creek. Dawn was simply a rose streak to the southeast, the beginning of another brief day. No one stirred. A few frosted ponies stood desolately, tethered close to the lodges, their breaths cloudy. Most of the lodge fires had died, and in this last hour before the camp stirred, the people lay buried in buffalo robes in skin tents that did little to turn the hard fist of winter.

Skye headed back to his own lodge, one of twenty-three here, and to his women, Victoria of the Absarokas and Mary of the Shoshones, who were used to his night-stirring and ignored it. But as he returned to his home, which was nothing but a thin buffalo hide that walled the bitter cold from those who lived within, a long-suppressed idea arose in his mind.

He needed a home. A real white man's home, with a hearth and stove, with beds and chairs and tables and windows and doors and escape from murderous winds and blistering heat and vicious deluges. He didn't want to live Indian style anymore. Victoria's people, the Absarokas, lived in lodges that they moved from time to time, and took their old and sick with them until the day came when the old and sick could be moved no more. And then the old ones were usually left to die, propped up under a tree with a little food and water. Sometimes they were left to die alone, in weakness and pain and a terrible cold infiltrating their bodies, because there was no other way.

Skye had watched the Crows leave old Indians behind. These were fathers and mothers, grandmothers and grandfathers, uncles and aunts. People he knew. Usually that was the choice of the old ones, who knew death was coming and accepted it. They asked to be taken apart and their wish was always granted. They wished to sing their death songs and be left behind, given to the sun and the wind and the spirits. It was something that the old themselves requested when the time was right and they were ready. Winter was more merciful to them than summer because they did not linger. Sometimes, though, when the village was in peril of death or disease or catastrophe, the old and sick were simply abandoned because there was no other way. There might not be horses or travois to carry them. So they were left on the spirit road, left to begin their long walk on the star-strewn trails of the heavens. Skye understood all of that, and yet he could not reconcile himself to it.

Now, in the middle of a bitter night, he hoped he might grow old and die in a house. As much as he had adapted to Victoria's ways, there was still the Englishman in him. And now the Englishman was hurting.

He pulled aside the flap with fingers already numb and stepped into the thick gloom. Above, in the smoke hole, ice-chip stars still were visible. A layer of frost coated the inside of the lodge cover, as well as the liner. It had been formed from human breath. His wives didn't stir. It was almost as bitter within as outside. He found his bed, two thick robes on the ground to protect against the terrible cold rising from it, and another he pulled over himself. But he scarcely warmed even after waiting for the thin heat to build in his bed.

He had ignored the rheumatism for years, but now he could not. Most of him hurt most of the time. He wasn't sure that rheumatism was the proper word, but it was the only word he knew for pain that radiated across his back, pierced his arms and legs, annoyed his joints, and often made his wrists and hands hurt so much it was hard even to chop wood. Whatever it was, it had sneaked into his life almost without his knowing it, and now he could not ignore it any-more. He wasn't so old, but his hard life had taken a toll. In the Royal Navy he had sometimes been colder and more miserable than he ever had been in North America. And here in the American West, he had waded icy rivers, been caught in blizzards, been soaked by cruel rains, and spent many a sleepless night shivering in wet clothes that could not be dried. And now he hurt night and day.

The heavy robes did little to comfort him. He lay impa-tiently, waiting for the day to begin. His wives would build up the fire and hope that the downdraft of wintry air wouldn't dampen the flames and fill the lodge with acrid smoke. He looked about him, suddenly dissatisfied with this thin layer of buffalo hide keeping the elements at bay. He wanted a house. He had never had one of his own in all of his years, and now he wanted a comfortable, solid, safe, spa-cious home, ten times larger than the largest lodge of the Absarokas, planted firmly in his own soil, surrounded by gardens and livestock and fields of grain and pastures.

He felt guilty. For decades Skye's home had been with Victoria's people, and sometimes with Mary's Shoshone people. Wherever they drifted, he drifted with them, as much at home on the plains or foothills or mountains as they were. Home was wherever they were, not just a white man's building on white men's land, surrounded by white men's neighbors. For the Crows and Shoshones, home was where the land offered meat and roots, lodgepoles, handsome mountains, rushing creeks, soaring eagles, and safety. They had never divided up the land, surveyed it, sold off pieces. It was all one to them. And it had been all one to Skye, too, for all these seasons.

But this bitter January morning, he knew he needed a home. He wondered how Victoria would feel about it, and how Mary would. They were traditional Indians, and home was wherever they happened to be. If Skye were to settle somewhere, how would Victoria feel about leaving her people? Home, for her, was being among her people: her clan brothers and sisters, the women who shared her day scraping hides or gathering roots or making moccasins. Home for her was a migrating neighborhood, not a place.

He peered at her, resting still and quiet and oblivious. She had slowed too. He had caught her straightening up after scraping a hide, caught the stoic look on her face that told him she ached in her shoulders and her back. She worked ceaselessly, as did Mary; there was no surcease from toil for a tribal woman. Even the very old women sat quietly working with awls or needles, making what needed to be made. Maybe Victoria, Many Quill Woman to her own people, might welcome a comfortable log home, as long as it was close to her own band. He would ask her after the day opened.

Mary, twenty years younger, was by nature more accepting, and Skye sensed that she would slip into a new mode of life well enough. But a certain sadness clung to her, and she seemed to pass through her days without the fire and joy that had drawn Skye to her when she was a beautiful Shoshone girl called Blue Dawn, a granddaughter of Sacajawea. Ever since Skye had sent their son, Dirk, east to be schooled, Mary had settled deep inside of herself, living within her own private world. Skye had often agonized about it, but there was nothing he could do. His son was gone.

Skye lay in his robes, wondering how he might get a house. He had no money and none of the skills that might earn him some. He was the son of a London export merchant, and ill-equipped to plow and harrow and plant. The beaver were trapped out; game was steadily vanishing, killed by the white men. The buffalo were doomed, though

Skye hoped the herds might prosper for another twenty or thirty years. But a man who hoped to build a home would need a way to sustain himself. Raise horses? They'd be stolen by the first raiding party. Raise cattle? Better, perhaps. Some cattle, horses, a garden, poultry, some grain fields, maybe these would support a man with a house.

Skye lay quietly, staring out the smoke hole, watching the gray light brighten. If he were young, he might manage. A young man full of energy could build his own house of log or rock or sawn wood, and mortar together a hearth and chimney. He could fell the logs and bark them and drag them to the house behind a stout horse, and notch them and jack them into place, one by one. He could split shakes and shingle the roof. He could raise the outbuildings, fence pastures and paddocks, sink a well, cobble together a homestead, plow the virgin earth and plant grain fields and gardens, scythe hay and fork it to a barn loft, feed it out to his horses and cattle in the winter, and somehow get along. But he was old now. Just when he needed a home, his strength had fled him.

Then he discovered Victoria, lying on her side, staring at him.

And as if by some mysterious communication, Mary yawned, sat up, and swiftly tugged a soft, thick robe about her, even over her jet hair. Their breaths steamed. Not even a lodge with an inner lining could stop the cold this morning.

"You have something to say," Victoria said.

She always read his mind. Skye sat up, clamped his ancient black top hat over his locks, and tried to warm himself.

"I do," he said. "After we are warm and have eaten."

"You are leaving us," Victoria persisted.

It had been her nightmare all these decades. Someday the

white man would grow tired of living the way her people lived, and walk away. How many times, over four decades, had she leaped to that? How often had he tried to assure her, only to run into dark flowers of fear.

"No," he said. He would say more when he was ready.

She threw off her robe. She was already in her doeskin dress. She wore it all winter, but in the summer she dressed as brightly as a flock of butterflies.

This time he watched her closely, and saw that rising from the bed of robes took determination. Not that she was old or feeble. Not that he was old. But no mortal steps into subzero air without determination and courage. The very sight of her struggling to wrap a blanket around her, and make for the bushes, hardened his resolve.

Only Mary didn't seem to mind the numbing cold. She slipped out of her robes, eyed him shyly—he always marveled at her shyness, even after many years of marriage— and plunged outside with little more than a thin summer blanket carelessly over her shoulders.

He thought to start a fire, even though Victoria would scold him. It was not men's work, she would snap, but she would be secretly pleased that he was thinking of her comfort. He made himself collect some of the kindling outside of their lodge, and with his skinning knife shaved bits of it, and added a pinch of gunpowder from his horned flask. He would not wrestle with flint and steel this morning, not with some trading post lucifers at hand. He struck one, watched the powder flare, and watched the tiny flame lick the kindling and catch. By the time the women returned from the brush, there would be a thin warmth in Mister Skye's lodge, and the nine-foot circle of his home would begin to welcome life.

Chapter 2

There wasn't much to eat. For two moons the village hunters had been stymied by cold so terrible that no one could leave the lodges. It was bad enough to look after the frostbitten, starving horses. No, this was a time to huddle around fires, sing songs, play the stick game, and endure.

Mary set a kettle of snow to heating, and added pemmican and some prairie turnips, to make a breakfast stew. The lodge warmed a bit. The frost coating the lodge liner melted and dripped onto Skye and his women. The fire gathered muscle and drove heat outward and smoke upward.

No one spoke. But they all knew this was a portentous moment, and that this day Mister Skye would say a thing that would affect their lives. He was always Mister Skye. Friends and family addressed him that way because he required it. When he had arrived in the New World, fleeing the crown's minions, he chose to give himself that title. He would be Mister Skye, and not just Skye, and so it had been for decades. Others laughed at him, thought it was pretentious, but he was always *Mister,* and if you wanted any sort of commerce with him, you would address him as he required.

With a good stout fire going, the lodge warmed, except underfoot, where the cold rose straight through the robes lying on the clay. The thin warmth helped, but both Skye and Victoria clothed themselves in red Hudson's Bay blankets even so. Mary ladled out the stew; it might not be a king's feast, but it would fill them. When they were done with the morning food, she silently gathered the bowls and horn spoons and wiped them clean.

They were waiting, he knew.

But he was stumble-tongued, as usual, and hardly knew where to begin.

"I want a home," he said. "For all of us."

"Is this not a home?" Victoria asked.

"A comfortable home," Skye said.

"Is this not a good lodge?" she persisted.

"I'm getting old," he said.

"Well, so am I, dammit. And so is she."

Skye ran bony fingers through his matted gray hair. He wore a trimmed beard now. His hands were stained to the color of walnuts by a life out-of-doors. He gazed at Victoria, who was dark and suspicious and already angry. Mary, with little gray in her glossy jet hair, waited patiently, her obsidian eyes masking her thoughts.

This was already brewing into a domestic fight.

"I don't mean away from your people," he said to Victoria. "Somewhere close by."

This resulted in a terrible silence.

"I have a great need—I'll call it a hunger—for a house. A refuge against wind and rain and snow and cold and a hot sun."

He knew that these women considered their lodge to be just such a refuge, and often it was. Some periods of the year, a lodge was a marvel of comfort. But in the blistering heat of summer, and the howl of winter, it could be miserable.

"It is harder and harder for me to live like this," he said. "I need chairs to sit in, a warm bed to sleep in. I need to stand up. I want walls that keep out the wind. Walls and a roof to keep out the cold and the heat and the rain and keep me warm. I would like a hearth, and a cast-iron stove, and maybe an oven. I would like to sleep off of the ground, so my legs and arms don't ache."

He saw not the slightest response in either of his wives.

"I am not as patient as your people," he said. "My own people, the English and the Americans, live in houses when they can. Log ones, or wooden frame ones such as we've seen in the mining towns. Glass in the windows. Roofs of shakes that carry the rain away. I'm hurting a bit and this would help me. I'm not planning on leaving this earth anytime soon. I want to be with you. I'd like to grow old in a little comfort. Maybe with our pastures and a garden and a woods where we can get fuel. A few cattle, a few sheep, some chickens to feed us. I'd like to build a shelter for Jawbone, now that he's hurting, and give him his own meadow, and lots to eat."

The silence returned and clung there.

"Where would this be?" Victoria asked.

"Near your people," he said. "Here we are, near the Birdsong Mountains. I would like to build my home over in the next valley, the Shields River, where everything is at hand, and everywhere the eye gazes, there is glory."

White men were calling the jagged and isolated mountains just to the west of this winter camp the Crazy Mountains, but Skye much preferred the Crow name, the Birdsong Mountains. What could be a more beautiful name for an isolated range of sharp peaks?

"But we would live there alone," she said.

"We would have many Absaroka visitors, and maybe we could care for your clan brothers and sisters and children, and they could care for us. Maybe they could help us build this place, and we could have them stay with us and take care of things."

Something dissolved in Victoria's spirit. Skye knew that

if she could have some of her people around her, she would be pleased. Home for her was not a lodge, it was a village.

"Sonofabitch," she said. "I'm going to have a big house. Biggest goddamn house anywhere. Big enough for my whole clan."

It dawned on Skye that if he built a house, it would have to hold thirty or forty of Victoria's relatives. But that was fine with him. There was a way to do this. He would ask his Crow friends for help, and together they could erect a house and the outbuildings, and then farm or ranch with him.

"I have always wanted to live in a house," said Mary. "A white man's house is a place of great medicine."

"And it would be a place for some of your Shoshone people too," he said.

She smiled so sadly that he felt stricken. Anything that reminded her of her Shoshone people also reminded her that she had seen very little of them as the winters and summers rolled by. Skye and his wives had lived among the Crows.

"This is women's work," Victoria said. "We will build the wooden lodge."

"It's men's work, and hard. We have to fell the trees, bark the logs, notch them, use a drawknife to flatten the top and bottom sides, split shakes, make a puncheon floor . . ."

"What is this floor?"

"Logs carefully split down the middle which will make a floor, curved sides down, flat sides up."

"Dirt ain't good enough for you?"

Skye was tired of clay; tired of walking on it, tired of the bugs crawling out of it, tired of mud and grass. "We can do better," he said. "If the right kind of rock is around, we can use flagstones for a floor. Wood is more comfortable."

A house. Nothing but a dream now, in the middle of deep cold and near starvation.

The more Skye talked to his wives, the less he hurt. It was as if the promise of comfort was sweeping away all the rheumatism in his body. He was aware that his women were studying him, receiving unspoken knowledge from his conduct. Let them study him. The more this great vision filled his imagination, the younger he felt. By the time he began building his house, he would be a young man again.

"I am thinking about the Shields River valley, just north of the Yellowstone," he said. That was a lush broad valley west of them, near the great bend of the Yellowstone. There would be running water, meadows for grazing stock, ample pine and cottonwood and willow and aspen.

"That is a good place," Victoria said. "The People visit there every summer. Magpie always makes great noises when we are there."

The magpie was Victoria's spirit helper, and she received occult wisdom from her communing with the insolent and raucous black and white bird.

The Shields stretched northward from where it debouched into the Yellowstone, through open country with the Birdsong Mountains rising to the east, and a great range white men were calling the Bridgers rising to the west. Skye had passed through that country many times. Some places might offer grander vistas, but no place offered so much of what the earth could provide.

And there was something else:

"The Americans are talking about giving the Crows a homeland south of the Yellowstone," he said.

"We got a homeland!" Victoria said. "What the hell is this?"

Skye dreaded what he had to say. "They say they want to settle your people on the land south of the river."

"How do you know this?"

Skye wasn't sure where he had heard it. Long ago he had concluded he could do little about the Americans flooding through Crow country en route to mining camps. For a few years they came up the Bozeman Trail, until the great Sioux chief Red Cloud stopped them, defeated the United States Army, and forced the Yanks to abandon the trail. Skye had made some money guiding wagon trains over that trail, through some of the most dangerous country in the West, but then the traffic stopped, and so had his income. So once again he lived as the Crows did, migrating from place to place, following the buffalo, defending their land against the Siksika and the Lakota. But someone, somewhere, told him the United States government had plans for the Crows, and they would be confined to a reserve. It was, he thought, the finest piece of land on the continent, and teeming with game, so there was solace in it. But it all heralded great change for Victoria's people, and for himself.

The Shields River country he would call home would be just north of the proposed reservation. That ought to suit Victoria, and it ought to suit the Yanks. They surely wouldn't boot him off the land he settled. Or would they?

"I don't know it," he said. "But the place I have in mind wouldn't be on that land."

"They make invisible lines, and say this is mine and that is yours," Mary said.

The world was changing so fast that Skye barely understood it himself; his Indian wives would have even more trouble with the future.

"First warm weather, we'll go and start," he said.

"Leave the People?"

"Find a place. I may need to ride into Bozeman City for tools."

"You gonna build this big damn house yourself?"

Skye considered the ache in his limbs and the way he got out of breath these days. "I'll need help," he said. "I can't do it alone. And Dirk's gone away."

Mary's wan smile appeared again, concealing her sadness.

"You're too damn old to chop down trees," Victoria said. "I'll maybe get the whole Kicked-in-the-Bellies to come do this."

"Maybe I should talk—"

"You leave this to me," she said.

Skye felt warm enough now to begin his day. He pulled a fur cap over his head, wrapped himself in a greatcoat made of buffalo hide, and pushed through the flap into the bitter air.

Jawbone stared at him. The old gray stallion was frosted from front to rear. Icicles dangled from his frozen lips, and from his belly and mane and tail.

Skye walked to his great medicine horse, fed it some cottonwood bark Victoria had cut, and leaned into Jawbone's withers.

"You and I are going to live out our days in comfort," he said.

The old horse stood mutely, alarming Skye. He noticed yesterday's meal lying untouched on the trampled snow.

Jawbone hadn't greeting him this morning, as he usually did.

Skye stared at the ugly gray, and Jawbone stared back, and everything was wrong.

Chapter 3

It was what did not happen this cold morning that worried Skye the most. Every dawn, for as long as Skye could remember, Jawbone had greeted him by butting his head into Skye's chest. It was a ritual. Jawbone would butt him, and Skye would yell at the horse, and Jawbone would butt him again just to let him know who was boss. That was their communion. But not this gray dawn.

Skye ran his gloved hand under the old stallion's mane. Something was terribly wrong. He studied Jawbone, realizing that the horse's long winter coat concealed the great hollows along his spine. The horse was starving and cold and listless.

He remembered how Jawbone had come to him seventeen years earlier, an ugly little colt that didn't behave the way horses behave, finding ways to be obnoxious. But in some mysterious way, Skye knew even then that this mustang that had appeared out of a wintry nowhere and he were mysteriously connected, and that they would share a life. For years, Jawbone had been a feared and admired sentinel, one-horse army, and protector of Skye and his family. He had also become a legend among all the plains tribes; even the enemies of the Crows hallowed and dreaded Jawbone. The horse annoyed white men so much that several had tried to kill him, but Skye had growled them off. Other white men had simply laughed: never had they seen a horse so misshapen and degenerate, with such a stupid look in his eyes.

Now the horse stood quietly, its head lowered, its back to the wind. As usual, it had posted itself near Skye's lodge. But the green cottonwood bark that Skye used to sustain Jawbone lay untouched in a scatter on the glazed snow.

Jawbone's teeth were no good anymore. Seventeen years of ripping up sandy prairie grass and masticating rough bark and chewing on dirt had worn them down so that the incisors didn't cut and the molars didn't grind. The tools in his jaws were worthless. It was a common malady in old horses, and why they slowly starved to death. Skye pulled his gloves off and grasped Jawbone's head. Usually the old horse would have snarled, but this time he just stood and let Skye run his finger between the horse's lips. He probed the incisors and found them blunt and rounded. The molars were flat and worn. What teeth were left were almost useless. Jawbone was dying, not from disease but from hunger.

In settled places there were some remedies. In Skye's own England an old horse could be fed warm sweet mash that could sustain an animal with bad teeth. But a good mash required rolled grains and molasses. There was nothing like that in this winter camp of the Crow people. There wasn't even any prairie grass. Only the bark, painfully harvested each day.

Skye felt the clawing of anguish.

Jawbone was not very old, and had more good years in him. He was a little lame, but eager and ornery as ever. Skye didn't ride him much anymore. It was enough to have Jawbone with him, guarding the family, enjoying the life they had fashioned. Jawbone was as much a part of his family as his wives.

Skye ran his gnarled hands over the animal, discovering shocking hollows under the coat, feeling the corduroy of ribs. Jawbone stood stolidly, and that in itself alarmed him. Jawbone was not usually stolid about anything.

"You and I are old, mate," Skye said.

He ducked into his lodge and found the women staring at him. They had heard him.

"I need a blanket for Jawbone," he said.

Wordlessly the women set to work. But there wasn't much to work with. Victoria found a large piece of buffalo hide that had been in the lodge cover until it grew too soft, and had saved it for moccasins. This would make some belly bands. There ought to be a breast band too. A blanket could be sewn to them. It would take a day.

Skye watched them cut the leather, cut thong, and fashion a blanket there in the confines of that small lodge. He kept the fire going, and tried to be helpful, but they ignored him.

"I'll build a barn. I'll build a stall for Jawbone. I'll get some grain and molasses from Bozeman City," he said. "He'll be warm and he'll have some sweet feed. I'll keep him going just as long as I can."

He caught Victoria staring coldly at him. The Crows would let a horse die, because death was a part of life and because it was good for old creatures to die. This was his white man's instinct, keeping the old medicine horse alive.

All that wintry day the women made the horse blanket, using their awls on the leather and lacing the straps to the blanket. Late in the afternoon when the cold was thickening and the twilight was vanishing, they finished. They nodded to Skye. Quietly he collected the blanket and carried it into the bitter twilight, and found the horse standing nearby, its head low, its legs locked. Victoria braved the cold, and between them, they threw the white and blue blanket over the old horse and tied the belly bands. It worked well enough. The blanket hung over Jawbone's back, covered his withers, and tumbled over Jawbone's hollowed croup. The chest band would keep it from sliding backward.

Jawbone lifted his head. Surely the horse would begin to feel some warmth now, a thin life-preserving warmth. Surely this great-hearted horse would survive the winter now, and never face a brutal winter like this one again.

It was growing dark. The winter night stole over them and drove them into their small lodge, and then Jawbone was outside alone. Skye glanced about the village, and saw not a soul out-of-doors. Smoke rose reluctantly from the lodges, and then lowered under the weight of heavy air. He felt almost as cold as Jawbone, and hurried in. There was not much firewood, but it was too dark to get some.

No one spoke. The women drew their robes tight and lay quietly in the dusk, and when the fire threatened to go out, Skye added a few grudging sticks of cottonwood limb. Tomorrow, no matter what the weather, he would need to cut a generous supply.

Skye could not sleep that night. None of them had eaten, and none wanted to eat. Skye and Mary and Victoria lay wrapped in blankets wrapped in robes, and still the cold pierced to them, through the lodge cover, through the layered robes that protected them from Father Winter this subzero night. He knew as he lay in the darkness that the women were awake too. If he had said something, they would have responded.

He heartened himself. He thought of that blanket warming Jawbone, good wool holding the heat in, protecting the vital areas, lungs and heart. Jawbone would be all right. Tomorrow he would try to grind up the cottonwood bark into tiny bits, the sort that Jawbone could swallow without grinding the bark with his useless old teeth. Tomorrow would be better. They had given Jawbone a lease on life.

It proved to be the longest and coldest night in Skye's

memory. Outside, there was only the silence. He itched to go out there, help the horse. He thought to bring the horse into the lodge, but the lodge was too small and the door hole too low. He dreaded the sound of a thump, the sound of Jawbone giving up and caving in. It was too black to find the bushes that night, so Skye did what he had to, just outside of the lodge. He did not see the horse.

Sometime in the small hours an understanding came to Skye, and he stared bleakly into the utter dark. He saw no stars up in the smoke hole, only unremitting blackness. There was Jawbone beside him, his flesh warm to the touch, his lop-eared gaze upon Skye, his muscles rippling, his mocking joy at the very business of being alive. There was Jawbone, waging his war against rival mustang stallions, stealing their mares, dancing his victory dance on every ridge. There was Jawbone, his hooves murderous when white men collected around him.

"Stay away from him," Skye warned.

"Does he kick?" they asked.

"No, he kills," Skye said.

The gawkers had stayed away.

Dawn came reluctantly, and as soon as Skye could see, he threw aside his robes, wrapped his capote around him, and plunged into the obscure light. He didn't see Jawbone. The horse was not at his usual post a few dozen yards from the lodge. Where had Jawbone gone? He peered into the murk, discovering nothing. Impatiently he circled the lodge, feeling the snow squeak under him. He hunted for Jawbone, dreading to discover some dark lump sprawled on the white snow, and could not find him. Maybe the cottonwoods, then? Had the horse blanket revived Jawbone's appetite? Was the medicine horse off in the thickets, gnawing at twigs, wolfing dead leaves and stalks and bark? Was Jawbone simply drinking from the steaming creek?

He could not know. It would be an hour before enough light would collect for him to find Jawbone. He squinted into the gloom, knowing he must wait, and that he must gather wood and stir the fire and blow on coals until the tinder caught, and warm the lodge and comfort his wives.

He slid into the lodge, more by instinct than by vision.

"He is gone," Victoria said.

"He's not there," he said. "I think he's in the woods."

"He is dead," she said.

"No, he's warmed up and the blanket is helping him."

She turned her back to him, which was always her way of saying that he wasn't listening to her.

After a while it was light enough. A grudging fire was warming the lodge. Its smoke wasn't rising, and they coughed now and then. It was time to find the horse. He pulled his capote over him, pulled the hood over his gray hair, and stepped into the deep silence of predawn. Now he could see. The woods were a dark blur. The village lay quiet in the menacing cold. The air stung Skye's cheeks and burrowed into his moccasins and sliced at his legs.

He saw no living thing. The horse would be deep in the snow-drifted woods. It was a little warmer there than in the open. Skye hiked into the silent web of cottonwoods and willows, the skeletal branches patching his vision. But he saw not a glimpse of Jawbone. He did not see any of the village horses here, but he didn't expect to. He wandered helplessly among the copses of trees, but Jawbone was not present.

Now at last the village was stirring. Old people, huddled deep in blankets and robes, were heading toward the willow brush. The sky blued, and then the rising sun caught the tops of the cottonwood trees, making them glow. But he did not discover Jawbone, and felt an odd and haunting worry.

Jawbone was gone.

Then Skye knew. The great horse wanted to do his dying alone. This was the stallion's final gift. Skye would never see the husk of the great horse after life had fled.

Skye understood. He lifted his arms toward the distant bluff and acknowledged what he knew, and then turned slowly to the lodge. But not before the people of the village caught it all, knew that Jawbone was no longer among them, and knew that Skye and Victoria and Mary had lost a mighty friend. They watched, all of them bathed in morning light.

He stood at the lodge door, watching the sun illumine the ragged foothills, and then slid inside.

"Goddamn," said Victoria, and threw her arms around Skye, and wept into his capote.

Chapter 4

Even before the April sun had pummeled the snow into the earth, Skye knew what he must do. He would find a good way to grow old. Jawbone's wintry death had made it urgent. Jawbone, far from old, was gone. What might Skye's fate be?

He was suddenly aware of things he had ignored. His vision was changing, and he could hardly focus on things close at hand. His long-distance vision wasn't as bad, but it was changing too. He could still hunt. He could defend himself—for a while more. He felt well enough, except for the rheumatism that afflicted his very bones.

Most of those he knew in the mountains were dead. Joe Meek had headed for the Oregon country to farm in a placid valley. Gabe Bridger was ready to settle on a Missouri farm and spend his days enjoying life on his front porch. Others, like William Bent and Tom Fitzpatrick, had become Indian agents for the American government, struggling to help tribes cope with the onslaught of white men. For all of those men of the mountains, the United States was home, and most of them had headed back East.

But not Skye. The United States was not his home. British Canada was not his home. There was no home to go to, no village or farm waiting for him, no relatives or friends or family. His only home, over a long life, had been Victoria's people, and wherever they drifted, so did his hearth and kith and kin. And yet there was a home, a place where his heart sang and his spirit was at ease, and that was the Yellowstone country. Somehow, in the midst of all his wandering across the American West, he had come to love the stately river of the north.

Maybe home would be the valley of the Yellowstone, a place still rich with game, filled with rushing creeks, pine forests, and breeze-tossed meadows. It was all the heartland of the Crow people. Montana was being settled west to east, the mining camps in the western mountains little islands of European life, while the plains, where Skye lived, remained a vast hinterland of untouched, unplowed, unknown country. That is how he wanted it. Maybe there would be a home for him after all.

One late April day he proposed to Victoria and Mary that they head west to look for a place to settle. The very idea, settling down, seemed odd to him, but he spoke it.

"No, dammit, you go alone, Skye," Victoria said.

That was unheard of. Through all of their years together, Skye had traveled with his women.

"You go now," she said crossly. "This is something you got to do."

"But it would be your home . . ."

"I'm in my home."

"Go, Mr. Skye," Mary said softly. "You go make a place for us. We will make a home with you. I have no other lodge in my heart."

Skye knew there would be no arguing with them. He knew from the sharp tone of Victoria's voice that their decision had been made and it would not be revoked. They wanted him to find a place where he might grow old in comfort. And they believed he had to make these choices without consulting them.

It wrought an odd sadness in him. He peered at his determined ladies, who sat in their warm lodge, and felt himself being torn from them. It was out in the open now: he, the European, could not possibly live to happy old age in their Crow or Shoshone fashion. Skye's roots and their roots were too different to bridge this last great gulf in their lives. He had lost his medicine horse this winter, and now his wives were building a wall between them and him.

This wasn't going well. He was saying to them that their ways weren't good enough for him. Long ago, Mary had hoped that when her and Skye's son, North Star, grew to manhood he would welcome his aged parents and Victoria into his lodge, and would care for them when they grew feeble. But that dream had shattered when Skye had sent his son away to be educated. Now there were no sons or daughters who could care for Skye and his women.

He left the next morning riding an ugly ewe-necked gray mare. He was partial to ugly horses, the sort that white men laughed at and Indians put in their cook pots. But she was good and faithful and had heart. He tugged behind him a mule laden with buffalo tongue and pemmican, cookware and blankets and robes, a duck-cloth sheet for shelter, and his fine Sharps rifle.

He wasn't going far. The Yellowstone country he hoped to call home stretched west forty or fifty miles from upper Sweet Grass Creek, where his Crow band had wintered. He would hunt for the mystical place he saw in his mind's eye. It would be a good place, well watered, sheltered from the north winds, with handsome views of the mountains, plenty of pine and cottonwood, rich with game. Maybe there would be a place on this earth to call home, a place for a homeless man.

His women stood sternly outside his lodge, seeing him off, never smiling, somehow understanding the gravity of all this. Nearby, his Crow friends and villagers watched silently. He had said his good-byes to Broken Head and

Sleeps In Rain, two of the headmen, and now he hurried the mare across the soft earth of spring, leaving the prints of his two animals behind him. Then he topped the ridge west of Sweet Grass Creek, and paused to look back. But his wives had vanished and the others had returned to their daily tasks. Victoria and Mary would give him no excuse to change his mind and return to the comfort of the lodge.

Soon Skye felt alone as he made his solitary way across a snow-patched prairie divide and into the Yellowstone Valley, where snow and earth mottled the landscape. The birds of summer had not arrived to trill their songs, and Skye rode through a powerful silence unbroken even by breezes. Or was he only getting deaf?

Uneasily he surveyed this corrugated land at the base of the Birdsong Mountains, and saw no sign of life. This was Indian country. Few, if any, white men ventured into it now, two years after the great Sioux war chief Red Cloud had banished the Yank army from this homeland of the plains tribes. The Yank army had lost that war, and didn't much talk about it. Skye didn't mind. Red Cloud's gift to the Crows was to permit them to live their traditional life a little while more.

Skye tugged his soft elk-hide coat tight against the cold, which penetrated to his flesh wherever it could worm its way past his armor. Victoria and Mary had fashioned the coat and quilled it and added a hood, and made gauntlets to go with it, and given it to him for warmth and comfort. He wore their moccasins on his feet and their leggings on his legs. These days he wore a flannel shirt and long johns gotten from the traders, but in all else his wives had outfitted him.

Away from the Crows, his caution sharpened. He was alone, an easy mark for anyone or any group or any animal, such as a rogue grizzly. But on this sublimely peaceful day he saw only some ravens gossiping on a distant branch. Did old ravens fly as well as young ones? What happened to a raven that could fly no longer? Ravens were smart birds. How did they die? Were they smart enough to choose death? Skye found himself entertaining questions that had never filled his mind before.

The pack mule came along willingly, carrying all Skye might need to survive in this lonely land. The odd thing was, Skye wasn't certain why he was making this journey. What exactly was he seeking? What did he need that the Crows or the Shoshones could not provide him? It was worth thinking about as he traveled.

Well, there were a few things. He wanted fields and pastures that would yield a living from gardens, grains, and livestock. He hoped to shelter himself behind a wall of thick logs, or rock, or adobe. A roof. A door that would stop arrows. He yearned for comfort: a real bed, with a real mattress to ease the pain in his aching bones. But that was only a part of it. He had, he knew, a white man's urge to sink roots deep and true, to take up land as a possession, a holding. That flew against the visions of his wives' peoples, who never dreamed of holdings, and considered the breast of mother earth to be beyond possession.

He rode across open country, most of it the giant shoulders of the snowy mountains north and west. As the day waned he started to search for a secluded place only a few miles from the Yellowstone River where he intended to camp. It would be almost invisible now, with only a few spidery branches to reveal it and he wasn't sure he could find it. This was monotonous country before it greened, and the brown reaches were deceptive. Far across the Yellowstone Valley lay foothills, and the great chain of the Rockies, running east and west here. He topped a ridge and could make out the distant Yellowstone Valley, which was veiled in haze. But he continued to hunt for the place, and just before

dusk he dropped down a slope and saw his oasis, just as he
had remembered it. He hurried the ewe-necked mare to
the intimate valley, and paused at the water's edge. There
were several algae-lined pools and a faint smell of sulphur
released when the hot water reached the air. He took hasty
care of the mare, put her in a cottonwood grove where she
could gnaw on green bark, and returned to his campsite. He
collected dry wood for a fire, and started it burning, using
a lucifer instead of flint and steel.

He tested the waters with his hand, found a pool to his
liking, as hot as he could stand, and then pulled away his
leather clothing and his ancient union suit, until he was bare,
and then stepped gingerly into the purling hot water and slid
slowly into it, until he was immersed to his nose, and thinking this was an old man's heaven. He toasted himself, pad-
dling occasionally, letting his limbs float free, letting the
water redden his flesh, until he could no longer stand the
heat and he had to clamber out on some cold rocks. He found
a small pool farther down, milder now, and slid into it, letting the tepid water cool him. Then he crawled out and dried
himself at his fire. For this little while, he actually lived
without pain, but by morning he would be hurting again.
That's what old age was all about. He wished there was a
hot spring where he intended to make a home. But from the
Great Bend of the Yellowstone there were several hot springs
not far away.

He camped that night under a south-facing bluff back
from the springs. For much of this chill spring night, the
sun-warmed bluff would spread its heat over him, and he
would take his ease. He lay quiet under his blankets, knowing why he was looking for a place to settle. It was simple:
he wanted a comfortable place to grow old. He would like
to sit in a rocking chair on a veranda and watch sunsets,
or feel the night-chill creep toward his door. There wasn't

anything more to it. And yet there was. A true home was more than shelter and more than comfort. It was rooted in family and friends and neighbors.

He knew perfectly well where he was going. There were a dozen likely places along the Yellowstone River, but only one filled his mind. He would find a place somewhere near the great bend of the river, where he could see the craggy Birdsong Mountains aglow in the sunrise, and watch the sun plunge behind the Bridger Mountains at dusk. He would look out of his front door at the majestic Absaroka Mountains, somewhere near where the river punched through them in a narrow canyon. He would look out his back windows toward the westernmost edge of the plains, or the Shields River valley. He mused, as he lay in the quiet, that this whole trip, presuming to hunt for a place to live, was a sham. He already knew.

But knowing the general area, and selecting a specific spot, were two different things entirely. He would hunt for a place where majestic cottonwoods lined the creeks, where there was good pasture grass, where a man could put in a garden, where cold springs would make delicious drinking in summers and keep food in a spring house during hot times. He would find a place that could not be surprised, where a man would have a few moments to reach safety. He would find a place where his eyes would feast on the world, and his flesh would rejoice, and his nostrils would suck in the scents of wild roses.

The next two days he made his solitary way up the Yellowstone River, seeing no one at all. Sometimes he left pony tracks in decaying snow. At other times he took his horse through mud. His passage would be easy to follow, and for that reason he paused now and then to study the land behind him, sometimes watching from a forested spur of mountain. But he saw no sign of human life, and his journey began to take on the quality of a trip across the Atlantic in a rowboat.

But he didn't mind. He rode carefully, knowing there would be no help if he got into trouble, broke a bone, took sick, or got caught in a cruel spring snowstorm. He had lived over six decades, much of it in wilderness, by being careful when he was alone, and strangely, by loving this land so deeply that he was nurtured and sheltered and fed by it. In some places the placid Yellowstone ran between yellow bluffs; in other places it ran through cloistered bottomlands guarded by rolling prairie. In other places along towering gray cliffs that hid the snow-clad Rocky Mountains to the south. That day he shot a yearling buck, apologizing to it for taking its life. The meat was good, and the weather cold enough so he could carry the meat with him for days.

Then at last, after circumventing one impassable gorge, he drifted into the country that he intended to be his home the rest of his life. The great bend of the Yellowstone lay only a few miles ahead. And even before he reached it, he felt at home.

Chapter 5

Skye hurt. Instead of sitting his horse and absorbing the area that would be his home, he slid painfully off and eased to the stony turf, knowing that the minute he alighted sharp pain would shoot up his legs. He had ridden horses all his life, but now it was all he could manage to sit a horse for an hour. The hurt would drive upward from his knees to his loins to his hip and back, and then he would have to dismount and walk awhile until the pain lessened.

Now he eased to the grass and felt his moccasins touch earth. He was used to pain. He had bullet wounds, knife wounds, a nose pulped by brawling early in his life, giant scars and scratches, and more recently the pain of all his years, lancing his bones and settling in every joint.

This would be the place of his old age, and he wondered why. Of all the ranges and prairies and hills and deserts he had roamed over a lifetime in the American West, why had he come to this place? He couldn't say. It was beautiful, but there were many vistas across this country that were more so. It was not a lush land, and would not afford much of a living. He stood on a brushy and uneven flat that had once been riverbed. One would not plow here because the blade would strike the river cobbles that lay just below.

Off to the south was a steep notch in the slopes, where the Yellowstone had washed through the mountains, and beyond that a broad valley flanked by snowy ranges. The trappers and men of the mountains had often camped here, and that was how he first became acquainted with it. Sometimes they had wintered here, built their miserable huts against the wind, harvested game, cut firewood, and then gambled and storied away the cold days and nights. Skye had been among them. He knew this place and it was just as real to him as the pain lacing his bones.

The wind here was incessant and cold, and now it slipped through his leathers and chilled him. He would need a good stout house to turn the wind, and a good stove to heat it enough to ease the pain in his joints. He wondered why he would build a home in a place notorious for its bitter winds, and had no answer. There were winter days here when the wind was so cruel that no man would venture out.

He eyed the sky, finding scattered frying-pan clouds with black bottoms skidding low over the ridges. They might snow on him. The setting sun silvered the edges of these galloping clouds, turning the sky into a kaleidoscope. He put a hand on the withers of his horse and felt it tremble.

The silent wilderness absorbed his gaze. The brooding mountains caught the last light, and now the river flat settled into obscure shadow. This place was incalculably old. For as long as the stars rose and fell, this place had nurtured life and welcomed death. These mountains rose and fell. This river had scooped away rock and cut a gorge. This was a place of mystery, the sort of place that made Europeans huddle closer to their hearth fires and listen for the unknown and unknowable just beyond the pale light.

He headed for the thick riverside brush, knowing he could find shelter there, and soon found a good gravelly flat surrounded by willows and cottonwoods, a place hidden from prying eyes, where he could light a fire that would never be seen. Why did he still keep his guard up? It was ancient habit. From silent places came silent arrows.

He unsaddled, and turned the horse and mule loose on

brown and matted grass. They would gnaw a few twigs as well as last summer's grass and do well enough to sustain life. He chose a gravelly ridge, once a sandbar in the river, that would shed snow or rain. Falling water here would not pool, but would filter into the thick gravel beds beneath him.

He collected an abundant supply of deadwood and heaped it nearby. The more he moved, the better he felt. Just doing chores drove the pain away. It never left him entirely, but he could drive it back until it lurked beyond the fires, with yellow wolf eyes, waiting to pounce on him again when he pulled his robes over him.

He checked his Sharps rifle and set it next to his bedroll.

He heard an animal stirring. At dusk deer came to water, but it might be something else, so he waited. But nothing loomed out of the quietness, so he turned to his supper, a pemmican broth that would warm and comfort him.

The sole noise was that of his own making. Nearby, a latticework of naked limbs raked the stars, and little air stirred. The limbs looked like jail bars, keeping his spirit pinned to earth and preventing him from knowing all things. Earth was home, but also prison. He used lucifers now; strikers and flints were too much work and too chancy. He shaved a dry stick, built a tiny fire, added twigs, and soon had a hot little blaze, just right for his cook pot. He had learned to feed himself with only a copper cook pot, his knife, and an iron spoon, and that was all he had with him. He dipped the pot into the Yellowstone River, and set the cold water to heating, along with some jerky and pemmican and some rose hips he had harvested along the way. He wouldn't need much. His appetite had faded over the years, and now he was indifferent to food.

He lowered himself quietly to the dry gravel, a good place to be during the muddy season when sometimes there was no dry bed ground to be found.

Was this home? Had he come all the way over here only to find that home is not a place, but a collection of memories and loved ones? He could not answer it. Did anyone on earth possess a real home, a sanctuary that put all the clawing pain in one's bosom at ease? Was the only true home death itself?

He lay on his back, watching for meteors in a sky patched with clouds, but he absorbed only the silence. He could not sleep, and even the usual drowsiness that signaled sleep did not approach him. Had he come here for nothing? He had imagined a home right about where the Shields River tumbled into the Yellowstone, and now that he was here and this was real, he couldn't imagine why he had come. It was naught but a foolish fancy.

The fire reduced itself to orange coals. The night was cold but he had often endured worse. His kit departed from Indian ways in one respect: he slept inside a blanket that was inside of a good duck-cloth bag that turned water and dew and wind, and captured heat, and opened easily along one side. His wives preferred the old ways, a buffalo robe or a trade blanket.

Restlessly he arose, impatient with himself, and stretched. A chill penetrated his leathers and reached his soft woolen shirt. There was only a sliver moon, and this night was very black. But he could see even so. He knew this place so well that everything was stamped upon his mind, every skyline and peak. Starlight glinted in the mysterious river purling by twenty yards distant. He was not afraid.

Moving about spared him pain. He hurt most after deep sleep, when his whole body ached and his muscles refused to obey. It was only by working his muscles in the morning that he drove the pain out of them. It was as if the pain were like some poison that needed constant flushing.

His horse and mule stared at him, aware of something

different in the shifting quiet of the night. He began walking along the river until he found himself on open rolling meadow devoid of river rock. The going was easier, but still he walked deliberately, a pace at a time, because his only lantern was the stars and a sliver of moon behind him. Across the river a snowy pyramid of a peak caught an odd glint out of the heavens. South of the river the meadows quickly gave way to black forests and foothills, and finally the vaulting mountains of the Absaroka Range.

He was standing on home.

He saw this place better in the void of night than by day, and the contours of the land were ingrained in his soul. A few miles to the east the view was just as handsome, but there were rattlesnakes. Here they were rare. Here were smooth grassy meadows and the majesty of nature from every prospect.

The land was very old, but not virgin. Trails came through this very country, followed by barefoot and moccasined people, and those with shoes and boots. There were the prints of shod and unshod horses and mules, the split hooves of the bovines, the ruts of wagons and carts, the furrows of travois, the prints of dogs. From here a road led over the western mountains to the distant mining towns. Trails ran north to the Missouri, and south to the headwaters of the Yellowstone, at a place Victoria's people called the roof of the world. In this land one could find flint arrowheads, and some made from obsidian collected from cliffs to the south. One could find old arrows, and great stone spear points, knife blades and buttons, horseshoes, bits of worn harness.

Skye liked that. He was a sociable man who enjoyed people and welcomed them to his hearth. He would not build a home in some remote place never visited by mortals. A night zephyr caught him, and drove cold into his clothing, so he retreated in the depths of night to his camp, flawlessly heading to the right shadow and the right gravel bar where his gear lay undisturbed.

This time he fell asleep swiftly, and didn't awake until sunlight pried his eyes open. Someone was staring at him. He quietly surveyed the empty gravel bar and the surrounding meadow, and discovered a bullock there, watching him. It was an ugly beast, splotchy brown and white, all skin and bones except for a huge set of horns that spanned six feet or more and arced forward into murderous weapons.

But not a bullock. Probably an abandoned ox. Worn-out oxen were scattered all along the old Bozeman Trail, cut loose when they were too weak to drag wagons anymore. Some died, some survived. The Indians left them alone, preferring buffalo to the stringy meat of the oxen. Still, it was odd to see a domestic animal here. Skye contemplated the animal as he lay in his bedroll. The ox neither approached nor ran, but stood there, guarding the ground.

Skye wondered whether to shoot and eat the beast, and decided against it. A rested ox in good flesh was worth a lot of money. He rose slowly, fighting back the usual pain, while the ox watched, and then the ox trotted into the brush and hid. There was something tantalizing in all this, and Skye forgot how much he hurt.

Chapter 6

Skye brewed some tea. It was a habit that rose from his very bones, and many mornings he cared for nothing more. He let the leaves steep in his pot, and then let the pot cool so he could drink from it.

The day quickened, and the low sun prized the flanks of the dark mountains south and west, sometimes burnishing the ridges until they shone like new pennies. But the sunlight was a cheat and the day didn't warm. Skye felt heavy air rolling out of Canada. He pulled his blanket about him to allay pain, and knew all over again why he needed a sheltering home.

The tea stirred his pulse, and he was ready to introduce himself to his land. He hiked slowly east until he came again to the ground that spoke to him in the night, and stood upon it. He felt some ancient stirring that could have no name, as if the earth beneath his moccasins were speaking. Maybe gravity was heavier here, making him feel heavier, connecting him to the soil below him. He saw a great meadow sloping toward the river bottoms. Behind him the land convulsed upward into grassy hills.

He ached for Victoria. She had medicine powers, and once in a while she warned him away from a campsite or some other place. He wanted her to stand beside him, and tell him what the spirits were whispering to her, and whether this would be a place of joy or danger or heartache. But she had begged off. Building a house was white man's stuff, and she wanted no part of it.

So Barnaby Skye would settle for his own wisdom this time. He noticed a shallow draw and walked to it, finding chokecherries and willow brush, and in the bottom, a thin trickle, not a foot wide. He hiked upslope and discovered a spring rising from an outcrop. He cupped his hands and lifted the water to his lips, and found it cold and sweet. The spring flowed from a vertical fault in gray rock, a good sign that it was not seasonal and perfidious. Its water could be diverted into a home, and it could cool a springhouse as well, and water livestock in a pasture, and water gardens and apple trees.

Ample wood was at hand. The meadows here were more in the nature of parks, surrounded by mixed stands of aspen, cottonwood, fir, and pine. Wood for hearth and stove; wood for timbers and planks and window frames and lintels. Copses sprang up from the meadows, especially where there was a bit more moisture in the soil. And just beyond the valley, fir and pine blackened the slopes.

It was a good and bountiful land, maybe not for a plowman but for a man who needed pasture and garden. Still . . . it was a long way from this open and virgin world to a functioning home. He had with him one small camp axe. He could no longer count on the toil of his body, his own sweat and blood and muscle, to build a house. He drifted across the parks, wrapped tightly in his blanket against the metallic air, wondering where houses came from and how he could conjure a good solid one here.

A bit closer to the river, he knew, would be good rounded cobbles just below the thin topsoil, cobbles to lift out of their ancient beds, placed on sledges and dragged to the building site. Cobbles to be mortared into foundations and walls.

He studied the woodlands, looking for stands of lodgepole pine, the preferred tree for log buildings because the logs were arrow-true and easy to work. But there were no lodgepole pines anywhere near. Only a little crooked jackpine, good enough for firewood but an anguish to builders.

The nearest sawmill was in Bozeman City, over Jim Bridger's pass, in the Gallatin Valley. He could buy sawn timbers and planks there if he had some money. He could have them hauled here, if he had some money. He could buy kegs of nails and window glass or even pre-made framed windows there, if he had some money.

He eyed the sod. He could build a sod house here. He still could dig each piece of sod with a spade without help, and set it into his walls without help. He could cut poles for a roof and put thick sod on the poles for a roof. That much he could do, even at his age and with his bounty of pain. Then he could live inside his dirt house, avoid the leaks when it rained, and chase away bugs and snakes and rodents and worms. He sighed, unhappily.

He saw flatiron clouds sliding along the northern horizon, and knew where the cold wind was coming from. Before the day was done there would be a spring storm here, and he ought to look to shelter. He turned his back to the heavy air and walked to his campsite, deep in the bottoms, where the trees subdued the wind a little and a man could find small comforts.

The temperature was plummeting even though it was midday. Rain slapped him. He peered upward and saw nothing but clear sky, and yet rain drove into him like tenpenny nails. The dark outliers still rode far north, deepening the mystery. There was no time to marvel at nature's perversities, so he hurried for shelter. He had lived in nature half a century, and knew what to look for.

In this case it was an ancient cottonwood lording over a

large grove. He collected his bedroll, dragged his packs to the top of the gravel bar where water would not pool under them, and then he hurried into the grove, while bullets of cold rain smacked his leather shirt and trickled down his neck. The mammoth tree spread naked branches over a wide patch of earth, but that wasn't the shelter he wanted. He studied the massive roots and found a hollow between them on the lee side, just wide enough for him to sit in. He wrapped his blankets about him, and then the duck-cloth bag, and lowered himself into the hollow. The roots rose beside him like stout walls, scraping his duck cloth, and then he pulled the cloth over his head and the ice picks falling out of the sky stopped pricking him. He settled in, noting the sweep of white rain across the parks and brown meadows. The mountains across the river vanished in fog, which soon white-blinded him to the rest of the world.

He had endured all this many times, and he would endure it again. A thin heat collected in his blankets. Water sprayed off his canvas, and rarely caught his face. He could no longer see sky; fog obscured it. He could not read the weather, and he knew this could last ten minutes or ten hours or ten days. He discovered sleet mixed in the rain, and knew the temperature had dropped. There would come a time when he was so stiff he had to stand, a time when he might need to drain himself, and when that time came, his haven would be violated, and he would return to water pooled where he sat.

The horse and mule stood with heads lowered, rumps to the wind. Their backs slick and black. A bit of slush frosted the packs on the gravel, and more was collecting here and there on dried grass.

In spite of his wraps, Skye felt cold. And worse, he was hurting again. He was breathing misty cold air, and his chest hurt too. He had weathered a thousand storms over half a century, but this was different because he hurt. As the minutes progressed to hours, his limbs ached, his back hurt, and his neck radiated so much pain that he found himself rotating his head this way and that, trying to ease the outrage of his body. A man of his years needed shelter, and he could never return to the outdoor life he had weathered for decades.

He thought he might build the foundation of river cobbles and mortar, and then add logs and a thick floor, and raise a hearth and fireplace and chimney of cobbles and mortar, and pile the logs up into walls, thick and airtight and sealed, and then raise a roof over all of that, a roof with shakes to drain the rain away and support the heavy loads of snow that would settle on them. He would add some store-bought windows, and a stout door, and a good iron stove to cook on and supplement the hearth fire. He would give Victoria and Mary rooms of their own, and partition off his own, but the rest of the house would be a great commons for them.

He would put a roofed porch along the front where a man might sit quietly and watch the future. He would build a massive outhouse in the back, where a man could sit without feeling the cold wind, and below the spring he would build a spring house to cool vegetables and preserve meat. In the bedrooms he would fashion sturdy beds wrought from poles and leather, and add stuffed cotton mattresses that could blot up a man's hurts and keep him warm and off the cold ground. Getting off the ground was the main thing. Even in a warm house, the cold of the ground in these northern places rose upward and numbed feet and made calves ache and stole warmth from each room. That was the trouble with lodges. The Crows had comfortable lodges that drew the smoke away and caught the fire-warmth, but the cold from the frozen earth stole upward, through layer upon layer of buffalo robes, and one never slept on warm ground in winter. Only on ground that made bones ache and old people draw deep into themselves.

After Skye had sat immobilized until he hurt all over, he stood, drew his covering about him, and walked through sleet and fog down to the river, where the silver waters flashed by. Slush worked through his moccasins and numbed his feet. He walked, feeling the cold muscle of his body begin to work, to drive away the pain that seemed to build up when his muscles weren't working.

So Skye walked. It was better than sitting tight. It was an old person's remedy. Old people drove away stiffness by walking. He could not see the heavens well enough to know when this storm might abate, but he would walk it out, walk until the cloud and fog lifted. He was not a good walker, his body compact and stout rather than lanky and lean, but walking would be his salvation now, and there was always this: walking took a person somewhere, and opened new prospects.

So Skye settled his soaked top hat on his locks and walked along the Yellowstone River, following game trails through brush. Walking felt better than sitting. He cold-footed his way through muck and slush, driven by some compulsion he didn't understand, to walk or die. He walked awkwardly, wrapped in his bedroll and duck cloth, but he never stopped walking. He had the sensation that walking meant life and stopping meant death, but he dismissed it. He might be old but he wasn't sick. He didn't know how far he was from his horse and mule and packs but that didn't matter either.

A stirring in the brush gave him pause. There had been only the deep quiet of the wilds, but now something stirred, and it was large, snapping twigs and piercing through brush. A grizzly, perhaps. Skye regretted that he had left his Sharps with the packs, and carried nothing but a belt knife.

The ox saw Skye at the same instant that Skye limned the ox. The startled animal lowered its giant horns, threw his head to either side, those deadly horns arcing one way and another. Then it snorted and charged. Skye had never been assaulted by a wild ox, and saw no way to escape. Brush hemmed him. The murderous horns cut a wide swath. Then it was too late. The left horn, swinging like an axe handle, caught Skye's leg and lifted him high into the fog and he felt himself tumbling back to earth, landing hard in slush and muck and brush, while the beast thumped by, its hooves missing Skye's writhing form by inches. Pain lanced him, white-hot pain shooting up from his leg, pain such as old age never knew. Then Skye drifted in and out of the world.

Chapter 7

Bright stars glinted above. Firelight wavered and danced. Skye lay on his back, buried deep under blankets that warmed him well. Lightning bolts shot up his left leg and thundered through the rest of him, but the night sky was clear.

He groaned. Immediately a man loomed above him. Skye focused carefully. This one wore a slouch hat and a heavy coat. Another man joined him.

"You come back to us?" the man said.

Skye nodded.

"Lucky we were close. Heard you howling and come look."

"Who?" asked Skye.

"Jim Broadus, that's me, and Amos Glendive. We're teamsters."

"Didn't know anyone was around," Skye said.

"You got thrown by one of them ox," Broadus said.

"Your oxen?"

"Wild ox. That's why we're here. We haul for the Bar Diamond outfit. They need oxen. Lots of 'em gone native around here along the old trail. They got wore out and ditched by folks. We got three span this time."

"Including the one got you, we think," Glendive said.

The memory was coming back now. That cruel horn hooking under his leg, lifting him, tossing him like a rag doll, and then the crash. He came down in a fury of pain, and howled, and then the fog rolled in.

A new bolt of pain laced Skye's leg and he groaned.

"Your leg's busted up some. Your knee ain't never gonna be the same, mister . . . mister . . ."

"Skye. Mister Skye."

"We got her splinted up, Skye, but that's all a man can do around here."

"I'd be dead," Skye said. "You saved me."

Broadus smiled slightly. "I reckon so. Leastwise, it'd be a long crawl to wherever you were heading."

Skye wrestled with pain a moment and stared about him. This was a good camp. A freight wagon slouched nearby.

"We'll take you to Bozeman City. That's where we're a-going."

"I can ride."

Glendive just shook his head, and Skye abandoned that.

"Your leg, it's some messed-up," Broadus said. "We didn't know how to splint it right, but she's tied up tight, anyway."

Skye knew the Bar Diamond Freight Company. Mostly they hauled goods from Fort Benton, on the Missouri River, down into the mining camps of western Montana. Big outfit. Always needing oxen, more oxen, more mules.

"Old man Baker sent us over here. He needs stock, and there's free stuff floating around here."

Skye craned his head, peering into the dark.

"It's all here, Skye. We moved your camp here. Your nags and all. You were going light."

Skye nodded.

"You hurting more than much?" Broadus said.

Skye nodded.

"It's gonna be a hard wagon ride tomorra. But we can carry you."

"I guess it's in store for me," Skye said. He was starting to fade again.

"You up to some broth?" one of them asked.

Skye nodded. Within moments, they were spooning some beefy broth into him, warming his innards. But he couldn't even swallow without his leg hurting him. He gave up after a few sips, and slid a hand down to the leg, discovered a tight-tied splint holding the leg rigid. He brought his fingers up looking for blood on them and found none.

"I'd say in some ways it could've been worse," Broadus said.

Skye nodded, a sea of brooding pain spreading through him again.

"Take a horse. It's yours," Skye whispered.

"No. You'd do it for us if need be."

"At least I can thank you."

"That ox, the one got you, he's under yoke now. Them wild ones remember. Whole trick is to get them into a yoke, and then they quiet right down, remembering old times. We got our ways," Glendive said. "Old man Baker, he's got forty, fifty oxen this way off the Bozeman Road. Baker sends us over here now and then to fetch him some more."

"Wouldn't mind if you ate him for breakfast," Skye said.

"You need anything, Skye?"

"You could amputate," Skye said.

They laughed uneasily. "We're here if you need us. You rest now."

Then Skye was alone with the stars and the pain.

He didn't sleep much. The throbbing in his leg never lessened. But as soon as dawn broke, Broadus and Glendive were stirring, and then bringing him some steaming coffee. Skye downed it gratefully.

"We're heading out. We got three yoke, and that's all

anyone thought we'd get. We'll put you in the wagon," Broadus said. "I imagine it ain't going to be comfortable, but it's all we can do."

They lifted Skye to his feet, and he clung to their shoulders as they helped him into the wagon bed and wrapped blankets around him while he trembled. The teamsters broke camp, added Skye's few possessions to the heap in the wagon, collected Skye's horses, and started toward Bozeman City. Every lurch of the wagon shot pain through Skye.

After a while, they stopped and checked on him.

"You all right?" Broadus asked.

Skye wasn't, but he nodded at the teamster.

Soon they were off again, the teamsters walking beside the oxen as they dragged the wagon upslope. Skye thought they might make Bozeman City by nightfall.

The day went much too slowly. He felt a helplessness he had rarely experienced before. He'd been gravely wounded several times, and managed to heal up and keep on going. Now he had a broken leg. Just what had snapped or shattered he didn't know, except that pain radiated from his left knee toward his ankle and toward his hip. Victoria and Mary were far away. Someone would have to care for him.

He put such speculation aside. He was alive, miraculously discovered soon after the trouble with the ox, and now he was safe in good hands. He tried to rest, but pain kept him wide awake.

It was just after sundown when the Bar Diamond teamsters halted.

Broadus loomed over him in the dusk. "We're at Fort Ellis. There's no sawbones in Bozeman City, but we thought there might be one at the post here. You want us to find out?"

"That would be good, Mister Broadus."

"Or we can take you into town somewheres. Livery barn, maybe. Those haylofts make good beds."

"I'd like a doctor, sir."

"I'll send Amos in to talk to someone."

Skye watched the teamster vanish among the stained log buildings of the post, and eventually he returned with an officer, who looked Skye over.

"Colonel Blossom here. You're the man, eh?" he said. "Know you. You're the old squaw man living with the Crows."

Skye nodded.

"Trouble is, our surgeon's cashiered. Clyde Coffin was a damned drunk and I sent him packing last week. We're waiting for a new man. Point is, there's no one here can set your bones."

"Anyone in Bozeman City?"

Blossom shook his head. "Not as I know of. Virginia City, maybe."

"I seem to be out of luck," Skye said. "I don't know what to do."

Blossom pondered it. "There's a thing or two I can do. I've got a lot of crutches around, and I can give you some. How tall are you?"

"Five feet some. I've shrunk."

Blossom nodded to his orderly, who trotted into the post.

"Well, Skye, if I can help further, call on me," Blossom said. "Have to go now."

Skye nodded. "I'll get along," he said. "You've helped me, and I'm indebted."

"No, old fella, from what I've heard, the army owes you a thing or two."

The colonel hastened back to the post. In time, the orderly appeared with some wooden crutches.

"Try these, Skye."

Skye slipped the crutches under his shoulders and stood. They would do. He could cradle his arms in them, take weight off the broken leg. That was a start.

Broadus and Glendive looked eager to get into town, so Skye clambered back into the wagon for the final half mile. The wagon yard was east of town on the edge of the military reservation.

"I don't know what to do with you, Skye," Broadus said.

"Could you take me to a livery barn?" Skye asked. "I don't know where else to go."

They could. At the freight yard the teamsters corralled a deliveryman named Glad Muggins, who harnessed a spring wagon and helped Skye into it. He added Skye's gear and tied Skye's ponies on, and drove into town.

Muggins climbed to the seat and slapped the lines over the dray horse, and the wagon creaked westward. The horse fell into a quiet walk and Skye watched the April clouds hurry past. April was a rainy month. Luckily it wasn't raining now. Beyond the freight yard the Bridger Mountains rose high, still choked with snow.

"Now where do you want to go?" Muggins asked.

"Is there a livery barn?"

"Kangaroo. North of Main Street some."

"Take me there."

Skye didn't have a dime to his name but livery barns were the usual refuge of the desperate. There might be a bunk in a hay pile, and he had a packhorse to trade for a few weeks of chow and horse feed. He thought it would be a month before he could put weight on that leg.

Somehow he had survived. They would not find his bleached bones out on the trail. Maybe he could find someone who would reach the Crows, and let Victoria and Mary know where he was. A livery barn was the right place to find travelers.

Bozeman City was strung along a miry street that nearly coagulated traffic. A few boardwalks over the wetter spots provided the only passage for pedestrians. Rills from the surrounding mountains laced the ramshackle town. False-front frame stores, some whitewashed, lined the street, and a few grimy residences south of the grubby road completed this outpost of civilization. Skye pushed himself up on his elbows to see what might be seen. He scarcely spotted a woman. The place had functioned as a farming and ranching town supplying gold camps to the west with grains and meat. It was also becoming a crossroads, the market town of the vast green valley it dominated.

Muggins turned up a side street, at least it might have been a street, and headed for a weathered board-and-batten structure several hundred yards north. A white-lettered front proclaimed it to be the Clyde Kangaroo Livery, Stock Sold & Bought.

Muggins swung the wagon around and stopped. A chin-whiskered gent in bib overalls, armed with a pitchfork, burst out of the barn alley, and boiled down on the wagon.

"What's the company unloading on me this time, eh?"

"Mister Kangaroo, this here's a man with a busted leg, looking for a place to stay."

Kangaroo reached the wagon and peered at Skye. "I get stuck with every vagrant comes through here, and none earns me a dime," he said.

Skye found himself staring upward at a skinny gent almost devoid of chin, with bulgy eyes. A venerable slouch hat capped some dark hair.

"I'm Barnaby Skye, sir. I broke a leg. I'll trade a horse for some accommodations."

"Trade a horse, will you? You call those items horses? They look like injun ponies to me."

"You have it right, sir," Skye said. "I'll trade one for a

month in your hayloft, plus feed for myself and the other horse. Take your pick."

"A month of chow and feed, you say? You suffer delusions, like most owners of nags. You want to sit in my outhouse and shit away three squares for a month, and pay me with that? That thing?" He waggled a gnarly finger at the packhorse.

Skye saw no reason to respond. He lay quietly while Kangaroo circled the packhorse, lifted feet, examined hooves, pried open the mouth, studied teeth, ran a hand over withers looking for fistulas.

"You a talker?" he asked.

"What do you mean?"

"I can't stand talkers boring me half to death. I got work to do. If you're a listener, we'll handshake it. Me, I always need listeners. I'm here alone. I'm a born talker. You come here, you gotta listen and don't talk back, and I'll put you up. Maybe I'll take that lousy packhorse, maybe I won't."

"It's a deal," Skye said.

Chapter 8

The town crier, Blue Tail Feather, announced that the People would begin their spring exodus to summer grounds on the Big Horn River. Many Quill Woman, Victoria, was a little deaf, and required that Mary repeat the word from the council of elders.

"We go to the Big Horn Valley now. Summer is here," Mary said in English. "The omens are good. The elders have spoken."

The Big Horn Valley was a good place to be during the warm seasons. There were deer and elk and antelope, and bear up in the Big Horn Mountains, although not many buffalo. It was a protected valley, not easy to reach, and mostly the enemies of the People just left them alone there. Out on the plains, to the other side of the sacred mountains, things were different. The Lakota were still stirred up after driving the Americans away, and now they patrolled that country and lorded over it and pounced on anyone entering it. There were many more Lakota than there were of Victoria's people, the Absaroka.

Victoria stood stiffly. The winter had taken a toll on her, and her body ached. More and more she depended on Mary to do the chores, gather wood for the small lodge fire, gather roots, butcher meat kindly brought to them by the camp's hunters. Sometimes all Victoria wanted to do was sit in a white man's rocking chair and rock and see all things. She wouldn't admit it though.

Mary returned to her toil. She was scraping the underside of an elk hide that had been given to her, cleaning off bits of fat and decaying flesh. And that was only the beginning of what must be done to turn it into soft, fine leather.

Victoria eyed Skye's younger wife, and saw no change. Mary was caught in sadness, but Skye scarcely knew it because Mary always flashed her brightest smiles at him and hid what was slowly eroding her life away.

It had begun years earlier when the boy was just past seven winters, and growing into a good stout son. That was when Skye arranged with Colonel Bullock, his agent and friend at Fort Laramie, to take the boy, Dirk, or North Star, to a place called Missouri, for an education offered by the blackrobes. Victoria wondered about educations. Why must the boy be taken away? Couldn't Skye teach Dirk all the things that white men called an education? But Skye had only said he wanted his son to have every chance to make something of himself, and he needed to learn to read and write and do his arithmetic.

One fall, when Colonel Bullock was quitting his post, he took Dirk away with him, and that was when Mary changed, and hid the change from Skye. After that, Mary had no child to care for, and Victoria didn't either, and a great sadness hung over Skye's lodge. But it was the way of women to hide all that, and there were good moments because Skye was a man who brought happiness and good humor to his wives, and sometimes they laughed and had good times and met all sorts of people. Except that Skye never saw Mary shivering in the dark some nights outside of the lodge, all alone. There had been no more children. Who could say why? More children would have gladdened Mary's heart and Victoria's too. The barrenness was a mystery beyond knowing.

Victoria watched Mary scrape, noting the quiet resignation, the long lines on her still-young face, and the refuge Mary took in ceaseless toil. Mary worked compulsively now, never taking any time to gossip or sit with other women or play the stick game or tell stories. It was always work, work, work, for Mary, and Skye only saw Mary's big smiles.

It was Victoria's privilege, as Skye's senior wife, to make the decisions, and now she did. She settled beside the younger wife and joined in the scraping, feeling the familiar tug of the flint-edged scraper as it fleshed the hide.

"We will go find our man," she said. "Maybe he needs us."

Mary nodded.

Victoria scraped the elk hide some more, until her back hurt, and then she stood.

"I will tell them," she said.

She straightened her winter skirt, this one of softest doeskin, and headed for the lodge of the village headman, greeting many wives along the path. The Absaroka headman now was Gout Belly, and so boyish that Victoria marveled. The headmen were all scarcely weaned in these times, she thought.

She didn't need to scratch at the lodge door, because Gout Belly was enjoying his morning nap on a light-skinned buffalo robe, letting Father Sun caress his caramel flesh.

"Why, Grandmother," he said, rising, because Victoria held a position of great honor in the village, and was known for her medicine as well as her advanced years. And it was no dishonor to be married to Mister Skye, either, though she thought it might be sometimes.

"It is a warm day, good chief Gout Belly, and I have come to slap flies away from you while you enjoy the sun."

"I imagine you have something to tell me, then. There are no flies as yet, so man and horse still await their bites."

"We will be going to Mister Skye," she said.

He considered it. "Then the village will be the worse without you."

"We will go with you to as far as the Yellowstone Valley tomorrow. Then you will go east, but we will travel up the river."

"Grandmother, there will be no man to protect you and the Shoshone woman."

"Who says we want to be protected, eh?" She grinned wickedly at Gout Belly.

"Then may a dozen Siksika catch you," he said, referring to the Blackfeet, mortal enemies of the People.

"I will turn them all into boys," she said, enjoying the banter.

He smiled. There were stories about Victoria, Many Quill Woman, told around many an Absaroka campfire deep in the night, to the sound of owls hooting.

The next dawn the Kicked-in-the-Bellies band of the Absaroka Nation slowly assembled into a column. Mary and Victoria pulled the willow sticks from the lodge cover and let it sag to earth, and then folded it and carried it to the travois. Then they undid the lodgepoles and hung them in bundles from a packsaddle. They had put their possessions into Skye's canvas panniers, and soon were ready.

At midmorning the procession wound away from the campsite where they had wintered. The place stank of waste and was shorn of firewood and was grazed down to the clay of the meadows. The Kicked-in-the-Bellies headed down Sweet Grass Creek. When they reached the valley of the Yellowstone, it was time for Victoria and Mary to leave the Absaroka People, and head west.

They watched the band until it was only a small dark line on the eastern horizon and then there was only silence and loneliness. Victoria nodded to Mary. It was time for them to head upriver. Mary sat inertly on her pony. When they were younger, she was often in the lead, eager to go wherever there was to go. Her face was still young and smooth, not like Victoria's seamed coppery face that had seen so many winters. Mary was still young, but now she was acting old and weary.

They rode their ponies over a faint trail that descended pine-dotted hills into the valley of the Yellowstone. Riding a pony wasn't so easy anymore for Victoria. The sharp bony vertebrae of the horse seemed to slice Victoria in two. That was one thing about age. Everything hurt, even things that once were pleasant and joyous. But Victoria sternly set aside her hurts and focused instead on the ride, on safety, on taking themselves, hour by hour, to Mister Skye.

They reached the riverbank during a spring squall, and continued westward along a worn trail, while wrapped in good blankets. That cold night they raised the lodge and found warmth and peace within.

It was only then that she realized Mary had barely spoken all day. Mary had not resisted anything, balked at anything, shown discomfort at anything, but neither had she laughed or chattered or exclaimed, for instance, when a flock of geese rose en masse. There was only that silence, and a haunted look in Mary's face. It had taken Victoria a while to discover it.

She watched Mary collect wood and silently build a small fire, silently fill a kettle and set it to boil, silently stare into the hazy twilight, her mind some vast distance from this place and this company. It was as if Mary weren't even present; that she had left Victoria in another world. Victoria kept her peace, said nothing, and watched closely.

Perhaps it was only a mood.

But as Victoria lay in her robes that early spring night, she realized that this silence had been present in Mary a long time. Present even when Skye was there, before he said he wanted a house. Mary had not visited with people in the village much. Winter times are merry times, when the People gamble, play games, flirt, and, above all, tell bawdy stories to while away the short days and bitter nights. But Mary had taken to staying in the lodge, and was often asleep, caught in her robes, when Skye or Victoria returned from a good night of storytelling and gossip.

Victoria lay in her blanket, shocked at herself for missing this change in Skye's Shoshone woman. She sensed that Mary of the Shoshone was so desolate that she scarcely cared about tomorrow. It was worse than sadness. Mary had been sad for several winters. No, this was something darker. And with another rush of understanding, she knew that there would be no happiness in Mary until the boy, North Star, would be returned to her. And that would never happen. The boy was far away, learning how to live as a white man.

Chapter 9

A cold gray dawn filtered through the smoke hole of the little lodge. Victoria knew what she must do. She arose quietly, padded into the frosty dawn, washed her face at the river, and then composed the words she would say to Mary.

When she pierced the door flap, Mary was sitting up, looking as listless this morning as she had in the twilight.

"Go to the river and wash. Then come back and heed my words," Victoria said.

Mary wrapped her blanket about her and vanished into the cold April dawn. Victoria waited, hunting for the words she still needed.

It was time for Mary to return to her people. Over a long life, Victoria had watched captive women slowly wither away, lonely and lost, wives of tribesmen whose tongue they did not know, treated harshly by senior wives, little better than slaves. There was nothing left for them, and sometimes they walked into a bitter winter's night never to return. She knew of Absaroka women taken by Siksika or Lakota warriors, women who never saw their own people again and simply died at an early age from the worst of all sickness, the disease of despair. Victoria had seen the reverse too, captive women taken by Absarokas in war, who spent the rest of their days in listless servitude right there in Absaroka villages. They died young and unmourned. It wasn't always like that. Some women did well in other tribes and lived happily. But some didn't.

Mary, or Blue Dawn, had never been a prisoner, but had married Skye freely long ago and the marriage brimmed with promise. But ever since her sole child, North Star, was sent away to a white man's school, Mary had slid farther and farther into solitude, which she had concealed with bright smiles. Victoria felt certain about the course she would take. Mary would go home to her people. If it angered Skye, Victoria would bear his anger. But Mary must leave, and this was a good moment for it, when everything was about to change. Maybe, among her brothers and their wives, life might return to Blue Dawn. Maybe not. But even as Victoria reasoned it out, she felt a hardening of her will.

At last Mary slipped into the lodge and sat down, awaiting whatever might come.

"I want you to go away from me. Go to your people. Take the lodge. I don't need it."

"But, Grandmother . . ." Mary said, using the term of greatest respect.

"Blue Dawn," Victoria replied, using the Shoshone name, "I want you to visit your people. Your brother, The Runner, will be pleased to see you."

"But, Grandmother, I am the younger wife of Mister Skye."

"It is my command," Victoria said roughly.

Blue Dawn slid into her silences again.

"Ahead is a crossing place, shallow and gravelly. And when you're across, start downriver and turn off where the trail goes to the Big Horn Valley. You know it well. And when it reaches the Shoshone River, you will be in your people's land again. Go!"

"Yes, Grandmother, if you say it."

"You will take the lodge. I cannot raise it alone."

Mary started to protest. It was true. It was beyond Victoria's powers now to lift the heavy lodge cover and pin it in place with willow sticks.

"The lodge will tell all who see it that you are Mister Skye's woman."

"It will say that. All the people know that lodge."

"There is a desert crossing, long and hard, before you reach the Shoshone River. Water your ponies well, and do not forget to take water for yourself."

"Yes, Grandmother."

"And honor the Shoshone people with my regards."

"I will tell them."

"And because you will be alone, go with great care."

"The spirits will guide me, Grandmother."

"We will know where you are and someday we will come for you. Now let us be off. The crossing is not far ahead."

For the first time in many days, Mary smiled.

They broke camp swiftly and loaded the ponies. Mary would have three, two for the lodge and her saddle pony. Victoria would have only her quiet old mare. She would have her blankets, a piece of canvas, a sack with some provisions, her bow and quiver, and her small rifle. It would be fine.

Two hours later they reached the crossing, and Victoria watched Mary lead her horses across a gravelly bar and negotiate the deeper channel on the far side, without trouble in this time of lowest water, just ahead of the spring flood. Then they stood a moment on opposite banks of the great river the white men called the Yellowstone. Mary lifted one brown hand high, and Victoria replied. Then Skye's younger wife mounted, settled her skirts, and rode downriver, the packhorses just behind her.

Victoria watched her go, knowing it was a good decision. A time with her people would lift Blue Dawn's heart. Skye would approve. The low sun slanted toward the stream, raising sparkles wherever its rays touched the water. Mary's trip would take an entire moon or so, and there would be danger in every step. She would follow the Yellowstone until it had flowed past the mightiest of all mountain ranges, the Beartooths, and then she would turn south and pass between the Beartooths and the Pryor Mountains, and then cross a terrible desert, and at last she would arrive in the lands cherished by her people, but she still would have many days of travel after that.

Victoria eyed the trail westward with apprehension, not because of danger but because she felt her years and everything was harder to do. It was harder to stay warm, harder to find food, harder to find shelter. Harder to fend off wild animals. She felt an odd sadness, but pushed it aside. She would not surrender to sadness.

All alone now, she braved a brisk west wind and walked her pony along a well-worn riverside trail. Her task was to find Skye. She had been his woman when they were young; she would be his woman now, until death separated them. She would be his woman until she was helpless; or maybe he would be her man until he was helpless. She didn't need much care. She ate little more these days than a sparrow would. The only darkness she saw at all in great age was the lack of comfort. Neither she nor Skye could find much comfort these times. Their backs hurt, or their muscles, or they were too hot or cold, or their feet ached, or their food disagreed with them.

"Sonofabitch!" she said to the wind. "I want some whiskey."

Spirits still killed the pain. But they rarely had any and couldn't afford to buy any from the white men. With a few jugs of whiskey, old age wouldn't be so hard. She'd once

heard an old white man call it painkiller, and now she knew
why.

She loved whiskey sometimes, but not always. It took
her senses away, and it was cruel too. There were other
things she learned of long ago, when she received the healing wisdom of her people, good things that did no harm
and brought spirit and body together. Now that she was old
and hurt much of the time, these things had taken new
meaning in her mind. She wanted to be whole, to make
spirit and body one again, and not at war. There was one herb
she carried with her for that. She prized the peppermint leaf
above all else, and often made a tea of it. Deep in her kit,
she had some. Just a little. Maybe she would find more. The
peppermint, as white men called it, grew along riverbanks.
This was a good tea, gathered and used by women. So was
willow bark tea, which subdued pain and blessed the lower
back, where pain gathered in old men and old women. She
had some of both, and this night she would brew a little tea,
and maybe that would give her strength and sustain life another day.

There were other herbs known to the Absaroka People,
and not a summer went by that she failed to learn more, for
the quest for medicinal herbs was a passion with her people. There were herbs for every malady of the human body.
Herbs to stop nosebleeds, reduce swelling, teas to quiet an
unruly stomach, herbs to calm the spirit, herbs to bring visions to those seeking them. Teas and herbs that brought
comfort to the very old. She hoped to share these things
with Skye in the days ahead, when their bodies troubled
them more and more. Was she not a medicine woman of the
People, with great powers?

But this night, alone in the great valley of the Yellowstone, she would find a place to brew peppermint and sip it

and welcome the air spirits and the earth spirits to come watch over her through the cold night. Her entire kitchen consisted of one small copper pot and a knife. It was enough.

She rode quietly up the Yellowstone River. The waters of this river tumbled out of the Roof of the World and raced eastward toward the Big River. The water was icy and teeming with trout, but no Absaroka would stoop to eating fish. She despised fish, and thought that eating fish was the reason white men and women were sick all the time. But the water was icy and sweet, and sometimes she paused at the gravelly bank just to sip some.

She saw no one. Ever since the Lakota had stopped white men from using John Bozeman's trail two years earlier, the road had grown weeds and fallen into silence. Now it was rapidly disappearing as rain and snow smoothed the ruts and grass hid the campgrounds. Was this the end of white men? Had the Lakota driven them away forever? Foolish question. It was just a small time of quietness before the noise of the white men started again.

It was a good road for wagons but she felt no need to follow it. Her pony took her anywhere she wished, and not just along a trail calculated to let wagons pass over the land. So she watched eagles hunt, and hawks patrol, and listened to ravens comment about every passing thing. Her spirit helper, the white and black magpie, flitted here and there. All her life, Victoria and magpies knew each other and helped each other. Now she saw half a dozen of them making a ruckus about something, so she strung her bow and nocked an arrow, drawn from the quiver at her back, and rode ahead, not knowing what she might see.

It proved to be a black bear out of her winter den, probably ornery, hunting for food just when nature provided little. A newborn cub appeared from a hidden place in the river brush, already knowing how to hide itself at his mother's command. Victoria gave the mother bear wide berth, something her nervous pony seemed to appreciate. Let them live and grow. She honored bears as her sisters.

Later she came across a pregnant antelope, restlessly circling a sunny valley, looking for a safe place to birth. Victoria lowered her bow. Let the mother live; let the newborn suck on her teat, find life, and enjoy the spring breezes. The older Victoria got, the more something in her resisted taking female life. It did not matter why. This is how she felt, so this is how she would conduct herself. But she would kill and eat any brother male sonofabitch.

That night she brewed willow bark tea to drive away the pains of her body, and then rested, sitting against sunwarmed sandstone, her robe around her. If she didn't eat, what did it matter? What she wanted of life now was escape from the pain in her bones.

The next day was much the same, but she knew she was getting close to Skye. She entered a narrows where the river had punched through some gray and brown rock, and here the trail took her across wind-scraped slopes until she could descend again. She passed by some mule deer at sunset, and kept on because the great bend of the river was not far, only an hour or so more and she could be with Skye this evening, and maybe hold him and make jokes with him, and rub his back if he hurt, which he always did.

But when she reached the great bend in the early dark, she found no one there. It was as quiet as if no noisy white man had ever been there. She saw no cook fire. She hunted for his campsite and found nothing new; some very old and lonely-looking. She knew he was careful in danger, and might have moved his camp away from the river and into the foothills, or maybe up the Shields River to avoid someone or something. So she searched all the places she knew he would choose, and found no sign of him, and as dusk closed she puzzled where he might be.

But this was a large place, and he could be anywhere. The night thickened, and the last alpen glow vanished from the giant shoulders high above, and she could no longer see.

She built a noisy white men's fire, sending sparks high into the night, knowing he would see it and scout it out. Then she withdrew from the flames and shrouded herself in darkness some distance away, and waited. Surely her man would come, understand, and begin a search that would reunite them.

The cold settled around her, and the night grew still and dark. She undid the halters of her ponies and let them graze freely, and settled in her robes, and waited patiently for dawn and the stories it might tell her.

Chapter 10

The moment Mary crossed the Yellowstone and stood on the far shore, a river apart from Victoria, she knew herself as Blue Dawn, the Shoshone. Mary had vanished from mind. That was unexpected. Now she was Blue Dawn, en route to visit her people, maybe stay in the lodge of her brother, The Runner, until she was called to Skye's lodge at some unknown time.

But there was more. She had become a different person, too, just by crossing that river. For many years, she had been Skye's woman, Skye's younger wife, and had made no decisions of her own. Whatever Skye and Victoria did, her fate was to go with them, believe what they believed, love what they loved, befriend whomever they befriended. Now, suddenly, Victoria had given Mary her liberty, a time apart from the Skye household among the Crows.

Those had been happy times at first, time when she brought North Star into the world and loved the child and nurtured him and the three of them all raised the boy, and life was sweet. Those times glowed in her mind. She had a son, she was the woman of the greatly honored Mister Skye, and she had marveled at all the new things that came to her, things that might never have brightened her if she had become the woman of one of her people. No other child came to them, though she hoped more would. It was a mystery.

Then Skye changed everything. He wanted the boy to be

schooled in white men's mysteries. Her son was taken far away, where the Big River met the Father of Waters. And that's when the sadness seeped into her life, and she learned to smile at Skye and laugh when he and Victoria laughed, and did her tasks faithfully and with many smiles. But it was not good. Who could say whether she would ever see this flesh of her flesh again? She loved the sturdy boy, and when he was taken away he was torn too, because he was too young to be ripped from his mother, and he looked desperately at her, that one last desperate look, when Colonel Bullock drove away in a buggy carrying her son with him.

The letters came once in a while, addressed to her in a child's hand, and Skye read them to her whenever they stopped at Fort Laramie, where the letters collected. And she wrote her boy, or rather had Skye make the marks on paper that signified what she said, and she sent her letters to St. Louis.

And so the years passed, and all that while Mary smiled at Skye and Victoria while her heart grew heavier and the days grew longer, until she thought she could not bear another hour of another day. But she hid it all. Now she stood on the far bank, seeing Victoria wave to her, and already she was changed. For the first time since she had reached womanhood, Blue Dawn had no master or mistress saying what must be thought or done or hoped for.

The sense of it was huge, so huge that she could not fathom what was happening inside of her. When Victoria had proposed that she spend time with her people, she had not dreamed that she would become another person, someone new and old at once. She knew at once who this new and old self was: she was North Star's mother now, and not Skye's younger wife. She watched Victoria collect her horse and ride slowly west, upriver, and vanish. Blue Dawn sorrowed. She loved Victoria. She loved Skye. But now some inner force was rushing through her, and she knew her first task was to cache the lodge. She didn't want it. She looked for cliffs hemming the south bank of the river, and saw none. Better to cache something like that high in a cliff, where it would stay dry and undiscovered, than in any low place.

She traveled east until she found a decayed cliff with some hollows in it, well above the river. It would do. She unloaded the lodgepoles and the lodge cover and pushed them to the rear of a dry shelf where they would escape most weather. And then she hung the rest of her kit on the pack frame of one pony, and retreated. At the base, she studied the place for a landmark, found one—an odd column of striated rock—and knew she would remember how to reclaim the lodge someday.

Now, riding one pony and leading two others, she headed south through a lonely land on a chill spring day. She knew the way. She would find a home with her brother, The Runner, and renew her life. But not right away. Not for a while. Not for many moons. That insight startled her, just as everything else had startled her the moment she was separated from the iron rule of Victoria. Day after day she rode through a chill spring, alone and unnoticed, quietly following the Yellowstone as it hurried east, marveling at the change within her.

For the first time in her life, she was free. She marveled at it. She was alone. It was strange, something she felt more in her chest than in her head. Skye had made all the family decisions. Victoria had not been a bossy senior wife but had expected Mary to join her in whatever needed doing, whether it was collecting firewood or sewing moccasins. When it came to raising the boy, Victoria and Mary were both mothers. And now Mary traveled with no one beside her, the hollow land spreading away from her in all directions. It brought an almost unbearable ache to her bosom. She could turn her ponies and go west if she chose, or east, or north, or south. She could stop if she chose, start if she chose, ascend the nearest peak if she chose. It made her giddy at first, but then it made her hurt.

The vision of North Star, far away in a white man's school, made her ache inside, ache as she never had ached except for the day when he was taken from her. She wanted just to see him. This hunger arose in her breasts and womb, not her mind. She had a maternal hunger she could not drive out of her, a hunger that rode the crest of her sudden liberty, a hunger that formed visions of the eight-year-old boy in her mind, where the images burned and smoldered and built into a flood of anguish. The sun rose in the east each morning, rose where North Star must be.

St. Louis was a long way off. It lay in some mysterious place far across prairie country, and then across hilly country, and finally at the throat of the rivers. Once she had heard that it would take two moons to walk there. She could scarcely imagine it. The white men had built a railroad for their steam wagons, but she didn't know whether it would take her to St. Louis. She did know that the steamboats would take her there, down the Big River, but she had no money for that. And she didn't know whether they would permit a woman of the People to travel there alone. White men had strange rules, and she had never fathomed them or where they came from or why they existed.

The farther she rode, the more determined she became. Should she find her people first, and tell her brother where she was going to go? Should she find the Absarokas and tell them? That might be good, but it would not be her way. She had settled on a way, and now she would follow it, no matter where it might lead her.

Would she even recognize her son? Of course she would. Now he would have fifteen winters. She would know him on sight. And he would know her. She hardly dared imagine what might happen then; whether they could spend time together, renew the ties of kinship, of mothers and sons together. Since she didn't know, she set that aside. She only knew that she would follow the path to this place called St. Louis, and she would find her son, and then the future would take care of itself.

She knew how to go there, more or less. She needed to reach the Big Road, the one that went past Fort Laramie, where she and Skye had been many times. The Big Road would not have many travelers on it now that the steam wagons were going on the iron rails. That would be good. Her ponies could graze.

She wasn't sure how to reach the Big Road from the Big Horn Valley, though. If she could find the trail she had traveled many times with Skye, she would be all right. But she didn't need a road. Her pony would take her almost anywhere. White men needed roads, but Shoshones needed only a keen eye.

She traveled quietly, not thinking about anything. Once she spotted a group of white men on mules on the north side of the Yellowstone. She feared them more than warriors from other tribes. These were probably miners. They had spread across the land, wanting to tear up the earth and rock. There was no telling what was in their minds, or what they would do with a lone Indian woman.

But they did not see her. That was because she traveled lightly across the breast of the earth, blending in to rock and clay and brush, moving slowly, as a grazing animal might move, so that she didn't stir up the ravens and magpies, and no crows scolded her. It took many days before she reached the turnoff and headed south, leaving the Yellowstone behind her. But it was all as she remembered it. She was not lost.

The great basin of the Big Horn ran north and south, and was guarded by snowy peaks to the east, and to the west barren, gloomy hills that slowly rose to high country, and the great backbone of the world, still wrapped in blinding white. It was spring in the basin, but winter above, and sometimes the winds reminded her that Father Cold had not departed and was waiting to bite her cheeks.

She stayed well away from the Big Horn River, wondering whether she might run into Victoria's people, the Kicked-in-the-Bellies band, making their summer home on lush pasture along the great stream. Her trip to St. Louis would be a secret from all the people. They were all her friends and would welcome her with smiles and much honor, but they might also ask too many questions and she was not in a mood to answer them. So she ghosted south, clinging to the barren foothills, where there was little game. She did not suffer for food, for she could make a meal of almost anything, and now tender buds filled her cook pot, and little new roots, and fresh-laid eggs stolen from nests. She did spend time at all this, but did not hunger and was content.

One night she weathered a sleet storm and bitter winds, but she turned her sleep-canvas into a poncho, and rode her pony while inside of her little tent, and kept Father Cold at bay.

The next morning frost lay thick upon the land, and every stem of grass was whitened, but that did not stop her ponies from grazing it.

She thought she knew where the Absaroka People were summering and gave that place a wide berth so that no tribal elders would stay her or ask where she was going. She did not feel that she was doing anything wrong; only that she had chosen a Way, and she intended to walk the Way, and it was not anyone else's business where she walked, or why.

But if she avoided contact with the Absaroka, she dreaded even more an accidental meeting with her own band, where she might find herself the guest of her brother The Runner, a great headman among them, and then she might be required to tell them where she was going. Then she would be forced to divulge her secret. In truth, she would be less free with her clan, and they might not honor the Way she had chosen for herself. But they were most likely on the Wind River, far south, with the Owl Creek Mountains lying between this valley and that one. That was their true home, except when they went hunting for the shaggies. She would not go that way. There was a creek named after Mister Skye's friend Jim Bridger that would take her across the eastern mountains to the Big Road.

She drifted south, and her ponies fattened as they walked, nipping at the tender spring grasses that now were pushing exuberantly toward the heavens. She chose a path that took her across the foothills of the Big Horn Mountains, a path that was not easy because it was up and down, but a path that let her follow her Way. Her resolve hardened in her. She had wavered for many suns, wondering what her man, Mister Skye, might think. He might not like her new Way, but she couldn't help that.

Several times, while she sat quietly on her pony on a pine-dotted slope, she saw horsemen far below, small dots moving in a hurried way. She could not tell who they were. She could not even say whether they were one of the People or white men.

One day, in the middle of what white men called May, she found the road up Bridger's creek and took it. This was a wagon road, but not much used anymore, and now the ancient ruts were filled with grass, and places where the white men had carved into slopes or built little bridges were washing away. She had been on it several times with Skye and Victoria; it would take her to the Big Road and Fort Laramie.

It was also a twisty, hilly road and that was what bought her trouble. She rounded a shoulder one moment, and there before her was a cavalry patrol, ten bluecoats, all mounted, with several packmules behind.

Within moments they swarmed around her, eyeing her from under their duck-billed hats. Their leader, a one-bar-on-the-shoulder, motioned her to halt.

"You speekee white?" he asked.

She thought better of replying, and slowly shook her head. It was safer to say and do nothing. One never knew about blue-belly soldiers.

He tried a few hand signs he had picked up somewhere, signs that read, Who are you? What tribe? Where are you going? She smiled and shook her head.

They were eyeing her ponies and the little that she was carrying, mostly her bedroll and a small kit of personal things.

"I guess we'd better take you with us," the officer said after a few moments of impasse. "Can't rightly say what a lone squaw's doing around here."

Chapter 11

Mary wondered whether it had been a mistake, hiding her English from them. Now they wanted to take her somewhere, make a prisoner of her.

She chose to speak in Shoshone, telling them that she was Blue Dawn, of the Eastern Shoshone people of Washakie, and she was going to Fort Laramie now.

"I think that's Shoshone," said a three-stripe sergeant tanned to the color of cedar bark.

He eyed her, and made the wavy line in sign language that signified her people.

She nodded slightly.

"Squaw's a Shoshone, all right, but that ain't what they usually wear," the sergeant said.

"Can you talk it?" the one-bar-on-the-shoulder asked.

"Not enough to say anything to her. I can listen it a little."

"Try telling her she can't leave the reservation. Washakie's got himself a home over on the Wind River, and now they got to stay there."

Mary bridled at that. What was this? Making her people stay on the river?

The seamed old sergeant tried a little sign language, a few Shoshone words, and a few English just to salt the talk a little.

"See here, little lady," he said, his hands making signs. "You got to go back now. You got a nice place, and you got to get a paper from the agent to leave."

She refused to acknowledge what she was hearing and seeing, but sat sternly on her pony. How could this be? Were the People prisoners now?

She didn't want to know any more. She would ask Skye about it.

"I don't see she's doing any harm here," the sergeant said.

"Search the panniers," the one-bar said.

Mary slumped deep into her saddle, pushing back an anger that boiled through her.

A one-stripe got off his pony and opened the pannier, poking around at her kettle and flint and steel and bag of pemmican. Then he lifted up the packet of letters, the ones from North Star that came to Fort Laramie, the ones Skye patiently read to her, over and over.

"She's got some letters, looks like," the one-stripe said, and handed them to the one-bar-on-the-shoulder.

"Sent to a Barnaby Skye, care of the post sutler, Fort Laramie. Never heard of him."

"I have," the sergeant said. "Old squaw man. Thought he was dead long ago. He was a mountain man before he settled in with the Crows."

"Still alive, looks like," the one-bar said. "Postmarked this March."

"She's just checking the fort for Skye's mail," the three-stripe sergeant said. "Probably some slut of Skye's, sent down to get the news."

Mary reddened.

The one-bar turned to her. "Fort Laramie?" he asked, slowly enunciating La-ra-me.

She nodded.

"Well, no harm in it. Now if you were a buck, we'd march you back to your reservation."

He returned the packet to the one-stripe, who put it back in her pannier and closed it.

"Free to go," he said to her. "I imagine you understood some of this, if you're tied up with the squaw man."

Mary didn't acknowledge it.

The patrol formed into twos and headed toward the Big Horn Basin. She suppressed a tremor and urged her ponies south. She needed to think about this insult. And about this penning of the People.

The whole world looked different now, as if the sun had decided to travel from west to east, or as if Father Winter decided to be warm and Brother Summer decided to freeze the toes of the People. How could this be? The Absarokas had talked of it, but she hadn't paid much attention. Skye didn't talk of it at all, which told her much.

Whose land did she now walk upon? She walked over the breast of the earth, and it was the privilege of all to walk upon all the earth. What were the soldiers doing? Looking for hunters or war parties, to send them back to their new prisons? And how was all this arranged? Who agreed to it?

She remembered that two summers earlier there had been a great gathering at Fort Laramie, in which the white fathers had proposed homes for the several tribes. And her chief, Washakie, had agreed to it. He was their friend. But did this now mean that the People were prisoners, unlike white people, who could go anywhere they chose?

Was this what her son, North Star, was learning in this school in St. Louis? What of him, half of one blood and half of another? If they looked at him as Mister Skye's son, he could go anywhere and live anywhere. If they looked at him as her boy, they would make him stay on the Wind River Reservation, and not leave without permission. He would have to stay inside of some invisible lines, best known by the white men who drew them. Was this right? Was that why Skye had sent him to the school, so that he would be free?

The encounter with the bluecoats had changed everything, but she didn't quite know how. She would sort it out as she traveled. She hurried along the road—the white man's road—that would take her over the mountains. Whose mountains now? Did these white men own the sun and stars and moon too? Did they claim the rivers and lakes? Was all the fish and game theirs now? Were the blessed buffalo and elk and deer and coyotes theirs now, except when they crossed a homeland of a tribe?

The land looked just the same as she had remembered it. The rushing creek, just beginning to swell with snowmelt, raced beside her. The cliffs that hemmed the creek and its valley were ancient beyond measure, gray rock that no man could ever own. The pines that scattered themselves in the watercourses of this dry land belonged to no one. As she gained altitude the cold grew intense, and soon she was in rotting snow, which wearied the ponies. She wrapped the bright cream blanket with red stripes—a white man's blanket—tight about her as her pony slopped through slush.

Did the slush belong to white men? Did the grass her ponies ate belong to white men? Did white men have the right to graze their ponies on the homelands of the tribes? Did the white men own all things in the earth and water and high above?

Late that day she reached the summit, and walked her ponies through soggy snow, dirtied by dust and the passage of animals. Now she could see the prints of the shod hooves of the soldiers, caught in cold shadow where they would remain until Father Sun caught them.

Dusk caught her well down the southerly flanks, on a grassy flat that had warmed all day in the tender spring sun. She scouted for a place to make a camp; the whole world was wet and there was nowhere to lie down without an icy soaking. She turned toward distant cliffs, knowing those

would be her sole comfort. She easily found a hollow under
an overhang, and knew it would do as well as anything. She
was well off the trail, but that was good. She had no protection at all except for a few knives, one sheathed at her
waist, the others in her kitchen gear.

The hollow had lion scat in it, and not at all ancient, either. A mother had nursed her cubs here. Mary didn't know
how she knew that, but she did. Women found safe places
and made homes of them.

She turned the ponies out on the grass. They were docile,
and would graze deep into the night, unless a wolf or a lion
prowled. She would forgo a fire this night, and instead settled in the back of the hollow, wrapped tightly in her
blanket. She felt comfortable in this woman's place.

She had rarely seen a white woman. The men had pushed
into these lands, gangs and pairs and columns of them, leaving their women behind. Even Skye had come alone, without a woman, long ago. Now it was men, not women, who
were drawing an invisible line upon the breast of the earth,
and making her people stay on one side of it. Would a
woman do anything like that? Men were mysterious, and the
cause of all change. She knew it was not her office to do
those things, draw boundaries, make war, make the earth
different. Her office was to gather food and feed the men,
and to bring her boy to manhood.

Maybe when she got to this place called St. Louis, she
would see lots of white women, and not just the handful who
westered with their men. She could talk to women. She
could share knowledge. She knew the best ways to gather
roots and seeds and cook them. She knew the best ways to
make elk-skin clothing for Mister Skye. She made the best
moccasins, better than Victoria's moccasins, and they lasted
longer too.

She knew it would be easier for her to go to this faraway

place because she was a woman. A Shoshone man might find trouble with every step. White people didn't like Indian men and were suspicious of them, and thought they would steal or kill. So it was good to be a woman going to the place Skye called St. Louis.

The night passed peacefully. She had dozed eventually, and had seen many night-visitors who had stopped at the hollow to see who was there. She sensed the mother lion had come and gone while she slept, and had left her alone.

In the dawn she discerned her three ponies grazing peacefully. Patches of fog hid the world. She felt good, had enjoyed a bone-dry night, and now it was time to ghost through the mist, ever downhill to the river the white men called the North Platte.

When she reached the Big Road days later she found it empty, and the reason was plain. It was so wet that wagons could not roll over it without miring. She saw awful ruts dug by iron wheels, and ox-prints deep in the muck, where weary animals had struggled to drag the gumbo-bound wagons. It was too early for the great migration of white people, and those who had tried it this time of year were undoubtedly regretting it.

The muck was hard even on her ponies, but she was not bound to the road, and found easier passage off to the side, away from the mire. She was in no hurry, either, and let her ponies fatten on the tender grasses joyously reaching for the sun.

When she did come across white men, they were usually with pack animals rather than wagons. They always looked her over with curiosity, but she never let on that she understood what they were saying. Sometimes their comments about savages or filthy squaws made her burn. Whenever they stopped to converse with her, she spoke only Shoshone and smiled quietly. It was good. One cheerful company of bearded prospectors even gave her a sack of flour as a gift, just because they felt like it.

"Lifts the heart to see a right pretty lady," one said.

She nodded, and acknowledged the gift with a bright smile.

By the time she reached Fort Laramie she had resolved not to stop there. Skye's friend Colonel Bullock was no longer operating the store. She didn't know a soul, and had no money or credit to buy anything. And she didn't need anything anyway, but some bright ribbons would have given her joy.

She was observed. All who passed the post were carefully observed and counted by the army. But she was a woman, after all, and what did it matter? So she walked her ponies past the flapping red, white, and blue flag, and the blue regimental flag, and the blue-bellies who were lounging on the shaded veranda of the store, and the others working at the stables or chopping firewood. There was scarcely an immigrant wagon parked there, but in this month of May, as they called it, who could travel? It was chilly, and she smelled the pine smoke from all the fort's fires drifting through the narrows that contained the post.

And then she was free, advancing eastward toward the great quiet prairies, where only the wind made a sound.

Chapter 12

Many Quill Woman—she used her Absaroka name more and more these winters—woke alone after a light doze. Skye was not at the bend of the Yellowstone. She padded down to the water's edge and washed her face and hands, feeling the icy water abrade her seamed flesh. There were young cattails rising from the mud of a slough nearby. Maybe she would make a breakfast of their starchy roots. But she didn't feel hungry. She often forgot to eat, just like so many of the old ones in her village.

She felt all right, except for the great weariness that comes to reside in one's body after a long life. She was used to it. But she thought she could never get used to the loss of vision, the thin yellow skim that softened everything and made the bright clean world hazy. Someday soon the only light that would reach her would be milky and the world would be white and without form.

She found her pony grazing peacefully, and bridled and saddled her. A simple hackamore and a light saddle built over a sawbuck frame sufficed. She had made a hundred of them over the years. A saddle provided a place to hang her feet and kept the pony's backbone from sawing her in two. She rolled her few things in her blankets and tied the roll on the cantle. She would not bother with breakfast.

She began a spiral circle, looking for anything she did not wish to see. Her eyes weren't good, but she would not miss what she dreaded to see. She stopped at the ashes of a campfire, dismounted, and studied the area. She could not tell how old it was. She remounted, circled wider, probed adjoining gulches, and studied the land from ridges.

He was not there. He had not died there, either, unless the relentless river had washed him away. She hunched into her saddle a moment, drawing her old coat tight against the probing May breeze, and then turned toward the mountains. Beyond them was white men's land, and the place called Bozeman City.

She ascended into winter, and the next day descended into spring, riding past Fort Ellis, built to protect white people from the wild Indians to the east. No one at that sprawling complex of log buildings noticed. She was a bony old squaw, and thus not important. She reached Bozeman City a while later, passing a wagon yard first, and then a barn, and finally a scatter of wooden buildings, some of sawn wood, some of log, some whitewashed, most of them weathering gray with the sun and rain.

No adult noticed. Who cared about a lone squaw? But finally some children collected, trotting along beside her as she sat her pony. Boys, mostly, wild little things without the manners of any Absaroka child.

"Hey, you speak English?" a blond boy yelled.

"You're goddamn right," she replied.

"Oh!"

"Hey, how come you talk that way?" a freckled kid asked.

"So white boys will shit their pants," she said.

"Boy, wait till I tell my pa about you!"

"Where you going?" asked another, this one smaller.

"I'm going to scalp everyone in town and burn it," she replied.

"How come?"

"Because I'm a warrior woman, that's why."

"You ever kill a white man?"

"You bet your ass," she said.

That subdued them a little. They trailed a little behind, and finally out of arrow range, and she steered her pony along a mucky street lined with sagging mercantiles with false fronts, most of which looked ready to burn away at the slightest excuse. The tawdry little town darkened the golden expanses of the Three Forks country beyond, and she wished it would turn itself into dust.

Now that she was in Bozeman City, she scarcely knew what to do, where to look, what to ask. She felt safe enough. Age and femaleness protected her. If she had been a young Absaroka warrior riding proudly into town, things might be different. She felt an ancient helplessness she had known all her life when it came to dealing with white men.

Was Skye here? The town wasn't so big it could hide him. She chose a saloon. She could not read its name, but she knew somehow it was a drinking place. Maybe Skye would be inside.

She slid off her pony, letting her old limbs adjust, and then drew her blanket around her. The blanket warded off the gazes of white men, so she pulled it tight, to make a barrier to their eyes. She opened the creaking door and confronted the rank odor and darkness of these places. This was lit by a small window and nothing else. A line of hairy and smelly men stood at a bar. They all stared at her. Skye was not among them.

"Hey, squaw, you're not allowed. You want a bottle, you come to the back door. And have cash. I ain't bartering," the barkeep growled. He wiped his hairy hands across his grubby apron.

"Goddamn outhouses smell better than here," she said, and walked out.

There was no place for native people in this new world, she thought. Maybe Skye was right, sending the boy to be made into a white man. Maybe her people were dying out, never to return. Maybe she was the last generation of the Absaroka.

She looked for his ponies. She tried a clapboard mercantile, where the suspicious clerk, wearing a black sleeve garter and chin whiskers, followed her every step through the dry goods, obviously determined to prevent imminent theft.

"Shit on you," she said pleasantly at the door, which jangled as she left.

She probed a grocery, wandering past cracker barrels and pickle jars, again followed by a slit-eyed boy who carried a rolling pin as a defense against ancient redskins.

"Go to hell," she said.

She peered into the window of a saddlery but did not see him. She entered another saloon, but the barkeep barreled down on her, pointed toward the door, and pushed her through it. She did not have time enough to see if Skye was there, but his horse wasn't tied to the rail in front of the place. She circled around and checked the alley just in case he was lying in it.

To hell with all white men, and maybe Skye too, she thought. White men with their bread-dough faces and wiry beards and greedy eyes.

She peered into a restaurant, this one operated by a matronly woman wearing a black eye patch who frowned at her, and she did not see Skye there. Nothing but hairy white men eating away. She discovered a bank, one of those mysterious places she knew little about except that money issued from them and they took money away from others. She thought Skye might be in it, and discovered a great silence within, with two whiskered men locked into cages eyeing her. But no one said a word. They stared at her; she grinned at them.

"Goddamn," she said.

"May we help you, madam?" yellow whiskers asked.

"I want money. I think I'll be a rich sonofabitch," she said. "Build us a goddamn house."

"You will want to talk to our mortgage department," orange whiskers said. "And he's out foreclosing on a ranch."

She didn't know what that was, but it sounded bad. But she liked this whiskers. He had orange hairy cheeks, but he cut off the hair at lip level. And he wore an orange bush between his lips and his nostrils. He probably didn't like the way he looks, if he did that, she thought. Skye didn't care one way or another, and had himself a big hairy beard. But this one shaved in patches, smooth here, hairy there. Maybe that said something about him. Damned if she would ever understand white men.

"Hey, my man wants to build a big house. You got money for him?" she asked.

"He could apply for a mortgage," whiskers said. "He would need to have good credit."

"What's that?"

"Assets. Something to protect our loan to him."

"Like what?"

"Oh, deeded land, a business, a mine, a herd of cattle, investments. Does the gentleman have these things?"

"Hell no," she said. "He's got a lodge, two wives, a Sharps rifle, and bear medicine. He's got a bear-claw necklace, biggest goddamn claws you ever saw. You want collateral? Bear medicine is it. No one got medicine like Skye."

He pursed his lips. "That would make it more troublesome. We need tangible assets." He paused. "What does he do?"

"He sits in the lodge all winter and makes love first one wife and then the other."

"Is he a big chief?"

"Hell yes, biggest goddamn chief ever lived. I'm his older woman, and he's got a younger one too. More wives you got, the richer you are. How about that?"

"Ah, that wouldn't be collateral," whiskers said.

"Young wife, Mary, she's still pretty."

"Ah, madam, I'm afraid—"

"Damned if I know what this collateral is, but when I find him I'll drag him in here as soon as he's sobered up and we'll get you some. He's off sucking a bottle somewhere. Then we'll figure it out. Two wives, that's good collateral, eh?"

Whiskers smiled. "You make an interesting case," he said.

"Hey, goddamn, I'll be back," she said.

She perused the rest of Bozeman City, saw no sign of him, checked the alleys behind the saloons, where he wasn't, and finally realized the sonofabitch was somewhere else. On her way out of town, she passed the livery barn, saw his nag in the pen, got off her pony under the suspicious gaze of the owner, and approached.

"Where are you hiding the sonofabitch?" she asked.

The liveryman yawned and jerked a thumb toward a hay barn. "I got him where I want him," he said. "He's got no choice. He's the worst audience I ever had. I'd like a little respect but I don't get it from him."

She tromped into shadow, was struck with the sweet, pungent smell of hay, and found Skye lying on a spread-out canvas on a plateau of soft, prickly hay. She stared. His leg was bound up. Her man had a broken leg. Maybe he fell down in a saloon.

"I thought you might find me," he said.

"Goddammit," she said. "I leave you alone for a few days and you get into trouble."

He didn't laugh. She looked into his face and saw gauntness and pain there. There was more. She saw a broken man, hemmed by age.

"Now I listen," she said. "Tell me. You get drunk or something?"

"I got thrown by an ox," he said.

"You what?"

"Thrown by an ox! Don't you hear me?" he snapped.

Wearily Skye told her what had happened at the bend of the Yellowstone, and how he was rescued by some teamsters looking for livestock, and how the very ox that had caught and thrown him with its horns was now at work dragging a freight wagon.

"Still hurt some," he said. "But I'm here, and they're feeding me. I've got a roof over me and a bed."

"Oh, Skye," she said, and knelt beside him, then clung to him.

Chapter 13

The man looming above Skye as he lay in the hay barn proved to be the town marshal, Magnus Cropper. Skye assumed as much, noting the man's black frock coat and the steel circlet pinned to his lapel.

"I've been looking for you," Cropper said. "Complaints is what I'm dealing with."

Behind him, Clyde Kangaroo hovered, bristling with curiosity.

Skye felt Victoria tense beside him.

"This old squaw, she's not welcome in Bozeman City, scaring white boys half to death with her foul threats."

"They deserved some scaring," she said.

"Who are you?" the marshal asked.

"Mister Skye."

"A drifter, I suppose. Squaw man, looks like."

Skye sat up and clamped his ancient top hat to his locks.

"This is my wife, Victoria, of the Absaroka People," he said. "And you, sir?"

"Cropper, Skye. The law here." He had the look of someone not expecting trouble.

"I prefer to be addressed as mister."

Cropper smiled. "Don't matter how you want to be called. You're leaving town. Vagrants and tramps and foul-mouthed squaws, they ain't welcome. We're a proper town."

"He's a border man," Kangaroo said. "Been here forty,

fifty years. He come to this country long before there was any Bozeman City. He led them fur brigades."

"Am I supposed to be impressed, Kangaroo?"

"He's got him a real reputation. I know all about him. He don't say nothing about himself, but I found it out. You ever heard of Jim Bridger? Well this one's twice Jim Bridger."

Cropper ignored the liveryman. "Don't matter," he said. "This pair ain't respectable white people, and that matters. And from the looks of them, they don't have a plugged nickel, so they're beggars, vagrants, and I'm shipping them out."

"I've a broken leg," Skye said.

"It matters not to me. Use a crutch."

"Goddamn savage," Victoria said.

"Public cussing, that's a misdemeanor," Cropper announced. "Taught some boys to foul their own mouths is what you did. I heard about it fast enough from a few folks. Here's your choice. You git out right now on your own, or I'll break your other knee."

"He didn't do nothing," Kangaroo said. "He's paid up for two more weeks. I traded him a month of chow for a pony."

"Then I suppose you owe him two weeks of chow," Cropper said.

"Marshal, this here man, you ask the old-timers who he is."

"He ain't welcome. We're civilized now," Cropper said.

Skye nodded to Victoria. "I can ride," he said. "My knee won't like it, but I'll deal with it."

Victoria stared bitterly at the marshal and headed for the pens where Skye's buckskin horse stood quietly, as well as her own pony.

"I tell you, Marshal, this here man is more than you think," Kangaroo said.

"What I think is that this hobo in greasy buckskins is on his way out of town."

The marshal hadn't backed down an inch. Skye looked him over. A bull of a man, with a boxer's build and stance and a lantern jaw. He seemed unarmed, but who could say?

"Any houses for sale in town?" Skye asked.

Cropper stared. "You couldn't afford an outhouse," he said.

Kangaroo vanished and Skye thought he was seeing the last of the liveryman.

"You took up with the Crows, so go back to them," Cropper said. "Go live in a skin tent."

The sheriff was somewhere in midlife, his face seamed from hard living. He was tough but his gut was bulging. He had Bozeman City in his pocket.

"Help me up," Skye said.

The marshal did so, lifting Skye by the shoulders. Skye stood on his good leg and leaned against a post.

"It ain't you bothers me, it's that foul-mouthed squaw. I don't want that kind of trash in my town. If it was just you, a white man, I wouldn't give a damn," Cropper said.

"That's a shiny badge," Skye said. "Too bad it doesn't shine."

Cropper spent some time processing that, looking for the insult, and finally snarled.

"Get on that nag and get out."

Victoria brought the saddled ponies up and helped Skye up. His knee howled, but there was nothing he could do about it. He tried to keep it pushed forward rather than bent, but it didn't do any good.

Then Kangaroo emerged toting a burlap sack.

"Here's two weeks' grub," he said. "Fair's fair. You didn't stay a month."

He handed it to Victoria.

It was all Skye could do to keep from fainting. The savage pain at his knee laced his leg, his thigh, his hip.

"Don't come back," Cropper said smoothly. "Next time, I'll get rough."

"A goddamn savage," Victoria said, loud enough so Cropper couldn't miss it.

"You want a night behind bars?" the marshal retorted.

They rode a well-worn trail toward the mountains.

"What's a vagrant, dammit?" Victoria asked.

"A drifter with no money or job."

"Well, hell, my whole tribe's vagrants."

"That's just about how the marshal sees you."

"But we got food and good ponies. We got houses and bows and arrows. We got everything we need."

Victoria took them east, going slowly to keep Skye from jarring his knee any more than necessary. But Skye knew he couldn't last long, and he felt sweat build in his brow. He wondered whether he'd manage one mile. But he hung on. Damned if he'd quit.

He lasted about as long as it took to reach Fort Ellis, three miles from Bozeman City, and then Victoria had to help him down. He tumbled heavily to the ground, his descent barely checked by her, and lay flat on his back. This was open meadow, close to the post. He didn't know how he could go on.

It didn't take long for the command to send a pair of bluecoats to them.

"Trouble, sir?" asked a corporal.

"No, I'm just fine, and my wife's just fine, and the world's just fine."

"Trouble, then."

Skye was too worn to respond.

"Get my man a wagon, dammit," Victoria said.

In time, Colonel Blossom appeared.

"You, is it? Something go wrong in town?"

"The city marshal decided we're vagrants."

"I insulted some boys, goddammit," Victoria said.

A faint smile bloomed in the middle of Blossom's beard. "I'll get you settled, and we'll talk," Blossom said.

Skye nodded, too wearied by pain to say much.

They brought a spring wagon, gently lifted him into it, and drove him into the post. Skye listened to the debate about what to do with the civilian and his squaw, but hurt too much to care. Eventually they cleaned out a harness room, brought in a stuffed mattress, and settled Skye in the stables.

"Bring them a ration every mess," someone said.

Skye felt lucky, and soon felt luckier. He had a visitor.

"Mister Skye, I'm Balboa, the new post surgeon. Mind if I have a look?"

"It can't hurt any more than it does now, sir."

The man was surprisingly gentle, and set about to replace the splints the teamsters had used to encase Skye's leg with a proper cast.

"I don't know for sure what's what in there, but nothing's poking through. Your tibia's probably broken across here, but you're too swollen up for me to tell. The fibula's broken here, where the hardness is. It's bad, and you'll limp. I'm going to give you some powders," Balboa said.

Skye nodded and downed a pill. That was the last he knew. He awakened in darkness and awakened in daylight, and the world turned over, and the pills they gave him leached the pain away, and he slept some more. Sometimes he awoke thirsty and they gave him cool water. He wasn't hungry, but the water was good. Victoria held the cup. Then they began slowing down the pills, and night and day slowed down too, until one day he awakened clearheaded and as weak as an infant.

They helped him sit up.

"It's been a while," Colonel Blossom said.

The man was sitting on a keg beside Skye's cot. Victoria sat on the rough plank floor.

"How long?"

"Five days. Your leg's not so inflamed, I understand."

Five days? Five days and nights lying in this harness room?

"I got your story from Mrs. Skye. I also talked some with Marshal Cropper, and Clyde Kangaroo, and a few others. Some of the teamsters too."

"You're going to send me back to Victoria's band, then?"

The commanding officer shrugged. "That's up to you. The story I've got from Mrs. Skye is that you're looking for a place to settle down. You'd like a hearth and a stove in the winter, and a veranda with a view in the summer."

"It got hard for me to winter with her people. They're good people, and they've taken care of us. But I need a home. I set out for the bend of the Yellowstone, that being the place with a good view every way a man looks, and that's where I ran into trouble."

"From an ox."

"Yes, an ox. Not a bear, not a catamount or a wolf, but a bloody ox. The country's full of wild oxen, abandoned along the Bozeman Trail—before the war."

"Dr. Balboa tells me you'll have a limp. The leg is pretty well locked up at the knee. That might change your plans."

Skye hated it. All his life he'd been fit. It would take a fit man to build a house. He had no money and would have to build it the hard way, the way the Yank pioneers did theirs, with an axe, a drawknife, and a stone boat.

"Not if I can help it," he said.

"I'm not here to discourage you, sir. You'll find out soon enough what you can do—and can't do."

"I'll do whatever it takes."

But Skye knew it was bravado. A log home might not be possible now, not if he intended to build it himself. Age and injury were murdering a dream. Had it come to this?

"At any rate, Mister Skye, you have the hospitality of Fort Ellis for as long as you need it." The colonel rose. "Glad you're coming along. Balboa's a good man."

Skye watched him go. He turned to Victoria, discovering that she had bedded herself on the floor of the harness room all this while, with nothing but her blankets. They had not offered a mattress to the squaw.

She sat beside him. "It's been a damned long time," she said roughly.

He felt all right, but his leg was a numb thing he couldn't move or flex even if he wanted to.

"You're not looking at me," he said.

"I don't want to see your face," she replied.

"What's wrong with my face?"

"You're no good at hiding what you feel."

"I feel fine."

"Bullshit, Skye. You look like the sun will never shine again."

Chapter 14

Skye's bones healed steadily, but not the rest of him. One May day he was on a crutch the army lent him. One June day he hobbled around needing only a staff to cling to. Then the post surgeon, Balboa, cut away the plaster, and Skye discovered his leg was not going to flex at the knee anymore. The rotation at the knee didn't amount to much. Skye stared at the offending limb, and then at Victoria, and shook his head.

It was time to try riding. He managed to sit his pony, but only with the sore leg hanging free, out of the stirrup. Still, he could ride, and soon was able to go awhile on horse before the pain forced him to the ground.

He developed a new gait, one in which he furiously arced his injured leg forward and progressed with a rolling lurch. It took so much energy to walk that way that he soon wore out, and then his face was drawn and white, and his eyes turned as black as obsidian. Pain lines radiated from his mouth, and a perpetual frown furrowed his brow.

Still, he was tough. No man of the borders was ever tougher, and Skye was learning new ways to endure. He was alive, and was flying his flags. Victoria had never heard a word of complaint. And not a word about the pain running through his body. There was just obdurate silence, quietness, and determination.

It was time to leave Fort Ellis. Victoria had dreaded the moment but the Skyes had worn out their welcome. Skye had said nothing of his plans. Whatever their future, it was locked in his mind. Victoria felt left out, isolated, and sometimes angry. It was as if he had crawled into himself and would not come out. One June day Skye thanked Colonel Blossom, and he and Victoria turned their ponies toward the mountains.

She didn't know where he intended to go. She sat easily on her pony, even though her own bones ached these days. But she was used to that. She was aging in a different manner, turning into a dry husk of a woman, and filled with an odd lightness. She didn't query him about anything. His plans would all come clear—if he had any plans. That was the terrible reality of age. The future simply vanishes. If he was heading for the Bend of the Yellowstone, and planned to stay there, she would know his plans were unchanged. He would build a house there or die trying.

She couldn't imagine it. She had watched white men build permanent houses. First they gathered rock for the foundation, dragging it from quarries on sleds they called stone boats. Then they trenched the earth with their spades and made it level. Then they mortared the rock into low walls. Then they built a framework of timbers for the floor and covered it with thick sawn wood. They felled straight pines, preferably lodgepole, barked them, skinned away the irregularities with a drawknife, notched the ends with an axe, and raised log walls with block and tackle, log by log by log. They sawed out a doorway and windows and cut lumber to frame them. They raised log rafters and laid down thick roof planks gotten from a mill, and shingled them with shakes they split off of short chunks of log. They added an iron stove or a big hearth of mortared stone, and framed rooms within. And that was just the beginning. They added doors and windows, stairs, porches and outhouses, a kitchen, a spring house, a well or piped-in spring water. They built sheds for their horses and hay. It took a lot of men to do all that, and it wasn't done quickly. And if they had livestock they would need to fence the land, and plant gardens, and build a paddock for the horses. That was one thing about white men she admired. Some of them worked ceaselessly, unlike the Absaroka men, who gambled and hunted and told stories and made war, and died, but rarely toiled at anything.

They made only a few miles that day, but the next day they topped the divide and descended a drainage that would take them to the Yellowstone. The day after that they were back in what the white men called Indian Country, though it was only twenty-odd miles from Bozeman City. Skye rode to the place where the ox had destroyed his body, and pointed. There was nothing to see. Whatever happened was locked in Skye's head, and he would not share it.

He sat on the horse, surveying the place he obviously loved, the place that had wrought dreams in him. Spring rains had greened the slopes. Puffball clouds hung on snowy peaks. The river, gorged with snowmelt, sparkled in bold sunlight.

She watched him quietly, knowing something of what was passing through his heart. He didn't move for the longest time, but she knew the exact moment of surrender. Something in him changed. He was letting go of this dream, defeated by age and wounds and a hard life. Instead of sagging into his saddle, he stiffened, sat more rigidly, clamped the old top hat tighter. It was as if, in defeat, he would fly all his flags.

"Mary's with her people?" he asked.

The question rose out of the mists.

"I told her get the hell down there."

"You had a reason."

"She ain't herself, dammit. I told her to visit her brother. Talk to all them goddamn nieces and nephews and aunts

and uncles and cousins and clan. Talk Shoshone with all of
them Snakes around there."

"Where's the lodge?"

"I told her to take it."

"I always liked Chief Washakie," he said.

And so it was settled.

But the Eastern Shoshone were far away, and it would
take many days to reach them. He didn't want to say what
both of them were thinking. Mary was younger and strong,
and would help care for them.

But Victoria felt a searing pain, not only her own pain
but his, for in that moment he was surrendering his dream
of a homestead at this place that sang to him, a home with
a great porch where he could watch the last light of the sun
fall upon the vaulting mountains that formed the spine of
the whole world, and gild them.

They rode quietly eastward. Both of them were thinking
the same thing; she didn't know how she knew that, but she
did. To reach Mary, they would have to cross the Yellowstone, which now was at flood tide, wide and cold and swift
and cruel. This was the time of year when gravelly fords
vanished, hidden logs careened down the river, ice floes
jammed themselves into temporary dams, and the water
was barely above freezing. Still, they didn't have to deal
with any of that for a few weeks. They were many sleeps
away from the place where they would turn south.

They struggled downriver. Skye had turned stoic. Sometimes he looked ashen, his lips compressed, the ridges of
corded muscle lining his face. A June thundershower pelted
them where there was no shelter, and they endured the slap
of rain and the spray of hail. Afterward, they found a dry
place, built a fire, stripped, and set their clothing and unrolled blankets to drying on a rustic frame. She still enjoyed
the sight of Skye naked, all fishbelly white except for his

face and hands and neck, and his venerable hat perched on gray locks. Nothing was quite as amusing as a naked white man. She was brown everywhere, brown and slim, with withered arms and small breasts.

A magpie had joined them, gaudy black and white, bold and raucous. She nodded. This one perched on a limb, then on the heap of driftwood she gathered, and then paraded back and forth, its lurching walk different from that of any other bird.

"Go to hell," she said to the magpie.

The bird heckled her and flapped away.

Skye cleaned the rain off his Sharps while she gathered wood to keep the smoky fire blazing. Everything that took work was now up to her. She unsaddled the ponies, haltered and picketed them on good grass. She dug into the burlap sack, extracting more flour she would turn into fry cakes. They had enough stuff from the liveryman for a few more days. June nights in the mountains were plenty cold, but with luck they would have their wet clothes dried before they were chilled.

A night fog descended just about the time when Victoria thought the clothing might be wearable, and they were glad to crawl into the slightly damp leather and pull blankets over them. Skye carefully settled his leg, and then drew the wool around it. Warmth mitigated the pain a little. Victoria studied the night sky, hoping it would not rain again. This time of year, it rained often and hard, and sometimes hailed. She wished they might have their lodge, but that was far away, and they had no ponies to carry it.

"We could go back to your people," Skye said.

"No damned good," she said. She was thinking of Skye's age and bad leg, and the way her people moved about all summer and fall, gathering, hunting, and warring. The Shoshones were more sedentary.

"Where then? Up to you," he said.

That shocked her. Up to her?

"Magpie," she said.

She would go where her spirit sister, the magpie, led her. Skye didn't respond at first. He lived in a different world, with one Creator and no spirit helpers. They had talked about this many times, and it had come down to respect. He respected her beliefs; she respected his white-man religion.

"Suits me," he said.

She didn't like it. She didn't like this deep change in him. She wanted the old Skye, bold and strong and decisive, look-ing after her and keeping her fed and safe and warm. She tried to imagine what life was like for him now. Always be-fore, he could command his body. It had been injured many times but he still lorded over his body, made his legs work, ignored pain, did what needed doing, whether it was hunting or fighting or finding shelter, or protecting her from a lion or a bear. But now his body was weaker, and it hurt, and he could not tell his leg to bend and walk and carry his weight and take him across meadows to the very horizon. His life was lost in a haze of pain now. She knew pain her-self, the pain that came with many winters, that crept across her shoulders and collected at the small of her back and made her legs wobbly. But there was no way to get their youth back.

Her heart ached for him. He had the harder life, from a pressed British seaman to a mountain man to a guide, to a man living with her in the fashion of her people. He's the one who had to adapt, surrender his London upbringing, make himself a new man in this world of mountains and plains she knew so well. Had it been a good life? She was shocked at her own thought. Placing his life in the past, like that. He was alive beside her. He had never complained, never even talked about the pain that wracked him. She reached across to his blanketed form and touched his arm.

Two days later they had run through the white man's food the liveryman had given them, and Skye said he would hunt. He could not walk toward game, so he would wait beside the Yellowstone for game to come to him. His Sharps was too heavy for her now, or she would hunt with it, and her strength had waned so she could no longer use her bow and arrows as she once had as a young huntress.

So he settled himself beside a fallen cottonwood, downwind of where he thought game might come to drink, and waited until twilight for game to come. He rested the heavy Sharps across the log, tried to make his bad leg comfortable, and eyed a place in the riverbank where he had seen the split hoofprints of deer. And then one did come; actually two, a doe and a newborn fawn still on her teat, a small spotted waif of a deer-child. The mother looked everywhere, her tail twitching, and then drifted toward the riverbank, across the sights of Skye's Sharps.

But he did not shoot. He could not say why, except it had to do with his age and a reverence for new life. He watched the doe drink for a few moments, and then drift into shadow, the baby a few paces away, and then vanish into brush.

"Goddammit," Victoria said. "I was afraid you'd shoot her."

Chapter 15

Blue Dawn of the Shoshone People was a curiosity to every passing wagon company. The Big Road wasn't crowded but she passed companies every little while. Most of them were entirely male, and they walked beside creaking wagons drawn by oxen. A few companies consisted of families, and these usually had wagons with the big sheets curving over the tops. Once in a while a single family traveled on its own, risking trouble but going at its own pace.

She rode beside the river the whites called the North Platte, with her two spare ponies behind her. Once in a while she shifted her high-cantle squaw saddle to another of the ponies, so that all bore her burden. The breeze-curried prairies stretched endlessly in all directions, and at some distant place they merged with the sky. Often they were rough and hilly, and in these places she feared trouble, apart from the eyes of other travelers.

She had evolved a way of dealing with these white people, and stuck with it. She never spoke English but only her own tongue, though she understood them well enough. She scarcely knew what to expect. The all-male companies sometimes eyed her in a way that worried her, their assessing gazes obvious. Other times, when westering families crowded around her, parents sharply warned their children to stay away from the filthy squaw.

"Don't you get close to her, hear me? You'll get nits."

"Hey, Ma, a wild injun! You think she'll kill us?"

"Diseased, that's what. Look at her, dark and savage, them eyes full of fever."

She pretended not to hear. It was safer. But sometimes men who knew a thing or two about sign language or Indians waylaid her.

"What tribe's you, little lady?" an ex-Confederate soldier asked. He was still in his shabby grays, but the stripes had been ripped off from his arms. He was walking beside a mule-drawn wagon with half a dozen bearded young men.

She ignored him.

"You understood me well enough, I'm thinking. Was I to guess, I'd say Snakes. You a Snake?"

She saw he knew something, and finally nodded.

"You going somewheres?"

She shook her head.

"I'd say you's going somewheres. We're inviting you to dinner, little lady."

She stared, and moved to go, touching her moccasins to her pony, but this one caught her hackamore.

"Such a rush," he said, grinning. He had watery blue eyes and a gray slouch hat, and a hairy face. She read his intentions all too well.

There wasn't much she could do with only a sheathed knife at her waist, and half a dozen of these rather young drifters eyeing her. For the moment she would stick with her silence. They caught her ponies, peered into the panniers, found the packet of letters, and read them.

"Looks like these are for some squaw man named Skye. But you ain't Crow, far as I can see," the blue-eyed one said. "You got you a man named Skye?"

She simply refused to acknowledge anything.

"You git yourself off that pony, sweetheart, and join up with us for some chow and we'll pass a jug around after she gets dark," he said. "Don't pretend you can't understand me.

I read you mighty well, and I know damned well you've got every word I'm saying."

She saw how it would go. Once they started drinking, it wouldn't be long before they would have their way with her, and then maybe kill her.

"Miz Poontang, off that pony now," one said.

"I do not know that word," she replied.

He grinned. "Likely we'll teach you."

"I am on my way to St. Louis to see my son. He is in a school run by Jesuits."

"Yeah, they got a school for breeds and bastards."

"I don't know those words."

"Half-breeds, Miz Poontang, whelped by whites and colored."

"I am very happy to go see my son."

"Well, we're right happy to spend a happy night in this happy place with a happy lady."

"Please let go of the horse. I will go now."

"Get down, little lady. We're going to have us a party."

The others were igniting a fire of kindling and buffalo chips. They looked as eager as this unkempt veteran in gray, but were leaving the matter to him. There was no one else in sight. They were a mile or two from the North Platte River, where she might escape in the underbrush, but here they were in open prairie.

"Guess I'll have to help you down," he said.

"I don't know your name."

"Johnny Reb," he said.

In one fluid move, he slid an arm around her waist and lifted her down. He pushed her to the ground and held her there with a strength that surprised her.

"Got some ponies here," he said to one of the others.

That one gathered the lead lines and led them into the twilight.

"Nice party, Miz Poontang. We got a little jug we've been saving, just for this heah evening."

Once they began sampling the jug, she would be lost. The others looked uncommonly cheerful as they did their evening chores in a lingering twilight.

"My husband, Mister Skye, was with the Royal Navy. Then he was a big man with the American Fur Company. Then he was a guide."

"Husband, is it. You mean he took up with you."

"I was given by my family, the Shoshone way."

The talky one grinned. "Sho 'nuff," he said. "What did the white man pay, eh?"

"He gave the gift of blankets and horses."

"And you went off and whelped."

Why did this man talk like this? As if it was all bad or wrong or cheap? Mary thought maybe she knew.

"Colonel Bullock took my son to St. Louis when he was eight," she said. "I have been sad ever since then. Many winters have passed, and now I will see him. It is said he learns well, and knows words and numbers. I am very proud of him."

"Breed," her captor said. "Just a breed."

"Our friend Colonel Bullock watches over us."

Johnny Reb grinned. "Yank colonel, eh? That ain't the way to make friends with me, Miz Poontang."

"This man, he comes from a place called Virginia. He says it's a very good place."

"Likely story, squaw."

The company had completed its evening chores and was gathering at the fire now, an eager anticipation flushing their faces. She thought she had sealed her own death, letting them know of her connections. They could not afford to let her go, now.

She studied everything in the twilight, noting where her ponies were picketed, where her packsaddle was, where they had put her halters and hackamore. Darkness would be her friend, if she survived that long. She eyed them coldly, a deep dread in her, but one mixed with resolve. She might never see her son, but some of them would never see another sunrise. She feared it had come to that.

Why did they dismiss her so? Her race, maybe. These were those who had black slaves, or at least fought on that side. Anyone colored like her could be beaten and used. They might do both, beat her and use her before they killed her. It would all be fueled by the fiery water in that crockery jug. Maybe if they had enough of it, they would fall senseless and she could escape. But maybe they would force her to drink, hold her arms, pry open her mouth, and pour it into her. She had heard of such things.

She knew then what she would do.

"Hey, Johnny Reb. You want a party? Let's party."

He grinned at her. "We'll take our time, Miz Poontang."

"You got two jugs? Three jugs?"

"Just this one, sweetheart."

"I'd like a jug all for me."

The others were paying attention now, smiling. She wondered if they were going to eat, but no one was cooking anything. Apparently the evening's entertainment trumped hunger. But the dark was the only friend she had.

"Hey, how about some eats, all right?"

"Who needs food?" Johnny Reb asked.

"I do. You keep me here, you feed me."

"Nah, Miz Poontang, you don't need a mouthful."

"You make food. I make food."

But she heard a cork squeal out of its socket and laughter. The plug was gone from the tan jug, and now the six men were all smiles. They settled into a small circle, legs the spokes in a wheel, as the night thickened. The smoky fire threw wavering orange light on them.

"Oh, it do smell like heaven," one said.

"Want it neat, or cut?"

"What do ya take me for?" One of them lifted the jug and sipped.

"Ah!" he said, and laughed.

The jug went around. It came to her. She took a tiny sip.

"Oh, no, that ain't how it'll be, Poontang. Drink!"

She pretended. They watched hawkishly.

"You drink or we'll pour it down you, bitch."

She sipped slowly, not swallowing, and passed the jug along.

"Swallow, bitch!"

They were staring wolfishly at her now.

"Makes me sick," she said, and spit it.

"Then get sick, squaw."

But the jug had passed her by that time, and now the slugs going down male throats were longer and fiercer.

When the jug returned to her, Johnny Reb grabbed it, grabbed her, stuffed it into her lips, hurting her teeth, and poured hard. She gasped, coughed, and splattered whiskey over her heavy skirts.

"Drink!" he snarled.

He jammed the jug into her face and lifted it.

She clasped her hands around the jug to steady it, and then he let her hold the jug.

That was her moment. She lifted the jug upward, and then threw it with both hands into the smoldering fire. It shattered. The whiskey spread, and then flared in yellow flame.

"Goddamn bitch!" her captor cried, and threw her to the earth.

She rolled and sprang up, ran away from the flame, her heavy skirts slowing her progress.

He cursed, raced after her, grabbed her, and threw her down again.

She fought crazily, raking him with her fingernails, biting and writhing, but he caught her hair and yanked hard, throwing her head back with such violence that she felt something snap in her neck.

Then he was riffling her skirts, jamming them upward, his big chafed hands rough on her legs. She bit his arm, her teeth drawing salty blood, and he howled. She slammed a knee into him, catching his groin, and he howled again, his body folding. He let go of her, grabbing his crotch, and she rolled free. She didn't wait, but staggered to her feet and plunged toward the mercy of dark, stumbling over prairie until she tumbled into a shallow depression, a foot or two deep, and there she threw herself to earth and stretched tight in the lee, where the bold orange light from the whiskey-fueled fire would not probe her. She scraped air into her lungs, quieted her gasping, and then forcibly stilled her body in the shallow safety of the gully.

"Goddamn squaw," her captive yelled. "She's out there."

"Get the horses in," someone said.

"Thieving redskin'll steal 'em."

"What'd you give her the jug for, goddammit?"

"Oh, shut up, damn you."

"A tin cup. Shove the tin cup of it down her throat."

"Go to hell, Jackson."

She heard someone come close, and this time she pulled her skinning knife from its waist sheath and waited. If it was to be blood and death this night, then she would give and take, even if she was one lone woman among hard young men.

"She ain't far, and we got her nags," someone said.

"I'll kill her. Breaking that jug. Goddamn squaw."

"Who cares about the jug? I was looking for some entertainment."

"Who'd a thunk a squaw'd fight back? They just roll over."

"You think she'll give us trouble?"

"We'd best find her and shut her up for good."

"Fat chance in the dark. She's down to the river by now."

"We'll find her. Get the horses in, and if she comes for them, we've got her."

Mary listened bitterly.

Chapter 16

The higher the half-moon rose, the more danger she was in. The shallow trough that protected her from firelight did not protect her from the cold white glare from the sky. The fire had died, and the men had fallen into their blankets. She peeked, and was disheartened by what she saw. Her packsaddle and saddle and horse tack had been placed close to the fire, within the circle of their bedrolls. Her ponies were picketed close. The chance of collecting her things and escaping in the white of the moon didn't really exist. What's more, one man was propped up against some harness, a rifle across his lap. She could not tell whether he was dozing, but he surely was a sentry.

She felt a moment of desolation, but quieted herself. All those years with Skye and Victoria had hardened her, given her a cast of mind that refused to surrender. She slowly raised her head again and studied the scene, thanking Mother Moon for giving her light. The high-walled wagon stood nearby, its tailgate down. Its mule team, six mules in all, were picketed some distance away. A saddle horse was tied to the wagon. On its back was a saddle. The men had a mule team plus one saddle horse, apparently kept ready to ride if trouble arose. She had seen this sort of thing before. The saddle would not be cinched.

She eyed her own saddle, with its bedroll, two blankets, rolled up and tied behind the cantle. But it and the packsaddle were within a few feet of three of the men. If she tried to lift either one, they would snare her.

She reluctantly gave up on that. They well knew she would be back and would try, so they made themselves ready for her. The same with her ponies. The picket pins were only a few feet from the men. If they caught her, who could say what they might do? These were the ones from the South, and what did they care about people whose flesh was darker? If they cared nothing for their black slaves, why would they care about her, with her copper flesh?

She eyed their saddle horse, which stood, head lowered, half asleep, one leg cocked. Would it startle if she approached? She saw no other choices. She crawled slowly along the trough in the earth, glad she was dark and was wearing a blue blouse and black skirt. She absorbed the light. She reached a place where the wagon cast a moon shadow. The horse was alert now, and she feared it might bolt. She stood slowly in the moon shadow, and the horse actually quieted. That was good. She took her time, studied the sleeping men, especially the one propped up on harness collars. Nothing changed.

She reached the horse, which turned and sniffed her. She ran a hand under its mane, and then under the surcingle, and found it loose, as she expected. Her fingers told her this was the type of girth with a buckle. She slowly tightened and buckled it. She located the reins, tied to a ring on the wagon. She might have an escape now if this horse didn't give her away. She ghosted around to the tailgate, which was partially lit by the moon, and studied what lay within the wagon. Something white intrigued her and she tugged at something made of heavy fabric and discovered it was a poncho. That lifted her spirits. This time of year, a poncho was more valuable than a bedroll. She felt around, her fingers clasping on a small copper pot, and then on a cotton

NORTH STAR   423

bag of something she thought was cornmeal. Food, a little
kettle, a poncho. She laid the sack and the little pot in the
poncho and rolled the poncho over them. She needed something to tie her kit together, and saw the heap of harness,
with its lead lines. With her skinning knife she sawed some
lines free, tied her bedroll kit together, and anchored it
behind the cantle of the horse.

Someone stirred and she froze. A man rose, stared,
headed toward the very trough that had hidden her, urinated,
and returned to his bed, while she stood stock-still. These
men were not caught in deep sleep, not with a white moon
pouring light over them. She feared that they would follow
her even though they would have three ponies in exchange
for their saddle horse.

She waited until the camp quieted again, and then sawed
through the tugs, the thick leather bands that collected the
harness to the wagon. She could not get to her own hackamore to saw it in two, but she could cut the rest and give
them a day or two of repairing. That would teach them to
respect a woman of the Eastern Shoshones. She sat down
and patiently cut here and there, her knife purring and muttering its way through leather until she was sure this company would not be moving soon. Her own ponies were
staring at her, which was dangerous.

It was time to go. She paused in the moonshadow of the
wagon, untied the saddle horse, which finally began sawing its head nervously, and then tugged. The horse followed
along after a moment's pause. She surveyed the country. If
she headed straight east, she would be in sight a great distance, in this cold light. If she reached the woodlands along
the Platte, she would swiftly vanish from view. She would
walk north to the river, then, and hope they slept.

She took one last look at the camp. The man lying against
the collars had sat up and was staring. She had apparently

made enough noise to stir him out of his doze. She froze. He stood, alert, but not knowing where to look.

She had intended to lead the saddle horse away and mount it later, but now she tried to wait him out. The wagon was the one area he was not looking. He was eyeing the mules and her ponies, looking at the way their ears were cupped. Only then did he turn slowly toward the wagon. She stood in shadow, and was grateful she wore dark clothing. Still, he was not satisfied, and finally drifted toward the wagon. She knew she had only moments, so she put foot to stirrup and lifted herself onto the saddle, as the horse sidestepped nervously, unfamiliar with this rider.

He saw her then, shouted, and she kicked the horse hard. It bolted toward the river. She heard another shout, and a blast, and felt her horse react to something, even as something stung her arm. A fowling piece. The horse pitched and then settled into a hard run, but she had no trouble hanging on. It leaped the trough that had sheltered her and thundered hard toward the loose-knit cottonwoods ahead. She heard a few more cracks, rifles now, and some distant shouts, and then she fled into the moon-dappled shade of wide-spaced cottonwoods and willows, their leaves throwing darkness here and there. She reached the North Platte suddenly, pushed through thick brush, felt her horse sink in muck, remembered that this wide, shallow river sucked horses and people to their doom, and yanked the horse sharply right. It floundered a moment, gathered itself, and plunged out of the sucking sand onto firmer ground. She halted, and it stood trembling, its breathing harsh and desperate. She itched to move, but knew she was a long way from the men, and let the horse regain its composure. Then she steered the horse free of the band of brush and into the moonlit woods. She paused, looking for the men, and heard distant shouts and curses as they discovered the extent that she had immobilized them.

She thought she was free, and steered the horse quietly downriver, but then she saw that one had saddled her pony and was trotting hard toward her. The others had caught her other ponies and were obviously rigging makeshift tack.

She kept her horse at a walk, but steered him into deeper woods, until the horse was slowed by fallen limbs and brush, and then let the animal pick its way. This was noisy. The horse was snapping limbs, lurching through brush, and advertising itself. The other rider gained ground over open grassland and eventually passed her, which troubled her. Now one of the others was coming her way also, having rigged some sort of bridle for one of her ponies. Something glinted in the man's hand.

So it was not over. Still, she had shadow; the others had moonlight and open meadow. The second one rode by, and now two were downriver from her. They would wait for her. They knew she had gone into the bankside band of willows and cottonwoods, where she would be slowed. They had sprung a trap that might not catch her in its jaws until daylight. Still, she had shadow. She slowed her horse and let it pick its way quietly. Through the leaves she saw the two riders far ahead of her, still out on the open meadow.

She thought she must say good-bye to her boy, The Star That Never Moves, fifteen winters of age, and say good-bye to Skye, and to Victoria, his older wife, and then say good-bye to life, for these men with guns would end it. They were in a rage, and they were good horsemen, probably former cavalrymen, and they would know how to run her down.

It was best to give her horse a free rein, so she did. This horse had a bit in its mouth, and was easy to guide, but she stopped guiding it entirely. She touched her moccasins to its flanks. It veered a little and drifted along a narrow trail where it made no noise at all, maybe a trail used by deer or elk, or even the great brown bear, but a trail even so, and she let the horse go where it would, even when the trail turned toward the wide, shallow, treacherous river that white men called a mile wide and an inch deep.

The trail ended at water's edge, but not far out lay a large island, mostly covered with brush, but with a few gauzy trees. She slid off her horse, untied her moccasins, lifted her skirts, and stepped in, probing one step at a time for quicksand. But she was walking on gravel, and slowly made her way out, tugging the horse behind her. The water never reached her knees. But she was wading under an open sky, where the moonglow made her visible to anyone on any shore. Still she continued, step by step, and then slowly climbed onto the island and led the horse through thickets and onto a grassy patch well hidden from both shores.

It would do. She quietly unsaddled the horse and let it graze.

Mosquitoes hummed, but she had a partial remedy. She untied the poncho and slid it over her black braids, and swiftly felt its protective comfort. She undid her braids and let her hair fall loose.

"Ah sure don't know where that little bitch got," someone said.

She peered discreetly at the near shore, but saw no one.

"Find her. She got mah horse and saddle, goddammit."

"We got three of hers."

"Never no mind that. I don't much care how many ponies and saddles and what-all; I just ain't of a mind to let some redskin git away with this."

"Looks like she did."

She could see them now, back from the water's edge,

studying the shoreline. She hoped her new horse wouldn't whinny. After some peering around, they gave up and crashed their way through the belt of trees and she heard no more.

For them, it was the principle of the thing. Three horses, a packsaddle and riding saddle, and a pile of gear weren't a good trade for what she got because she was a Shoshone, because they intended to use and kill her and keep everything she had, and keep their own stock too.

She turned quietly back to the center of her island, her small refuge in a moon-whited river. She wondered if she would recognize her half-white son if ever she found him in this place called St. Louis, or whether she would like or trust him if she did find him.

Chapter 17

Victoria heard the cattle first, a great lowing and bawling just around a bend, and didn't know what to make of it. Then riders appeared, white men with broad felt hats, dressed in a fashion she had never seen, with leather chaps and neck scarves. She stopped at once. These men were well armed, and she wished to be careful. Skye pulled up and watched as the herd, which numbered many hundreds of long-horned cattle, bawled and bleated its way west, guided by numerous riders who walked quietly ahead, behind, and on the flanks of the herd.

Two of them rode toward the Skyes, who waited quietly in the broad valley of the Yellowstone. The riders were wary, with carbines across their knees, but the Skyes gave them no reason to be alarmed.

Eventually the pair, both bearded young men in broad-brimmed hats with creased crowns, reined up before the Skyes. Victoria didn't like the looks of them.

"Howdy," said one.

"Good afternoon, sir," said Skye.

"You injuns?"

"I'm Barnaby Skye, sir, and this is my wife Victoria."

"Injuns, then. What tribe?"

Victoria wondered how these white men could mistake Skye for one of the native people. He was weathered to a chestnut color but hadn't the face or bones of her people.

"I am Mister Skye, sir, from London, and this is my wife

of many years, of the Absaroka People." There was an edge in his voice.

"Just checking. We like to know who we're dealin' with."

"So it appears. And who are you?"

"Harbinger's the last name, Slocum's the first. Texas born and bred."

"Your men, they're Texans?"

"What else?"

"You're running true to form," Skye said. "And where are you headed with all those animals?"

"The big bend of the Yellowstone, Skye. That's good country. This heah's the second herd; I ramrod for Nelson Story. He brought the first bunch up in 'sixty-six, right through the injun wars, and pastured it in the Gallatin Valley."

"It's Mister Skye, sir. I prefer to be addressed in that fashion."

"It don't make no never mind to me, Mister Skye. I'll call you whatever you want. We'll have you just sit heah until them cattle trail by, so you don't booger them."

The herd was drawing close now, with a slobbering wide-horned multicolored bull leading the whole parade. Other of these Texans were drawing close as well.

"In fact, Mrs. Skye and I were thinking of settling on the bend of the Yellowstone, sir. Maybe we'll be neighbors."

"No, Mister Skye, we ain't gonna be neighbors. Nelson Story's done took it, all that country."

"By what right?"

"By the law of armed force is how. Any questions?"

"By land-office claim?"

"I don't suppose it matters none to a Londoner. But no, we'll take the land and keep it. We got there fust. There ain't no land office within hundreds of miles, but we don't need one. There's land, lots of land. There's twenty-four of us, all

Texas men, and that's all we need to hold it. That was enough to get us past the goddamn Sioux. They didn't want no fight with Texans with repeater carbines. The redskins ain't so strong, anyway. Degenerates, ain't gonna be around much longer."

"The army found them invincible, sir."

"Yank army. Rebs would've walked through them savages. We drove these here animals a thousand miles, and we're going to sell beef to the mining towns."

"On the Bozeman Trail? The closed trail?"

"The same. Not one sonofabitching white man on it. Good grass all the way."

"And no Sioux?"

"None as wanted to test our repeaters."

"You came without army protection, then?"

"Now, Skye, why would Texicans want protection from a Yank army? Know what we saw? Lot of ash, where them Yankee forts got burned down by Red Cloud."

"You are brave men," Skye said.

The herd flowed by them now, and several more Texans drifted by, curious about the Skyes but staying close to the skinny red, brindle, black, gray, and multicolored cattle that seemed to be all rib and no meat.

"And what's your business, Skye?"

Skye stared long and hard. "Just passing through," he said softly.

"It figgers. I knew it when I saw you. A squaw man, looks like. Well, we got some ambition heah. We got white-man plans, and we're going to make our way."

Victoria listened with growing irritation. "Sonsof-bitches," she said.

Harbinger grinned, revealing gapped teeth. "This heah squaw talks my language," he said.

The cattle flowed by endlessly, strangely disturbing Victoria. These were white men's meat animal and intended to replace the buffalo that had fed and clothed and sheltered her people for as long as her people could remember. Hundreds of cattle, more than she could count, slobbering, skinny, wild of eye, mean-spirited. She found herself hating these animals, which had none of the courage and dignity of her brothers the buffalo.

More riders passed, eyeing them curiously but continuing to flank the herd. Men in red shirts, gray shirts, tan shirts. Men without women, young and bearded and bristling with weapons, six-guns at their waists, carbines in sheaths or on hand, looking ready to shoot anything that moved.

And now they were simply taking away the land, claiming it for themselves, and holding it by force. She marveled. She marveled that they could tell Skye to settle elsewhere, to go away, because they would not let him settle there, in the place he had dreamed of for many years.

Long ago, Skye would have put up a fight. But now, he sat his pony, his lame leg dangling out of the stirrup, his eyes sunken and his hair gray, and she knew there was no fight in him, at least not that kind of fight.

"We'll be seeing you, Mister Harbinger," Skye said.

"I don't suppose so," the man replied, and turned toward his herd. "Nice to pass the time with you all."

Skye and Victoria watched the last of the riders, the drag, trot by. The air and the ground quieted. But no bird flew or sang.

"There was enough land for everyone once," Skye said.

Victoria slid into a crabby mood. She didn't know what to say. These things unsettled her. Everything was changing, and too damn fast. Nothing but a faint dust in the air remained of the herd, that and a few green cow flops that

sat moistly in the peaceful light. She hated the sight of the
cow pies, hated them for what they meant. Cow pies instead
of buffalo chips. Great herds of stupid animals, surrounded
by men with guns, taking away land for their own use.

"Let's get the hell out of here," she said.

They resumed their ride downstream, but somehow the
world seemed violated. It wasn't just the cow flops lying
moist everywhere. It was something else, more subtle, as
if nature had retreated and now this was simply ranching
country. Victoria couldn't quite fathom why the very land
had changed, but it had.

They camped at one of the favorite places of her people,
where the Stillwater River tumbled out of the mountains and
emptied into the Yellowstone. Now the river was flush with
snowmelt, and it proved difficult for the horses to negotiate, with water hammering at their bellies. But in time they
reached the east bank, picketed their ponies, built a fire, and
cooked antelope steaks. June rains threatened, but the Skyes
had no lodge and the best they could do, if showers started,
would be to burrow into the woods.

That's when three large ox-drawn wagons arrived, each
the property of a westering family. In minutes the area was
chock-full of people, including women and children. They
didn't see the Skyes at first, and began the many twilight
tasks that occupied any wagon company. They unyoked the
oxen, picketed horses, collected wood, started water boiling, spread bedrolls, all before they discovered the Skyes,
off a quarter of a mile.

Then the men of the company descended on them, most
of them armed with rifles or scatter guns.

"Good evening, gents," said Skye.

The men collected around the Skyes, studying them,
eyeing Victoria, noting her Indian features.

"I'm a goddamn Absaroka," she said.

"Barnaby Skye here, and you?"

"Oliver Skaggs," said one. "She safe to be around?"

"No, I'll cut your heart out in the middle of the night," Victoria said.

No one laughed.

"I'm Mister Skye's sits-beside-him wife. He got another, Mary, she's a Snake. She's a lot prettier than me, and keeps him happy."

This wrought a deeper silence.

"She's off ahead of us. Otherwise you'd get to meet the whole family."

Skye's eyes glinted at Victoria, telling her to shut up, but she wasn't in the mood for it.

"Where's your tent?" asked one of the scowling men.

"Who the hell needs one?" Victoria said.

"How do you protect yourself from prying eyes?" asked Skaggs.

"Nighttime, that's all we need. We pull off our stuff and howl at the moon and dance around nakkid."

Skye sighed. Victoria was on a tear, and she wasn't going to slow down for him.

"We have some antelope we'd be pleased to share. Shot it this morning. Would you join us?" Skye asked.

"Any more of you hidden around here?"

"Just us."

Victoria could see women and children boiling toward them, and then an odd thing happened. Several of the men swiftly corralled them and kept them perhaps fifty yards distant. She saw much gesticulating and waving of arms.

"We'll stay with our own mess," one said.

"You people heading west?" Skye asked.

"Gallatin Valley."

"You came over the Bozeman Road?"

"Oh, no, not with the Sioux there. It's closed. We came

up Jim Bridger's road, and a poor road it was too. A wagon near tipped over," said Skaggs. "But there were no redskins, thank the Good Lord."

"The Gallatin Valley's a good place," Skye said. "You going to farm?"

"We're merchants and farmers. We've got seed potatoes. Got orchard stock. We've got a lumber man with a small mill. But we hear there's Indian trouble."

"Goddamn Blackfeet," said Victoria. "Scaring the hell out of everyone. Bloodthirsty bastards."

They stood about silently, absorbing that. Behind them, where the bonneted women and a dozen children of all descriptions were halted, there was a great deal of talking, and then one of the bearded men approached.

"Skye, would you mind camping somewhere else? You and your squaw's upsetting our folk. Scaring the children."

"I guess a man and wife can camp where they choose. Free country," Skye said. "You're free to move somewhere yourself."

"I guess I shouldn't have put it as a question, Skye. We're not asking you, we're telling you."

"And if we choose to stay here?"

"Someone might get hurt, and it ain't gonna be us."

Victoria wondered if her old man would do what he might have done long ago, but he didn't. He arose slowly, balancing on his game leg, using his Sharps as a crutch.

"Did you bring some spades?" Skye asked. "Start digging our grave. We're not moving an inch. The only direction you'll move us is six feet down."

Victoria listened to the bark in his voice, and thrilled to it.

"We'll haul you off on a wagon, then," one said.

Skye ignored him and lumbered painfully toward the children clinging to their mothers a few yards distant.

"Hey, where you going?" Skaggs yelled.

"I thought to get me a little girl and boil her up."

The women shrieked.

Skye continued to limp toward the children.

Then Skaggs laughed. The other men laughed, uneasily. Some mothers looked flustered, ready to bolt.

Skye reached a woman whose son had buried his face in her skirts.

Slowly he leaned over, even as the men of the company hastened to surround him.

"Hello, young man," Skye said. "I'm Barnaby Skye. Who are you?"

The boy eyed him suspiciously.

"Your folks heading west? There's good farm land there."

The little boy tugged himself tighter to his mother.

"I was here before there were a hundred white men in the whole western mountains. Now I live the way the Indians do, and I have an Indian wife. That's her, over there. She's a Crow, and very pretty, and I love her just the way your mother and father love each other."

"Is she a witch?" the boy asked.

"She's a medicine woman of her people. She has great powers. She's also a warrior woman, very good with a bow and arrow. Would you like to meet her?"

The question occasioned a flurry of worried glances among the adults, but then the boy nodded.

"Come along now, all of you," Skye said.

They hesitantly followed Skye as he limped back to Victoria, and let them gather around her.

"This is Many Quill Woman of the Absaroka People. I didn't know her tongue at first, so I called her Victoria, after the Queen. And she is a queen. You might call her a princess. That's a good word for her, because she was given great powers to help and heal people."

They stared at Victoria, seeing an Indian for the first time.

"Is she a real princess?" one woman asked.

"I would say so," Skye said.

Victoria felt the glint of wetness forming in her eyes.

Chapter 18

Barnaby Skye sliced the antelope haunch thin and used up the last of it. The company hadn't had meat on its tin mess plates for a week. Some of the women contributed boiled spuds. Skye hadn't had a potato in years, and relished every bite. The women from another wagon boiled a kettle of parched corn. With a little salt, it tasted just fine, and built a comfort in the belly.

They all eyed the Skyes, sometimes furtively, sometimes boldly. They studied Skye's top hat, this one the fourth or fifth he had owned, gotten at a trading post. It was a silk one because beaver had gone out of fashion. It sat rakishly on Skye's gray locks, and never moved, as if it had grown from his scalp.

Skye thought that Victoria had exhibited great restraint, remembering not to cuss in front of the smaller children, except for a few hells and damns, which they had already mastered from their fathers. Victoria had never quite understood tabooed words. There were none among the Absaroka People. All words were good. So over a lifetime she had derived a vast repertoire of forbidden white men's words and phrases, which she employed with great relish.

Soon the women hustled the children off to their bedrolls, which were laid out under the three wagons, and then most of the adults hastened back to the bright campfire, which the men of the company had built up to drive back the darkness. Skye never was quite comfortable with fires like that, which turned them all into targets. But he was too old and crippled to care now.

The adults drifted to the campfire as soon as chores were done, all of them eager for what was to come. This would be a night of stories, and Skye knew they intended to pump him for all he could tell them. Much to his astonishment, these westering people pulled two rocking chairs from wagons, and these were soon occupied by elder women, the dowager queens of this wagon company.

"Ah, Skye, did I hear you say you had a younger wife?" asked one of the gents named Monroe.

"I do, sir, Blue Dawn of the Shoshones. I call her Mary. She's quite a bit younger than I, sir, and a beauty."

"Ah, Skye, that's very unusual."

"Not at all. In most plains tribes, men of prominence have several wives, and the more wives, the more prominent they are. A chief might have several."

"How does the Mrs. Skye with us feel about this?" asked a graying woman, in a rush.

"Hell, I pushed and shoved for years to get my man to take one. I even made the match. The old cuss, he kept saying one was enough, but I would have liked a dozen. I'd get to boss 'em all around, because I was the first."

"A dozen wives? Surely you're making a joke!" said a lady.

"Hey, wives do all the work, see? The more wives, the less work for me. I gotta scrape a buffalo hide for weeks if I'm alone. Get a bunch of wives, and I'll scrape a hide and tan it in a day or two. I get tired of cooking. Give me a few wives, and I'm happy."

"But how . . . do you have separate teepees?"

"Hell no, we're all in there together. Me and Skye and Mary, we got one little lodge."

"One lodge! How do you manage? I mean, privacy?"

"I don't know that word," Victoria said. Skye laughed softly. Victoria knew the meaning exactly, but it was more fun doing this her way.

"It's dark in there," Skye said. He was starting to enjoy this.

"Where is she now?" someone asked.

"With her people, the Shoshones, far south of here," Skye said. "That's where we're headed."

"I would think each wife would want a lodge of her own. Just to tell the children apart," said a woman in brown gingham.

"Children, they're all the same. I got children I never had," Victoria said maliciously. "Every time I look, there's a new one."

Skye thought he heard breaths released.

"I don't suppose these were proper Christian marriages, were they?" asked a frowning young man.

"We were married according to the customs of the Crows and Snakes," Skye said. "A pleasant ceremony in which the parents give away the bride."

"Did you pay a lot?"

"A gift to the family, sir, not payment. You offer a gift. Some horses, or a rifle, or blankets. You offer the biggest gift you can, and the bride's family decides whether that'll do. When you get married, they gift you back, help you set up your household."

"Sounds like buying a woman to me." The stuffy fellow was determined to prove the moral superiority of whites.

"Oh, white women sometimes come with a dowry. Their parents are buying a husband, I suppose," Skye said.

"That's different," the fellow persisted.

"I'd like to buy a few white men," Victoria said. "I'd like half a dozen."

That stopped the talk for a stumble or two.

"Tell us about your days in the fur trade," an older man asked, obviously steering away from plural marriage. "Were you ever comfortable, living in nature?"

"Hardly ever," Skye said. "We lived in the wilds. We took our ration of rain and sleet, of heat and starving. We took arrows and sickness, broken bones and tumbles off of horses. We froze at night, hurt all day. Some Yanks, they make it sound romantic, but I assure you, sir, it rarely was pleasant. My bones hurt just thinking about wading a river in winter. There weren't a hundred comfortable days in a year."

"How many grizzly bears did you face?"

"More than I want to remember. See this?" Skye lifted up his repaired bear-claw necklace "Those are grizzly claws, and they give me my medicine."

"What's medicine?"

"Inner powers, I suppose. Other things too. Bear wisdom. Bear whispers in my ear, sometimes, so I stay away from a cave, or watch out what's on the riverbank, or I study the sky because weather's coming."

They stared at the old necklace, that Skye had restrung half a dozen times in his life, including the time last fall when he stumbled upon a denning grizzly. Those six-inch claws were formidable.

"You put a lot of balls into a grizzly? I've heard it takes ten or fifteen to kill one," a man named Peters asked.

"The grizzlies are my brothers," Skye said. "They know another bear when they see one, and leave me alone. We see each other and turn away."

"You pullin' our leg, Skye?"

"It's Mister Skye, sir. Form of address I prefer. When I was a seaman in the Royal Navy, the officers were all 'mister' or 'sir,' and the rest of us, we hardly had first and last names. When I got to the New World, to this place where ordinary men could be misters, I took to it. From then on, I was as good as any officer in the Royal Navy. Call me Mister Skye, and I'll be grateful."

"You left the navy?"

"I deserted, sir. I was pressed in, right off the streets of London at age thirteen, and it took me seven years to escape. That was at Fort Vancouver, on the Columbia River, in the twenties. I jumped ship with nothing but my clothes and a belaying pin. I've been on my own ever since. I haven't regretted my escape, not for a moment. And I don't apologize for deserting. They made me a slave and I escaped their slavery."

"Amen to that," said Skaggs.

"You fight injuns?" That question rose from a nervous young man with muttonchops.

"There's no way I could have survived, sir, without defending myself."

"Which tribes are the worst. The most ruthless?"

"Goddamn Siksika," Victoria snapped. "Blackfeet."

Several women began fanning themselves with their hats.

"The Crows and the Blackfeet have a few grudges," Skye said. "I think the fiercest I've ever faced were the Comanches. I tangled with them once, taking some people to Santa Fe. They don't fear death and like to give pain. They are the world's most terrible torturers," he added. "We saw it, and we'll never forget it."

Victoria looked grouchy. She considered the tribes of the southern plains to be toothless.

"Cheyenne are better," she said. "Old Cheyenne women, they'll tie you to a tree and skin you alive, piece by piece."

That caused a stir.

They listened to Skye tell about that trip, and his other trips from his years as a guide, and the people he had taken into the unknown American West, the peers of England, the missionaries, the scientists, the army officers, and even a traveling medicine show once. He told about meeting Victoria and courting her, and learning about her Otter clan and family and Kicked-in-the-Bellies band. He told them about the rendezvous of the mountain men, and the artists and noblemen and adventurers who showed up at them. He told them about Jawbone, the strange fearless colt that became his horse-brother, a ferocious warrior in his own right, and a sacred animal known to all the tribes of the plains. The ugliest, strangest horse that ever lived, but also the greatest of all horses.

And before they knew it the hour had grown late, and these weary people were drifting off.

"Well, Skye, ah, Mister Skye, this has been quite an evening," Skaggs said. "We're lucky to have run into you. We've never met a mountaineer before."

"Or a medicine woman, either," Skye added.

Skaggs seemed discomfited.

Skye watched them settle. The men unrolled blankets under the wagons. The women and children crowded into wall tents. This company paused for evening prayers. Skaggs offered up the Lord's Prayer, and then they drifted to their beds.

Victoria was smiling broadly, as she always did when she had done the most mischief.

They had hardly settled in their blankets when lightning whitened the western heavens, followed by a distant roll of thunder. They both sprang up at once. They had no shelter and needed one fast. June thunderstorms could be vicious, cold and cruel, and often dumped hail on unwary people. There were a few cottonwoods around, but they offered no protection.

They had settled on an open flat at the confluence of the rivers. Behind a way, the south cliffs of the Yellowstone rose high, but these were half a mile off. They didn't hesitate. Skye caught the picketed horses and threw on the blankets and saddles and pulled hackamores over their heads. Victoria rolled up their blankets and their handful of possessions, and tied them behind the saddle cantles. Gamely, he clambered into his saddle, while she climbed aboard her pony. They reached the majestic cliff about the time the sky whitened regularly, and a drumroll of booming thunder seemed never to stop. The wind picked up, eddying cold moist air over them, with its promise of torrents. An overhang eluded them, and Skye was just surrendering to the idea of an icy drenching when Victoria steered her pony up a crevice in the cliff and under an overhang. A bright white flash of lightning informed them they would share the refuge with an angry black bear sow and cub.

There was perhaps twenty yards between the bears and the ponies. Skye halted. It was only the continuing lightning that revealed the presence of the bears.

"We're staying here," he said to the sow. "Sister, you're not going to scare us off."

She rose on her hind legs, while the cub ran behind her. Lightning caught her at her most angry, her claws extended.

"We're staying here, woman. Look after your cub," he said.

The rains swept in, a sudden rattling and clattering everywhere, and Skye was grateful for the refuge. It was even better than his lodge. The winds gusted moisture over them, but that was nothing compared to the torrent a few feet away.

Somehow, the rain settled the sow, and she returned to four legs and then drove her cub to the far edge of the overhang, another few yards distant. There she paused, just before a sheet of water, and halted. It would do.

Sister Bear would let Skye and Victoria live.

Chapter 19

Mary regretted slicing up the harness of those men. Now she was stuck on a mosquito-ridden island while they repaired it. She wore the poncho, and it helped, except around her ankles and neck and forehead. But the horse suffered, and the constant lashing of its tail did little to relieve its torment.

And across the channel of the North Platte, those former Confederates were no doubt riveting or tying their harness, unable to move until they could hook the mules to their wagon. If they had rivets they could make repairs easily; if not, they would have to bore holes in the leather and then lash the severed pieces with a thong, a slow and miserable process.

Mary bitterly endured, knowing the men were not far distant, beyond the band of riverside trees. She was fairly safe behind walls of brush and trees on her island, but the whine of mosquitoes maddened her and the horse. She finally led the miserable animal to a place where there was mud stretching into water, and patiently coated the horse with it. One handful at a time, she ran a protective coating of mud over its rump and flanks and withers and neck and chest, and then its belly and legs. The horse eyed her gratefully, she thought, and quieted. She rubbed mud over her own neck, without doing much good.

At one point the horse's ears pricked forward, and Mary feared it would whinny. She crept to the edge of the island

and peered across the channel. Downstream a little, the men were watering their mules and her three ponies. She ached to have her own ponies back, but remained still. She glided back to her new horse and gently rubbed its nose, hoping to keep it from signaling the other horses. Eventually the men and the livestock left the riverbank.

Mary hunted for food, but the bird nests she found were already deserted, and she spotted no turtles. She saw whiskered catfish, loathsome creatures, and would have eaten one if she had to, but she was spared that. She found bountiful cattails, and systematically pulled them up from their swampy habitat. They had gnarled white roots that could be pulverized and boiled into a thick paste that was nourishing, though vaguely repellent. She would do what she had to. Rocks were hard to find on that island, but she finally found what she needed and mashed the white roots, and added them to a growing heap in the copper pot.

She built a small fire directly under a stand of cottonwoods that would dissipate the smoke, lighting it with the flint and striker that hung in a pouch from her belt. And then she waited for the water to soften the cattail roots into something she could stomach. Much to her surprise, this had consumed her day, and as twilight overtook her she doused the fire, let the mush cool, and then ate it with her fingers.

She would not endure another night in this mosquito-misery, and resolved to use the friendly dark to escape, no matter that those men were nearby and might discover her. As darkness settled, she brushed mud off her horse, settled the blanket pad over its back, dropped the saddle and tightened it, and bridled the horse. She rolled up her few goods in the poncho, braving the whining mosquitoes again, and tied the poncho tightly to her saddle. She was as ready as she could be. She mounted, eased the horse across the gravel bar to the south bank without discovery, and made her way downstream, worried that she would be halted at any moment. She stayed in the loose-knit woods, finding just enough light to avoid copses of trees. No one stayed her progress.

She startled a deer, which startled her, but soon she was some good distance from the men and wagon, and steered the horse out to the well-worn trail and into a starlit night. She did not pause, but rode steadily east, the Star That Never Moves always on her left. She rode past a wagon with people bedded down, and was glad her horse and their horses didn't exchange greetings.

She rode most of the night, and only when the first blue line of day stretched across the eastern skies did she look for a place to rest herself and the weary horse. She found a low knob, scarcely twenty feet above the country, and took her horse there. It was a much-used place, but there were no mosquitoes, and its contour concealed her from prying eyes.

She rested until the day was warm and velvet. She saw no one. The Big Road was used mostly by people who could not pay to take the steam trains rolling over the nearby rails.

On the south slope of the hill she discovered yucca plants, and she rejoiced. A large one dominated a dozen more.

"I will leave you, Grandfather," she said to it, but selected a sturdy one for her purposes. She had no digging stick, and would need to use her knife to cut the yucca free, which she did with great care because she did not wish to break her knife. She dug patiently until she could pull the yucca out by its roots, which were thick and long. These were her treasure. She cut off the top of the plant, but kept the roots.

She eyed her mud-streaked horse and herself, and headed down the hillock and toward the river half a mile distant. The North Platte was lined with thick forest on both sides of its slow-moving current, forests that would shield her from the world. The sun had stirred a soft breeze that carried the scent of spring flowers. She thought she smelled roses, but maybe it was lady slippers. She could not say. She passed through lush grasses joyously reaching for the heavens, and wandered through copses of willows and trees she didn't know, and finally to a riverbank where there was a soft curve of sandy shore. She scared up red-winged blackbirds, and alarmed a few crows, and then she found herself alone.

At the river she cut the roots into small chunks, then mashed these between two rocks, dropped them into her copper kettle, and added water. She manipulated the pulped pieces and soon had foaming suds filling her kettle, a rich lather to wash with.

She shed her clothing in the hushed bower, and stepped into the flowing water. She was tall and bronze and thin, and the years did not yet show in her, except for the beginnings of gray in her hair. She undid her braids, letting her rich jet hair fall free, and then knelt in the purling water and let her hair float in the stream. The water wasn't cold, as it once was tumbling out of the mountains. Here it was mild and slightly opaque, carrying a little silt on its way to the distant sea. She sudsed her hair with the lather from the yucca roots, which she called amole, and felt the lather cleanse her hair until it felt silky. Then she rinsed it in the gentle flow of the river and washed her body with the amole. She ran rough willow bark over her flesh, abrading it gently until it tingled. She knelt in the shallow water, rinsing herself and then letting the river strain through her hair one last time. She finally felt chilled, though the sun warmed her in this quiet glade.

But she was not done. She immersed her clothing, piece by piece, in the river, washed them with the yucca lather, and then twisted the water out of each piece. Then she spread her skirts and blouse on the grasses, and began the long wait for the sun to dry them.

She led the horse into the river and washed it carefully, sudsing away the mud until its coppery coat shone. It was a good horse and it stood patiently while she cleansed it. She combed its mane and tail with her fingers, plucking thorns and debris from the horse hair. She rinsed it with kettles of water, and let the horse shake water off its back with several violent convulsions of its flesh. Then she led it back to grass and picketed it once again.

She spread the poncho on the grasses and lay down upon it, letting Father Sun finish her cleansing. She loved the warmth of the sun on her tawny flesh, and for the first time in many moons she felt utterly clean. She wished for sweetgrass, so she might bathe in its smoke and might take onto her body the scent of the sacred. But she was far from the places she knew and the herbs and grasses she knew. White men called this place the territory of Nebraska, but she knew no more than that. She spent much of that day lying in the sun, screened from the Big Road by a band of forest, waiting for her clothing to dry.

There were no mosquitoes there, at least not yet. With evening, things would be different. She dressed late in the afternoon, eyed her contented horse, and decided to ride a while. Her son was calling her. In some mystic way, she could hear him within her heart, calling for her to come to this place called St. Louis, where he resided with the black-robes called Jesuits.

She dressed in slightly damp clothes and found her way back to the Big Road, heading east once again. The road was empty, and that pleased her. It felt good to be washed and clean. The horse was well rested and set an eager pace. This night she would be that much closer to the big city, and that much closer to her son.

She passed an encampment of several wagons and could see various men at their evening chores. Some were gathered at a cook fire. She saw no women, and thought it would not be a good place to stop, so she rode onward, but then they were shouting and mounting their horses and coming after her.

"Hold up there," one yelled.

She dreaded it and kept on walking her horse.

A shot from a revolver changed her mind. She reined in the horse and waited, while half a dozen bearded white men swiftly overtook her and surrounded her.

"That's her! That's the nag!" one said.

"What is it you wish?" she asked, not concealing her knowledge of their tongue.

"Stolen horse, chestnut like this, proper shod, and taken by a squaw!"

She addressed an older one, with massive shoulders and a hard look in his eye. "This is my horse."

"No it ain't, woman. We're taking it. Feller came by yesterday, said look out for just such as you. Said 'twas his saddle and tack too."

"Did he tell you he took three of mine, and all I possessed?"

"Likely story. Squaw story, you ask me."

"Did they tell you they tried to force themselves on me, and I barely escaped? Do you approve of violating a woman?"

"I ain't here to argue that. I'm here to get that horse and send it forward. Them fellows are ten, twelve miles west and we're going to take this nag to 'em."

"Did they tell you they planned to kill me after they had used me?"

The bull-shouldered one only smiled. "You'd better fetch yourself off that nag, or we'll pull you down, and maybe you'll get used after all."

He had ahold of her rein. The others crowded close, eyeing her.

"I'm on my way to visit my son in St. Louis," she said. "He's in school there."

"Sure you are," one said. "More likely you're just findin' ways to make a nickel along the road."

"Would you speak of your own mother in that way?"

"Where'd you learn English so good, eh?"

"I am a Shoshone. My husband was born in London and has been in the fur and robe trade all his life. We live in the territory of Montana."

"Stealing horses from white men, I imagine. West's full of renegades, and more'n half are hitched up to squaws." He paused. "Off!"

She saw how it would go, and slid off. She started to untie her kit, the cornmeal and cook pot wrapped in the poncho, when he snarled at her to leave it alone.

"I wish to have what is mine."

"That fellow, Willis, he said the horse and every damned thing on it was took."

She saw half a dozen men looking for an excuse, and quietly subsided. With luck, maybe she could walk into the thickening dark with the clothing on her back.

Chapter 20

Darkness cloaked Mary. Or maybe it was the indifference of those men that really cloaked her. Once they took the horse, they didn't seem to care much. She slipped beyond the campfire light and no one stayed her. The river would be to the north, so she studied the heavens and found the Star That Never Moves, and walked that way. This was an inky night, and she scarcely knew where she was walking. She dropped into a slough, pulled her wet moccasins from the muck, and worked around it. She didn't know she had reached the wooded bottoms of the river until she ran into a limb, which knocked her flat.

She stood, waited, saw vague limbs lacing the starlit sky, and knew she was close. It was time to sit. The men wouldn't find her. She felt about, and then settled against a tree trunk and waited. It didn't take long for a slim moon to rise, and with that lantern casting its ghostly light, she made her way through a thickening forest, then canebrakes and sedges, and then a spit of sand surrounded by wavering water.

She settled there, and took stock. She was an Indian woman alone, with no food or weapons, save for her skinning knife, no shelter, no horse, and no friends. This was country where one could run into Peoples from many tribes, or white men, or the bluecoat army, or bears or wolves or coyotes. It was also a long way from the place called St. Louis, where she would see her son, if they would let her. She wasn't sure she would be allowed to see him.

She might keep from starving if she stayed close to the river. The Oregon Trail often ran a mile or two away from the river, working in straight lines rather than following the meandering bank. But the Big Road was too perilous for a lone woman of the People, and the river offered a chance to find food. The river was full of the fish with whiskers, which she despised but maybe they would keep her alive.

She thought about turning back, making her way to Fort Laramie and then to her people, but without food or a horse that would be even harder than continuing downriver. She might perish. A woman alone might die apart, trapped or destroyed or captured or sickened. The bitter reality was that she was caught. Maybe she should sing her death songs, and lie down and let the spirit fly away. Maybe she could send a spirit messenger to Skye, the man who filled her heart with tenderness every moment she was with him, and tell him she was going to fly away to the Long Walk.

She found the sand dry and soft, and lay down for a rest, cradled in the softness of a quiet June night. She drifted off, and the night was quiet, and then light was in her face, and a man was nudging her with his boot, and she looked up into the face of a young hard stranger with angry eyes.

She clawed her way up, not wanting him to look down on her.

He was not alone. Two others stood back. The one who had nudged her was clean-shaven, with a revolver at his waist, and he had a flair for dressing. He wore a blue shirt and black vest and a flat-crowned hat. The others were dark and had ill-kempt beards, and heavy bandoliers laden with copper cartridges. Still more lined their belts. Each carried a repeating rifle. She had never seen men so heavily armed.

"What do you suppose she's doing here?"

"Don't rightly know. No horse, no nothing. Not a kit or a bag. Just one lone squaw."

"Think she talks English?"

"Hey, you." She was being addressed by the shaven one. "You speaka da English?"

She elected to hide her knowledge. It might save her life. It also might give her a clue of her fate.

She stared blankly at him.

"Hey, Kid, she can cook. We need a cook."

"Yeah," the Kid said. "She can cook and we can figure out what to do with her."

He prodded her forward. A camp came into view, and in it were several more young men, all busy with camp chores.

"Looks like we got us a squaw," said the Kid.

"Well, hell, ain't that nice," one replied.

He addressed her. "Go make johnnycakes." He pointed. She stared. "Hey, squaw, cornmeal and grease, and water, and fry 'em up." He pantomimed.

"I will," she said.

"Ah! I thought so. Where you come from?"

"I am Shoshone, Snake, going to St. Louis to see my son. He's in school."

"Goddamn educated injun," a bearded one said.

"You with anyone?"

She debated what to say, and opted to tell her story. "I lost everything. I had my ponies and my saddles and things, but white men stole them and were going to use me and kill me. Twice this happened."

The one called Kid yawned, and motioned for her to get to work. The men were hungry. Now they collected, eyeing her as hungrily as the others. Maybe she was in even worse trouble than before. She knelt, stirred cornmeal into mush, added grease to the hot fry pan and the meal, and began forming patties with her hands.

"Thought you'd know how," the Kid said.

She started the johnnycakes frying, and hunted for a spatula to turn them. She found none.

"I would like something to eat," she said. "I have nothing."

"Why should I feed you?" the Kid asked.

"Why should I cook for you?" she retorted, and started to walk away.

"Ah! I like that. A real bitch squaw! You eat, woman. What's your handle?"

"I do not know this word."

"Name."

"My husband calls me Mary."

"Where's he?" But before she could reply, a motion from the Kid sent a couple of men out to guard the perimeter. "Around here?"

"Yellowstone River," she said.

"You want to stick with us? You get fed."

She returned to the fire, found a knife stuck in the sand, and flipped the cakes while they watched. She eyed the knife, eyed them, and slowly plunged it back into the sand. Kid did not ignore the gesture.

"Sweetheart, that knife was a little test. You don't know bad when you see bad. I'm bad. I'm badder than bad. I'd cut you to ribbons if I feel like it. All these gents are badder than you ever saw or ever will see."

She shrugged.

"I'm the Choctaw Kid," he said. "That's my business. Being bad. Ain't no sin on earth I ain't done a hundred times."

She gazed up at him, finding cruelty in his face. He was a breed himself; she could see that.

"Why did you go bad?" she asked.

"No reason except I feel like it. There's posters in every burg around here. I'm wanted by a dozen lawmen. Army wants me. Over to Fort Kearney, they have a reward for me, dead or alive."

"I don't know what bad is. Shoshones don't have bad."

"Don't hand me that. You get a killer, what do you do with him?"

"He's got to pay the family of the dead. Or else they get to kill him."

"That the law?"

"We don't have laws. Only white men have laws. We have justice. Someone hurts you, you get revenge. It all works out."

"This lady, she's got no laws!" the Choctaw Kid said.

"All right," she said, pointing to the black fry pan.

These men scooped up the cakes on their knife blades and took them off to cool. She started some more cakes while the rest watched her closely. She did not know how this would end, or whether she would ever see her son. Probably they would take her with them, and her only escape would be death in some lonely place.

The Kid ate his in a moment and waited for another.

"What do these men look like? That took your horses?" he asked.

"Bearded men, in gray, with a mule wagon."

"Saw them pass," he said. "The other bunch must be the ones around here last night."

She nodded.

"Maybe we'll kill 'em. Kill 'em real slow and long."

She averted her gaze.

"Would you like that?"

"It's not for you to do," she said.

He smiled darkly. "We do what we feel like doing. And these wouldn't be the first I've killed. And won't be the last."

"And then the army will kill you."

He shrugged. "Not many in my line of work live long."

"Then why do you do it?"

"Lady, you ask too many questions. Now git them fry cakes done. I do whatever I feel like doing, and if I feel like killing a few, I'll do it."

"What are your bloods?"

"Half and half, and it makes me crazy. Don't never trust a breed."

"I do not know Choctaw."

"Now you do. My ma, she was Chocktaw. My pa, he was Dutch. Don't never marry Dutch to any injun because it'll come bad."

She fed them a second fry pan of johnnycakes, and waited. But he signaled her to scrub out the pan and clean up. The men left her one, which she ate quietly. It tasted oddly delicious.

"What's your son?" Kid asked.

"His name is North Star in my tongue, Dirk in yours. He is a grown man now. The blackrobes have him. I want to see him. I haven't seen my boy in many winters. Maybe he will not know me."

"He'll know you. If he don't like his Snake ma, I'll kill him," the Kid said.

That shot a chill through her.

"Religion ruined everyone," he said. "Plumb ruined me. I almost was good until I got smart."

"What are you going to do?"

"Rob and ruin until I die."

She stared. He meant it. He had worked out his future, knew it wouldn't last long, and wouldn't change a particle of it.

"We're tired of this here Oregon road. We're heading for the Union Pacific next. Them rails down on the Platte, below here. We're going to cut wires and clean out trains like you never saw, until we got the whole cavalry on our ass."

"Why?"

He eyed her. "I'll tell you why. Someday you'll tell people you met the Choctaw Kid. You tell 'em and they won't believe it. You tell 'em what the Kid did. Promise me that?"

"What the Kid did?"

"The Choctaw Kid. Not any kid, the Choctaw Kid."

"If you want to be known, why not be bad in St. Louis?"

"Don't ask stupid questions," he said.

"Here, no one knows you're bad," she added. "Maybe you not bad."

He turned to the ones with the bandoliers. "Fix her up. Two horses and a kit."

"For me?"

"Mary, we're going to get ourselves two horses for every one we give you. That's what's going to happen this day."

Men headed for the picketed horses, selected two small ones, saddled and bridled a bay, collected a big buckskin, haltered the big horse and added a blanket and packsaddle, and then strapped on panniers. Into these they added a kit. Bedroll, fry pan, pot, a bag of cornmeal, another of rolled oats, and various other things she could not see.

The Kid led the bay mare to her. "Up," he said. "I'll look to your stirrups."

But the stirrups were fine. She sat, amazed.

"These here got no brand, and no one knows where they come from. But I'm gonna write out a bill, just because you're a redskin and they'll be picking on you."

He dug into a saddlebag, found a pencil and a sheet of paper, and wrote on it.

"What does it say?" she asked.

"It says I, Harry Kidder, sold you two nags. Sold to Mary

of the Shoshones for consideration of twenty-five dollars of service, June twenty-five, eighteen and seventy."

"And you signed it?"

"I did. Show it to your son." He handed her the paper. She slipped it into the pannier.

It was true. There were no brands or marks on these ponies that she could see; not even an ear notch. They had come out of nowhere.

"They're not shod, and you'll want to go easy on rock."

"You are a good man," she said.

His face darkened, and she thought she had made a fatal mistake.

"Go!" he snarled.

She touched her moccasins to the flanks of the bay mare, found her responsive, and slowly made her way downriver. Behind her, the bad men watched.

Chapter 21

His old black top hat flew off his head even before he heard the distant crack. From ancient habit, Skye dove off his horse, feeling pain shoot through his bum leg as he landed. He snatched his old Sharps from its sheath as he went.

Victoria had done the same, and now they stood behind their ponies. The shot had come from some vast distance far ahead and to the left, probably in the bottoms of the Big Horn River. She strung her bow and nocked an arrow. The ponies sidestepped nervously. Skye peered over the neck of his, wondering what lay ahead. He saw nothing. But someone had just tried to kill him. He wished his eyes were as good as they once were but now age blurred the horizons. He checked his Sharps. It was ready.

He retrieved the top hat, which had fallen ten feet away, and found a fresh hole through it, just above his hairline. He had been an inch from death. This was his fifth hat. The first two had been beaver felt; the last three silk.

A rage built in him.

There was only silence. No crows flew, no wind whispered. They were proceeding south along the arid Big Horn River valley, on a trail laid out by Jim Bridger, the old mountain man. They had thought they were alone.

"Goddamn white men," Victoria said.

Indians wouldn't snipe at them from several hundred yards.

His leg hurt. He had landed squarely on it, and while his knee didn't capsize or break again, everything ached anew. He squinted at the silent bottoms of the distant river, ready to shoot back.

After a while they moved slowly southward, walking between their horses, and thus walking within a living fortress as they had often done in the past. Occasionally Skye studied the river bottoms, ready for anything. But they proceeded peaceably south without hindrance.

That lasted only a minute or two. A gaggle of horsemen boiled out of the brushy bottoms, heading straight for Skye and Victoria. Skye continued quietly, his bum leg paining his every step. There were six in all, skinny horsemen in slouch hats, all except one. A fat man, bulging at the belly and thighs, mounted on a thicker horse, followed along just behind. They were spread in a half circle, ready for whatever trouble they faced.

They swiftly surrounded Skye and Victoria.

"Hold up there," the fat one bawled.

Skye waited quietly. This was a tough outfit, with mean thin men sporting an unusual amount of facial hair along with revolvers and saddle carbines.

"Gents?" Skye asked.

"This here's claimed land, and we don't allow no goddamn redskins on it," the fat one said.

"I'm Barnaby Skye. And who am I addressing?"

"It don't matter none. This is my range, and you're on it, and you're going to get yoah ass off it."

"That's interesting. I didn't know there was a government land office anywhere around here," Skye said.

"It don't mattah whether they is or ain't. Yoah getting yoah red ass off. Ah'm claiming this heah Big Horn Valley, top to bottom, mountain to mountain, and that's that."

"I didn't catch your name, sir."

"It's Yardley Dogwood, but never no mind; I could be God and it won't make a bit of difference to you."

Skye had lived among the Yanks long enough to detect region in a man's voice. These were Texans, he thought. Bitter men, defeated in war, swarming out of a ruined South, reckless of life and law.

"Texans?"

"We sure as hell ain't Indians. Now you turn around and git. We don't allow any trespassing here. You git or face what you get."

"Just passing through. Visiting my wife's people."

"Did you heah me? Git out!"

"Did you bring a shovel?" Skye asked. "Dig a grave for two people passing through?"

Dogwood glared. "We don't give a damn who you are, what you are, or whether you git buried or just rot until the coyotes eat what's left of you."

"Got a few longhorns? I don't see them."

"There a-comin' and you're a-going."

"Who are you going to shoot first? My wife or me?"

"You're both going to buy the ticket, mister."

"Mister Skye, yes. That's how I prefer to be addressed. Do you prefer to be called Mister Dogwood?"

"Enough talk." He motioned to his men, who withdrew revolvers. Skye found himself staring into half a dozen muzzles. "That's how I talk, redskin."

"Born in London, sir. This is my wife Victoria, born among the Absaroka People. And who are these gentlemen?"

For an answer, Dogwood lifted his hog leg and drilled another hole through Skye's silk hat. It flew off again. Skye winced.

"You fat sonofabitch," Victoria yelled. "You miserable bastard. I own this land. You get your ass off. This land's mine. I've owned it since before you were born, fatso. My people owned it before Texas was. This is my home, and you can damned well take your fat ass out of here."

The whole lot stared at Victoria, whose drawn bow was aimed square at fatso's chest.

"Kill me, go ahead, you pile of grease. Only you get an arrow before you do."

Skye marveled. Dogwood sat, breaking the back of his nag, utterly paralyzed. One of the cowboys began easing sideways, out of Victoria's vision.

"One more step by that bastard and you croak," she said.

The cowboy stopped.

"Looks like there's a standoff, Mister Dogwood," Skye said. "Now, are you going to let us through, or do we die? We're old; we don't mind dying. You're what? Thirty?"

"Tell that squaw to put the bow down."

"Tell your cowboys to holster their guns."

Dogwood plainly didn't wish to do it.

"Did you bring a shovel, Mister Dogwood? Three graves, one for you, two for us."

"I'll tell you what you're going to do, you fat bastard, you're going to turn around and ride away, and when you're out of range, we're going to go ahead and cross my people's land. And then you're going to take your cowboys and your cows and get out of here."

Dogwood was hefting his revolver, twitchy, daring himself to shoot her.

Skye deliberately reached to the grass and plucked up his hat, which lay between his and Victoria's horses. When he was down, he swung his Sharps around. He put his hat back on, and his Sharps was at his waist, pointing at fatso.

"Looks like you put another hole in my topper, Mister Dogwood," he said.

But Yardley Dogwood was staring at the huge bore of the Sharps, which now pointed blackly at his chest.

"I don't mind dying, but I guess you do," Skye said. "You back off now. Turn your men around and get out of here."

Dogwood slowly, carefully, holstered his own Navy revolver and wheeled his stout gray horse. He nodded to his men, who followed suit, and soon the horsemen were retreating toward the bottoms. No tricks. Skye didn't trust them, and rested his Sharps across his saddle, ready for a long-distance shot.

The horsemen were soon beyond the effective range of their own carbines, but Skye didn't move. Not yet. He waited until they were deep into the river bottoms, where they probably were camped in the middle of the mosquitoes awaiting Dogwood's trail herd.

Skye was in no hurry, and stood on an aching leg for a while more.

Victoria eased her bowstring, returned the arrow to her quiver, but did not free the bowstring. Not yet.

"Can they do that? Take land?" she asked.

"No Yank government's here yet," Skye said. "They just claim it, and drive others off it, and call it their own."

"The goddamn government's worse than the cowboys," she said. "One of these days they'll tell my people to go to some damned place with four invisible lines around it and stay in there."

All that day they rode hard, wanting distance between themselves and fatso. The Big Horn Valley was flanked by the Big Horn Mountains on the east, and rolling arid hills on the west, and was easy to travel. Skye's leg hurt from the new insult, but he concluded nothing was damaged. They scared up some mule deer, but Skye was slow to draw his Sharps, and the deer vanished. Old age wasn't helping him keep meat in the cook pot, which was still another reason why he was feeling the need to settle somewhere and raise his own beef.

Midday heat suffocated them but Skye felt compelled to keep going, and as the day waned he knew they had traversed a long stretch of the arid valley. This arid land was going to fool fatso. Only the green bottoms along the river offered much feed for the longhorns, and most of that was brush-choked.

Along toward dusk, Victoria grew restless.

"Something ahead," she said.

"I don't hear anything."

"You're deaf as a stone, Skye."

It turned out she was right. Just about when Skye was about to call it quits for a day, they rounded a river bend and discovered a sea of cattle ahead, longhorns of all shapes and colors, brown, brindle, bluish, spotted, black, gray, bawling and milling, many of them along the riverbank. And herding them were a dozen or so men on horseback, some barely visible in the distance.

"More goddamn cowboys," Victoria said.

"Fatso's herd coming up the river."

This time they rode straight toward the camp, where a fire was blooming. They were noticed, but no one was pulling weapons or showing any signs of trouble.

But the foreman did pause and await company.

"Evening," he said, looking Skye and Victoria over.

"Evening. I'm Mister Skye, and my wife Victoria Skye. We're angling through here and thought to say hello."

"I reckon you're welcome," the lean man said. "Light and set."

Skye and Victoria gratefully slid from their ponies, picketed them, and joined the busy trail crew. The lowing of the cattle wrought a constant sound, almost a wail, as the animals watered and spread out on thin grass. Here were a dozen more of these wire-thin men, trail-worn and tired.

"Name's Higgins," the man said. "Seems to me I've heard tell of you."

"I used to guide once, and before that I led a fur brigade."

"You a friend of Bridger's?"

"Sure am, Mister Higgins. You're on his road. Old Gabe worked this out, mostly for wagons, but you've taken a herd over."

"You pass my outfit north of here?"

Skye nodded. "Maybe twenty-five miles. That's Yardley Dogwood, right?"

"They let you through?"

"It took some persuading, Mister Higgins. That fellow, he's a big target."

Skye laughed. Higgins laughed.

The foreman turned to several of his men. "Gents, this heah is a fine old man of the mountains, Mistah Skye, and his woman, Victoria. They been here before we were born. He's rassled grizzly, put bullets into Blackfeet, taken people where white men never been, and he's too tough to eat so we ain't going to roast him for dinner. They's passing through, and we're going to welcome them. We got us a quarter of a beeve to eat this heah evening, before it turns rank on us, and pretty soon now we'll be roasting the meat, soon as that fire gets hot. And you, Mistah Skye, you're going to tell us some stories."

"Some good beef for a few yarns? I imagine that's a bargain, Mister Higgins."

"Goddammit, Skye, you call me Mister one more time and you can just starve."

"Higgins, you call me Skye one more time, and I won't tell stories."

"You got any booze?" asked Victoria. "He don't tell stories good until he gets himself sauced up."

Higgins sighed. "I'd give a dozen steers for a bottle," he said. "But we're out of luck."

Chapter 22

Blue Dawn of the Shoshone People made her way east along the Big Road. She was no longer Mary, the name Skye had given her. She was no longer the woman of a white man. She was what she had been born to be. She sat perfectly erect in her saddle, and did not slouch like white men. She sat with her head high and her back straight, and thus she told anyone who saw her that she owned the world and was a woman of the People.

But she met very few westering parties, and they paid her little heed. There was something about her that discouraged contact, and that was how she wanted it. Skye would count miles, but she never fathomed those invisible marks, and instead counted horizons. On a good day she rode past several horizons. She was now some unimaginable distance from her people and from Skye and Victoria. It was so far she had no word or concept for it; and yet the land never ended, and the only thing she observed was that the grass was thicker and taller, and there was more standing water and evidence of generous rain. But each day she was a little closer to her son.

When North Star had been old enough, Skye had taught the child the mysterious signs Skye called writing, and taught the boy to read these signs. Sometimes Skye would draw them in charcoal on the back of a piece of bark, or an old paper, and then have the solemn child learn the letters. Then Skye taught his son words. Often this was early in the morning, before the world stirred much. Sometimes Skye found a book and taught his son the meaning of each word, even as Mary listened. She often thought that she, too, could read with a little help, but he never offered to teach her. He only told her he wanted their son to have a chance at life, a chance that was taken away from him when he was young.

Skye had been a patient, cheerful teacher, who never reprimanded the boy when he could not fathom a letter or word or idea. Skye often illustrated the words, making up little stories, or telling the boy all about the place called London, with its streets and half-timbered houses and fog and thousands of people and frequent rain. So the boy had soon connected words and letters to these magic things, so different from the buffalo-hide lodge that was his real home, far from any sort of building.

She had watched this mysterious ritual proudly, watching the boy discover a word and point a finger at it, watching Skye rejoice whenever his son had made a bit of progress. North Star was a patient boy, but sometimes he got restless when Skye detained him too long in their lodge on a winter day, or outside when the weather was good. Her son wanted to run and walk, like other sons.

She only vaguely knew what this schooling was all about. Her boy would learn the magical powers of white men and be able to do the things white men did, and know what they knew. She knew this would take her son away from her, bit by bit. He would not be a Shoshone boy when he had mastered all this, but a white boy. That was a great sorrow to her, and yet she also was proud that he was learning Skye's ways.

"He needs to know these things," he told her. "If he learns these things, he can choose the sort of life he wants to live."

That seemed strange to her. Why would one choose a

life? What was wrong with the life they were sharing? Did Skye have some sort of plans for the boy that she knew nothing of?

Sometimes North Star would pull out a scrap of paper and read words to her, pointing at each one. The child scarcely imagined that only one parent had these mysterious secrets hidden inside, and that she knew nothing of writing and reading. But she could at least teach him the ways of her people, and she showed him how to draw language-pictures, how to make the signs that were understood by most plains tribes, and she taught him all the words of her own tongue that she knew, and Victoria taught him the words of her Crow tongue as well, so the boy grew up trilingual, switching easily to her tongue, or Skye's, or Victoria's whenever he was addressing one of his three parents. This was a beautiful thing, for the boy had drawn close to each. He was quiet and sunny, and she had watched him proudly as he grew into a person, and left his infancy and childhood behind him. But what did Skye intend for him?

Skye had seemed driven to teach the boy his words and his writing, and it troubled Mary because it was as if Skye were investing something in the boy that she couldn't understand. All he would say was that he didn't want Dirk to be trapped in the life that Skye had lived after being put on a ship and sent into the Big Waters. It amazed her that Skye's people would snatch him away from his father and mother as a boy and put him on a boat and keep him from ever seeing them again. Surely that was a terrible violation of Skye and his parents, and it made her wonder about the English. No Shoshone boy would ever be captured and forcibly taken from his parents. It was unthinkable. These English, they had no respect for the liberty and rights of the family they had torn asunder. They must be a very hard people, she thought, to permit such a thing. Hard and cruel. She liked her people more, because each boy could choose his own path, and was not stolen from his family.

Skye was a hard man, she thought. He could have taught her to decipher the letters and words, and shape them into language. He could have taught her, the same as he taught their son. He could have taught Victoria too. But they were women, and he never thought to teach them how to put words on paper with marks. That was for white men. She didn't mind much. She liked being his woman, and gathering nuts and berries, and firewood, and mending the lodge cover, and nursing the boy, and making quilled shirts and moccasins for him. But he was hard, and more often she could not fathom what went through his head. White men's thoughts were so different from hers, and sometimes he seemed to be an utter stranger to her.

Still, it had been a happy lodge, the four of them, his late-in-life boy, she and Victoria sharing the work and Skye's arms. North Star had prospered. The Absaroka boys taunted him because he was different, but he gave back as much as he got. He was Skye's son, and that gave him an aura of mystery, for Skye was a legend among them, the strong white man who had come to live with the Crows and fight beside them.

Then one day, her happiness fell apart. North Star had lived eight winters. They were at Fort Laramie, and Skye was talking with his friend Colonel Bullock, who was the sutler. They talked for a long time, and Skye brought North Star to the colonel, and presented him, and the men all talked a long time, while she and Victoria wandered outside. She knew it had been a bad year for Skye; he could not pay the colonel what was owed. Fewer Yankees wanted guides to take them into the lands unknown to them, be-

cause now the country was known, and there were trails.
And Skye went ever deeper in debt.

Then at last Skye appeared on the veranda of the post
store, looking solemn. He was searching for words, trying
to bring himself to say something to his wives and son, and
the more Skye struggled, the deeper was the dread in Mary.
He was having such trouble that even the boy caught the
malaise, and stared.

Skye ran a weathered hand through his graying locks, and
settled his old hat, and began.

"The colonel's retiring," he said. "He'll no longer be my
agent. He's sold his inventory to a new post sutler named
Harry Badger. The new man won't extend credit. I owe over
two hundred seventy dollars, and we'll be unable to buy
anything until that's paid." He stared glumly at Victoria.
"We'll do without."

That was bad enough, but then it got worse.

"I don't want my boy to grow up without a chance at life,"
he said. "He needs schooling, and a trade, so he can make his
way. He'll need to support a wife and family someday.
He'll need to read and write and pay bills and earn his way.
I just can't give him that here, with a few old books and
newspapers."

Skye looked so uncomfortable that Mary took alarm.

"Colonel Bullock's leaving for the East tomorrow. He's
retiring in St. Louis, and he'll be taking Dirk with him."

A sudden desolation broke through her.

"It's all arranged. The blackrobes have a school for
Indian boys in St. Louis. This is Father de Smet's dream,
helping native boys get an education and passing that along
to their people. They'll take Dirk and give him an education. They're good people. They'll teach the boy whatever
he needs, and start him on his way."

Skye had been talking about Dirk almost as if the boy weren't there, listening to every word.

"But, Papa," he said.

"How long will this be?" Mary asked. One winter, maybe. That would be forever. One winter, and then her son would come back.

"Until he's sixteen," Skye said.

It was as if she had fallen off a cliff and were tumbling down, down, down to the cruel rocks far below. Eight winters.

"But he will have no mother!" she said.

"The blackrobes will care for him. And Colonel Bullock will look in on him. There is a dormitory, a place where he'll be with other boys, safe and warm."

"Eight winters."

She felt dizzy as grief overtook her.

"Sonofabitch, Skye!" Victoria snapped.

He started to reply, and subsided into silence. He tried to draw them to him, but she went stiff and wouldn't let him touch her, and Victoria stalked off the porch. He tried to catch his son, and soothe him, but Dirk had gone pale and was sliding deep into himself. In that moment Skye's family had shattered, and it didn't seem possible that it would ever be put together again.

"I can't even pay my debts anymore," Skye said.

That made no sense at all to Mary, but sometimes white people made no sense to her. She glanced furtively at her son, as if she shouldn't be looking at him because he wasn't hers anymore, and felt something shatter inside of her.

Skye knelt before his son, and clasped the boy's shoulders in his gnarled old hands.

"It's for you, Dirk, not for me. It's to give you the chance to make something of yourself. You'll be grateful someday. You'll be lonely and homesick for a while. But then you'll be too busy to worry about that. And the blackrobes will help you grow up to be whatever you want to be."

But Dirk's face had crumpled into fear, and Mary ached at the sight.

"They took me off the streets of London and put me on a ship," Skye said. "I never saw my family again. I had to learn how to live, how to survive. It won't be so hard for you. You'll see us in a few years, and we'll all be glad. You'll be better off than we are."

But it was as if Skye were talking to the wind. There was only the terrible reality that Skye's son Dirk, and Mary's son North Star, was being torn from the lodge.

"Now, son, it's time to say good-bye to your father and your mothers."

But the boy could not manage that. He simply stared, a tear welling in each eye. Skye took him by the hand and led him to his mothers. "Son, you'll see them in a few years, and we will all be proud of you. Colonel Bullock and the Jesuit fathers are giving you something precious, something that will help you to have a good life."

But Dirk simply stood mute and miserable.

"We'll say good-bye now," Skye said, but no one did.

Finally, helplessly, Mary watched as Skye led her son to the clapboard house where Colonel Bullock resided. She watched a woman welcome the boy, and then the door closed, and so did her own life.

Chapter 23

Skye awoke with the sense that something was wrong. It was an ancient feeling, honed from a long life lived in a way unknown to most white men. It was not yet dawn, but a band of light cracked the eastern horizon. He peered quietly at the slumbering cow camp. The cook was already up and building his morning fire near a wagon with bowed canvas over it. The cattle were grazing quietly. He saw a night herder sitting his horse, unmoving.

There had been a light shower in the night, pattering down on Skye's canvas-covered bedroll and annoying his face and hair. The air this June dawn was moist and fresh and sweet. He peered into the darkness, unable to banish his malaise, but he saw nothing amiss.

The evening had been enjoyable, though not for Victoria, who had sat bitterly among those who were occupying her homeland, a valley the Absaroka People had considered their refuge. But the trail crew had sawed off some thick beefsteaks for Skye and Victoria, and after beef and beans they had peppered them with questions about this country. Victoria had subsided into silence, staring flintily at these bearded Texans, but Skye had relaxed some. These were working hands, without large ambition, unlike their employer and the men two days' travel downriver, the ones who had nearly killed him. Skye didn't hold that against this trail crew, but he knew Victoria did.

They had mostly wanted to know about the valley they

would be settling; what tribes visited, what creeks ran
through. This was home to the Snakes and the Crows, he
had told them, employing white men's names. It was arid,
caught in the rain-shadow of the great chain of mountains
lying to the west. It wasn't prime buffalo country, but the
river bottoms would support plenty of longhorns. He never
did tell any yarns from the old days. These drovers wanted
only to know about the present.

Now he peered about the slumbering camp, taking inventory, but he saw nothing amiss. Victoria still slept. He
threw his bedroll off and lumbered to his feet, wrestling
with his stiff and pained leg. The river brush wasn't far, and
he headed there in the deep silence. Dew caught at his moccasins. Even as he relieved himself, his gaze roved because
his sense of malaise wouldn't leave.

When he returned, limping painfully, he saw Victoria sitting up in her blankets.

"Something's wrong," he said.

She nodded curtly. She hadn't liked being here last night,
and still didn't. She rose easily, her age affecting her less,
and studied the camp. The cook busied himself, and ignored
them. Their ponies were picketed on good grass.

"Go?" he asked her.

She nodded.

She would fetch the ponies. He couldn't get around much
anymore. So he shook out his bedroll and tied it tight. Then
he shook hers and tied it. Then he took his over to his saddle to tie it behind the cantle, and that's when he discovered what was wrong.

His Sharps rifle was not in its sheath. Had he pulled it
out, as he often did, to keep it beside him as he slept? He
didn't remember that, but checked the ground where he had
slumbered. No rifle lay there. He limped in widening circles. Had he left it at the campfire? He hadn't. Was it lying

with Victoria's stuff? It wasn't. Her quiver and bow rested beside her Crow-made saddle. Was the light tricking him? No, the widening dawn skies were concealing nothing.

He had owned the Sharps for decades. It used an old technology now, but that didn't matter. It had been a great lifesaving weapon, a weapon that had kept him fed and safe, for as long as he could remember. Its throaty boom had aided his wife's people in their battles with the Sioux and Blackfeet. Its big bullet had dropped buffalo for her people and kept her Kicked-in-the-Bellies band fed and sheltered. With the Sharps, he had earned enough in buffalo hides and tongues to support his wives and son. The robes and hides he had brought to the traders had kept him in powder and caps and paper or cloth cartridges, had purchased pots and knives and thread and awls and calico. Long after the guiding business had faded, his Sharps had brought precious Yank dollars to keep his wives and himself alive.

Now it was missing, and he felt deprived and, in a way, naked. The Sharps was still his meal ticket and his safety. He stared at the empty sheath, willing his rifle to be there, willing it to be on the ground under his saddle, or close by. But it was gone, and without miracles, he could not replace it.

"We'll look," he said, not yet ready to make accusations.

She nodded. They separated, each drifting toward a group of slumbering drovers. She in particular had a way of gliding through unseen. No one paid attention to an old Indian woman. He watched her pause at each bedroll, pause at a pile of gear near the horses, and even stoop at one point to examine something closely. He drifted toward the cook and his fire and wagon. The cook was a cranky old gent, as disapproving of the Skyes as he disapproved of everyone else in his company.

"Looking for something of mine got misplaced," Skye said.

"Nothing gets misplaced in my kitchen," the gent said.

"I lean on it a lot," Skye said.

"No sticks around here I haven't burnt up to make coffee," the cook said, dismissing him. Skye peered in the covered wagon.

"Ain't nothing in there for you. Iffen you're hungry, you can wait like the others."

Skye had seen nothing resembling a rifle anyway.

Some of the hands were stirring now, rolling up their blankets, stretching, washing down at the river. Two night herders were riding in slowly, and Skye waited to see what was hanging from their saddles. But, in fact, neither had a saddle scabbard or a rifle on board. If they had lifted Skye's rifle, they had hidden it somewhere in this brushy river-bottom country.

Someone had it. He hadn't lost it. He didn't know how to deal with it.

Victoria slid close.

"Some sonofabitch stole it," she said. "Good at it too."

Her grudging admiration was drawn from her own culture. The Crows were some of the best camp robbers on the plains, and were masters at lifting valuables from any white party wandering through their country. Only this time the game was reversed.

Skye debated the proper course. There was no good way to deal with it. Accuse them? Threaten them? Systematically tear into their gear while they bellowed at him? No. The Sharps would not be in this camp, and would not be picked up by its new owner until the Skyes were long gone, and then it would be a source of great good humor among these drovers. But at least he'd put them on notice, one way or another. Some trail bosses ruled with an iron hand and wouldn't let a guest at their campfire be harmed.

Victoria brought the ponies in and saddled them. Skye

watched her lift his saddle over the blanketed pony and draw up the cinch. The scabbard hung uselessly from the right side.

Higgins approached. "You ain't staying for a little coffee and cakes?"

Skye seized the moment. "Mister Higgins, I'm missing my Sharps rifle. It wasn't in the sheath this morning."

The foreman absorbed that for a moment. "Must be lying around here somewheres, then."

"We've looked."

Higgins studied the Skyes' campsite, as if expecting the rifle to materialize.

"You used it some as a crutch. You reckon it got left in the bushes?"

"We've looked."

"I don't recollect seeing it when you-all rode in yestiddy."

"I had it."

Higgins paused a long time, and came to some sort of conclusion. "I imagine it's around heah somewheres. I'll ask. Let me do the asking, friend."

Skye watched the foreman approach knots of men and converse with them, and watched them shake their heads. Higgins headed out to the horse herd, where other of the drovers were saddling up for the day, and once again the same questions wrought the same shake of the head in them all. Higgins must have directed them to start a search, because half a dozen yawning drovers began a broad sweep of the camp, the herd, the brush along the river, the riverbank, and the surrounding meadow.

They turned up nothing, which was what Skye expected.

Higgins ducked his head into the cook wagon and poked in there, and finally withdrew with nothing in hand. He returned to Skye and Victoria.

"It sure ain't showing up nowheres. Maybe some thieving redskin come in the night and took her off."

"In other words, it wasn't your outfit."

Higgins absorbed that a moment, and then agreed. "It sure as hell wasn't any of my boys, and if I see one toting a Sharps, I'll fix to get it to you. You going to the Shoshones on the Wind River, right?"

"Yes. They have an agent."

"Well, Mister Skye, I'm plumb sorry. It makes the Republic of Texas look bad, and that makes me feel bad."

"You tell Yardley Dogwood he owes me a new hat and a Sharps."

"I don't suppose I'll tell him that. What happened to your hat?"

"Those bullets holes are what happened to my hat."

Higgins had nothing to say after that.

"I suppose if a Sharps turns up in your outfit, Texas will be disgraced," Skye said.

"I'm afraid that would be true."

"And so would Texas and Yardley Dogwood, and each of you."

The foreman stared.

There was no point in dragging it out. Skye painfully clambered onto the buckskin pony, and Victoria lithely settled in her squaw saddle, and they rode away, feeling the stares of a dozen men on their backs.

He and Victoria rode silently for an hour, wanting to escape that place and those men, and finally a certain tension lifted and they relaxed a little.

"I am watching the death of my people," Victoria said.

"I'll get a new one somehow," he said. "Muzzleloaders are cheap."

But the thing he had shoved to the back of his mind, the

bottom of his heart, and the farthest reaches of conversation welled up in him, and he could not banish it. His vision was going bad. More and more, distant things were blurred, and words on pages were blurred, and he had been hunting now for two or three years in dread of not seeing clearly what he was going to kill, and that dread had so suffused him that more often than not he had let blurred moving objects pass by, for fear that he was shooting at a friend's horse, and not the wild animal he wanted for meat. And he was more and more afflicted in his near vision too, often asking some white man to read something to him because he couldn't make out the letters and words and sentences. Nor was that all. He had acquired a slight tremor, one he hoped was not visible to Victoria and Mary, but one that weakened his aim and required him to use a bench rest as much as he could.

The terrible reality was that he was not far from having to set aside his fine old Sharps because age had caught up with him. He had intended to give it to Dirk when Dirk returned, or rather if Dirk ever returned. There was one more year of school with the Jesuits, and then Dirk would be sixteen and free to choose his life: Indian like his parents, or white. It was odd. He had driven Dirk from his mind, refused to think about the boy, loathed his decision to send his son east for schooling. But now he found himself aching for his son.

Chapter 24

Victoria watched Skye ride a little ahead, unbalanced in the saddle, his stiff bad leg twisting him. He was riding with his spine straight and rigid, his shoulders thrown back, not with his usual slouch. He was riding as someone new to horses would ride, ill at ease in the saddle. She stayed a little behind him, aware that she was seeing something fraught with pain. Skye didn't ride like that.

She elected to stay back, knowing his silence meant something also. Sometimes in the past they had walked their ponies side by side, communing with each other out of ancient love.

His rifle sheath bobbed uselessly on his saddle. He ignored it. An empty flaccid sheath, a lost rifle, an old man. Wearily, for she no longer rode easily for long, she followed, letting his silence command the hours. They were two days from the Wind River Reservation of Mary's people, two days from Mary herself. Mary would pitch Skye's lodge near her brother, and her brother would be looking after her, and they would all welcome Skye and Victoria.

Ahead the treacherous Wind River canyon blocked any direct route to the land given to the Shoshones by the white fathers. Skye steered west, up a red rock canyon that would lead to a divide and down an ancient route much favored by the Shoshones themselves. And in a while they would all be together again in Skye's lodge, and Mary would look after them. More and more, Victoria was glad that Skye's small family encompassed the younger Shoshone woman. Victoria wearied easily now.

They nooned in an enchanted park encased in tumbled red rock. A clear creek ran through. The red walls were decorated with ancient stick figures, the language of people long gone. But the stories told by the figures were sometimes clear enough for anyone to read. This small avenue over the arid mountains was a sacred route, filled with mystery and holiness.

Skye eased off his pony but landed badly, gasping when his bad leg shot fire through him. Victoria watched helplessly. She led their ponies to the creek, where they nosed and swirled the water before lapping it.

Skye, afraid to settle into the verdant meadow without a crutch, chose to sit on an old cottonwood log.

Victoria washed her face in the icy water, enjoying the shock of cold that stung her skin. Then she settled in the grass near him, planning on a brief nap in the breezy shade.

"I was going to give it to Dirk," he said.

It had come out of the blue, and she puzzled a moment to connect these words to anything. But he was talking of the Sharps.

"I can't see much anymore." He stared at her. "Next year. He's supposed to come back here next year. The rifle, that's what a father gives to a son."

She marveled. She had known for a long time that his vision wasn't good, knew that when he hunted he wanted her along. Knew when he asked about things ahead, or moving animals, he was making sure. He couldn't see things close at hand, either, and had stopped studying those mysterious signs in books, stopped reading. But never until now had he confessed to it, and somehow he had even been able to hunt well enough. He knew from the way animals

moved what they were, knew the stolid walk of the buffalo, the bounce of a running deer, the race of antelopes.

Now, for the first time, he was acknowledging it. And for
the first time in many winters, he had spoken of his son, as
if the boy were back from the dead.

"Will he come here?" she asked.

"I don't know. Eight years of schooling. Who knows?"

"Next year, he is free?"

Skye lifted his hat and stared into the red-rock high country. "I don't know that he'll want to see us. He's been away
a long time, and he's got a good schooling now. He's used
to the city. He wouldn't like it here. Stuck with an old man
who hasn't seen the inside of a school for half a century."

She marveled. He had not talked about Dirk for years on
end, and sometimes she thought the boy was dead, and Skye
wouldn't mention his name, the way the Native people didn't
name the dead. But now, suddenly, sitting on this cottonwood log beside a clear creek, he was talking about a boy
who was ripped away and scarcely heard from again, except for a perfunctory letter waiting each spring at Fort
Laramie saying he was well and learning his lessons.

"This school. Is it like a white man's prison?" she asked.

"I haven't ever seen it," he said. "But there's a dormitory
for younger boys, another for older boys, a dining hall, some
classrooms, and a church and rectory."

She hardly knew what all that was about. "The blackrobes?" she asked.

"Jesuits. Society of Jesus. You've met Father de Smet on
his travels."

She had liked Father de Smet, the blackrobe who liked
Indians and defended them against sickness and the Yankee soldiers and government.

"What will he be like?" she asked, dreading the answer.

Would there be a terrible gulf between his Indian mothers and the educated boy?

"If he comes. Who's to say?" he asked. He peered into her eyes. "I didn't do it for me. If it was for me, I'd have kept him here, showed him everything I learned here. He could be looking after us now."

"Will he hate you?" she asked, the thing that had been smoldering in her breast for many winters.

"He was too young to rip away from us," he said. "But Bullock was leaving. It was then or never."

She didn't like the brittle tone in his voice; this was something he had been rehearsing and reliving and regretting for all those winters past. And the lack of any more children only deepened Skye's desolation. Skye had sent his only boy away and torn his own small family apart.

He rose abruptly, and Victoria knew she must not ask any more or mention Dirk again. He limped to his horse, his back stiff against her, almost in rebuke for opening this subject. He pushed himself heavily into his saddle, and she slid into hers, and they turned their ponies up the red-rock valley and the distant pass they must surmount.

She rode behind, aware that something valuable had happened there, while they rested themselves and their horses. She never did understand goddamn white men, and she had understood Skye not at all when he had sent North Star away and broken the heart of his two mothers. But it had broken Skye's heart too, and that was what she marveled at now. She had never realized that. He had sent Dirk away for the boy's sake, so the boy could find a good life. And he had suffered for it, every day of his life since then. She didn't know the meaning of all this, but she knew, at last, what had gone through the heart of the man she loved.

They rode uneventfully over the high saddle that would take them toward Mary's people, and descended Muddy

Creek, through a quiet afternoon. Skye rested often, mostly
to relieve his tormented leg. Victoria was grateful for the
rests as well. Once she saw a doe and fawn, and resisted
drawing her bow. The Texas foreman had given the Skyes
enough meat and biscuit to reach the Wind River Reservation. She watched the doe lead the speckled fawn toward
safety, and thought about the drovers and their vast herd of
beef, which would all be killed and eaten someday.

She wondered whether white men apologized to the spirit
of the animal they had just killed, the way many of her people did. She had a ritual prayer. I am sorry to have taken
your life, she would say to the downed animal. And she
would wish the spirit a good voyage to the place of spirits.
She meant to ask Skye whether white men ever felt sorrow
for taking the life of one of their cows or sheep. But somehow she could not bring herself to ask him that.

They reached the banks of the Wind River the middle of
the next day, and made their way upstream, toward the towering peaks in the distance, following a well-worn trail
along the cold river. This was Mary's home. She would be
there with the lodge, and there would soon be a joyous
reunion of Skye's family.

Within the hour they reached Fort Washakie, and discovered log buildings, and also a cluster of log homes,
along with some traditional lodges. There were even some
white clapboard structures that she thought were government buildings. These had fieldstone chimneys, some of
which were leaking gray smoke. Plainly, the Eastern Shoshones were acquiring the ways of white men. Their great
chief, Washakie, had befriended white men and wanted to
teach his own people the ways of these Europeans who
were filtering through their country. He was as old as Skye
but more vigorous, and had an almost mystical power over
his people. He knew English and French, having learned it

from the trappers, and this had enabled him to deal with the Yankees and win for his people a great and beautiful homeland along the Wind River.

Now, as she and Skye wandered into this sprawling but tidy settlement, she looked for Mary and the familiar lodge, but she saw neither. Skye reined in his pony, unsure where to go or what to do, and then started a systematic search for his lodge, even as Shoshone children and women, and a few elders, congregated around them. They all knew the Skyes, and they greeted the Skye family joyously—except for one thing.

"Where is our Blue Dawn?" a woman asked.

Skye knew enough of the tongue to understand. "Isn't she here?" he replied.

They stared at one another. Mary, it seemed, had not come to Fort Washakie at all, and no one had seen her for many moons.

An unease built in Victoria. Surely Mary would have sent word. But it was plain that Skye's younger wife had never arrived, no Skye lodge had been raised here, and the Shoshones had no knowledge of her whereabouts.

Victoria was well aware of all the troubles that could befall a lone Indian woman traversing a vast land. Bears, storms, hail, sickness, injury, a broken leg, a lamed pony, death at the hands of hostile tribes, and something more. White men. Had that ugly bunch with Yardley Dogwood caught her, saw how vulnerable and beautiful she was, used her, and then killed her as they would kill some camp dog?

The thought must have crossed Skye's mind too, because she found herself staring into his worried eyes. Those savages from Texas knew no boundaries.

About then Mary's brother, The Runner, gray at the temples now, pushed through the throng.

"It is thee," he said. "Art thou here for a visit?"

Skye had always loved The Runner's Elizabethan English, gotten from studying the Bible and Shakespeare given to him by a white teacher long before.

"We are. It's good to see you, my brother. And where is Blue Dawn?"

"Thou hast asked a question I cannot answer."

"She came ahead of us. Victoria left her on the Yellowstone. She was coming here."

But The Runner could only stare, sadly. "Brother and sister, come to my house. We will await Blue Dawn there. See my house? It is built the way of white men."

Skye nodded reluctantly. "Has there been any word of trouble? Are there hunting bands from other tribes in the area?"

"No, only the sweetness of spring doth fill the air . . . But yes, word hath come that some white men with many cattle are upon the Big Horn River."

Skye's dread was palpable to Victoria. She thought that she and Skye might soon retrace their steps, this time looking for a hasty grave.

Chapter 25

Mary found herself at a place where the iron horse ran on silvery rails. For a day or two, she had heard the wail of whistles and the distant clatter of the steam cars, but she had never seen a railroad or a train. Now she halted her horses at the sight of a graveled road running along the Platte Valley, and on this road were wooden cross ties, and metal rails, stretching mysteriously east and west. An iron horse would not alarm her. She had seen the fireboats on the Big River, the fires making steam, which pushed a piston, which drove the paddlewheels.

Surely the iron horse would make as much noise and be as ferocious as the fireboats. Sometimes the fireboats had scared the ponies, and she didn't doubt that these horses, given her by the Choctaw Kid, would take alarm too. Still, for reasons she could not fathom, she abandoned the Big Road, which ran closer to the Platte River, for this arrow-straight iron road, and led her horses eastward along it. No iron horse came for a long time, and when she reached a place where there was a big tank of some sort on stilts, she stopped. It didn't take any effort to see that this was a place where they ran water into the iron horse, to make steam.

She stood there, contemplating these wonders, when she did hear the distant chuff of a train, this one behind her, going east. There was the same chuff as the boats, but there was also an odd roar or rattle. She steered her horses back to a grove of box elders nearby, and waited, curious about this thing. She dismounted, for fear that the horse would buck or become unmanageable, and simply waited. Off a way she saw a plume of smoke, and then the iron engine rounded a gentle bend, and behind it was a string of boxcars. She knew at once this train carried freight, not people, and she was grateful because it was white strangers she feared most, especially here. She thought maybe she should not be here, and faded deeper into the grove of box elders.

The chuffing engine, belching smoke, slowed and then she heard a great squealing and didn't know what that was about, but the train was grinding to a stop. The nervous horses yanked at the reins she held in her hand, but didn't balk or bolt. They had seen the iron beast before, she thought, and didn't panic.

The engine halted directly under the tank on stilts, and then seemed to die, or sag into a temporary death. It sat on four big iron wheels, and four smaller wheels in front, and smoke issued from a conical chimney at the front. An iron grille at the front was plainly intended to sweep aside anything in the path of the iron horse.

A man in blue coveralls emerged from the cab on the engine, climbed upward, swung the chute of the water tank to a place on the little car behind the engine, and opened a hatch there. Then he spun an iron wheel, and she knew water was flowing from the big dark tank into the little car behind the engine. Other men climbed to the ground. One lit a cigar. Another turned toward the track and urinated on it. A third, walking along the cars, seemed to study the wheels of each one. The cars looked to be empty, their doors open to the wind.

Her horse snorted, and they saw her then. For a moment they did nothing, but finally two of them headed her way. She did not flee, but held her ground. In fact, she chose to push forward to meet them, so they would know she was not afraid.

"Damned squaw," he said, eyeing her. "Where the hell did she come from?"

She responded at once. "I speak your tongue. My husband taught it to me. I am Mary, of the Snake people. I have never seen the iron horse."

"Snakes, lady, you're a long way from home. Where's your man, eh?"

"I go to St. Louis to see our son. He is in the blackrobe school."

"That's a long way. He couldn't buy you a ticket?"

She didn't know how to respond to that, so she kept silent.

"That's a long way you got to go, lady," said the other, this one with a trim dark beard and kind eyes.

"I wish to see my son. His name is Dirk, but I call him another name."

"Dirk? That's a rare one."

"My man is from this place called England."

"Well, I'm Will Mahoney and I never saw an Englishman I liked."

She didn't like the tenor of this, and started to wheel away but Mahoney stayed her.

"You want a ride? We ain't going to St. Louis, we're going to Omaha, but you just go down the Big Mo from there."

She was confused.

"These are deadheads, empties," he said. "I'll take you if you want."

"I have no money."

"Naw, free ride, unless the railroad dicks chase you off."

"Omaha?"

"Upriver some from St. Louis. You git off, the Omaha yards, and I reckon you can go on down the river road to wherever your boy is."

"Why you doing this, eh? What do I pay you?"

She wanted it plain. There were things she would not do, and white men supposed that they could do them with any Indian woman.

He shrugged. "Deadheads. Most of our freight goes west. Might as well help a lady out."

The one working the water chute had finished, and was cranking a wheel closed. They would go soon.

"I don't know how to feed or water my horses in there."

"I know a car with some hay in it. That suit you?"

"How do I put my horses in one?"

He pointed at something, a wooden structure near the tank. There was a pen there too.

"How do I get them out when I leave?"

He grinned. "Trust us."

The other one, the cigar smoker, yawned.

"I will," she said.

"Beats riding them nags five hundred miles," he said.

They led her to the pen, and showed her the chute that her horses could climb to enter the car.

"Wait here," one said.

A moment later the engine crawled forward until eleven cars had passed, and then stopped when the bearded young man swung a lantern. The car door was open wide, and inside was abundant scattered hay.

It took a sharp rap on the rump to drive each horse up and in, but in moments she was in the car with the gaping door.

"Easy, ain't it?" the bearded one said. "I'm the brakeman. Will Mahoney. I'll keep an eye on you."

She wondered how foolish she had been, but saw only a cheery smile behind that beard.

"My man, Barnaby Skye, would be very pleased with you."

"Maybe I'll make an exception," he said.

He vanished from the door, and a moment later she felt a soft jolt and a thump and the car began to roll east. The nervous horses circled around, but she unsaddled them and tied their bridle rein and halter rope to a rail on the wall. They tugged at the lines, and then settled down, even as the train gathered speed and Mary began to see the trees and meadows whirl by, faster than anything she had ever seen before. She made a soft place in the hay for herself to sit, and then let one horse at a time dig his snout into the hay while she held the line.

Sometimes the boxcar lurched violently. Other times it rolled so smoothly she marveled at it. Sometimes they rocked between woodlands, where the road cut through forestland. Other times the Platte River vanished from view. She could scarcely imagine her good fortune. From her doorway she saw running deer, alarmed crows bursting into the sky, a coyote paralyzed at the sight of the huffing train. And once she saw a wagon on the Big Road, its oxen plodding west.

Still, she realized she was now a prisoner. She could not jump down, and neither could her ponies. They could take her wherever they wished, do whatever they wished, and she could not escape them. She eyed the roadbed passing in a blur before her eyes, and knew that if she tossed herself onto that gravel, she would break bones and abrade her flesh. But trains didn't always go fast. They slowed now and then. They would stop for more water, or more of the black rock that burned.

She resigned herself to a long wait, and settled on a bed of hay she swept together. Then she watched the prairie go by, and the river bottoms pass from view. This iron horse was taking her where she wished to go, and that was all that mattered.

A long time later, the train slowed and then ground to a halt. Some whitewashed buildings stood in an orderly square, but the place looked deserted. She peered out the door, and discovered Will Mahoney approaching.

"Stopping here, if you have needs," he said. "This is Fort Kearny. Used to be a big place when the Oregon Trail was the way west, but now they're fixing to close it. One company's all that's left."

"Soldiers? Will I be safe?"

"Long as you don't scalp someone."

She slid over the edge of the car and dropped to the ground. "It is good to stand and walk," she said.

"I should tell you, this here's where you should get off if you want to ride direct to Independence and St. Louis. From here on the train goes to Omaha."

She had no idea what to do, but he sensed her confusion. "If I was you, I'd just stay on. In the Omaha yards, I'll get you off and you just ride down the river three, four days to where you're going."

"I will do that, then."

"Tell me. Is this son of yours a hellcat?"

She stared, frightened. "I do not know . . ."

"Oh, hellcat. Is he wild as a catamount?"

Mary retreated into silence.

"Reason is, I got me a Pawnee woman. I fetched her out of a cathouse and now we've got a boy, half wild Pawnee, half wild Irish, so I'm wondering if he's going to be like your boy."

"My boy—I haven't seen him for a long time."

Mahoney grinned. "Got rid of the little devil, eh? Well, I figure I'm raising a wild little beast. There's no law, no rule I don't want to bust, and my woman, she never heard of God. I just got the notion my little tiger, he's like your little tiger, he's half civilized, half savage."

She started laughing. "Mister Mahoney, I like you," she said. "But you must understand. In my marriage, my man, Barnaby Skye, he's the savage, and I'm the civilized."

Will Mahoney stared, bright-eyed. "By God, next time I lift a mug, I'll salute you."

She didn't know what all that was about, either, but it didn't matter. They both had mixed-blood boys, and that was what bonded them.

Soon they were rolling again, and night fell over the car, and she could see almost nothing, and lay quietly in the hay through the strange night. But not long after dawn she saw an occasional building, and planted fields, and once a man riding a buggy, and then more buildings, mostly white-washed places, and finally the train pulled to a halt in the place called Omaha, where there were many tracks side by side, and many buildings glowing in the early sunlight.

Then the train started to crawl slowly, and she heard voices, and then it stopped. Directly out of her door was one of those ramps leading down to pens. She could unload her horses here.

Mahoney appeared. "I had 'em pull up a bit so you could get these nags out," he said.

In moments, she had unloaded her ponies into the pen, while he collected her saddles and gear.

Now she was in a strange place, with many rails, and many buildings, and she felt utterly helpless.

"You go see your hellcat," he said.

"But, sir, I don't know . . ."

He saw her fear.

"Hey, I'm done. I got to go to that building over there, and then I'll take you down to the river and put you on the road. Whatever you do, stick with the river and go down-stream. You'll go through a bunch of towns like St. Joseph and Kansas City, but you keep on going to the biggest one, where the Missouri meets the Mississippi."

"Many days?"

"It's a way, lass. A week or more, I reckon."

She went with him to the building, and soon he was leading her through the city, with its broad streets and shops and ornate houses, larger than she had ever seen. People stared at her, seeing an Indian woman in quilled leather. She lifted her head and sat proudly. She would let them see she was a Shoshone, and proud, and nothing would frighten her.

Mahoney led her down a steep grade, past more handsome houses, and finally to a worn dirt road that ran alongside the great river.

"I guess this is it," he said. "Good luck. Me, I got two hellcats to visit. Pawnee women, Jesus, Mary, and Joseph. It's more than I can handle."

But he laughed infectiously, and Mary decided that a three-hellcat family was probably a good one.

She watched him trudge up the hill, plainly weary after his long hours as a brakeman. Something in her loved him.

Chapter 26

Cold rain soaked Mary, but she endured. She had no other clothing than her blue chambray blouse, red-quilled elk-skin vest, and doeskin skirts. It had rained constantly, usually in afternoon thundershowers, but there was nothing she could do, and rarely did she find shelter. The moist climate had bred mosquitoes and flies, which often swarmed her, but there was little she could do about those, either. So she endured. The sun dried her clothing and the clouds soaked it with their tears. Sometimes she thought it was a way of keeping clean.

St. Louis frightened her. Now, as she plunged deeper into its outskirts, she brimmed with anxiety. What if North Star didn't wish to see her? Or was no longer there? Or was so changed by life with the blackrobes that they could only stare at each other across some chasm? Finding him would not be easy. She had only two names. The school was St. Ignatius, named after the founder of the blackrobes. And she knew Colonel Bullock had retired in that place, after years at Fort Laramie.

So she endured the rain, endured the curious stares of people on the river road, endured the occasional boys who raced along beside her, shouting "Injun! Injun!" She knew about boys. Many a time when Skye and his wives entered a strange village, the boys clotted around them, sending mock arrows at them, raising a hubbub. White boys were no different.

The vast valley of the Missouri proved to be a good place to feed herself, with all its berries now in season. She lived on the bountiful raspberries and blackberries, on wild asparagus and green apples, and familiar roots. The land was not so settled or farmed that she failed to find safe havens at night, well hidden from the people nearby.

Soon she would see her son. She would see how he looked as a young man, adult by her standards, almost so by Skye's. Fifteen winters he would have now, and he would have his full height, and broad shoulders, and a man's gait.

Would he even recognize her? Worse, would he care?

Of course he would. She heartened herself with that belief, and continued to travel the river road, now running east toward St. Louis. Now things crowded her senses. She passed farmsteads, with plowed fields and laundry flapping on lines. She passed tall freight wagons drawn by ox teams, driven by profane teamsters, hauling mountains of whiteman things to the outlying settlements. Some of those men eyed her with something more than curiosity, and she hurried past them.

She formulated a plan of action. First she would try to find this school herself. She would resort to Colonel Bullock only if she could not find it. She had enough English to ask directions. Where were the Jesuits? Where was this St. Ignatius school that took in Indian boys? She feared that if she went to Colonel Bullock first, he would dissuade her, or even forbid her to see her son. She didn't know why. White men were mysterious to her. But what if the Jesuits refused her? Would they keep her son from his mother? She dreaded that, dreaded not even having a glimpse of him, locked behind stone walls and iron grilles, hidden from her hungering eyes.

The road took her along the waterfront, an area of grim brick buildings and rough wooden structures side by side.

A bluff separated this part of St. Louis from the rest, and above she could see homes shaded by stately trees, and women strolling. Occasionally steep roads connected the rest of the city with this waterfront. Some of the buildings had signs she could not read, but plainly one was a saloon. Before it a wagon stood, its big draft horses quiet in their harness, while burly sweating men in grimy aprons unloaded big wooden casks and carried or rolled them into the dark building. Downriver, she saw steamboats docked at the riverbank, tied in place by great hawsers wound around wooden pilings. Some were being loaded; others sat idle, no fire in their bellies.

This did not look like a place where the blackrobes might have a school.

She saw not one woman here, but men of all descriptions, a few in black suits, but most in rough workmen's clothing, such as those unloading the kegs. She trusted workingmen more than men in suits so she edged closer to one burly man in a filthy apron, with cinnamon chin whiskers and watery blue eyes. He paused, eyed her up and down, and grinned toothlessly.

"I am looking for help," she began. "I want to know where the Jesuits are."

"A squaw that talks English. I'll be goddamned. And a couple of dandy horses too," he said, his eyes surveying Mary and her two good animals.

He simply grabbed her bridle. "Looks like maybe I can tell you," he said.

His freckled hand held the bridle, and she knew she was trapped.

"I am visiting my son. The blackrobes at St. Ignatius are teaching him. Please tell me how to go there."

"Got me a pretty squaw," he said, his toothless grin widening. "Got me a couple of nice horses too. What say you come visit me? I live in there. I'll show you how to get around the city. You can pay me any way you want." He was leering now. She understood the leer, which crossed all peoples and cultures, and was very plain.

He had her horse. No one paid the slightest attention. And she knew no one would heed anything an Indian said. If it came to an argument, his word would win. He would accuse her of stealing his horses, and he was just getting them back. Something like that, anyway.

She didn't intend to give up her horses to this man, even if he weighed twice as much as she did. But she was not without a few ploys, some of which Skye had taught her. She dismounted, sliding off the horse, which lifted her skirts a little as she settled on the brown paving blocks that surfaced the street.

"Hey, you want a good time?" she asked, drawing close. "I'll give you a good time. You want a squaw? You'll get a squaw."

He grinned, and nodded toward the building. He was still holding the bridle.

She stood before him, alluring and tall and slender, and she smiled.

"Go on in there, squaw, and I'll be right along," he said.

"What's your name?" she asked.

"Oh, you'll find out," he said.

She edged close to him, smiling, until she was practically in his arms, which he enjoyed. But he was still holding the bridle. She brushed against him, closer now, eyeing him carefully because she would have only one chance, and if she failed he would probably beat her senseless.

She caught his eye. "You big man?" she asked, even as she lifted her knee smoothly, fiercely, and with deadly aim, into his groin.

"Yooww," he bawled, his arms flailing outward and then

down to his crotch. He folded like an accordion, holding himself and wheezing. He was gasping, red, his mouth a big Oh, his lips drooling saliva. She dodged back, recovered the rein of her skittering horse, threw herself upward and over, before the bearded man recovered enough to roar and spring toward her. But he missed, and she was clear, her packhorse too.

She hastened away, but he stood there watching, and strangely laughing. It was all in a day's work for him.

But she had other ideas. She would never seek directions from a man again.

The city was strange, a world utterly amazing, and she wondered what to do. Mostly from instinct, she took one of the steep roads that led away from the muddy river, and when she topped the slope she found herself in a different world, a place where people lived in buildings unlike any she had ever seen. Some were made of brick, and had tall glass windows and wooden porches. Others were made of wood. Great trees cast shade over emerald lawns. She wandered aimlessly, past stores that displayed goods in their windows, or had signs swinging in the morning breezes. Some buildings seemed beyond her fathoming, and she had no idea what happened inside of them.

Horse-drawn buggies rattled past, and big freight wagons drawn by massive horses rumbled by, or paused at a store to deliver crates and cartons. She wondered where the horses were fed because she saw no pasture anywhere. She wondered where she would feed her pack and saddle horses. Pasture would be a long way away, and her horses would be very hungry soon.

She saw young women carrying empty baskets she thought were intended to carry their purchases, while others wheeled small carriages with babies or children in them, and she marveled. The women wore long, full dresses and covered their arms, even in the moist summer heat, and wore bonnets or hats. The men usually wore black suits and white shirts, but the workingmen dressed in rougher clothing, but were just as covered as the women. She could not fathom it. In any camp of her people, on a moist, hot day like this, the men would wear very little, maybe just a breechclout, and the women would be sleeveless at the least. She eyed these people, thinking how much they had to suffer through the fierce heat. She could not imagine why anyone would live with such discomfort.

She herself endured the rain and heat, but the moist air was not pleasant. It made her flesh oily and she yearned to return to the mountains. She discovered that St. Louis seemed to have districts, some with old, narrow streets and ancient houses, and some newer. She occasionally attracted attention, especially from children, who swarmed around her until she feared her horses would kick at them, while they studied her angled face and strong cheekbones and the clothing that told them that she was from one of the tribes. She smiled, and they tentatively smiled back.

But this was an urbane city, and it largely ignored her as she wandered her helpless way through it. She had utterly no idea where this place of the blackrobes might be, or where she might find North Star in a city that contained more people in it than all of the Shoshone, east and west, every branch.

A carriage sailed by, pulled by a pair of high-stepping white horses, reined by a man in a shiny black silk hat rather like Skye's, and beside him was a red-haired woman in gauzy white, with sleeves that were almost transparent. Mary thought it might be a chief and his woman, because she could wear something more pleasant on this sopping hot day. The air was so heavy and moist that she felt suffocated, and every instinct in her cried to flee to the country where there was real air.

Some great bells began to bong, and for a moment she was paralyzed with fear. Would the noise signal soldiers? But no one on the cobbled streets paid heed, and she realized that these bells were ringing in the towers of a great stone edifice nearby, one with endless steps climbing upward, and crosses topping the towers. The crosses she recognized. Ah, now she knew where the blackrobes would be, so she turned her horses that direction, up a mild slope toward this great and frightening building, taller than four or five buildings piled on top of one another.

Father Sun had climbed as high as he would go this day, and burned down from above, making the heat all the worse. She knew one thing: she would never, not in a thousand winters, choose to live here. It was so hot that not even the flies lingered in the sunlight, and very few buzzed about her horses.

Then she saw a blackrobe walking down the steps of this great building, and she rejoiced. She steered her horses to the foot of the wide stairs and waited, and when he approached, she spoke.

"Sir, could you direct me?"

He peered up at her, and she marveled. He was gowned head to toe in black, but he showed not a drop of sweat in his face. His gaze took in her native dress, and he frowned slightly, as if not approving of her.

"Madam?" he asked.

"I wish to go to the place of the Jesuit blackrobes called St. Ignatius."

"I'm not a Jesuit," he said.

Her heart sank. This one looked like the blackrobes she had seen among her people.

"But yes, I can direct you. And why do you ask?"

"I have come to see my son."

"Ah," he said. "Yes, they school some red boys there." He eyed her doubtfully. "It's four blocks that way, two more, over the bridge, and then back one."

He was waving his black-encased arm this way and that.

"What is a block?" she asked.

"I see," he said. He eyed her amiably. "Follow me," he said.

He strode away from the river, his pace fast, his robes flapping, and she followed behind, past streets and people and houses and a small green park given to trees, and she soon didn't know which direction she was going, but he never paused until at last he came to another building with towers with crosses, and a high brick wall surrounding whatever structures lay within.

"There," he said, pointing to a narrow grilled gate.

She nodded her thanks, but he had already wheeled away, his black skirts flapping, and soon was gone.

Here was the place she had sought months earlier, the place where her own North Star lived, where her flesh and blood slept and ate and learned. She thought of all the days and moons she had traveled, the perils and starvation she had endured, the gifts of those who had helped her, and the hope that had inspired her. If only she could see her boy. If only she could gaze upon him for a while. She tied her horses at a hitching post with an iron ring in it, turned toward the grilled gate, found a cord, and pulled it.

Chapter 27

Mary struggled with an instinct to flee but forced herself to stand quietly. When a man appeared, it was not a person in black robes, but a man wearing the suit of the white men, and wire-rimmed glasses perched far out upon a bulbous nose. He peered at her.

"I have come to see my boy," she said.

He looked doubtful. "But it is class time . . ."

"I have come from the mountains to see my son," she said.

The mountains meant something to him, and he softened. "You are?"

"I am Mary, the woman of Barnaby Skye, and Dirk Skye is my son."

"Oh, Dirk," he said, warming a little.

He opened the grilled gate and she entered a serene courtyard, with somber buildings surrounding it. Somewhere, somewhere near, would be the Star That Never Moves. Her pulse lifted. In truth, she hadn't the faintest idea what she would do when she saw him. But that was all she wanted. She had come all this distance, all these moons, to see him.

He led her to an austere reception room, white plastered walls, a crucifix, some chairs, a small window opening on the yard. He nodded her toward a wooden chair and vanished through a door.

She felt utter confusion then. Why had she come here? What did she expect? Who was she, that she had abandoned her husband to come here? What would her son look like? Would he accept her? Would he smile? Would he turn his back to her?

It took a long time, and she resisted an impulse to flee to the safety of the street, collect her horses, which she had tied to a hitching post, and escape.

But then she heard noises, the door opened, and she beheld a thin young man in white men's clothing with warm flesh, medium height, dark hair, the strong cheekbones of her people—and blue eyes.

She gave a small cry. It was North Star. She uttered his name in Shoshone, but he looked puzzled.

"You are Mary of the Shoshones?" he asked in English.

"Oh, my child."

"Are you my mother?" he asked, his own bewilderment as large as her own.

"Seven winters, seven winters," she said, a river of anguish flowing through her now. "Seven winters ago."

He stood quietly. "That was what Papa wished for me," he said.

But she could not speak.

"Ah, I'll leave you to your reunion," the man said. "Dirk, you'll not want to miss chapel."

The young man nodded. The graying man in the dark suit vanished, and then Mary was alone in the austere room with her only child.

"I have only a few minutes," he said.

"What are minutes?"

"Ah, little bits of time."

"Then you must go?"

"We cannot miss chapel, not ever."

"Sit here," she said, motioning him toward the other chair.

They sat, staring at each other. She could not fathom him.

Everything had vanished behind his white man's mask. She understood even without words that the years with the blackrobes had driven his Shoshone nature from him. He looked uncomfortable.

"Can you speak the tongue of the People?" she asked softly.

He stared, and finally shook his head. "The words might come back, but offhand I don't remember them," he said.

"Then we will talk in Mister Skye's tongue," she said.

He nodded. "I am wondering—why you came now. Is my father here too?"

"No, I came alone."

"Is he—dead?"

"He and Victoria are old but they are well enough. He is very stiff, and his eyes trouble him."

"He never came here to see me," he said.

She knew this was painful ground, for her son and for her.

"I know. It was because . . . it would hurt too much."

"Does he want me now? Is this why you came? To take me back?"

She carefully chose her words. "No. He is old and proud, and won't say that he needs you, even if he does. I came to see you by myself."

"All alone, across the plains? To see me?"

She nodded.

He smiled suddenly. "You came to see me!"

"It is my way. I wanted to see you now, with fifteen years upon you."

"I am doing well. I get high marks. They say maybe I will be like a white man. Tell Papa that I get good grades." But then his bravado faded. "I wish I knew Papa. It's like . . . I am an orphan. Year after year, I waited for him to come visit me here."

She didn't want to hear that. He had ached for Skye and

her to come see him, spent the months and years waiting and hoping. And Skye had let him down.

There was another pregnant pause, and finally she broke it.

"Are you happy?"

"I am treated well. They tell me I can be a clerk or a teacher someday. The good fathers are kind to me. They say that a mixed-blood can do as well as a full-blood."

"Is that good?"

"I suppose it's better than living in a buffalo-hide lodge, freezing all winter, wondering where the next meal will come from." He eyed her uncertainly. "I am very fortunate. They tell me hardly anyone from the western tribes has the good luck that I have."

Her son was staring at her, absorbing her, his gaze missing nothing. No doubt comparing her to the white people in this city.

Sunshine and shadow crossed his face as he wrestled with strange and conflicting feelings. "I don't know your world, or my father's anymore. My memories don't go back that far. My life really began when I came here. So it's not easy, seeing you, knowing you are my mother, you raised me in a lodge, and my father hunted and kept us alive." He brightened. "You are all that I dreamed you would be," he said. "I had no mother. I lived with other boys, but you were only a memory. And the full-bloods . . ." His voice trailed off.

She understood at once. Mixed-bloods were not respected. "Do the blackrobes treat you well?"

He shrugged. "I don't know what that is. I don't know what being treated badly is, either. They have always been kind to me."

"Do they favor other boys, North Star?"

He nodded, slowly. "They are very kind to the Lakota boys."

The Sioux. "Do they let you have your Shoshone name?"

"North Star? No, the blackrobes call me Dirk Skye."

"Would you rather be North Star?"

"Please don't ask me!"

She sensed she had transgressed.

"We were free," she said. "We went where we wished. Now they have put us on a reservation, with lines around it we cannot see, but we are forbidden to cross them. Things will be different now. Chief Washakie is helping this to happen."

The youth stared dreamily out the window, which opened on the lushly planted courtyard. "I dream sometimes," he said. "Of you and my Crow mother and my father, and a world where we could go anywhere, anytime we wished." He smiled slowly. "But it is gone."

"I have two horses," she said.

He stared at her. Not until she said it did she admit to herself that the entire purpose of this trip was to bring him back to his people, and his family. Skye and Victoria needed him. She needed him. She suddenly grew aware of something that had burned in her bosom all those days of travel.

"Your father, he needs you. Your Crow mother, she needs you," she said.

"Are they failing? Dying?"

"It is hard to live when you hurt. He hurts. She hurts worse but doesn't show it to anyone. We cannot help him. Before I came here, he left us to find a place where he could build a white man's house, with a bed in it and a chair in it and a stove and a fireplace in it, and a porch where he could watch the clouds skim across the peaks."

"Where would this be?"

"The upper Yellowstone."

"That is a good place to grow old," Dirk said.

"For him and Victoria," she said, leaving herself out of it.

"They tell me I am bright and there isn't much more they can teach me," he said. "They want to teach many boys with Indian blood, so that the boys will go back and teach the tribes."

"Teach what?"

."All about God. Farming. Cattle raising, plowing, blacksmithing, living the way white men live."

"And how do they live?"

He smiled. "I wouldn't know. I have scarcely left here, but once in a while they take us to the cathedral."

"You cannot leave?"

"A little. They watch over us."

"You see no one? Just the students and the blackrobes?"

"Once in a while Colonel Bullock came. He sat there where you sit, and he would ask me how I was doing, and whether I wanted anything, and what should he tell my father? And then two years ago he stopped coming. I learned he had died. He grew old and his lungs would not take air. I haven't seen anyone from outside since then."

"No girls?"

"Especially no girls." His face clouded. She saw a melancholy in him so deep she could barely fathom it. She saw all the spirits standing above him, sighing in the quietness. It was more than melancholy; she saw anger and frustration and loneliness too.

"There are full-bloods here, and there are breeds like me," he said. "The full-bloods, Blackfeet, Pawnee, Assiniboine, the Jesuit fathers like them and treat them like chiefs."

"And those born of two bloods?"

"Born in sin," he said.

She found courage to ask one of the big questions. "Was it hard—going away?" she asked.

"Not at first. I sat with Colonel Bullock in the stagecoach. It was an adventure. I looked at everything through the windows. It was only here, when I was given a narrow iron bed and a small locker in a dark room with other boys, that it was hard. Then my sunny world stopped. Do you know what I missed? Sunshine, open country, with you and my father bathed in sunlight. My new world was dark; dark walls, small windows, dark classrooms, teachers in black, darkness everywhere. That is the world of these Europeans."

"Is it still hard?"

He looked away. "I am a white man now. I take my solace in work. They tell me none do better. I make the time go by with work. The suns and moons and winters of time, I make them go past me. I read the classics. I know French. I do algebra and geometry. I have learned their history. I know their authors, the storytellers. I can compose a letter or a pleading or an index. They have even made me a mechanic. I know about iron and wood and the tools to shape them. I know about farming, even though I've never farmed." He smiled. "See? I am a white man now."

She scarcely knew what he was talking about, strange words, strange studies. Did he know anything of his own people? Had he sat with the elders and learned? No, and he couldn't remember the tongue of his childhood. He was as mysterious and difficult as any white man, and strange as Mister Skye.

She remembered how hard it had been for her to fathom her man, once the blush of her marriage had faded and she found herself trying to learn his ways. Now this son was like his father. That had been Skye's intent. Send North Star here so he might become a white man, and not one of the People.

"Star That Never Moves," she said in her tongue.

"It has been a long time since I heard that," he said.

"We gave you two names, and now you have chosen."

"No, I never chose it, my mama."

"The blackrobes, they chose it, then."

"No, they didn't choose it either. It just happened. When I was a boy, I called myself North Star, and it was lost."

The words ceased then, and they gazed at one another, and she felt him slipping away, and she wondered why she had come. She knew it would end like this. She would look at him and be glad, and then he would slip away, and she would sorrow. Now there was a gulf between her and him. He would call her a savage, and tell them he had a savage for a mother, and she would carry this in her heart.

A low, mournful bell tolled.

He smiled. "Vespers," he said.

"What is it?"

"It is a small service late in the day, offered to God."

"Do you follow the same path as Skye?"

He paused, hesitantly. "No," he said.

The door opened and a blackrobe swept in, this one young and dark, with almond eyes.

"Vespers, Dirk," he said.

The boy bolted upright out of his chair. "I must go, Mama. It is time for chapel. Good-bye. I am glad you came."

The father stood amiably in the door, waiting. He smiled at her. "Ironclad duty," he said to her.

"Give my respect to my father," he said.

North Star followed the blackrobe through the door, and she saw the door close behind them. She sat in the small silence of the waiting room, with a heavy heart.

Was this it, then? Had she come across the mountains and plains and rivers, through these nearby woods, across great rivers, for this moment, now passed? She had. She always told herself she only wanted to see him, just to see him, and now she had seen him, and had feasted on him, this

slender, serious, two-bloods boy with blue eyes and strong
cheekbones and warm flesh.

The soft bonging of the bell ceased, and faint on the air
came the sounds of solemn song, boys' voices, many voices,
singing something that sounded a little like the songs sung
at a Shoshone campfire by old men, to the sharp syncopa-
tion of the drums.

She could not bring herself to leave, not with North Star
so close that she could hear the singing, so close that one of
those male voices must be his. So she sat in the starchy
room, listening, until at last the song ended, and she imagined he was going to his bed. She rose, stiffly, glad that she
had seen her son, glad that he was alive, and he was very
bright and pleased the blackrobes. She looked around, uncertain how to navigate to the ponies tied outside, but she
found her way out the door, into the yard, and she saw no
one. Maybe they were all at this vespers. She found the
grilled gate to the street, and saw how to open it, and stood
one last moment, knowing she would never see North Star
again, knowing that her journey was complete. She saw
birds flocking in the lush trees, trees of a sort she didn't
know, and then she stepped through the iron grille and
closed it gently behind her, and stood staring at the moss-
covered wall, which was crowned with vines, which grew
in profusion from the moisture and heat.

The horses stood quietly, their tails lashing at the clouds
of flies. She felt sticky from the heat and wet. Beside her,
the great edifice of St. Ignatius rose silently, its walls a
reproof to this world of the street.

She slowly undid the rein, and also the lead line of the
packhorse, and climbed onto her saddle horse, and turned
to leave.

The gate clanged, and she turned to see him there.
"Mama, wait," he said.

Chapter 28

Skye had known loss all his life, and now that familiar and ancient grief flooded through him. Mary had vanished. No one in the village had seen her. She should have been there long ago. Victoria stood stiffly, her loss as large as his, her lips taut.

Mary's brothers and clan could offer nothing. Skye found himself cataloguing all the ways that people died in the wilderness. Snake bites, grizzlies, sickness, broken bones, a tumble down a cliff, getting bucked off a horse or stepped on by one, a runaway horse plunging into forest, a poisoned spring. And that was only a beginning. A lone, beautiful Indian woman in her middle years was prey. She might be a slave of the Arapaho or Sioux or Cheyenne. Or still worse, she might have become the plaything of those Texans in the Big Horn Valley, someone to use and abandon.

The bleak catalog scrolling through his mind could embrace only a few of the possibilities. He probably would never see Mary again, nor would he discover her fate, and as the days and weeks and months rolled by, all hope would fade and there would be only loss.

He had first known loss when a press gang had plucked him off the streets of London and he found himself a powder monkey in the Royal Navy. He never saw his mother or father or sister again, nor any of his cousins or other relatives. That had been the greatest of all his losses, but he had lost friends, horses, clients, and colleagues over the decades

in the North American wilds, each loss vivid and mysterious.

Now his younger wife.

"We'll go look for her," he said to Victoria.

But she seemed afraid. It had been all he could manage
to ride here to the Wind River Reservation. Her odd expression told him that she doubted he would have the strength
to go look. And it seemed a futile enterprise anyway. Look
where? There were many thousands of square miles to
search, and each one contained its secrets.

He and Victoria would be welcome with any of Mary's
clan or brothers, but somehow without Mary it wouldn't
seem right. He thought maybe after he had rested they
should return to the Crows and wait. And wait. And wait.
But even as he contemplated this, a youth arrived, and the
lad spoke a surpassing English he had gotten somewhere.

"Sir and madam," the bronzed boy began, "our good
chief, leader of all the Eastern Shoshone, wishes the honor
of your presence."

Skye nodded. "Tell Chief Washakie we will be along
directly, and thank him for inviting us," Skye said.

The slim boy smiled slightly, and trotted toward a white
clapboard cottage, one of the first at the Indian agency.

Skye and Victoria excused themselves from Mary's clan,
and led their horses across a green sward toward the cottage where the great chief awaited them on his porch. He
wore a denim shirt and black britches and a flat-crowned
felt hat, but kept his jet hair in tight braids, in the style of
his people.

"Ah, it is you, Mister and Mistress Skye," he said, waving them up the wooden steps to his broad roofed porch.

"Shall we go in? I live like a white man now. Come and
see," the chief said.

And indeed, Skye discovered an interior furnished very

like the homes of white people, with a rocking chair, Morris chairs, stuffed horsehair couch, a dining table and chairs, a well-equipped kitchen and two bedrooms, each with a brass bed frame. His women stood shyly, in gingham dresses.

"Tea for the Skyes," Washakie said, steering his guests to the parlor.

Victoria perched primly on a seat. This was big medicine to her, and she looked to be ill at ease.

"Your beautiful wife is missing," Washakie said.

Skye nodded.

"I have received the news. Anytime someone comes to the agency, I hear everything. So our own Blue Dawn was due here long ago, coming down from the Yellowstone, and she is not here. Have you any understanding, Mister Skye?"

"No, sir, we learned of this only a while ago, and neither Victoria nor I can offer the slightest reason. But all trips have their peril."

"And Texans flood into our lands with their cattle. And these are a particularly—shall I say undesirable?—lot of men."

"They worry me more than anything else, sir."

"Yes, that is my worry, as well. Your Shoshone wife is famous for her skills at travel, her powers over the spirits, and her courage. She can subdue a brown bear with a smile. She can quiet a horse made mad by a rattlesnake. But I am not sure she would be a match for some of those men who herd the cattle onto our lands."

Skye glanced at Victoria, who was keeping quiet. The Absarokas claimed the Big Horn Valley too, and probably had a better claim to it. Some of the tribe wintered there year after year.

"We will go look for her, Chief."

The Shoshone paused, gently. "You look worn, Mister

and Mistress Skye. You have traveled far. Even if you should return over the trail from the Yellowstone, you would be covering a vast land, with great mountains, rushing rivers, grasslands as far as the eye can see, thick dark forests, snow-fields, strange places where the spirits gather, places where ancient peoples have built rock cairns for their own purposes. Who can find one small, lone woman in all of that?"

"We will go look, sir. Mary is my wife, and beloved spirit sister of Victoria, and the mother of my son, and the woman to whom I have pledged my love and life."

"Well said, Mister Skye. But you are worn, and even as you sit you favor that leg, which hurts so much you cannot let it rest." He paused. "You have come a great distance, lon-ger than old people should have to travel. And if you leave us, looking for this beloved woman in this country we call our home, I will understand, and will make sure you carry some pemmican with you." He smiled slightly. "And your chances would be poor indeed. I have a better idea. It is our home. My young men know it and keep its secrets. I will send them out, all that will go, to look for Blue Dawn. They will cast a wide net, clear up to the Yellowstone, and before long you will have a good understanding of Mary's fate. They have sharp eyes. Young eyes. They see the distant eagle on the wing, and the field mouse at their feet. They see the moving dot on the hillside. If they find Blue Dawn, her heart will be freshened by her tribal brothers. And they will heal her and help her . . . in any case, you will have news. So come, stay here with Mary's clan; I welcome you as hon-ored guests of the People."

Skye choked back his sorrows and nodded. It felt strange, surrendering the fate of his wife to others. All of his days, he had acted on his own, done whatever needed doing, no matter what the risk or the hardship. But now younger men would fan out along Mary's path. He would be grateful to them. Old Washakie had said it gently: they would search with young eyes, sharp eyes, eyes that saw the moving dot on the hillside.

One of Washakie's many women, this one in blue gingham, appeared with a tea tray and poured tea for Skye and Victoria. Skye took it gratefully. He missed tea, which he received only rarely, and which not only tasted fine to him but wrought nostalgia for his ancestral home. And here was a great chief of the Indians serving it to him.

Skye eyed the steaming cup. "This is home, home for me. Please thank the young lady."

"She is my daughter, Wantabbe."

"You are teaching her new ways."

"It is good," he said. "I am following the new road given us by the fathers in Washington. It is not easy. Many of my people resist and say the old ways are good. But the old ways meant we starved when game was scarce, and we had no berries and roots if there was drought, and our lodges didn't protect us from bitter cold. We need to scratch the earth and plant our food, and herd cattle for our meat. I have seen it is good. And we will have houses too, houses like this. And we will be safe from our enemies, and have a great land given us forever, and we cannot be driven off of it. The other Peoples will have their own lands, and they will be protected too, and that is good. The new ways are better than the old. I say it and believe it."

"I hope you're right," Skye said.

The chief stared. "I hope I am too," he said. "It is a hard road."

The chief was nobody's fool, Skye thought. The Yank government made treaties with the tribes, only to break them whenever the Yanks felt like it.

This tea was bitter and harsh, and it suited Skye just fine. He let it cleanse his mouth before swallowing it.

"But my friend Mister Skye, you must tell me about the boy, Blue Dawn's boy, of our blood. How does he do?"

"I believe he is well. I haven't heard otherwise."

"Ah, I remember his name. The Star That Never Moves, what you call North Star, and at the time of eight winters, you sent him to the blackrobes."

"I did, Chief. You remember Father de Smet? He came west many times and visited your people. He offered to school the boy. He wanted to teach Indian boys so they could return to their people and teach them."

"I remember de Smet. He is a great and good man, who brought us the Book."

"But it took Colonel Bullock, at Fort Laramie, to make it possible, Chief. He offered to take my son east and look after him. So I sent the boy to St. Louis, and he's there now. He'll have a chance at life, a chance that was taken from me."

Washakie stared. "A chance? There was no chance for your son among the People? You chose not to bring him to our elders for schooling. You chose not to show him our Ways, or teach him how we govern ourselves, and how we live." Washakie nodded. "This I understand. To give your boy a chance, you sent him to the white men."

Skye found himself deeply discomforted, and scarcely knew how to respond. But Washakie rescued him, with a smile.

"You did the right thing, Mister Skye. Our ways will fade. The ways of the white man will settle upon the breast of the Mother, at least for now. Before white men came, we did not know about wheels, or guns, or metals. We made our tools of stone and bone. We did not know the secrets in the holy book, and the one God of all the world, and all the other worlds, and all the skies and all that is under the world. Maybe someday the white men's ways will be overcome by the ways of someone else. But you saw that the ways of the Snake people are not good ways for your son, and so you did what a good father would do, you gave your son something better."

"I never thought—your Shoshone ways are greatly to be honored, Chief Washakie."

"Have more tea, Mister Skye."

"If Dirk returns, we'll make sure he learns your ways, sir. That's his inheritance."

"If he returns?"

"I don't hear from him, sir. The letters stopped coming to Fort Laramie."

Through the window, Skye saw Shoshone youths preparing to leave. They were saddling their horses, collecting gear, and waiting for the laggards to join them. In a moment, they would ride away, looking for Skye's missing wife.

Chapter 29

Her son stood at the gate. She turned toward him, her legs going weak under her. He looked agitated and she feared he might be in trouble.

"Shoshone woman. I am glad you are still there. Stay for a little while. I'm going with you," he said.

"To the mountains?"

"To the People, and my family."

"Dirk . . ."

"I am North Star." He stood uncertainly, and then came to some decision. "I'll get my things and tell them."

He vanished into the schoolyard, and she stood beside her fly-plagued horses on the quiet street. She felt tense. He was gone a long time, and she wondered whether she had imagined what had happened, or whether Coyote had played a cruel trick.

But at last he appeared at the grilled gate, carrying a canvas sack. A young bearded blackrobe followed him.

"Are you sure this is the thing to do, Master Skye?"

"I am needed."

"So close to finishing? One more term. Just one."

"You have taught me well, Father."

The Jesuit turned to her. "Is this the wish of his parents?"

"I am his mother."

The blackrobe surrendered. "We hope you'll take what you've learned to your people," he said to the youth. "Remember the Lord who watches over you in all things."

North Star smiled. "Please thank the fathers. I've been given many things."

The Jesuit nodded, a small tight smile, and he turned into his school. The grilled gate creaked shut, and Mary beheld her son, freed from this blackrobe world, and somehow a man, even if sallow from the lack of sunlight.

"Star That Never Moves," she said. "I must tell you this. I came without the blessing of your father. I came because I wanted to and the need came into me."

"Then we are together in this, Shoshone mother. I am leaving the school without his blessing or knowledge. Aiee! He shall not like this. He shall ask why I threw away the gift he gave me. He shall send me back here. But I shall go to the mountains. I have made my choice. I shall make my own life. Maybe he shall not welcome me but I shall welcome him. I was a boy and now I am myself."

"Yourself, Star That Never Moves?"

"I have two bloods, Mama. I am not the same as you. I am not the same as my father. I am not the same as the Jesuits. Not the same as the full-blood boys in that school. I've learned the ways of the white men and I am glad I did and proud of it. But I am not of that blood. Now I wish to learn your ways too. I'm coming with you, Mama."

"My own son. I need to tell you I have no food. I have no saddle for you. Only that packsaddle, and nothing much good in the packs."

"Then we shall go to the mountains on faith. They were always talking about faith, about trust in the unseen God. Well, I learned my lesson. We shall go where we are led."

"I don't even know how to go to the road from here."

He smiled. "Then we'll find out."

He lifted his duffel onto the packsaddle and anchored it. "There's not much. A few spare clothes. A few small things. A blanket."

He led her confidently through the great city, and she marveled that he knew where to go. Plainly he had not been confined to that quiet schoolyard. The giant city vaguely alarmed her; yet they had no trouble, and people were not even curious about a youth and an Indian woman leading horses. There were so many of these white people, more than the stars above.

But eventually the city folded away, and they walked along a dirt lane between plowed fields and farmsteads and woods. The river was nowhere in sight and she kept craning her head to find it. She had followed it closely en route to the great city, making her own road but never straying far because the flowing water would take her to her son. But now her son was following the white man's road.

"This is the pike," he said. "It will take us to Independence."

She smiled at him, marveling that he knew so much. This was heavily forested country, and these farms had been cut out of the woodlands and planted with wheat and barley and maize and squash and things she didn't recognize. But her son seemed to know all these things.

She didn't mind walking, even if the afternoon was hot and moist, for she had her son beside her to lead the way, and she had her horse too if she grew weary. They stopped now and then, especially at berry patches, where thick bushes crowded the road, lush with blackberries. She found a place where asparagus grew, and harvested many stalks for their supper. And everywhere they looked, thick timothy grass grew, fodder for the horses.

They talked little. That would come later. For now, this son was a mystery and she was content to let him remain one. When he chose to tell her things, she would listen. But she watched him, letting him walk ahead so she could see her son. They continued into the evening, and finally she chose a place to alight for the night, a woods where they might make a fire and boil the asparagus for their supper. But the mosquitoes were bad so they hiked to a hilltop and found a hollow there that would hide them from owls and night spirits.

North Star knew all there was to know about caring for the horses, and soon had them watered and picketed on good grass. He eyed the skies, noting that clouds were building and it might rain, as it often did here. He dug into his duffel and pulled out a piece of duck cloth and began fashioning a lean-to.

"The fathers have these for their travels," he said. "We were taught many things, and not just from books."

He soon had a decent three-sided shelter erected from the limbs of Osage orange trees with an open side facing the cook fire she was building. She had never seen such a thing.

The storm held off until the middle of the night, and then it rained hard, but her son had chosen good ground, and the water drained away and did not soak her blanket. But the wind rattled her shelter, blew bitter rain into her seamed face, so she sat and endured, listening to the distant rumble of thunder.

This was a good thing. Her son would be a good warrior, at home in a strange world. This day she had learned much about him. He was a stubborn man, as stubborn as any she had known, more stubborn than his father. There would be sparks flying when he returned to the mountains. Sparks and thunder and anger, and then she would see how much of a man was this youth.

The next days passed peaceably. She had no trouble finding food. As they progressed along the pike, she collected wild blackberries, wild strawberries, blueberries, wild onion, and the tuberous roots of arrowleaf plants, which might be boiled into something very like potatoes. Whenever they discovered water lilies, she joyously harvested the large tubers that could be as fine a meal as a sweet potato, while the young leaves of the lily made a good spinach. She continued to collect the knobby white roots of ordinary cattails, which could be pounded and boiled into a white paste that sustained life. There were various types of wild tomato, and berries she didn't know, and sampled gingerly until she was sure they were edible. She and her son yearned for meat, but didn't lack for things to fill their stomachs and keep them going. That was fine for the moment, but in a little while, when summer waned, things would be very different. Soon there would be acorns and nuts in abundance to sustain them, and once they reached the plains, there would be prairie turnips. But as they passed through this moist land, they did not want.

North Star observed her closely, until he, too, was skilled at gathering a meal as they walked along the pike.

"They didn't teach me this at St. Ignatius," he said after she had collected a heavy load of water lily tubers that would sustain them for days. "I learned other things."

The pike took them to a large town that North Star called Jefferson City, a handsome place with broad streets, shade trees, and noble buildings, as well as great edifices that were plainly important, though they puzzled her.

"This is the state capital. It's where the chief of Missouri lives, and those who govern the people."

"Is this the place of the great father in Washington?"

"No, that's the United States government there, far to the east. This is where Missouri is governed."

The division of the lands by invisible lines mystified her. How could anyone know where the lines ran? They had put invisible lines around her Wind River homeland, and no one knew when they were on the allotted land or off of it.

"These lines, I don't understand them," she said.

"They have a way of measuring the surface of the earth," he said. "They have instruments that tell them where they are, and they measure all things. The boundaries of the nation are measured. So are the states, and in the states, the counties, and in the counties, the cities and towns."

"Aiee! It is beyond me," she said.

They trod unmolested through the gracious capital, while North Star quietly educated her. He told her what each building contained, and what the signs said. She marveled at this world she had scarcely imagined. No wonder her man, Mister Skye, had sent North Star here to learn these things. These were beyond her, but her son knew them all, and was at ease, while she felt taut and worried that trouble might come.

At long last they passed through the city and struck open country again, relentlessly undulating and still largely forested in spite of the many farmsteads dotting the hills. They found safe places to camp, choosing places away from the pike, where they might build a fire and boil the day's harvest of tubers. Rain came so frequently that she found herself glad to live in the mountains, where the air was dry and sweet and she didn't feel soggy clothing on her flesh.

The horses fattened on the summer grass, and grew sleek and handsome. Mostly Mary walked, but sometimes when her legs wearied, she boarded a horse and rode, while North Star walked beside her, leading the packhorse. It was good. Her moccasins were wearing out, but somehow she would get along.

As they approached the town her son called Sedalia, they grew aware that railroads were nearby. On the hazy horizons, they spotted plumes of smoke and heard the wail of whistles, and sometimes even the clatter of cars rattling along some distant track. And when they did at last penetrate the outskirts, they found a railroad yard, with tracks side by side and various empty cars idled there. She had never imagined there could be so many cars in the whole world. Some were flat, nothing but a floor on wheels, while others had low sides and were open on top, and some were boxcars of the sort she had ridden, while many others had slats in the sides and were obviously used to transport animals. Now and then little engines, stubby and fierce, pushed or pulled the cars around.

This, too, was a white man's wonder.

"M, K and T," her son said. "The Katy. Missouri, Kansas and Texas Railroad."

She nodded, not quite knowing what that was all about.

"They bring cattle up from Texas," he said.

Sedalia proved to be a bustling town, with buggies on the streets, and many pedestrians, and delivery wagons pulled by giant drays. The pike took them near a great edifice in the center of the town.

"County courthouse," North Star said. "This is a county seat."

"What is that?" she asked.

"A smaller government. The cities have governments too."

"Aiee!" she said.

A lean man in a black suit stepped into the cobbled street and stopped them with a wave of the arm. She saw he had some sort of shining device on his coat, and was armed.

He walked across the paving stones, past horse manure, and looked them over, his gaze resting at last on the horses.

"Those sure ain't Indian ponies," he said. "Where you from?"

North Star responded. "I'm Dirk Skye. We're going to the mountains. This is my mother, Blue Dawn of the Shoshone People."

The names didn't interest this man in black. Mary thought

he might be a man of authority because of the way he be-
haved, and that shining device on his coat.

"Indian ponies, they're broomtails, with ewe necks and
flop-ears and two, three colors. These here horses, they're
showing good blood, nice build, clean sorrel and buckskin. They sure ain't horses two redskins should own.
Where'd they come from?"

"Constable, my father is Barnaby Skye, an Englishman,
living in the Northwest, sir. He has been a trapper and guide.
I'm returning from St. Louis, where I was schooled by the
Jesuits at St. Ignatius."

"Sonnyboy, I didn't ask you who you are, I asked you how
come you got two shiny well-bred horses that no Indian can
afford."

"They are mine," Mary said proudly. "I have the papers."

She walked to the pannier on the packhorse and pulled
out the papers that had been given her. She handed them to
her son, who eyed them, and handed them to the thin, mean-
looking man in black.

"Worthless bunch of scribbling," the man said. "Don't
prove a thing. Who you take them from, eh?"

Mary's anger built. "I took them from no man."

"I'm thinking maybe this runt of a boy, all dressed like a
white man, he took them, eh?"

"They are mine," Mary said.

The man in black, who gazed at her from smirky eyes,
merely smiled, tore up the bills of sale, and tossed them to
the cobbled street.

"I know the red kind of human better than you know
yourselves, and I know these ain't yours, so I'm confiscating
them and getting them to their rightful owners."

"Would you treat my father this way?" North Star asked.

"No, sonny, I wouldn't. Not at all. You ain't your father.
She ain't white neither. I would not treat any red-blood the

same as the folks here. Now, from the looks of you, you're vagrants. You got any means of support?"

This bewildered her, so she left it to her son.

"My father supports us," he said. "Always has."

"Your father, your father. I ain't seeing any father around here. You got means or not? Show me the purse."

Her son did not reply.

"Vagrants. I thought so. It's illegal to be a vagrant here, and that goes double for wandering redskins. I'm fining you whatever's in the packs. So git. It's over. Vamoose from town, hear me?"

"Those have our bedrolls, our camping gear, our clothes."

"You heard me. You got fined for vagrancy, hear? Do I have to lock you up?"

"Yes, lock us up. At least we'd be fed and have a bed," North Star said.

The skinny man laughed easily, yanked the reins and lead rope from Mary's hands, and grinned. "Git, before there's an accidental shooting."

Mary's heart sank, as this man took away her horses and her packs and left them standing there in the street.

"I'm taking these nags to the livery. If I see you again, your backs are gonna bleed when the whip lands."

North Star choked back whatever he was about to yell, and sagged. Mary shrank into herself. Several people were watching. Off a way, a train whistle moaned. The smirky-eyed man in black cheerfully walked away with everything.

Chapter 30

Mary's spirits sagged. They were far from home and had nothing. North Star watched the constable lead the horses away, and then quietly began collecting the scraps of paper lying in the manure of the street. He let none escape, and eventually had every piece in hand.

"We will go there," he said, pointing toward the large building called the county courthouse. "Let me talk."

She wanted only to escape this bleak place and its bleak people, but she reluctantly followed her son, wondering what a youth of fifteen winters could do. He paused, and finally decided where he was going, which was a corner street-level office.

She did not know what lay within, but the gold lettering on the glass seemed to inform him. They entered a small anteroom with wooden chairs. Beyond was an office, and sitting behind a desk was a vast man in an immaculate cream-colored suit, stiff white collar, and floppy black bow tie. His face was as wide as his waist, she thought, and made even wider by those bands of hair down the cheeks that white people called muttonchops. He surveyed them from watery blue eyes, sucked on his cigar, and motioned them in.

"Folks from far away, I imagine," he said. "What can I do for you?"

Mary glanced at North Star, who was steeling himself.

"Sheriff, I am Dirk Skye, and this is my mother, whose Shoshone name translates into Blue Dawn, but who is known to my father as Mary."

"Boggs here," the sheriff said. "Is there trouble?"

"We've just had our horses confiscated by your town constable," North Star said. "That and our packs for being vagrants."

Something bright bloomed in Sheriff Boggs's blue eyes. He drew on the cigar until its tip crackled orange, and then exhaled a plume.

"My mother showed your constable her bills of sale, but he said no Indians could have such nice horses. He looked at her bills and ripped them up." North Star placed the shreds on the sheriff's desk. The man eyed them curiously, and then eyed Mary.

"Horses branded?" the sheriff asked.

"No, sir, and not shod, either."

"What'd he do with the horses?"

"Walked off with them a few minutes ago."

"Maginnis Livery Barn," the man said. "What did Constable Barnswallow say?"

"He said we had to leave town fast or he'd whip us."

The sheriff smiled. "People of color never had much traction with Clete. He sure don't even like Italians or Spaniards and he's hard on Greeks."

"I'll help you put those shreds together. You can see for yourself," the youth said.

"Who's your father?"

"Barnaby Skye. Ask anyone at Fort Laramie. He's an Englishman, a guide now. American Fur Company, long ago."

"Yes, Pierre Chouteau's outfit," the sheriff said. "And you?"

"I've been in St. Louis at St. Ignatius, where the Jesuits teach Indian boys."

"Barnswallow, he don't like Catholics, either."

"We've done nothing wrong. We want our horses and packs back. He left us with nothing but the clothing on our backs."

North Star's voice was brave and strong. She looked at her son with wonder. He knew something about dealing with these white men.

Sheriff Boggs arose, revealing a vast girth, immaculate in cream except for a few cigar ashes. "You wait right here, boy. I'll be back in a few minutes. There's chairs out there."

With surprising speed, the wide man swept past them and out the door to the street.

Mary found a seat, but North Star stood rigidly.

"How did you know to do this?" she asked.

He looked broken for a moment, and then said something that astonished her. "My father was trying to protect us when he sent me to school."

A shelf clock ticked steadily behind the sheriff's battered desk. Beyond the office she saw two iron cages, and she knew this man had the power to cage them if he chose, and her fear deepened. Maybe this man would decide they were thieves, and put her and her son inside one of those cages.

It did take time, and the afternoon began to wither away when she saw the big man in the cream suit leading her mare, and another man leading her buckskin with the packs on it. They tied these horses to a hitching post out front.

"Mistah Skye, it seems the city constable outstretched himself, and I've recovered your nags and your packs. Barnswallow's not my man; he's the city's hire, so there's not much I could do except tell him I'll pound the crap out of him if he stops me, or you."

"Thank you, Sheriff," her son said. "I have a small request. We have no proof of ownership anymore, and—"

"I'll fix it."

The sheriff dipped the nib of a pen into an inkwell and scratched out a document, and blotted it up. He read it slowly.

"'To whom it may concern: this bay mare and buckskin gelding belong to Mrs. Barnaby Skye, known as Mary. I certify it. Amos Boggs, Sheriff, Pettis County, State of Missouri.'"

Mary marveled.

"We'll be going then. Thank you, Sheriff," her son said.

"Oh, you're mighty welcome . . . and by the way. You just set there a moment longer whiles I talk with this hostler."

He barged outside. The hostler listened, nodded, and hastened off.

"Seems to me the city ought to make amends, so I'm adding a sack of oats to your gear. I told the liveryman to bill the city."

In minutes the liveryman returned, shouldering a heavy bag of oats. He laid these before North Star. "I reckon these are yours," he said.

The sheriff had ignited a new cheroot and watched while North Star rebalanced the loads in the panniers to accommodate the oats.

"My old dad, he trapped some, working for the Bents. I think maybe I've heard the name of Skye once or twice," the sheriff said.

"Then he will remember your father, and will thank you," North Star said.

They escaped town and headed west again, this time with enough food to last a long time. The oats would boil into a tasty gruel. Mary chose to ride, but her son walked ahead, leading the packhorse. She eyed him contemplatively. Had he lived among her people, he would probably be a young warrior now, unless his spirit helpers led him toward something else. He had a warrior's body, lithe and strong, still filling out. But now it was encased in white men's pants and shirt and shoes, the very clothing he wore as a student sitting in quiet rooms all day.

He had not fought the white man who tried to steal the horses. Instead, he had made good use of what he knew about how the headmen ruled, and talked to the man named Boggs, and it had all worked out. If he hadn't been schooled in St. Louis, how would he know such a thing? Just how the whites governed themselves was beyond her. There were too many parts: fathers who ruled over all, and fathers who ruled over smaller parts, and on and on, down to that constable. She gazed at her boy with a new insight: what he knew, locked inside his head, might rescue her people from constant trouble with these white conquerors. For the first time, her bitterness toward Skye softened. He had ripped her boy from her. But now her boy possessed mysterious powers unknown to any other Shoshone. Was that good? It was hard for her to say, but she was proud of North Star, and rejoiced inside of herself.

They walked through Independence and Kansas City virtually unremarked, perhaps because the residents of both of those towns were familiar with plains Indians and thought little of their presence. After that they followed the Kansas River northwest, on the Big Road once again. And soon they were in open country, where the hand of the white men could no longer be seen, and that lifted her heart.

The trip to the mountains proved peaceable enough. They reached Fort Kearny, but no one was counting wagons anymore. They proceeded along the south bank of the Platte River, often without seeing any travelers for an entire day. Now and then the railroad tracks came close, and then they heard the mournful whistles and the clatter of trains. Other times the rails went somewhere else but in the stillness of the nights a distant moan of a whistle reached their ears. The white men went by rail as much as they could, at least those who could afford it.

It was high summer, and the bottoms of the Platte offered her berries and roots in addition to the gruel made of oats, and they got along well enough. Such people as were heading west on the Big Road had passed by in the spring, as always, when the grasses were up and the trail was dry. As always, they started their trip with overburdened wagons, and soon were discarding the heavy items to spare their oxen. She scavenged all she could, acquiring skirts and dresses and shawls and blouses and one pair of brown shoes that fit her, a welcome find after wearing out her moccasins. Several times they discovered worn or wounded livestock, oxen, horses, loose in the bottoms, but these were skittish and hard to catch, and she and North Star had no luck with them. Then one day she found a lamed ewe, abandoned by her herder. It had a broken leg and was wasting away. She slit its throat, and she and North Star gorged on the first meat they had enjoyed in a long time, and kept eating until the meat turned bad. She skinned the pelt and began working on moccasins from it during the evenings.

The air lost its moisture and became more comfortable, in spite of furnace heat each afternoon. Her heart lifted. This was air she knew, air from the great reaches of the High Plains, and the mountains.

They passed immigrant families, and discovered that these white people spoke no English and came from places she didn't know. They were a little different somehow.

"Those were from Sicily," North Star said. "And the ones we passed earlier were from Hungary."

She marveled that he knew these things.

It was only when they were approaching Fort Laramie that he opened the topics that had remained a barrier between them these many days and nights.

"Are you and Father separated?" he asked one afternoon, when she was least expecting it.

"I don't know," she said.

She told him what had been intended. Victoria, Skye's sits-beside-him wife, had directed her to go to the Wind River Reservation and wait for Skye and Victoria. But Blue Dawn had been drawn east by some spirit guide, drawn east in some way beyond her own willpower to resist, as if the wise and frightening owl had compelled her to go.

"I'm not sure where they are now. I think with my people on the Wind River. We will look for them there, because that is where we were to meet."

Then, realizing how little North Star knew of recent times, she narrated the recent past.

"He hurts now, and it is hard for him to lie on a robe and sleep. It is hard for him to get up off the ground, and sometimes he wishes he had a chair, one of those rocking chairs. The cold comes through the robes on a winter's night and makes him stiff, and then he hurts all the more. Last spring, even before the snows melted, he said he wanted to build a house and have a stove in it and beds and chairs and a fireplace, and the place that would lift his spirits the most would be the great bend of the Yellowstone. He rode away one day, leaving Victoria and me with her people, because he said he wanted to choose the right place. But he didn't return, so Victoria went to get him, sent me away, and more than that I don't know."

"Will he turn his back on me?"

In truth, Mary was not sure of that. "He is torn, Dirk," she said, using that other name for him. "All the while you were gone, he could not talk to me, or Victoria, about you. But you were there in his mind, every moment, every winter, and I think he believed you would need to make your own decision when you left school. To come back, or live there with the white men." She paused. "He knew you could help the Shoshones the most if you learned all the secrets of the white men. But it would be your decision."

"I've already made it," North Star said.

Chapter 31

Skye ignored the distant white man with the rakish hat perched jauntily on his head. He patiently hoed a row of potato plants, breaking the soil and chopping away weeds. Each strike of the hoe hurt, but he didn't mind. He was helping raise food for Mary's brothers, and that made him feel useful. There at Fort Washakie, the Shoshones were slowly adapting to white men's ways and raising crops.

But progress in that direction had not been easy. The Shoshone men considered it women's work and refused to labor in the fields. Male Shoshones hunted, made war, and gambled. Women toiled. But there would be potatoes this season, Skye thought. The rains had come and the frosts had held off, and no hail had destroyed the tender plants. Potatoes might not be as satisfying as a haunch of buffalo, but these people had little choice. The Yank government was decreeing how they must live.

So he chopped and weeded and felt a thin sweat dampen his hatband and his shirt, and he counted the time well spent. And maybe the sight of a white man patiently growing food might inspire the younger Shoshone boys to at least try the new life.

The white stranger stared around, looking for something in that pleasant Wind River Valley, and finally strode toward Skye, who imagined it would be another Indian Bureau functionary with new commands or restrictions or rebukes. But this gent was too gaudy and looked more like some dandy from the nearest saloon than a government man. He wore a black waistcoat with a gold fob stretched across it. Gold-plated fob, at any rate. The man studied Skye, made up his mind, and headed down a row of potatoes toward his quarry. The man sported muttonchops and a mustache, and peered at Skye from watery blue eyes that flanked a veined nose that suggested a long acquaintance with spirits.

Skye straightened up slowly to ease the pain in his back and rested on his worn hoe.

"Ah, there you are, Skye!"

"Mister Skye, sir."

"So I've heard. I know more about you than you may think."

"Then you have the advantage of me, sir."

"Buntline here. Ned Buntline at your service." The man seemed to be waiting for something, perhaps recognition, but Skye had never heard of the man.

Skye lifted his hat and let the dry breezes evaporate the sweat on his brow. "A good name, Mister Buntline. I knew that term when I was a boy," he said. "Buntline's the rope along the base of a square sail."

"Ah, we have it in common!" Buntline said. "I was a sailor, and now I'm a scribbler."

"A reporter, maybe?"

"No, no, I spin yarns of the great West, true stories, carefully documented, about the towering border men who opened these lands. I'm going to do a story about Cody, called King of the Border Men, and I want to do you too."

"Do me?"

"You're the one who became king of the mountain men, aren't you? Then king of the guides? Then king of the Indian wars?"

Skye stared, at a loss. "You have the wrong man," he said, and took up his hoeing once again, the strokes of the blade rhythmically opening the soil and vanquishing a creeping vine.

"Ah, a modest man. But I think you're wrong, Mister Skye. There's no man in all the West more honored than you."

"I really need to hoe these potatoes before the weeds take over, sir."

"You're the man, all right. You have not one but two wives, sharing the very same lodge. You've taken scientists and preachers and doctors into the wilderness and got them out safely. You've fought the Blackfeet and Comanches, the deadliest of all tribes, and survived. You've taken white men into forbidden valleys. There's nothing you haven't done. Your name is known from St. Louis to the Pacific. They all say Skye's the man, Mister Skye. Write about him."

Skye leaned heavily upon his hoe. This was heavy work, and his bum leg was rebelling.

"Mister Buntline, how can I say this? I would rather have my privacy. There's nothing I did that dozens of others couldn't do. You want to write about a remarkable man, you just corral Jim Bridger and take down his story."

"Oh, Mister Skye, I don't take down stories, I invent them, always based on truth, of course. I don't really need to know your secrets. The name is enough. Trust me, within a few months yours will be the most celebrated name in every nook and cranny of the Republic."

"I think, sir, I'd like to return to my hoeing."

"And that's a story too. A brave man, giving his last for his wife's people."

Skye smiled. "It's been good to talk with you," he said.

"You're very like you were described, Mister Skye. I got some excellent descriptions of you, but they were wrong on one item. There's no London left in your voice."

That gave Skye his opening. "I'm not a Yank, so don't write about me. Go find a Yankee to write about."

Buntline smiled, his manner apologetic. "You know, Mister Skye, I've talked to people in St. Louis. You worked for American Fur and the Chouteau family, and they told me you were the best man out in the field. I talked to army men at Fort Leavenworth. They told me you're a legend. Whenever the army wanted something, they asked you. They said you'd fought more hostile Indians than any man alive. They said you're the bravest man ever to walk this continent. I stopped in Independence, and learned you're the most trusted guide alive. You got people through."

Skye listened incredulously. This man was inventing things.

"The trouble was, no one knew where to find you. They said you might be with the Crows, you might be with the Shoshones, you might be anywhere. But the best bet was to go to Fort Laramie and ask, so I did, by train and stage, and I asked, and they weren't sure either, but then a young Indian Bureau fellow said he'd heard you'd come to the Wind River agency, and I got a horse and came here. And here you are. I'm hoping you'll hear me out."

The man had crossed a continent for nothing. Skye wasn't sure how to cope with it. "They probably told you, Mister Buntline, that I wouldn't be very cooperative."

"Oh, they did, but of course that just gets my dander up. I've had trouble lining up Cody, and even more trouble lining up Hickok."

"I suppose I should know who Hickok is, sir, but I don't. What I do know is that I live a quiet and private life and it's going to stay that way."

"Well, I'm not done, not done at all, Mister Skye. There are rewards, compensations, good things in your future."

Skye was feeling more and more testy. "I apologize, sir, for not being civil. You'll excuse me now."

Buntline grinned cheerfully. "I thought maybe you'd like to get rich."

Skye was not averse to the idea, and decided to give the man a few moments before evicting him from the potato patch.

"My backers and I plan to do stage shows, sir. These shows simply pump in cash. We'd like to do one starring yourself, called Trapper Skye, King of the Mountains. We'd have you say a few lines, talk with your two wives, get into a staged battle with some redskins, and discharge your piece now and then—it's marvelously deafening inside a theater. How about a hundred dollars a week, for starters?"

"Mister Buntline, I'm sorry you came all this way. The answer is no."

"You say the word, and we'll pay your way by rail to St. Louis, where we'll organize the show. Yes, bring your wives, and we'll give you a few lines to memorize on the train. The minute you walk onstage, and the audience sees you're the real thing, and the roughest cob that ever came east, they'll sit spellbound, and throw dimes onstage when you're done. You'll pocket a few dollars of dimes right off the boards every show."

"Are you through, Mister Buntline?"

"Oh, no, not at all. Shipping both ways, one season, bonuses if you pack the house, and plenty of good dime novels about you to spark interest. Do that for a year or two, and you won't be hoeing potatoes. You'll be living like a prince."

"A prince? Me?"

"Onstage for six months, just one season, a hundred dollars a week. You'll have room and board, traveling money, and a bottle anytime you want it. I'll tell you what. If you stick it out, I'll add a bonus after the season, yes, let's add four hundred. That's around three thousand dollars, sir, for one season. Think about it! A home of your own. Something to retire on. Money in the bank. Think on it, Mister Skye. Just for walking onstage and saying a few lines. I promise you, sir, you'll fill up every theater from Kankakee to Pittsburgh."

Skye could barely absorb it.

"How about it?" Buntline asked.

"Mister Buntline, I may have lost my wife Mary. She's gone. I'm awaiting word."

"Well, that's no problem. I know a few Italian actresses who look Indian in front of the gaslights. We'll just dye their faces. In fact, this is even better. We'll give you three or four wives and that will be an even better draw."

Skye roared, swung his hoe at Buntline, missed him, and started after the man. But the impresario was faster and had no limp. Skye lunged again, but too late. Buntline ran over several rows of potatoes and headed for the safety of the clapboard agency buildings. Skye watched him go, his heart hammering, and then settled the venerable hat on his head. The hoe lay two rows away, so he collected it as he watched Buntline vanish inside of one of the buildings.

He hoped Buntline would complain loudly to the Indian agent. That would be the only entertainment the afternoon offered.

He used his hoe as a crutch because he was hurting again, and began to make his way across the potato patch, when Victoria intercepted him.

"What the hell was that about?" she asked.

"Oh, nothing."

She glared at him.

"That man wants to put me in a theater with a bunch of Italian actresses playing my wives, while I run around stage killing Indians."

"Sonofabitch!" she said. "I'll kill him."

"Not a bad idea," he said. "He offered me three thousand dollars."

"He what?"

"To shoot Indians. To cozy up to several wives. That would amuse an audience."

She stared at him.

"I did what I had to do. I've never taken any pride in fighting or killing. When it happened it was because I had no choice. I won't glorify this in a theater. I won't pretend or make believe. I won't turn myself into a hero when I'm an ordinary man. I won't have little boys wishing they could be like me. I won't turn myself into something I'm not and never was. I can't be bought, not for three thousand dollars, Victoria. So I told him my wife was missing and I was waiting to learn of her fate."

"Mary will come back," she said.

He knew better than to ask how she knew that. All his life with her she had visited mysterious insights upon him, and usually was right. But he didn't believe it. Mary was gone. She had crossed the great divide, and nothing would restore her to him. He had been quietly grieving as he hoed the fields each day. Hoeing was the only way he knew to let go of Mary. He hoed one row and then another and another, burying her.

Buntline vanished the next day, but not without leaving an elaborate contract with the agency. An owl-eyed clerk handed him a thick envelope with his name written on it in an elaborate hand. Skye's eyes weren't good, but he managed to decipher the blur by holding the papers at arm's length. Sign right here and you'll be a theatrical star and make enough money to last the rest of your life.

Skye read the amazing document, and carefully stuffed it into the agency stove and watched flames lick it. He had burned Buntline out of his life. The whole thing had left him with an unsated curiosity. Why would some novelist and impresario track him down? There had been nothing unusual in Skye's life. He had survived decades in the wilds, but so had others. He had adopted the ways of the Indians and had become their advocate, but so had others. He had guided a few people, led a few trapping parties, explored a few areas unknown to the outside world. But so had others.

He toiled through another day of heat and dryness, and then the searchers returned. Victoria summoned him from the fields, and as he walked toward the agency buildings, he saw the young warriors collecting at the frame house of Chief Washakie. He saw no paint, which might have signified battle or victory or death, but only bronzed young men, mostly in breechclouts, sinking off their unpainted and unadorned ponies.

The old man appeared at once, and surveyed the quiet young Shoshones as they gathered at his porch.

"I do not see Blue Dawn," he said to Fast Bird, who had led the search.

"Grandfather, she is not anywhere," the young man said. "We looked for her bones and saw none. We looked for her ponies. She has gone to the place of eternal mystery, and we know nothing more."

"How far did you go?" Washakie asked.

"We rode to the Yellowstone, and then we rode along the banks in both directions. The trail would be very old, but we looked. We were thorough. The owls said nothing to us. The coyote did not lead us."

Washakie turned to Skye and Victoria. "Blue Dawn is not among us anymore," he said. "I am sorry. We will not say her name. She will be the One Who Disappeared."

Chapter 32

North Star felt some mysterious tug as he and his mother worked their way up the Wind River. Something ancient and powerful was awakening in him. It seemed almost a physical force, though he knew he had scarcely been in this place, and only when he was too young to remember much about it. There was majestic beauty, with snowy peaks rising to the west, but along this trail was greenery and shelter from the winds.

The white man part of him told him it couldn't be familiarity, because he had spent most of his childhood among the Crows of his mother Victoria's people, and he had scarcely been here. But the Shoshone part of him whispered that he had come home, that this very land was the ancient and primal land of his people, and all that he saw was his to possess. His mind had worked like that for years now, a dual way of seeing the world, and he didn't mind. If he was a man of two bloods, then he really wanted to see the world in each way. But just now, he was pure Shoshone, walking beside his Shoshone mother Blue Dawn, just a little apart from a place he and she had not seen, Fort Washakie.

"I do not know this," she said, the sweep of her hand encompassing planted fields, small log cabins situated well apart from one another, and up ahead, some white frame buildings with a flag flying above them. The new agency, he supposed, given by the Yankees to his people. The thought was a little cynical. The Yankees had forced his people onto a homeland, with borders around it that made it an invisible prison.

Still, this was a good place. He saw smoke curling up from the chimneys of the cabins, and knew life progressed within. He and his mother proceeded into this settled area unnoticed. There was no town crier anymore to herald the arrival of visitors, as there had been when his people lived in lodges and moved camp whenever it was necessary. They saw some women toiling in the fields, patiently using wooden or buffalo-bone hoes to hack down weeds. They saw squash and maize and beans and potatoes and grains, some of it well tended, the rest patchy and in need of hard work.

"This place . . ." Mary said. "We once raised our lodges here. We met with the other bands and had games and feasts. The families arranged marriages, and it was good. Now a plow has torn up the grass."

But the closer they got to the white buildings, the more North Star sank into himself. What would his father be like? When at last, when they stood man to man, would he welcome his son and his wife? What would he think of Blue Dawn after her long absence? Would he and Victoria even be here? Neither he nor his mother were sure.

He could not answer these questions. But this was his home, and he was in a good place and his heart was good.

The sun had dropped to the top of the distant mountains in the west, and now the long light gilded the land, burnished it with gold, so that the cottonwoods were golden, and the grasses too, and the sunlit sides of the log cabins, and the sunlit sides of the agency buildings. And opposite every gilded object was a purple shadow, a shadow that was crawling along the earth as the sun sat for a while right on the distant ridges.

They both saw Skye at the same time. The gold light lit his ancient top hat and turned his white hair bright and caught his ruddy cheeks. He was in a field, hoeing, and there was no mistaking him. Mary cried out suddenly, her hand flying to her face. His own heart tripped, and for a moment he was anxious.

She steered her worn horse toward the distant man, her man, his sire, who hoed in the golden last light, and now they progressed between rows of some plant he thought might be potatoes, and at last Barnaby Skye noticed, and set down his hoe, and lifted his old hat from his head, so the gold light caught all his white hair, and the old man seemed to straighten up, grow taller, as he stood waiting. For it was plain the old man recognized his wife and his son, and now walked toward them, limping slightly, his hoe as his staff.

They reached him and stopped. Mary slid from her horse and went to him. North Star halted, afraid now, seeing the great puzzlement in the old man's face.

"Mary! And you?" his father said, peering first at his wife and then at his son. "You?"

His mother stood stiff and proud, for she was making a presentation. "Yes, Mister Skye. We have come to you. Here is your son."

He didn't speak for a moment, but stood, the breeze riffling his unkempt gray hair. Then, searching for words, he spoke. "I'm glad," he said. "Gladder than I've ever been."

He collected his wife and hugged her, and collected his boy and embraced him, and then stood back to gaze again at these two.

"Now my life is complete," he said. "But don't explain it. Let it be a miracle."

"Mister Skye, we will call it a miracle," North Star's mother said.

Now the sun slid beneath the western peaks, leaving a rim of white fire as the gold faded away into indigo shadows.

North Star had no wish to talk. There was no need for words, and besides, all the feelings within him now were Shoshone, but he had lost his mother tongue and his English seemed poor and inadequate. His father was glad. So it was enough to stand still while his father took the measure of them both, his gaze, which seemed uncertain, absorbing his wife and then examining his son.

"What name shall I call you, son?" Skye asked.

"That name that draws you closest to me, Father."

"Then you are Dirk, lad. And a proud name it is, owned by your grandfather in England.

"And you, my beautiful wife? What shall I call you?"

She grinned. "I'll whisper it in your ear sometime."

He laughed, a rumbling chuckle that wrought memories in North Star. "Let us make the circle complete," Skye said. "Victoria hates cabins and stoves and is probably cussing her way through some cooking." He turned to Mary. "Your brothers gave us a cabin. They are starting another."

They walked through the fields, three people and two horses, in the gathering twilight, and no one noticed them. The first stars emerged, and Dirk looked as always for the Star That Never Moves, his natal star and one that wrought odd feelings deep within him.

They reached the door, Skye set his old hoe against the logs and pushed the door open. Victoria turned and stared.

"I'll be goddamned," she said.

She set down an iron spoon and examined the youth and the mother, and then she studied Skye, looking for something within him. Whatever it was that Victoria saw in him, she seemed satisfied.

"I am pleased to see you, Mother Victoria," North Star said.

"You are here. You are alive," Victoria said. She turned to Mary. "We stopped saying your name."

Dirk knew all about that. The names of the dead were never spoken.

"There isn't much in the kettle. We don't eat much anymore. You're both thin."

It was true; she had only a few cups of stew boiling on a sheet-metal woodstove. "Eat this," she said. "I'll start some other."

"Let me cook," Mary said.

There was meat boiling slowly in that stew, and the scent seemed heavenly to North Star. They had scarcely enjoyed a mouthful of meat for days on end.

Victoria headed first for the younger wife, and touched her cheek. "It is Mary of the Shoshones," and then she touched North Star's cheek. "What name have you taken, boy?"

"I wish to be Dirk to my father, and North Star to my mothers."

"Aiee, this is good!" Victoria said.

North Star waited for the questions that didn't come. He waited to justify himself. He waited to tell them why he had left school. He waited for them to ask his mother where she had been. About the long trip. About how they connected. About what had inspired her. But Skye and Victoria asked nothing at all of him.

He was ready to tell them that he had done well with his lessons. He was good at arithmetic. He knew some geometry. He could spell. He could write. He could keep accounts. He had read many books written by Englishmen. He had learned the history of the Americans. He had learned theology, and knew the history of the Jesuits. He knew mechanics. He had done some carpentry. He could glaze a window or plane a door.

If he was weak, it was in composing sentences and writing paragraphs and papers. His thoughts were too unruly, and the nib pen too slow in his fingers. And yet, the good fathers had told him he was quick and bright, and they had little left to teach him because he was doing better than most of the other boys. They had told him he could do as well as any white boy. He wondered about that. Could he do as well as any full-blood too? What was it about being a mixed-blood?

But his father didn't ask. His father kept staring at Dirk, staring as if he was trying to puzzle away the gap between the eight-year-old boy he last saw and this youth he was examining now.

So the questions didn't come, and neither did they rain on Mary, and it gradually dawned on Dirk that this was acceptance; that he would not have to justify himself to his father and Victoria, and neither would Mary have to justify what obviously was a long and perilous trip. His father and Crow mother would learn about it in good time, and they were leaving it to him to choose the moment.

So Mary and Dirk spooned the savory stew while another meal was boiling, the new one without meat because the antelope meat had been the gift of Mary's family, and it was all the meat there was.

The cabin could contain them. It had no furniture in it, but at least it had a straw-covered clay floor with robes scattered about. It was as close to the interior of a lodge as a small structure could get, and it awakened ancient memories in North Star. It was a lodge, but with log walls and a shake roof and a sheet-metal stove.

There was only a small window, and it had no glass, but shutters against the cold. Now, as the last light faded, it grew dusky in the cabin. He could see that Victoria was bent and worn now, as thin as ever but her back had curved and her head rested forward. And Skye had lost weight, and had bent also, but there still was fire in his eyes. Fire in the eyes of both of them.

Someday soon they would know the story. Mary would tell of her impulse to see her son; he would tell of his rushed decision to return with her. She would talk about the long trip on the Big Road, and tell them where her horses came from, and the troubles they had. He would tell them of his honors at school, and what he could do and what he had learned. But not this night, when they paid him and his mother the greater honor of not asking.

"Father and Mother Victoria, I should take care of the horses," he said.

"That's good, Dirk, and I will show you," Skye said.

Together they slipped into the twilight and undid the packs and the packsaddle and the riding saddle and brought them inside. Dirk knew that they would feel very light in Skye's hands. They contained no food at all, and few other things. The trip had consumed whatever small things Mary and he possessed.

Skye gathered the reins. "Good-looking horses. Are they yours?" he asked.

"They are my mother's."

Skye started slowly toward the fields, his limp slowing him. "The herd's off that way. Not many left."

"Stolen?"

"No, eaten. These people don't get the rations they were promised by the government. Either that or the Indian agent skims much of it off. So they're half-starved and living on horse meat until the next shipment of flour and beans comes in."

"I didn't know. I shouldn't have come."

"You can help, son."

They hiked a while more along a lane between planted fields, and then Skye quit.

"My leg's giving out. Here, take these over to that grove of cottonwoods and let them loose. They'll find the herd."

Dirk took the reins, led the horses another quarter of a mile to the trees, slid the bridle and halter off, and let them go. He saw no other horses and wondered if he'd ever see these again.

His father was waiting for him.

"We're living on charity, Dirk," Skye said as they started back. "These people can hardly feed themselves, much less a Crow and a white man. Tomorrow, you get yourself enrolled with the agent. You and Mary. It's worth some flour and beans. Erastus Perkins is his name. Major Perkins. They're all called major, all the Yank Indian agents."

"Where are my uncles?"

"In a lodge upriver, four, five miles. They turned over the cabin and said they'd live the old way for a time. But no one can leave the reservation without the major's say-so, which means they can't go after buffalo out on the plains, which means that they're worse off than ever. Victoria and I, we're thinking we'd best get back to our Crow people. Wild Indians have it better than tame ones, and we're just robbing them of food, staying here like this."

"It's an outrage, sir."

"It's that. It's slow starvation. They're out hunting rabbits and snatching turtles and trying to kill a few ravens for the kettle."

They reached the little cabin, and Skye paused.

"I'm glad you're here, Dirk. I'd like to help these people but I can't, not with my bloody busted leg, and I get worn-out fast. I hardly know what I'm going to do; everything I try, including hunting, hurts too much."

North Star felt a strange tenderness, and more. He felt that he was destined to return at this very hour. He was standing, man to man, beside his father. They needed him here. The moving finger had written his fate.

Chapter 33

The youth wandered aimlessly, wondering what had inspired him to abandon St. Louis. Dirk, or North Star, or whoever he was, drifted day by day, not knowing what to do. His two bloods were at war, but mostly he wasn't sure he cared. These were not the Shoshones he remembered from his childhood, when they were still a proud migrating happy people never far from buffalo or game.

When his mother had suddenly appeared in St. Louis, that ancient memory was kindled in him, and the joy of unfettered freedom, of riding open prairies, of climbing to mountain lakes, of dancing to the drums, of shivering at the sound of an owl's hoot, all trumped everything the Jesuit fathers had instilled in him, and suddenly he had to break free.

But this gaggle of huts being called Fort Washakie was not that place, and it all seemed bleak and unfamiliar. The valley itself was beautiful, but where were the people? They lived now in little cabins far apart, disconnected from one another, their dreams reduced to hoeing and drifting. On his hikes, North Star saw the shanties and the barely scratched plots of land, growing a few scraggly worm-eaten crops that would yield little when harvest came. He saw women alone by the river, rinsing out old clothing, and he remembered how the Shoshone women used to gather together and make their work communal, with gossip and jokes to make the toil pass by easily.

He saw men lounging, smoking, looking unkempt and bored, waiting for the next allotment day, when they would get their few pounds of flour or rice, or beans or sugar and maybe a slab of beef now and then. He wondered what had happened, why these men didn't have fire in their eyes, why they sat passively waiting for whatever would happen to happen. Where had their souls gone?

This wasn't the world of his memories, filled with strong, bronzed men and women in clothing wrought from deer and elk skins or trade cloth, sleeping in buffalo robes, tackling each day with joy. Maybe that world never quite existed, but it seemed real to the seven- or eight-year-old boy who was eventually ripped from it and plunged into another world, in another land. Maybe, had he been older, he would have seen weary, half-starved, diseased people locked in an unending quest to survive. But he did remember laughter, and jokes, and pride, and those who decorated their lodges and clothing and ponies with their own emblems.

North Star had thought there might be rejoicing when he and his mother showed up after her long absence, but there wasn't much, apart from a little curiosity about her. Her brother, The Runner, had come to visit, along with his women, but no one said much. A few people stopped to talk with him, but the Shoshones were spread for miles up and down the Wind River now, and were grimly trying to eke a living from the verdant meadows, and there was little time to rejoice in the prodigal who had returned. Had the heart been torn out of his mother's people?

Chief Washakie had welcomed him warmly, rejoicing in his mother's return. But even he was different. North Star remembered him as a traditional and proud chief living in a large lodge, wearing magnificent ceremonial robes, beaded moccasins, attended by his wives, his lodge a place of power and wisdom. But now Chief Washakie lived in a house with chairs and tables and a stove and a couch and a kitchen, and he wore collarless shirts, with black waistcoats and gray woolen trousers. Only his shining black braids remained as North Star had remembered them. Washakie seemed the only Shoshone on the reservation who still had spirit burning in him, and good cheer always radiated from his face.

"We are glad you have come to us, North Star," he said. "And we are glad that you bring with you the mysteries of the white man, which I hope you will share with the People, so we may be as wise as the Fathers who taught you all they knew."

Washakie blessed Blue Dawn too, and urged her to enroll herself and her son in the tribal ledgers kept by the agent, Major Perkins, in the white clapboard buildings. So Mary and Dirk duly entered the fearsome building, found the major with his boots resting on a cold stove, drinking some amber fluid Dirk thought might be whiskey. The man's beard was unkempt, and his clothing stained.

"Ah, yes, Skye's woman and boy," the major said. "Heard all about it. You should have stayed in St. Louis, boy."

But Gallipoli Sanders, his bespectacled white clerk, enrolled them, writing with a Spencerian hand, and henceforth on each distribution day he and his mother would receive some flour and beans or rice, and occasionally some beef butchered from a few stringy and stumbling cattle delivered by a ranch over in the Big Horn Valley. That meant that the Skye household had three allotments to feed four, because Victoria was an Absaroka woman and not eligible. But Skye himself, as a spouse of Mary, would qualify.

Each day Dirk watched his father crawl from his robes, struggle to his feet, dress and overcome his morning stiffness, and then pick up his ancient hoe and head for the fields, where he would patiently chop weeds away from squash or maize or beans or potatoes until he wearied. Dirk's father had welcomed his son, and yet there had been something unspoken lying between them. Plainly, his father had seen this new world coming, and at great cost to himself, to Mary, and to Victoria too, he had sent Dirk to his freedom and his future. But now Dirk was back, and this reservation was his future, and the youth found himself drifting from sadness to bewilderment, and occasionally to fits of action. He joined groups of boys who went hunting in the old way. He had no weapon and minimal skill with a bow and arrow, but he went anyway, hoping to add food to the larder.

Occasionally he saw his uncle, The Runner, who lived with his family in the traditional way now, having given the cabin to Skye. Mary's brother had been eager to embrace this new world, and had mastered some ancient English, but now he was too busy trying to feed his wives and some clan brothers and sisters. This was not The Runner of yore, either, and that disturbed Dirk. He felt he had walked into some vortex that was sucking him down into a pit. Sometimes the majestic mountains brightened him. Some early September snows had whitened the peaks, making them glow boldly with their promise of liberty. Flee to the mountains, for there is liberty!

Dirk noticed the girls too, quiet Shoshone girls, most of them too thin, some pretty, though he had an odd aversion to the heavy cheekbones he saw in them, and in himself. He thought white women were more delicate, with faces and figures he liked more. And yet occasionally a girl stirred him, and he sometimes talked with one or another, but they took alarm. He had not yet recovered his own tongue, though it was swiftly returning, and the girls shied from him as an odd and maybe dangerous person, who sometimes glowered at them instead of smiling.

Was this all there was to life? He wished he might have books to read now that the whole bright world of knowledge had been opened to him, but there was scarcely a book on the reservation. His uncle, The Runner, had once had a Shakespeare and a Bible, but the pages had been ripped out, one by one, to start fires, and now there were no books, not even in Major Perkins's office and house, except for a Bible, which the agent obviously not only did not read, but rejected.

September was harvesttime, and Dirk helped dig up potatoes, and pluck maize from stalks, and gather squash and stow these in a root cellar dug into a slope. Skye and Victoria and Mary worked steadily, not only harvesting the crops The Runner had planted in his patch of land, but also neighbors' crops, which had suffered from inattention. Few traditional Shoshones cared to garden, and most all of them greatly preferred good meat, even if it was the softer white man's beef, though they all yearned for the rich, textured firmness of buffalo meat.

Dirk sensed that his family was not happy. His mother and Victoria toiled silently, saying little. His father had drawn deep into himself, and seemed to be forcing labor from a body mostly spent and hurting. Dirk heard no complaint; his mothers simply did what had to be done each day and fell into their blankets at night.

The clay-floor cabin itself was not as comfortable as a lodge, and its stove ate firewood, requiring the women to roam farther and farther gathering deadwood. Both Victoria and Mary shouldered heavy packs on their backs, and walked a mile or so back to the cabin with enough wood to keep it warm two or three days. Dirk remembered the lodges, how the tiniest fire would heat the air inside the leather cone, how an insulating layer of robes on the ground would keep the chill off. And yet that was mostly unreliable childhood memory. Each day, as his father struggled just to get up, Dirk knew that a good bedstead would be a treasure for his father. And yet nothing happened. It was as if the whole tribe was waiting, waiting, for something.

There was something else: the silence was terrible. Dirk craved the company of his father and mother and Victoria. There were years of absence, a thousand stories, and a universe of wisdom and anecdote and always the mysteries, the things that had animated his mother's people. This was a cruel world, and was having a cruel effect on his parents.

These people were slumbering through life. The past had vanished, and there seemed to be no future. The agent, Major Perkins, didn't seem to care. He was a time-server, taking his pay from the government, maintaining some sort of minimal existence for his wards, and whiling away his empty hours drinking. And toying with the girls. The agent had two housekeepers, Shoshone girls in their teens, pretty and well fed, and Dirk wondered about them. The girls avoided his eye. One looked pregnant. On distribution days, there never was quite what had been promised, or the food was bad. Wormy flour, spoiled salt pork, bony cattle. Somehow, that never evoked any ire in the agent, though he was responsible for feeding these people and making sure the government was not being cheated by contractors. Dirk began to study the man, not sure what was happening. And the longer Dirk lingered on the reservation, the darker his spirits grew. What had he come west for?

One day, he peered into an empty clapboard building near the agency and discovered an unused schoolhouse, and an unused teacherage next to it. Through the windows he saw a completed school, with desks and a woodstove and a chalkboard. Through the windows of the teacherage he saw empty bedsteads, horsehair furnishings, a table and chairs, a kitchen. All as new and silent as the day they had been completed.

Impulsively he headed for the agency, and found the major more or less drunk.

He stood, hat in hand, because one was required to wait and be invited to speak if one was not a white man. Eventually Major Perkins nodded.

"You, is it? What's the trouble? More bad flour?"

"Sir, I wanted to ask you about that school."

"Oh, that." The agent yawned. "Another bungle. They can't get anything right. Build a school and then there's no budget for teachers or books. Congress won't spend a dime."

"Could we, my father and I, teach, sir?"

"No money, I told you. Not a bloody cent from those skin-flints."

"Could we move into the teacher house and teach, sir?"

"What makes you think you can? What are you, fifteen?"

"I was ahead of my class, sir. I can teach the alphabet, spelling, writing, reading, mathematics, some algebra, English literature."

"Oh, now, boy, half the students would be older than you."

"My father was schooled in London and was headed for the university."

"And was pressed at age thirteen, I gather."

"He knows a lot more than the boys here do."

"What's in it for me, young Skye?"

Dirk had no answer to that.

Chapter 34

Dirk Skye fumed his way to the forlorn cabin. Nothing was right on this reservation. And Major Perkins liked it that way. An October chill was a harbinger of what would soon descend on them. The dirt-floored cabin was worse than a lodge, and he knew his father and Crow mother would suffer, and maybe his mother too.

His father wore his age with dignity, not complaining and doing what he could to grow food for them all. But Dirk knew he hurt. His Crow mother Victoria hurt in other ways, torn from her own people and way of life, even as her body lost strength.

He plunged into the cabin just as his mothers were boiling a vegetable stew, there being no meat again. It took the women most of each day just to find firewood, and they were forced to search ever farther away. In the days when the People lived in lodges, they simply moved to a new locale when fuel and grass and wood were exhausted. But now there was no place to go, and few lodges to shelter them.

His mother glanced at him and frowned, well aware of the fury boiling through him. But she said nothing. They all had turned stoic, their goal to endure one bad thing after another. He wasn't even sure that they had hope of anything better.

They ate the stew eagerly, but it did not fill or satisfy them, because there was no good meat. But they could expect none until the next distribution day, and then it was likely to be a few pounds that must last all four of them the whole month.

Skye, too, was watchful of his son, and when they had all finished their meager meal, he addressed the boy.

"What is it, Dirk?" he asked.

"I despise this place," Dirk shot back.

The women were attentive now.

"Have you looked at the school? And the teacherage?"

"I have," said Skye. "Did you? What did you see?"

"Empty school, all ready for use, and a house all ready, with furniture and a stove. I went to Major Perkins and asked why it wasn't being used, and he said the Indian Bureau had no money for teachers or books or slates or anything. I said we'd teach, I can teach lots of things, and he asked what was in it for him."

"That's how the man does things here," Skye said.

"We could be teaching. I know my arithmetic and letters and spelling and grammar and a lot of other things. You know a lot more than I do. These people need what we can give them. It's not their world, and no one can help that, but we can help them into the new world."

Dirk saw how attentive they were, and felt heartened. This was the first time in all his days and weeks and months on the Wind River Reservation that he had cried out, that he had been anything but polite and subdued.

"We could be living in that house. It has a floor and bed frames and chairs and a horsehair couch. It has a kitchen and a kitchen wood range and a woodstove in the parlor. We could be there. Every day I see you get up, drive the stiffness out of you that came from lying on cold ground. You never complain." He appealed to them all. "You get up, begin a hard day, no matter that you hurt, no matter that dry firewood is two miles away and you must haul it here on your backs."

Victoria sighed. "A lodge. That's all I want is a lodge. All it needs is a tiny goddamn fire the size of a hand, and it is warm."

"A lodge would be good," Mary said. "This place . . ." She waved at the foul clay floor which soiled their robes, and the gloomy log walls, the one tiny window, scarcely a foot square because glass was precious, the flapping door hung on leather hinges. "It's so hard to live in it."

Skye rose stiffly. "Dirk, we'll talk to the agent."

"About what?"

"About the future."

Dirk's father dusted off his top hat and settled it on his gray hair and brushed his old leathers, making himself presentable.

"What future?" Victoria said.

Skye turned to her. "We don't need to stay here. We can go live with your people."

Victoria's face told Dirk everything he needed to know. For weeks, this ragged family had lived in deep silence, the women bravely enduring a miserable life in a place that was neither a village nor a new home for his mother's people.

Dirk followed his father toward the distant white buildings of the agency, the air sharp against his face.

Skye entered, lifted the top hat, and didn't wait to be summoned by the agent, who it turned out was snoozing, his feet on his desk, his bulk filling a wooden swivel chair. Major Perkins awakened with a snort, eyed Skye and Dirk narrowly, and carefully lowered his grimy boots.

"It's customary to knock," the major said.

"Our apologies," Skye said. "My son and I, we've been thinking about that empty school."

"Think no more. Nothing's going to happen."

"The people here are slowly sinking," Skye said. "We think we could help."

"You were pressed into the Royal Navy at age thirteen, Skye."

"It's Mister Skye, sir. A preference of mine. In the New World, anyone has the right to be a mister, including these good Shoshone people, and my son Dirk. Now, as it happens, something can be done to help them. I was thinking my boy and I could teach a lot more than reading and doing numbers. These people have been pushed into giving up their lodges and building these miserable cabins, but this new life isn't much good, sir. No one has enough firewood, and winter's coming on. It's not like the days when a village could take down their lodges and go to a fresh place with wood and grass. I'm proposing, Major, that we teach these people a little about business. I was a businessman in the fur trade, and as a guide, most of my life. I want to help these people. We need a firewood company, someone with a horse and wagon and a crew with saws and axes. We need a furniture company, someone who can join wood and make chairs and tables and bed frames."

"And earn a lot of coin," Perkins said, amused.

"Barter, sir. We have some potatoes. I'd trade some for firewood and furniture. What I propose, sir, is that my son and I start up a school. My boy will teach arithmetic and reading and spelling and all that. He knows some mechanics too. I'll teach these people how to organize services and businesses."

"I'm sure you'd draw crowds, Skye."

"I think, with Chief Washakie's help, we would."

"Well, the answer's no. I have no funds for a school."

"There's another thing, Major. This tribe needs its own herd. It needs something to replace the buffalo in the diet, and I'd like to see a few cows and a bull each month set aside from the beef allotment and kept on the reservation."

Major Perkins almost reared back. "I'll not permit it. I've a contract with ranchers to bring in thirty beeves a month, and I won't be undercutting these good folks who supply our beef."

Dirk wanted to yell at the man. What beef? The culls and sick animals driven here each month hardly fed anyone. Just putting them on pasture for a month or two would add plenty to the food supply.

"I will discuss that with Chief Washakie, Major. We all want to see these people properly fed and healthy and on their way to living a better life."

"No, Skye, you won't be competing with my suppliers. This tribe will not grow its own beef."

"Then release them to hunt buffalo," Skye said.

"No, if they feed themselves on buffalo meat, they'll take food out of the mouths of the local ranchers."

"You'd prefer that the tribes remain as they are, Major?"

"Exactly as they are, Skye. It's all orderly and peaceful."

"What about the school?"

"It would just be a magnet of discontent and rebellion. It would be best if it never opened its doors. In fact, I may have it torn down."

"You don't want them to live as white men do?"

"Well, Skye, that's the policy of the Indian Bureau, but we know what the chances are. These are stone-age people, without the wheel, without metal tools. What good would a school do?"

"I'm sure Chief Washakie would be interested in that viewpoint, Major."

Perkins stared. "You done, Skye? You want to register a complaint? Write my bureau? Stir up the Shoshones? Educate some boys?"

"We have one request: unlock the schoolhouse door."

Perkins looked amused. "I might. What's in it for me?"

"Commendation from the Indian Bureau. Anything you can report to Washington about schooling the Shoshones, making them self-supporting on farms and ranches, would win you advancement."

Perkins yawned. "The position doesn't pay, Skye. What's a thousand dollars, eh? A year of toil and grief and isolation for a thousand dollars? And neither does any other in government service. So what if I rise, and become a supervisor for two thousand a year? What if I reach twenty-five hundred a year, and oversee a dozen Indian agents, eh? What if I dine with congressmen and senators, and bring in a chief now and then and present him to the White House? What then, eh? Why would I want to advance, when everything is fine right here?"

Dirk fumed. This was a world he didn't know about, thanks to all the years he was confined in a quiet compound in St. Louis. But he was learning fast, and it was all he could do to let his father, so weary with age, conduct this exchange. The agent was absolutely in charge, knew exactly what he did not want changed, while he enriched himself.

Dirk wished he knew just how Perkins was doing it. Each month thirty beeves were supposed to arrive, but only twenty-eight actually came, and those were so miserable that two of them hardly equaled one healthy one. Each month each household got a flour and rice allotment, but it was always short. How did the major rake off a cut? Who got the beef and flour? Who paid whom? And here was the major, resisting a tribal herd, resisting a school, resisting even the teaching of agriculture to Dirk's mother's people.

Dirk's father seemed more accepting of this than he should be, and Dirk wondered if age had simply weakened his will or dulled his once-powerful sense of moral outrage. He had swiftly come to understand what age had done to Barnaby Skye. The man never stopped hurting. Dirk, at fifteen, could hardly imagine it, a body that hurt all the time, but his own eyes told him that his father lived with some unimaginable pain, and it was softening and withering him.

The major slowly lifted himself to his feet, smiled benignly, as one does in total victory, or perhaps in total power, and nodded. Dirk saw his father nod stiffly, and slowly limp out the door. But the major's gaze was not on the old man, it was on Dirk, educated by the blackrobes, and that gaze was not friendly.

But outside, where a chill wind whipped through their coats, Skye seemed to transform himself.

"Time to talk to the chief," he said. "We're going to go out on the biggest buffalo hunt ever to leave the reservation."

"But we can't!"

"But we will. And you and I are going to lead it. We're headed clear out to the plains. Out near the old Bozeman Road. Out in Sioux country, where the buffalo are still thick. And we're going to make meat. And make robes. And make jerky and pemmican and lodge covers."

"But we can't without the major's permission!"

"Exactly," said his father.

Dirk stared at a man who suddenly looked twenty years younger.

Chapter 35

Chief Washakie met them, as was his custom, on his front porch. He listened closely and came to a swift decision.

"I've been a friend of the whites and will continue. I've guided my people in peace. That is my road. I will not send word to join the hunt." But then he paused, a faint smile on his lips. "But I won't resist it."

That was all Skye needed. He thanked the chief and left.

"Saddle up, Dirk, and spread the word, up the valley first. We'll leave early the day after tomorrow from here."

"Where will we be going?"

"To the plains."

Dirk hastened to collect one of his mother's good horses and saddled it. He would be the messenger of a quiet rebellion, hunters leaving the ancestral home to pursue the buffalo, contrary to the express wish of the agent. It tore at him. He had learned much in St. Louis. He admired the Americans and he knew they held the future in their hands. Even their reservation system was at bottom an effort to give his people and other tribes a safe and productive homeland. His mother's people could only bend, and change, or wither away. But here he was, furtively spreading word of a hunt, in defiance of the Indian agent, a man who was backed by the bluebelly soldiers.

How strange and determined Barnaby Skye seemed in

that moment. This was not an old man, but a younger one with a will of steel.

North Star rode up the great valley of the Wind River, his message terse and clear: join Skye in the morning of the second sun for a buffalo hunt. Nothing more needed to be said. There were no remaining buffalo on the Wind River Reservation. The Shoshone hunters would arrive with whatever weapons they could manage, saddle horses, and travois horses. If the weather was good, and the hunting was good, they would bring back frozen quarters of buffalo on those travois. If the weather was warm, they would bring back jerky or pemmican. It would fill bellies during the long winter descending on them.

He found The Runner's lodge and stopped to give word to his uncle, who spoke an odd Elizabethan English derived from his self-study of a collection of Shakespeare's tragedies.

"Prithee what news?" The Runner asked, upon discovering his nephew at his camp.

"My father is organizing a buffalo hunt, and he'll leave the morning of the second sun. All are welcome."

"And where doth he intend to go?"

"The plains."

The Runner pondered that, looking grave. The Shoshones were ancient enemies of the plains tribes. He was not a young man, and his memory stretched back into the hazy past. There was white blood in him because he was a grandson of Charbonneau, and that was one reason Dirk felt close to him, and to his mother. The mixed-bloods were a people apart.

"It is something to be considered," The Runner said. "A trial fraught with peril."

He was talking about the United States Army, which had a small detachment right there on the reservation, near the agency buildings. It had started up as Camp Brown. "The plains, you say? That which was ceded to the Sioux?"

Dirk nodded. Double the jeopardy, the army and the Sioux.

"Is thy father, the honored Mister Skye, in possession of his senses?"

"He is twenty years younger now than he was yesterday."

"I will think on it," The Runner said.

On a frosty morning a dozen or so Shoshone men of all ages, plus several women, gradually collected at the cabin. They brought riding and travois ponies, and whatever weapons were at hand. Dirk had never hunted before, and now he examined these skilled hunters and warriors with respect. He would help with the skinning, or any other way he could. His schooling had taught him much, but not such as this.

In air as sharp as needles they proceeded toward the Wind River, directly under the eyes of the two platoons of soldiers at the army camp, but they paid no heed. The soldiers were busy erecting a new post, which was the true occupation of most enlisted men on the frontier. The comings and goings of a few Shoshones didn't interest them. Skye wanted it that way; everything out in the open. Dirk rode easily, but not comfortably because the icy wind whipped the heat from him. In time they made the river, far out of sight of the soldiers, and proceeded downstream through the majestic valley, flanked by some of the highest mountains in the Rockies. No one stayed them. Dirk half expected a squad of bluecoats to ride them down and turn them back, but it never happened.

For two days they rode east toward the plains, mostly under cast-iron-gray heavens that threatened to spill snow or icy rain over them. His mother rode comfortably; old Victoria hunched on her pony as if she had lived there all her life, and his father seemed more alive than ever. The

Runner and the other Shoshones began to enjoy themselves, and one of them shot a buck that would provide some good camp meat for this large group. These people, Dirk realized, were poor. They could not renew or repair their buffalo-skin clothing because they could not reach the buffalo. They lacked funds to buy wool or cloth, and their allotments scarcely kept them warm. A few had old fusils or smooth-bore rifles; only two or three had a modern weapon. Others were well armed with bows and arrows, and a few had lances.

Somewhere or other they crossed the invisible line; Dirk had no idea where it was, and the Shoshones understood it only vaguely. But they were no longer on their reservation, no longer within the "homeland" that the United States government gave them, along with two platoons of soldiers to keep them at home. Just where those lines ran was something Chief Washakie probably knew, but few of these Shoshones knew, and couldn't fathom invisible medicine lines anyway. It was a good home, but it also was a prison without walls, and white men were claiming every inch of land outside of those medicine lines.

The sparkling river took them east, and when it curved north toward the gloomy canyon that guarded the Big Horn River basin, the hunters abandoned the stream and continued toward the plains where the buffalo were thick. They slept out-of-doors, building brush wickiups against the icy nights, and relying on their robes for warmth. Dirk watched Skye and Victoria, fearful that the hardships of the trail would weary them. It was painful to watch his father ride, with his stiff leg poking out, always unbalancing him. His eyes were so bad that Dirk wondered if the old man would hit anything he shot at with an old muzzleloader he had somehow gotten. His birth mother found ways to ease the toil of the elders, but Victoria kept shooing her away, not yet ready to surrender to great age.

The cold weather held, and that was a blessing. Ice skinned the puddles each morning, and rimmed creek banks. Frozen meat would keep. But then one afternoon the thing he dreaded most fell upon them. A patrol of blue-clad cavalry soldiers cantered up and stopped, examining Skye and his cohort. Some of the Shoshones were taut and ready for trouble. The patrol's commander, surprisingly a major with oak leaves on his shoulders, looked dashing, with mustachios and sideburns, and merry blue eyes.

The officer addressed Skye. "Shoshones, I take it."

"Chief Washakie's people," Skye said. "I'm Mister Skye, and these are my wives Victoria and Mary, and my son, Dirk."

"Mister Skye, is it? That name's known, sir, from ocean to ocean. I'm Dedham Graves, sir. Call me Ded."

"Dead Graves?"

"Dedham Morpheus Graves. It runs in the family. My mother is Passionflower Nightshade Graves. My father was Oak Coffin Graves." He eyed the Shoshones and their dozen travois ponies. "Out for a Sunday stroll, are you?"

"It's a good day for a stroll, sir."

"Ah, Mister Skye, I can't let you stroll over to Sioux country. Ever since the Honorable Red Cloud licked the United States Army, they've been testy about wandering Shoshones and other undesirables sampling their private larder."

"That makes it hard on us, sir. We're some short of meat."

"Short of meat, are you? Don't you get thirty beeves a month?"

"We're supposed to, but it comes out to a regular twenty-eight, and culls at that. Not enough meat on them to feed half these people for one week."

Major Graves eyed him. "How about the other rations?"

"Always short, sir. The agent blames his suppliers."

"Perkins does that, does he? Who supplies the beef?"

"Big Horn Basin people, sir, as far as we know."

"Yardley Dogwood. We've had a few spats with him. He doesn't want any Yank blue-belly soldiers on his rangeland."

"I thought he might be the one, sir."

"He has the contract, all right. I don't know who has the contract for the flour and sugar and all that." Major Graves stared into the cold blue sky. "The army would like to see the Indians well fed and happy on their reserves, and learning to take care of themselves."

"Then you'll let us continue our Sunday stroll."

"I hear tell there's a few buffalo along the foothills of the Big Horn. You might take your Sunday stroll that way, steering well clear of Yardley Dogwood, of course."

"We'll do that, Major."

"I know a place," Mary said. "In our tongue it is meeteetse, the place of meeting."

"Very good, madam." Major Graves smiled cheerfully. "I must report this, Mister Skye. I'll let my superiors know I had a pleasant visit with you and your family who were out on a picnic."

He wheeled his horse to lead his parade, and then looked back.

"Mister Skye, don't confuse Dogwood's longhorns for wild game. It would cause no end of trouble."

"My eyesight's getting bad, Major. Never know what I'm shooting these days. I can't even tell if it's two-footed or four-footed."

The major laughed and wheeled his patrol west.

Victoria looked irritated. "When white men talk, I don't understand nothing," she said.

"He said he won't report us, and don't get caught."

"Then why didn't the sonofabitch just say it?"

"Politeness, I imagine."

"I'll never understand you crazy people," she muttered.

Skye turned his party north, where he would intercept the Bridger Road and could follow it into the great valley to the north.

"Dirk," he said, "tell our people that all's well. We can hunt, but not where the Sioux are buzzing."

Dirk let the others catch up, and quietly explained that the army didn't mind, and this hunting party would slip north, past the ranch there, and look for buffalo in the hidden draws near the Place of Meeting.

If the conversation with Major Graves had fascinated Victoria, it had fascinated Dirk even more. Here was something his schooling by the Jesuits had not touched upon, an entire visit in which the principal concerns of each party were scarcely addressed. Skye wanted to lead his hunters to the plains but didn't say it. Graves wanted to know why the Shoshones were off the reservation but didn't say it. Skye wanted the major to know that the food allotments were seriously short, but made no accusations. Graves wanted them to know that this state of affairs justified a hunt, with the army's blessing, but didn't say it that way. And the major said he would consider all this a Sunday stroll, and a chance encounter with Skye and his family.

Why hadn't the conversation been direct and open? Dirk grasped that there was a world among white men he knew nothing about, and his father was a master of it, using innuendo and guile, even as the major did.

Skye led them into the Big Horn Basin over the next days, where they cut west, keeping a sharp eye out for Yardley Dogwood's drovers. But it was a vast basin, and they never sighted the Dogwood company, even as they skirted the western foothills until they arrived in the place his mother called meeteetse, or meeting place, and found buffalo hidden in the nearby ravines.

Chapter 36

The hunt required only minutes. The butchering took the afternoon. They dined on tender, hot buffalo tongue that night, while the chill wind froze the quarters of three cows and two bulls. Never had meat tasted so fine. Never had they been so happy. They watched sparks fly into the heavens, and sang songs and settled into their robes. The world was good. The next dawn they left for the reservation with as much meat as they could carry or drag, all frozen solid. It would be a bounty for the hungry people on the reservation. People would laugh and smile once again. Two days later, not far from the reservation line, they ran into a patrol from the reservation, led by Captain Orestes Wall.

"The agent's some put-out that you left the reservation without permission, Skye."

"It's Mister Skye, Captain Wall."

"Well, whatever. Major Perkins requested me to confiscate any meat."

"Is it his intent to starve the Shoshones?"

"No, he wishes to teach you a certain lesson."

"There are over four hundred Shoshones on the reservation, sir. They receive twenty-eight culled beeves a month. Most of each month they have no meat. And live on short rations."

"You don't have to explain, Skye. I'll have to take that meat."

Bitterness flared in Skye, but he contained it. "All right then," he said. "We'll leave it here for you."

"No, bring it along."

A sorry parade of Shoshones, their spirits bleak and their hunting triumph ruined, rode wearily toward the Wind River Agency, escorted by soldiers with carbines in their sheaths. The soldiers wore heavy blue overcoats. The People wrapped blankets or old robes about themselves and hunkered deep into them. At some point they crossed the invisible line, a line scarcely understood by these people. The mounted infantry rode to either side, pinning the Shoshones between them, as if they feared that these people, dragging a heavy load of meat and buffalo hides, would escape.

"Bastards," hissed Victoria.

Captain Wall heard her and stared.

Skye eyed her. She was worn from the butchering, and so was Mary. Their dresses were smeared with blood and offal. Dirk stared bitterly at the soldiers, saying nothing, but Skye knew things were brewing in the boy's head. They had worked hard in a cruel wind to gut and skin and quarter the buffalo, wanting it done before the gore froze to their hands. Maybe it was all for nothing.

They rode under a cast-iron sky, past cottonwoods naked of leaf, past reeds and rushes faintly red or orange. Snow lay in patches on the hilltops. That last dozen miles was hard and cold, and worse, it was angry. The hunters fumed, whispered to one another, eyed the soldiers with frank bitterness, and Skye imagined some of them were thinking of causing trouble. He hoped they wouldn't.

At last the whitewashed agency buildings hove into sight. The wind was whipping the chimney fires downward, making the smoke crawl the tawny grasses. The army camp lay a half mile upriver. Major Perkins saw the sorry party coming, and was waiting for Skye on his veranda, dressed in a thick long buffalo coat with a hood.

The hunting party paused before him, and the soldiers spread out, ready for trouble and expecting it.

"Sorry about your meat, Skye, but you took my wards off the reservation."

"There's no game on the reservation, Major. Every last deer's gone. There's no elk or bear or wolves or coyotes or foxes or marmots or beaver, either."

"What is that supposed to mean?"

"There's no beef either, because two are missing each month and the rest are hardly worth slaughtering."

"So?"

"And not much flour or sugar or beans or rice, because not enough reaches here, or maybe enough does but it doesn't reach these people."

"Enough of this." Perkins addressed the captain, "Take the meat to the camp. It's yours."

Slowly, wearily, Skye dismounted, favoring his bum leg. He limped to one of the travois horses and settled himself on the heavy load of meat. The travois bent under him.

"Over my dead body," he said.

Dirk jumped off his horse and threw himself over another travois. "And mine," he shouted.

"Skye," Wall shouted. "Get off of there."

"You heard me."

Victoria staggered off her horse and threw herself over another travois. Mary descended to the ground and swiftly unhaltered a travois horse.

"Skye, I'm warning you," Captain Wall roared. "Get off. Get your family off."

But then The Runner leaped to the ground and threw himself against a packhorse carrying a quarter of a cow.

And the rest of the hunting party leaped to guard the remaining meat and hides.

"Over our dead bodies," The Runner said, sonorously, in a voice that oddly carried deep into the afternoon.

Wall turned to his squad. "Withdraw arms. Load and aim."

Reluctantly, the unhappy bluecoats unsheathed their Springfield carbines and leveled them at the hunters, at Skye and Victoria and Mary and Dirk.

"Now get off," Wall snapped.

Skye stared at the black barrels pointing toward him, the dark bores ready to spit flame.

"I suppose my time's come," he said. He did not move.

The Indian agent slid to the side, getting out of the line of fire.

A gust of wind caught the flag, flapping it hard, until it snapped and crackled in the gale. Wall glanced at it, at the Skyes, at the hunters, and at the agent, who looked frightened.

He turned to his men. "Sheath your weapons," he said.

His frightened bluecoats swiftly returned their weapons to their saddle sheaths.

"Take your meat to your people, Skye," Wall said.

"Insubordination!" the agent said.

"Yes, Mr. Perkins, it is that, all right."

Skye waited until every carbine was sheathed, and glared furiously at Dirk who began to stir. Dirk caught the glare and stayed quiet, his body across the buffalo quarter.

"Now, Captain Wall?" Skye asked gently.

"Now, Mister Skye."

Mary addressed her Shoshones and told them they could go, divide the meat, give to the poorest, and sing a song this evening.

Skye listened.

Wall turned again to his men. "We'll ride to the post now and let these people feed themselves and their kin."

The soldiers looked relieved. They knew these Shoshones as friends and neighbors, knew them by name. Slowly, they wheeled their horses about and rode to their encampment.

Skye lifted his old top hat and settled it, an ancient salute. He hurt again. He never stopped hurting.

Perkins retreated to his lair, slamming the door behind him. Skye watched the windows, fearful that something bad might yet befall them, but he saw no sudden menace crowding any window frame.

Victoria, old and gray and worn, walked to Skye and pressed her gnarled hand in his.

"You are a brave man," she said.

"You and Mary and Dirk give me courage," he replied.

She turned to Dirk. "Goddamn, you're a man," she said.

Dirk seemed to straighten and stand taller. He, too, had put his life on the line for his mother's people. Skye eyed his son, who eyed him back, and something fine passed between them.

Mary caught the shoulders of her son and gazed deep into his eyes, and then released the youth. Skye and his wives all knew that at this moment, the youth had passed into manhood. Maybe Dirk understood that too.

They found the cabin numbingly cold, and there was no wood for a fire. Victoria, too weary to go hunt for some, sank to the robes and pulled one over her. Wordlessly, Mary collected a hatchet and started for the door, but Dirk stayed her.

"I'll find some," he said.

Mary gratefully gave him the hatchet. Deadwood was now more than an hour distant, and it would be a long time before Dirk returned with enough for a fire. They had a buffalo tongue to boil, if only they could start up the stove.

Skye peered around the dreary cabin, wishing he had a lodge, where a small flame in the middle of the cone soon spread its delight. He sat down beside Mary, as worn as she, and drew a blanket around him, but it didn't offer much comfort.

At great peril he had won a small victory this afternoon, but it was no victory at all. A darkness hung over the Wind River Reservation, a homeland that was really a prison, where they were starting to starve. Maybe, if he could summon the strength, he could take his family back to the Crows, who still roamed freely in buffalo country. Not that the Crows' freedom would last long, either.

There was no escape from the encircling darkness. He slumped wearily, favoring his bad leg, and waited for Dirk. Even Mary, much younger, gave up her toil and climbed under a robe, trying to ward off the damp, rank cold of the cabin, a cold that reached right to the bones.

What had life come to? For the first time in all his years, giving up life seemed seductive to Skye. He stared at Victoria, and found her staring at him in the gloom, their unspoken thoughts plain to each other.

They were startled by a sharp knock. Mary rose swiftly, while Skye was still struggling, and opened to Captain Wall, who stood there with an orderly behind him.

More trouble, apparently.

"May I have a word?" the captain asked.

This was the man who only a while before had ordered carbines drawn and aimed at all of them. Skye nodded curtly.

Wall stepped in, noted the coldness, and the dead stove. "No wood?"

"My son is getting some."

Wall turned to his orderly. "Bring these people an armload of firewood, and don't forget some kindling."

"Yes, sir," the private said, and hastened into the gloom.

"We have no chairs, sir," Skye said.

Victoria sat on the ground, her robes around her. She looked gray.

"A lodge would be more comfortable than this, Mister Skye."

"Yes, sir." Skye wondered what this was about. Maybe an apology, though the army never apologized for anything, including massacres of red men.

Captain Wall stood awkwardly, and then slowly settled himself on the cold clay. "You'll have some warmth soon, Mister Skye."

Skye waited, not much caring what might be transpiring.

Wall was an older man, trapped by the army's glacial promotions, and not far from retirement. He had been breveted a colonel during the recent war. Now he was filling time at a lonely post. Skye knew that much about him, and had no wish to know more.

"This isn't right, Mister Skye. Not right at all, and the army is caught in the middle of it."

That faintly surprised Skye.

"Have the Shoshones been getting their full allotments?"

"No, Captain. Not even close."

"Let's start with the meat. The reservation is supposed to receive thirty cattle a month in good flesh."

"That's never happened, sir."

"Right you are, Mister Skye. Twenty-eight, and most of them so poor you'd get more meat off a deer. What about the grains?"

"The people here don't have scales, and many don't know what a pound or a gallon is. They take what's given them by Perkins and his two assistants."

"Badly short?"

"Not what was guaranteed in the treaty."

"How do you know that?"

"I spent much of my life in the fur trade, Captain. I'm familiar with every trading post trick in the books. The thumb on the scale, the finger in the measuring cup, the miscount or misweighing."

The orderly returned, bearing wood, was admitted, and swiftly built a fire and lit it. There would still be a long wait before any heat permeated this chill room.

"Thank you, Corporal, you may return to the post," Wall said.

The mustachioed corporal nodded and retreated into the twilight.

"Now again, Mister Skye, if you'd oblige me with a few more answers. Do you know whether these shipments are short when they get here, or something is held back?"

"They're short when they arrive, Captain. There never are thirty cattle."

"Mr. Perkins's books acknowledge receiving thirty."

"I never see anything shipped out, and I've never seen anything held back in the warehouses, Captain."

"Yes, it's all accomplished elsewhere. The army's looking into a few things, including large increases in his accounts in Washington. Have you or your people anything to add?"

"Yes, goddammit," Victoria said. "There's not a deer or elk or other game left. It's all been hunted away inside the invisible lines."

"We don't even have firewood," Mary said. "Before, we could move our lodges to firewood and game."

That seemed to end the discussion. The captain stood, hat in hand. "I deeply regret what happened today. The army is supposed to heed the directions of the agent in a time of crisis. I came to my senses much too late." He paused, in the midst of the deep silence. "We're looking into Major Perkins."

Skye nodded.

"You've answered the questions we had in mind. Perhaps we can help matters."

"Thanks for the firewood, Captain. Nothing could be more welcome than that wood."

The captain nodded curtly.

The beginnings of warmth began to fill the cabin as the stove popped and the fire within it began to crackle.

Skye was slow to his feet, but Mary showed the captain to the door.

Skye slid back into his robes, grateful for the tender heat.

Chapter 37

Early snow blanketed the valley and brightened the distant peaks. It grew harder and harder to heat the cabin. Dirk collected the half-starved ponies and threw packsaddles over them, and added an axe. He was forced to travel two miles to wood now; others were competing for the deadwood. His days were filled with little but hiking up slopes to find deadwood, hacking it to pieces, loading it onto his pack frames and tying it down, and returning to the cabin, where the stove ate his wood at a terrifying pace.

This cabin, erected by The Runner, had been located near the agency buildings but far from forest. Mary's brother was better off, living in a lodge the traditional way, able to move his household to fresh woodlots. And it was easy to stay comfortable in a lodge, with only a small fire. Dirk wondered what sort of nightmarish life he had returned to; nothing here resembled what he remembered from his earliest years.

Victoria looked gray, and spent her time in the buffalo robes, lost in deep silence. And Skye seemed old, or at least worn down, and unable to help much. So it befell Dirk and his mother to care for the older ones. Skye talked now and then of going back to the Crow people, and living out on the plains with them. There still were buffalo there, and the army left them alone even if the Sioux didn't. Skye knew now that his lodge had been cached on the Yellowstone, and it would probably still be there. The thought of going north tantalized them, but the weather was not cooperating, and they had too little food. Dirk knew little about hunting, and Skye's eyesight was weakening, and Victoria's strength with her bow was declining. So the whole idea of abandoning this miserable place seemed never to take wing, and they endured from day to day.

For a few days after the hunt they feasted on buffalo tongue, their share of the meat, but it was long gone and they hadn't seen meat since. It was said that the supplier, Yardley Dogwood, had not bothered to show up with animals when they were due December the first, and there would be no meat at all in December.

There were muted things happening at the agency; couriers coming and going, bluecoated military men in and out. But these events did not bear upon the Shoshones, who were struggling to get through a hard winter. Dirk thought that if things didn't improve, they would all soon be eating horses. But there was no fodder for the horses, and they were slowly starving their way toward spring, sometimes gnawing on green cottonwood bark to make a living. What sort of life was this? A life imposed by white men bent on making all this land their own, no matter who had first claimed it.

Then one day half a dozen cavalrymen arrived at the post, along with some freight wagons. Skye watched from a great distance, sometimes standing at the door of the cabin, but rarely venturing into the snow, which he found treacherous with his bad leg. Mary watched a moment also, and returned to her housekeeping. She had learned something of making things from flour, and was making flat, round loaves of Indian bread employing grease and flour, to sustain them all. The gray skies seemed lower, the days shorter, the dark more pervasive, and Dirk took it as a sign. He had come all the way from comfortable St. Louis—to this.

But one morning, the first sunny one in a week, that cavalry officer, Major Dedham Graves, came to call on foot, having negotiated a half mile of snowy turf.

Dirk remembered the man well. His mother admitted Graves, whose glance took in the state of affairs, lack of furnishings, the two older people swathed in buffalo robes as they sat against a gloomy log wall in deep cold. Graves settled on the clay floor near them, his eyes as bright and cheerful as the day they first encountered one another.

"Mister Skye, sir, it's my pleasure to bring some good news. At least the army thinks it's good news."

"I'm glad to hear it," Skye said.

"In a nutshell, we've cashiered Perkins. He was a bad lot, and we were able to catch him in wholesale peculation, and even as we speak he's being ejected from the agency and is being sent packing."

"Say that in words I've heard of," Victoria snapped.

"Perkins is a crook. We've gotten rid of him. He was raking off about thirty percent of everything. That's most of the reason the people here haven't gotten their full share. Others made a few dollars too, Yardley Dogwood was one. And some other scoundrels. So there's change afoot. The reservation is about to have a new agent. He's been appointed, in Washington, if he agrees to a few stipulations."

"If the people get their full measure, and if this is not a prison for them, that's all I care about," Skye said. "The actual agent is of no consequence to me."

"I'm talking about you, Mister Skye."

Skye bolted upright.

"Annual stipend, a thousand dollars."

"Me?"

"We've been burning up the telegraph lines. The Indian Bureau wants you. Army wants you. Some of your fur trade friends were excellent agents for their people. William Bent, Tom Fitzpatrick. So will you be."

Skye clambered to his feet, staggering a little on his bad leg. "I'm a wreck. How can I perform my duties with this?" He jabbed a finger at his leg.

"Broken-Hand Fitzpatrick didn't have any trouble."

Dirk was agog. This thing filled this gloomy little room and threatened to burst outside.

Major Graves played his ace. "Ask your wives, Mister Skye. They rule the nest."

"Rule the nest, do they? I'll send you packing out that door if you . . ."

Victoria was looking smug. "Take it, Skye."

"We're hoping you'll look after these good people, and see that they're properly cared for. The army wants nothing more than some happy Shoshones, working with their great chief, Washakie. We're calling the post Fort Washakie. Only army post in the country named for a chief. You'd better sign up and help these people."

Skye was standing now, his face more grave than Dirk had ever seen it. "It's an obligation," he said. "You might not like what I'll be doing. Your government might not like it."

"That brings up another matter, Skye. Citizenship." He reached into his portfolio and withdrew some papers. "You'll need to sign here, and I'll administer the oath."

"Citizenship?" Skye said.

"We can't appoint a Briton to be our Shoshone Indian agent, Mister Skye."

A dead silence fell over the room. Dirk knew all about Skye's occasional bitterness toward the Yanks, his habit of cursing Yank folly, his scalding comments about the way Yanks treated Indian people. But there always was more. His father had some difficulties with his own England, with its class and caste system. He always insisted on being called Mister Skye because in the New World any man was entitled to be a mister, a man on the same footing as anyone else.

Graves quietly dipped into his portfolio and withdrew a stoppered ink vial, and a steel-nib pen, and handed them to Skye.

"I can hardly see this thing," Skye muttered.

"You know, sometimes, Skye, the army manages to do things right." Graves withdrew half a dozen wire-rimmed spectacles. "Try 'em."

Skye did, one after the other, found a good one, and slowly his face lit up. "I hardly could see."

"Read it, Mister Skye. You commit yourself to citizenship in the Republic of the United States of America."

Skye looked remarkable, Dirk thought, almost eagle-eyed, his gaze focused on the document, his new spectacles propped on the majestic prow of his nose. He read, stared off into space for a little, and nodded. "Does this make my wives and son citizens too?"

"Your son was born here and already is. Your wives, by virtue of marriage to you, are eligible, and can make that choice anytime."

Dirk had never thought of himself as a citizen before. He had thought of himself as a Londoner's son. It amazed him. He was a Yankee.

Skye unstoppered the ink flask, dipped the nib, and scratched his name.

"I'll witness it, Mister Skye, and congratulations," Major Graves said. The officer added his signature.

"Now, sir, another small matter. This is an employment agreement. You'll agree to uphold the laws and Constitution of the United States, and to proceed under the direction of the Bureau of Indian Affairs. Your annual stipend will be

deposited wherever you wish. You will have the use of the
agency residence, the agency offices, the agency horses
and buggy and wagon, and will also receive expense allow-
ances for lamp oil, firewood, office supplies, and the like.
You can move in at once. Perkins is off the reservation, and
the staff have prepared your house."

Skye skimmed through the agreement, and signed.

Dirk marveled. Was this commanding man the same one
whose old face was etched with fatigue and loss only a while
before? Was this old woman, beside him, once so gray and
worn, now this eagle? And was his own worn mother, Blue
Dawn, so tall and proud ever before?

"I can weather a few years," his father said. "If I can put
this place on a sound footing, and help these people find a
way to live, and defend them from predators, and give them
something to live for, well, Captain, that would be all that
a man could ask of his remaining days."

"Mister Skye, half the things you want your superiors
will veto. Or Congress won't fund. But you probably know
that."

"Will I be able to call on the army, Captain?"

"No, not for much. The army's in worse shape than the
Indian Bureau."

"Has Chief Washakie been told of this?"

"We thought to tell you first."

"Will you tell him?"

"He's our next stop. We needed to find out whether you
would accept."

"Hey, how did this happen, eh?" Victoria asked.

"We knew Erastus Perkins was . . . pocketing whatever
he could. But that's not what you mean, Madam Skye. You
mean, how did your man get chosen, I take it. Your husband's a known man, I assure you. He's lived among your
people all his adult life. He's fought at your side. He's fought

us, sometimes. He's known for, what'll I say? Grace, let's say grace. An odd idea being mouthed from some old soldier, close to retirement. Grace it is. If any man can help your people, madam, he can. He knows us, and he knows you. He knows what to tell us, what's gone wrong, what won't work, what violates your deepest beliefs. There are some in the Indian Bureau who want to turn all of you into white men, but Mister Skye here is going to say no to them, and is going to help find a way of life that fits with who you are and what you believe." Graves paused. "I'm told that no one in Washington dissented. Not one."

Mary said, "Will my people now cross the invisible lines?"

"I think the new agent will allow it, don't you? But, madam, I wish to offer you a somewhat different idea. Those boundary lines are there to keep white men out, not keep you in."

Oddly, Dirk didn't much care for all this. One man, Skye, could not bend the will of the Yankee government. This would only mean no change, but now a man friendly to the Shoshones, and bound by marriage to them, would be telling them what to do and how to live. Now his old and ailing father would be an instrument of the Indian Bureau. It might all work out, and at least his father and mothers would be comfortable. But what would a mixed-blood man do with his life?

Chapter 38

Within the hour, army teamsters had moved the few possessions of the Skyes into the agency house, even as Mary and Victoria wandered through the small frame building, noting its kitchen, parlor, two bedrooms each with two narrow cast-iron bedsteads, and outhouse out back.

Two young Shoshones appeared, one a deaf-mute girl named Keewa, who understood sign language, and her mate, going by the name of The Walker, a general factotum whose days were largely devoted to cutting firewood for the agency house as well as the agency offices.

Dirk watched his weary father stare at the object of his desire for many months, a bed with a mattress, a haven for his aching body. His mothers, by some agreement, took one of the bedrooms, leaving the other to Skye and Dirk. Skye settled in a chair; his face filled with pleasure. He had scarcely sat in a chair his entire adult life, and often squatted on his heels, in the fashion of the mountains, until age and stiffness kept him from it. But now his father settled in a Morris chair, and then rose to try a horsehair settee, and then a straight-backed dining chair, all with such childlike joy that Dirk realized at last what pain meant to an old man, and how relief from pain could be a life goal and vision all in itself.

Skye even wandered to the two-hole outhouse, and settled on a seat in wonder, and then retreated to the warm agency residence. The mute girl followed anxiously, eager to please, and Dirk thought she might have been abused. Victoria watched her, and employed the ancient sign talk of the plains to tell the girl that she was welcome, all was well, and she was appreciated. She and her man had quarters at the back of the agency building, which they cleaned.

But something was gnawing at Dirk, and it had to do with this sudden luxury, while just beyond these walls his mother's people, his own people, were struggling to stay warm and fed. But after a grateful tour of the premises, Skye asked how much wood there was.

Dirk hastened out to the woodlot, and found what he thought was two cords.

"Tomorrow, early, harness the team, load half of that wood in the agency wagon, and take it to our people."

Somehow, Dirk's anguish eased. This would be Skye's first official act.

The whitewashed house was small, not grand, but it seemed a palace to the Skyes, especially that first night when each of them slept on a cotton-stuffed mattress in a warm house. True to his charge, Dirk arose before dawn, found the agency's barn and harness and draft horses, and soon began loading wood, until he thought he had half of it.

When he returned to the house, he found all his parents were up and cheerful.

"How did you sleep, Papa?"

Skye yawned and smiled. "Maybe I'll go back for another round," he said.

His wives laughed.

"Goddamn white men need soft beds," Victoria said. "So do old Absaroka women."

They looked uncommonly cheerful while Mary brewed some coffee.

Dirk drove into a frosty dawn, crystal-white haze on top

of a thin cover of snow, and made his way up the valley, the two draft animals exhaling steam. Dirk knew where to go: the isolated cabins dotting the great valley. But he found no one present at the first place, the stove cold; and the pattern repeated itself as he drove upriver. Then he discovered an encampment next to some woodlands, traditional lodges bleeding white smoke into a white sky, and he knew the people had solved their firewood troubles their own way, by returning to their traditional ways. Some lodges had been cut up to make moccasins and shirts and coats, but enough remained to shelter the Shoshones. He drove to the encampment and made a symbolic gift of a piece of dry wood to each household, including his uncle, The Runner, and in each case he told his people that his father would be their agent and this was his gift to them. This would be a good day, he thought. A very good day. The people, mostly wrapped in blankets or buffalo robes, smiled their greetings, and then set out to share the great news with all the rest. And so the trip to deliver firewood turned out to be an announcement.

His last call that morning was at Chief Washakie's home. The youth carried the gift of wood to the door, but the chief was waiting for him.

"It is a fine morning, North Star. I have heard the good news," Washakie said.

"Grandfather, it is my father's wish that each Shoshone household receive the gift of firewood from him."

"Ah, warmth. It is a fine gift. Warmth, North Star, is more of a gift than any other."

Washakie took the firewood and hefted it, and smiled. "You will come in now," he said.

North Star knew it was a command. He tied the harness lines to a post and entered. The chief motioned him to a seat, and vanished into the kitchen for a moment.

"The ladies will bring us tea," he said.

North Star nodded, wondering what all this was about, as the chief settled himself on the horsehair sofa.

"It is a good thing, our friend Mister Skye becoming our agent. My heart is lifted up."

"Mine too, Grandfather. There will be more food delivered on each allotment day."

Washakie stared into the brightness of the winter's day outside. "I despise allotments, North Star. They make beggars of us. We wait in line for handouts from the Yankee government. Do you know what I am saying?"

North Star did. The monthly dole of food had reduced this proud people to helplessness. Several times, North Star had watched his mother's folk shuffle through the line, be checked off by officious bookkeepers, and then receive a little of this and that, and drift away to live out their lives without purpose.

"The Shoshone People are broken," North Star said.

"I work ceaselessly for the day when there will be no allotments, and nothing is handed to my people," Washakie said. "And I know what must come. We must have our own herds, and plow our own fields, and then we will have food enough. That is how your father's people stay alive through the times when there are no berries and roots to gather, and the times when there are no buffalo or deer or elk to be found."

North Star sensed this was leading somewhere, and it would be best just to let the seamed old chief take the meeting wherever it would be taken. It didn't take long.

"We need more than allotments; we need the wisdom of the white men. They are very wise. They live with grain stored against hunger, wood against the winter, and cattle that can be slaughtered as needed. They have commerce, in which those who have skills produce one thing, and those with different gifts produce another, and they use money to make trades. This is good."

A girl returned bearing a tray with a teapot and cups. She was a beautiful girl, with blueberry eyes and jet hair and golden cheeks. She eyed North Star with demure curiosity, but he caught her glancing at him, and she caught his swift glances that absorbed everything about her. She wore a white velvet ribbon at the end of each of her two braids.

"North Star, this is my youngest daughter, whose name is Mona, and the reason I am keeping you here, even though I am sure you wish to return to your father and mothers, is to ask something of you."

Mona passed steaming tea to each man, and shyly vanished into the rear of the little white house.

The chief lifted the teacup. "I will sip in honor of this day, and of our good fortune, and of the appointment of Mister Skye," he said.

North Star followed the ritual, and smiled.

"It is my wish that all of my people be educated in all the mysteries of the white men. Some things about them are excellent. Some things make me wary, and some things worry me. But they are the future, and they have wonders we did not know, guns and wheels and metal and marks on paper they can turn into words. It is my wish, North Star, that you will tutor us all, and especially my daughter Mona. And if you will set a time early each morning, I will have us all gathered here, in the parlor, and we will receive your instruction. I would like for us to learn something of each of the things you know. Would you do it?"

"Grandfather—"

"We will share some of our allotment with you."

"But, Grandfather, I don't know much. I didn't finish the schooling. The blackrobes still had more to teach me."

Washakie smiled slightly. "I thought you might at least

teach what you know. It is more than we know. Mona is very eager to learn everything you might have to show her."

"I would be pleased to teach her, Grandfather."

"Ah, North Star, it is done, then. Now, we will be ready when the sun first shows himself, and we will learn from you. A little while each morning, if that is suitable."

"It is, sir."

The chief rose smoothly, and escorted North Star to the door.

The young man turned at the last, and saw Mona shyly peering from within.

"Grandfather, tell Mona I will be pleased to teach her everything I've been taught."

"I thought you might, North Star."

He untied the harness lines and returned to the agency with an empty wagon, the backs of his dray horses frosted, and after he had cared for the animals he entered their new house. And there, once again, was that Major Graves.

"Ah, young Mister Skye, this is fortunate. I came looking for you."

Dirk stood uneasily, wondering what he had done wrong.

"It was the Quakers, the Society of Friends, that got it done," Graves said.

Dirk had scarcely heard of them. Some sort of Pennsylvania society that was attempting to help western Indians cope with the tide of settlement. Dirk didn't know what to say.

"The school, my boy, the school. Would you like to teach?"

"Teach? Teach who or what? Why do you think I'm qualified?"

"They have it from the Jesuits that you'd do just fine, and could teach the ABCs, writing, composition, arithmetic, including addition, subtraction, multiplication, and division, and you'd be just fine with history, some geography, mechanics, religious instruction, and moral instruction."

"But who?"

"These good people. Here at the agency, in the government schoolhouse."

Dirk felt the weight of his youth on him. "I'm not sure I'm the one, sir."

"Ah, young Mister Skye, do you want to? Would you like to see these people master the skills they'll need in the future?"

Dirk stared out the window. A part of him said that he only wished the government would leave his mother's people alone to continue as they always had. But another part of him knew the world would never be the same.

"Yes, sir, I would."

"The Quakers can't afford much. It's all subscription for them, but they'll pay twenty dollars a month, and of course the government will supply the schoolhouse and teacherage, and handle basic expenses."

"But where are the slates, and primers, and all that?"

"Ah, a sticky business. My officer colleagues at Fort Laramie have rustled up some readers, a few slates and chalk, a few pencils and some paper. Enough to start. The Quakers are working on it, but it won't be until spring before you'll be adequately equipped."

"You think a person my age would be accepted, sir?"

His mother replied at once. "North Star, you are a man."

He had not thought of himself as a man, but now he would be stepping into a man's job. He would need patience and courage and idealism. He would need to persuade young people his own age to come to his class, learn, and make use of what they learned. There would be immediate utility in it: they could make their grievances known. They could make sure whatever agent governed them was acting justly.

"Let's go look at the goddamned place," Victoria said.

They rose at once, wrapped shawls and robes about them, and hiked across a snowy reach to the school, where Skye let them in. This place was a single room, with a potbellied stove, student desks, windows out upon a snowy world, and little else. But it came alive, even as Dirk walked the creaking wood floors. It came alive with Shoshone faces, young and old, with the radiant heat of the stove, with pretty girls and seamed old men, with ponies tied to the hitchrail outside. He would give them what he could. He would try to teach a practical education, so they might operate businesses, raise meat and grains, supply wood, build roads, repair wagons, and all the rest.

"Major Graves, I will do this," he said.

"The teacherage is yours if you want it."

"Maybe someday. Just now, I want to help my parents."

"Yes, helping Major Skye would be a welcome service," Graves said.

"Major? Major?" Skye asked.

"A courtesy rank, sir. Indian agents are commonly called major."

"Not I, Major Graves. I am Mister Skye. I have always been Mister Skye, a man without rank. To the day I die I will be Mister Skye."